The Fall of Whit Rivera

The Fall of Whit Rivera

CRYSTAL MALDONADO

HOLIDAY HOUSE • NEW YORK

HOLIDAY HOUSE is registered in the U.S. Patent and Trademark Office.
Printed and bound in August 2023 at Maple Press, York, PA, USA.
www.holidayhouse.com
First Edition
1 3 5 7 9 10 8 6 4 2

Library of Congress Cataloging-in-Publication Data is available.

ISBN: 978-0-8234-5236-1 (hardcover)

To anyone who has ever had an illness that felt all-consuming: you are more than your diagnosis. And to the PSL girlies: never be ashamed of what brings you joy.

AUTHOR'S NOTE

I started writing this book with only two things in mind: love and autumn.

But as I wrote, Whit's story took on a life of its own, and I began to share what life is like with PCOS—a syndrome I was diagnosed with when I was sixteen years old.

As you pick up this book, I want to tell you that I've done my best to cover all topics with as much kindness, empathy, and tenderness as possible, but you may wish to know that this story deals with fatphobia, diet culture, bias within the medical community, autism, socioeconomic status, parental abandonment, loss, and grief.

Take care of yourself.

Chapter One

What is it about fall that makes me SO basic?

Well before the sticky summer days have cooled, I'm salivating over leaf-peeping and farmers' markets and cider tastings. At the stroke of midnight on the eve of autumn, I turn into an apple-picking, pumpkin-spice-craving, boot-and-oversize-sweater-wearing *fanatic*.

Autumn is when my sleepy Massachusetts town sheds its old life: the leaves become a symphony of reds, oranges, and golds, then let go. I love the colors; the crisp breeze; the pumpkin patches; the bonfires; the delicious scent of apple cinnamon; the melody the trees make when they rustle in the wind.

Fall is catharsis: it's paying tribute to what was while making room for what's to come. It's possibility, wrapped in a crimson bow.

The season is honestly in my top five favorite things *ever*.

Whit Rivera's All-Time Faves

1. My tiny little family: me; Abuela; Abuelo (who we miss every single day); my little sister, Lily; and our cat, Patch.
2. My ride-or-die besties, Sophie and Marisol, and my (super-hot) boyfriend, Aiden.
3. Fall and every single thing about it, including the high school's beloved Fall Fest, a weeklong celebration.
4. My notebook collection and all my infinite lists.
5. Gilmore Girls.

6.   (And a final secret sixth addition: Intonation, the bestselling
      boy band that Lily, Abuela, and I have loved since I was in
      eighth grade. Shhh.)

At this time of year, everything feels hopeful. And right about now,
I could use a little hope—because my summer kind of sucked.

I had been ready for a productive yet charming summer. I pictured hard days at the coveted internship I'd secured at Empower(ed)
Teens—a selective summer program for aspiring special needs educators and therapists—where I'd be praised for my organizational
skills, leadership, and compassion. I envisioned late-night bonfires,
spontaneous road trips to the beach, the sweet taste of ice cream
cones, refreshing dips in the pool, sandy toes, and laughter with my
friends and boyfriend.

How incredible does *that* sound?

But I didn't get any of it.

Because my summer kicked off with a heartbreaking goodbye. My boyfriend, Aiden, moved *two hundred miles away* for his
mom's new job at the University of New Hampshire.

This then made me feel like a fifth wheel with my best friends,
who turned out to be joined at the hip with their partners from
May straight through August.

And then came the doctors' appointments…which I was too
embarrassed to talk about…so maybe I retreated a little.

I don't know.

What I do know is that the second my junior year concluded,
my whole body suddenly felt *off.* Actually, if I'm honest with
myself, I had been ignoring signs that something was wrong for a
while. I could no longer pretend it was normal that I hadn't gotten
my period in months. I was sprouting body hair everywhere, and I
was gaining weight really fast, mostly in my belly.

It was like I'd lost total and complete control over every facet of my life, in a way no Whit Rivera list or color-coded binder was going to fix.

I couldn't even work up the courage to tell Sophie and Marisol, and I sure as hell wasn't going to tell Aiden: the move had put enough of a strain on our relationship. I didn't even tell Abuela—too ashamed, too fearful, too reluctant to add anything to her already full plate. She had enough to worry about between being the sole provider, her own health, and her business.

But Abuela sensed something, as Latina matriarchs always seem to, and a few obsessive internet searches later, we had three words to describe what might be wreaking havoc on my body: polycystic ovarian syndrome, or PCOS.

I should've been relieved to have a name for this experience, to be able to point to a reason why my body no longer felt like my own. But the more I read about the syndrome, the more I realized that the medical world seemed utterly mystified by it. There were few answers and no treatments.

Still, we diligently went to doctors. In appointment after appointment, under offensively bright lighting with parts of my expanding body spilling out of a blue gown, I'd be told the same thing: lose weight.

The whole summer vanished as we careened from doctor to doctor. They couldn't—or wouldn't—confirm that there was anything medically wrong with the soft brown girl standing before them, insisting instead that it was the circumference of her hips that was her grave undoing. Over the course of the summer, I was referred to four nutritionists, two different fat camps, and no less than seven bariatric surgeons.

I spent so much time in and out of doctors' offices trying to get a confirmed diagnosis of what I *knew* was polycystic ovarian syndrome that I ended up having to resign from the Empower(ed) Teens internship I'd been so excited about. I burrowed into the comfort of our family shop instead, working there whenever I could.

It was the nail in the freaking coffin of what was supposed to be Whit's Perfect Summer.

But finally, a ray of hope: Dr. Dianalys Delgado, a slim, dark-skinned Afro-Dominican woman with the most beautiful accent. The first doctor to let me share *all* of my symptoms without interrupting. The first doctor to ask how I felt. The first doctor to actually look up at me from her notes and meet my gaze. The first doctor to *see* me. Dr. Delgado nodded as I spoke and was ready with a tissue when I started crying. She told me it sounded like my self-diagnosis was correct, and that she was proud of me for being so proactive. It would only take one follow-up test, she promised, and we'd know for sure.

Dr. Delgado was right. And so was I. But even with the official diagnosis to explain what was happening in my body, I couldn't bring myself to utter the words out loud. I didn't want it to be real. PCOS was my little secret—a weight I quietly shouldered throughout a season I wished would just *end* already, as if summer were the real cause of all my problems.

But that had to be it, right?

Because fall and I kind of have a thing. It would never treat me this way.

* * *

"Hey. You there?" Aiden's voice startles me out of my thoughts.

I let him recenter me, focusing my gaze on his hazel eyes, angular jaw, crooked nose; on the lips I've grown so fond of kissing; on the curly brown hair I've loved running my hands through; on the wide shoulders and muscular arms he'll wrap around my waist.

Suddenly, I'm being swept away by a special kind of daydream. I shake my head and rearrange my face into a grin. "I'm here! Sorry. Just mentally planning my back-to-school ritual. You know how I am about new school supplies." A little shrug with my left shoulder, a shy glance away; I hope it's the perfect mix of sheepish and sweet. Because, yeah, I totally zoned out while Aiden was filling me in on the latest details from his *amazing* life in New Hampshire.

It's not that I'm not happy for him (I am!); it's just that it's really hard to listen to Aiden talk about how much he loves his new town, his new house, his new friends, and his new adventures, when my life is now tragic enough to require its own commemorative holiday.

Aiden breaks into a dopey grin, and part of me aches for him, wanting to see that grin up close. "You *do* love your pens. What's that one you really like called?" Aiden's brows crinkle while he thinks.

"The Pilot G2 bold point?" I offer. It's definitely in my top three—the ink glides easily and holds up to the pressure when I'm notetaking. The .3 mm Le Pen series would be my favorite *if* it didn't bleed through most paper.

He snaps his fingers. "That's the one! You said it 'writes like butter.'"

"If butter were a pen!" I laugh.

"I've never met a girl who can rattle off pen names like you." Aiden grins. "You still have those sticky notes on your laptop, too?"

My eyes glance down to the reminders I've taped to my ancient laptop, an old Chromebook I inherited from Abuela's shop when she needed to upgrade. The notes read: YOU'VE GOT THIS and FLOWERS BREATHE AND SO SHOULD YOU.

"Sure do." I catch myself smiling—a real smile this time—at Aiden, fondly remembering things that might seem insignificant to someone else, but that matter to me. Aiden is my first real relationship. Sure, I've kissed people before, and I've had plenty of crushes on both guys and girls, but when it comes to the going-on-dates, holding-hands, making-googly-eyes-at-each-other type of relationship, this is a first for me.

At times, Aiden can be really thoughtful—like last year right after winter break when he surprised me with an impromptu road trip to a specialty stationery store. Or the time when I told him I wanted to be kissed under a streetlamp in the pouring rain and, during the next rainstorm, he made it happen.

I'm good to him, too. I've gone out of my way to learn about some of his favorite football teams so I can listen when he talks about Fantasy Football. I'm supportive whenever his little brother's pranks have gone a bit too far, and I always let him choose the music in the car because I know how much he loves introducing me to new bands.

But lately it feels like it takes so much *effort* to ensure that we still know each other, and the little nuances seem gone altogether. It's like he and I were just finding our footing as a couple, only to have it all ripped away. Now we're sort of struggling along without the thrill of shared kisses and, quite frankly, it sucks.

"It's sweet you remembered the notes," I admit.

He tilts his head. "Of course, babe. How could I forget?"

I give him a soft smile. "Well, it just sounds like things are going really, really well for you, so maybe part of me thought you might—I don't know—forget me?"

Aiden shakes his head. "No way! Even though, yeah, things are pretty awesome out here."

"That's amazing. I'm so happy for you," I say, doing my best to mean it. Can I help it if there's a small part of me that resents it?

"Aw, thank you, babe. You're so supportive."

That elicits another pang of guilt. "I miss you. Do you think you'll come visit soon? You're only a few hours away." He's the only one of us with a reliable car. I doubt my junker would survive a long drive.

He nods. "Definitely. Soon. It's just that I've been so busy, you know?"

Oh, I *know.*

Aiden's new best friend—who goes by the nickname of Moose, of all things—has basically cannibalized every spare second of my boyfriend's time: boat trips and cabin retreats and whatever the hell else people do in New Hampshire. (I wouldn't know.) The fact that Aiden's off hiking with some man named MOOSE just emphasizes how separate our lives feel now. With Aiden's social profiles practically defunct, I can't even keep up with him that way.

"And with football starting up..." Aiden's voice trails off.

I arch a thick eyebrow in surprise. "Football?" What I mean is: *More* football? Haven't I suffered enough with the whole Fantasy Football thing?

His eyes sparkle at the mention. "Yeah! I didn't want to tell you until it was official, but I made the team!"

Aiden looks so giddy sharing this, pushing his curly hair out of his face excitedly before launching into *what position he's playing* and *what Coach has been saying* and *how he's been getting so strong.* I let him talk, watching his hands as he animatedly mimics throwing a football and makes sound effects to illustrate some mind-blowing catch his teammate made. I try to nod at all the right parts.

In the back of my mind, though, I'm wondering how much longer our relationship can survive when it feels like we're two buoys in an ocean, drifting apart.

"All of that sounds incredible. I'm so proud of you, Bean," I say. "But let's try to figure something out soon, okay?"

"Absolutely," Aiden says, nodding. "And..."

"Yes?" I ask.

He hesitates for a moment. "Well, it's just that everyone's been calling me Ace now. And I really like it."

I blink at him.

"What?"

"Yeah, I was hoping you could call me that, too."

"But I've been calling you Bean forever," I blurt. "And I'm Jelly!"

I know I probably sound like a child, but *come on*. Don't take this from me, too!

"I know. I know! And, like, I want us to have our own special nicknames or whatever, but, like…it just feels like we're outgrowing those a little, you know? We're seniors."

I swallow. He's acting like we came up with our nicknames Jelly and Bean as children or something, when really they're nicknames *he* came up with when we started dating last fall. Are they obnoxiously cheesy? Yeah, totally. But I like them. When he asked me to the Fall Fest for our first-ever date, he gave me a ton of jelly beans that each read FF? He knew I loved jelly beans, so it was really sweet. (Never mind that he wrote in Sharpie on each one, making them totally inedible. I was still touched by his efforts.)

"I guess," I say, frowning. "So…am I not going to be Jelly anymore, either?"

He shrugs. "Your call. Why don't you think on it and let me know?" His face brightens suddenly. "Maybe Marisol and Sophie would have some ideas!"

Right. Because I want my friends to help me come up with a romantic pet name for my boyfriend to call me.

"Yeah," I say, trying not to take this request too personally. "Maybe. I'll think about."

My gaze darts to the clock at the top right corner of my screen and I see that it's nearly eight now. Since this call is doing nothing except give me a stomachache, I'd really like to get started on my annual pre–first-day-of-school ritual of organizing my belongings and backpack, selecting an outfit, performing my nighttime beauty routine, and finishing up with pre-bed meditation.

"You're the best." Aiden gives me a thumbs up, which is just about all I can stomach.

I cut in. "I should get going. You know how I am with my rituals and all."

He slaps his forehead. "Oh, right! Okay. See ya later, alligator!"

"Uh...after a while, crocodile?" My voice lilts up in a question.

And then his little box on my screen is gone. No heartfelt goodbyes, no whispered sweet nothings, no plans for another chat. Just...see ya later, alligator?

Cool. Cool, cool, cool.

I mean, am I overthinking this? Probably. I tend to do that.

Which is why I turn to my phone, which I had propped up just beside my laptop, and ask, "So, how was it?"

Sophie and Marisol are both grimacing on their ends.

"Could've been a little better..." Sophie starts, her voice trailing off.

"That was a freaking train wreck," Marisol blurts out. "I mean, no offense. But holy shit."

Ugh. We're doomed. That's why I all but begged (okay, fine, *actually* begged) Sophie and Marisol to listen in on this call. Maybe that's pathetic, but hello? My perfectly put-together life has gotten so far away from me that that's kind of the level I'm at right now.

Sophie shoots Marisol a look before gently asking me, "Have you guys talked, like, at all this summer?"

"Of course we have!" I insist.

Marisol arches an eyebrow. "How often do you guys FaceTime?"

I don't want to admit that this is only the third time we've video-chatted since Aiden left. I grab a hair clip and twist my curls into a messy bun on top of my head before answering carefully. "I'm not sure."

"Maybe you should try making that more regular? You could choose one night a week or something. Like a date," Sophie suggests. "You guys just need practice figuring out how to be boy-friend and girlfriend now that you're long-distance."

Marisol crosses her arms. "I *assumed* that's what you'd been doing all summer. Because you definitely weren't hanging out with us."

Heat creeps up my neck. "I've been working at El Coquí a lot with Abuela. And helping Lily with summer school."

"Well, nothing says you can't focus on making things better with Aiden now," Sophie says. "It sounds like he's going to visit soon."

I nod. "I'm hoping I'll be able to see him before the Fall Fest dance."

I leave out the part where I haven't pushed for Aiden and me to meet up this summer because it's saved me from having to reveal my bigger new body.

I hate to admit that, even to myself. The thing about Aiden is he's so freaking *hot*—like, conventionally hot, and *muscular*, and he always made me feel so tiny and delicate, as if I were a little ballerina. I may not have been small when we were together, but there's a part of me that's terrified he'd see me now and instantly be turned off.

I've been embarrassingly, shamefully hiding my blooming stomach and softening jawline with tricks of the light and cam-era angles in hopes of—well, I don't know what. Stalling, I guess. Rebuilding a foundation that isn't so physical.

"That's something!" Sophie enthuses. "Hopefully things feel better between you two soon."

Marisol uncrosses her arms and nods. "Yeah. Hopefully."

I can't blame Marisol for what is only a half-hearted attempt at making me feel better about this floundering relationship—especially not when she's upset with how MIA I've been. Suddenly, it hits me how selfish I was to ask them to give up part of their night on the eve of the first day of school just to listen in on my call with Aiden.

"Thank you so much, guys. And thank you for doing this. I really appreciate it," I say. "I'll let you go so you can get everything ready for tomorrow."

"Are you still planning to meet up with us in the courtyard before homeroom?" Marisol asks. It's our tradition, and I take it as a promising sign that Marisol wants to continue with it.

Without hesitation, I nod. "Promise. I wouldn't miss it."

And at that, Marisol gives me a small smile. "You better not."

Sophie smiles, too. "See you tomorrow!"

"See you," I say with a small wave, before all-too-happily ending my second disastrous video call of the night.

Chapter Two

Down the hall, I can hear Lily and Abuela chattering above the jarring sound of a local furniture commercial, and I find myself annoyed that its stupid jingle will be playing in my head over and over all night long.

I'm not really annoyed at them. Or the commercial (even though that is kind of irritating). I'm more annoyed at myself, I think, for being so emotionally drained after talking to the people I should love talking to.

That's what I get for isolating myself so much this summer. Of course things feel off.

Right now, I should be focusing on my pre–first-day ritual so that I can clear my mind and be forward-thinking. Instead, I glance over at my laptop, at the way I angled it perfectly so that my double chin wouldn't be as visible on the call with Aiden, and imagine everything I won't be able to ignore any longer with the start of the new year.

Patch, our chubby tabby cat, nestles up to my hand. "You're plump and *you* rock it," I whisper, scratching between his ears until he purrs. "So why can't I, too?"

But I know that's easier said than done.

I've been this fat before, in tenth grade. But then I shrank. Don't get me wrong: I wasn't thin by any means. Just thin*ner*. And in this fatphobic society, that matters. I had small-fat privilege.

The world was suddenly a little kinder. I didn't just see the shift in how everyone—classmates, teachers, strangers—looked at me, I felt it. I felt it in the way I was given spare smiles. I felt it in the way people no longer scooted away from me whenever I took the bus downtown. I felt it in the way people just let me do my thing without aiming glares at me.

I've tried to brace myself for what it'll be like when I step into school tomorrow: the whispers and the knowing looks and the loaded glances as everyone realizes I've gotten bigger. It doesn't matter that I don't actually mind so much, because others will have opinions. Even if no one says anything at all, can we all agree that the silence is its own special kind of torture?

When I lost a lot of weight the summer before junior year, *everyone* seemed to comment on it: the classmates I'd never exchanged a word with, the people I'd known all my life, my tías, my teachers. It was like my body had suddenly become public property and every single person felt it was their right—no, duty—to inform me that I had vastly improved it.

I'll admit that I reveled in the compliments. I took so many selfies. I hung notes on the corkboard near my desk that said things like IF YOU'RE NOT HUNGRY ENOUGH TO EAT AN APPLE, YOU'RE PROBABLY NOT HUNGRY and FACE YOUR STUFF; DON'T STUFF YOUR FACE. I was so smug about it, even donating all my "fat" clothes. I gave lip service to fat folks deserving dignity while reveling in my newfound smallness.

Fat hate, always internalized, sinks into every pore like poison.

It's only because I'm big again that I've had to have an internal reckoning with myself. Like, girl, you thought you had healed from the trauma society places upon you, but really, you just got better at fitting into society's expectations of beauty.

What a hard pill to swallow this summer, alongside...I don't know? The rest of my life being in total and utter shambles?

I gulp as I walk over to my closet, which used to be brimming with cute thrifted items. Now the selection is much more curated, a mix of Goodwill gems Abuela and I managed to find among a sea of matronly dresses and unsold MLM merchandise. The best items I have, Abuela has carefully tailored for me. Because each was altered with so much care and love, I treasure them…though I admit I find myself missing the days when I could waltz into any secondhand shop and enjoy a huge range of options.

Thankfully, I feel good about the outfit I've chosen for tomorrow. Since summer in New England has a tendency to linger well into September, I've opted for a sleeveless black bodysuit tucked into boot-cut jeans under an oversize houndstooth blazer. Paired with some chunky white sneakers, loose curls, gold hoops, and beautiful makeup, it's giving just the blend of sophisticated and stylish that I'm going for.

I hold the bodysuit up to myself in the mirror to confirm it was the right choice, and I smile. I'm going to look great. I just hope others can see that, too.

Mostly, I *haven't* changed:

My giant pile of dark hair—a melting pot of S Curls, DNA spirals, and waves like the ocean, hair that springs to life with even the subtlest of movements. (Abuelo would sometimes grab a strand, usually one of the curly Qs, and pull it just to "watch it dance.")

My carob-colored eyes that glisten like fire in the sun and darken like onyx when I'm sad.

My legs, which may be short but which are also strong and muscular.

My dimples, which hide when I'm expressionless but reveal themselves when I smile—something I inherited from Abuela.

I step closer to my mirror, examining my face and double-checking that a pimple hasn't decided to start forming because that would be Just. My. Luck.

My brown skin looks smooth and mostly blemish-free, except—

I toss the clothes I've been holding over to my bed and squint.

Is that a SMATTERING OF GIGANTIC BLACK HAIRS ON MY CHIN?

I practically smash my face into the glass trying to get a better look, but it's hard to see in the dim light of my room. I whip my bedroom door open and rush to the bathroom.

"Everything okay?" I hear Abuela call from down the hall, likely startled by the sound of me practically Kool-Aid Manning my way through the door.

"All good!" I shout. The last thing I need or want is for Abuela or Lily to come down to the bathroom while I get up close and personal with my hairy face in the mirror.

Dr. Delgado said the unwanted body hair on my stomach was totally normal, and she gently explained it could also pop up on my face. I guess I latched onto the tiny glimmer of hope in *could*, because I was not prepared for this. Why me? And why *now*?

My eyes blur as I examine the small but very-much-there dark hairs peppering my jaw. How long have these been there?

It's no use; the tears I've been fighting escape from the corners of my eyes and roll down my cheek. This is not the revelation I needed to have on the night before my first day of my senior year—not after everything else.

All I can think is that I need to shave ASAP. I turn on the water in the sink and grab my shave gel, squirting some in my palm. But only a small lump of foam comes out before it fizzles.

I'm out of shave gel. Of course.

Someone thunders down the hallway. I can tell it's Lily by the cadence of her steps. Her timing couldn't be worse, though I guess she doesn't know that. Quickly, I swipe at my cheeks and wash my hands under the cool water, splashing a bit on my face.

"Whit, you missed it!" Lily's voice says through the door.

I take in a deep breath and pull on the doorknob, giving her my best smile. "I missed what?"

"This little kid is singing 'Girl Be Mine' and he's sooooo good," she gushes.

"What?" I ask, distracted. I barely register that she's talking about one of the singles by Intonation, the boy band we love so much.

"Just come!" Lily snatches my arm and drags me all the way to the living room, where I see that she and Abuela are watching some kind of children's talent competition show. I vaguely remember hearing Lily talk to me about this—she loves all things music—but I can't even remember the name of it.

On the television, there's a replay of the kid singing. Under any other circumstances, I'm sure I would find him adorable, plop down on the couch with Lily and Abuela, and maybe even start to reminisce about our Intonation days...but this? This is serious. The bearded lady is out of shave gel on the eve of her first day of senior year.

Abuela puts her hand over her heart. "¡Que lindo! Isn't he the sweetest?"

"Yeah, Whit, see? He's so good!" Lily says, pointing at the TV. "He even has his hair styled just like Lucas!" (Lily is referring to the lead singer of Intonation, her favorite, though I always had a soft spot for the tattooed bad boy, Rider.)

"I see that. Very cute," I say, trying to hurry this conversation along, "but I have to run to the store."

Abuela raises an eyebrow at me. "Now?"

"Yes! I need something for school tomorrow."

"You nearly bought out the entire school supply section when we were there the other day," Abuela teases. "What could you have possibly missed?"

I ignore her good-natured ribbing and press on. "I'm just gonna run to the pharmacy really fast. Okay? I'll be quick."

Lily starts to rub her hands together the way she does whenever she's excited. "I wanna come!"

"No," I say sharply, causing Abuela to startle and look my way. "I mean, it'll be quicker if I go alone. You know." With my eyes, I try to communicate to Abuela that I really don't have the time for Lily to dawdle down the aisles.

Lily looks away from me, crossing her arms, and I can see that I've deflated her. But come *on*. I'm midcrisis here.

"Okay," Abuela finally says, glancing at me skeptically. Then she looks at Lily. "Lily, would you like anything?"

Lily keeps her arms crossed and her head facing the TV, as if ignoring me, but her eyes sneak a glance in my direction.

"Well?" I ask.

Lily says nothing and I look over at Abuela, who gives me a sympathetic shrug.

Wordlessly, I grab my keys, a scarf I have hanging by the door, and my purse, and head to my car. I wrap the fabric around my neck despite the warm evening, because I absolutely cannot take a chance on letting anyone see me like this. Who knows how many already have?

Thankfully, my car roars to life without hesitation, and I make it to the store in a blur. There, I grab what I came for in the beauty aisle (plus some tampons, a new razor, and a Mountain Dew) before making a beeline for the self-checkout.

I'm home lightning-fast and rip off my scarf before bolting inside.

"Jeez, that was quick!" Abuela remarks. "Did you fly?"

"Basically," I admit, slightly out of breath. "Sorry."

"What'd you need at the store that badly?" she asks. I reach into the paper bag and hold up my tampons. She frowns. "On the night before you start school? Cruel."

"Right? I hate never knowing when it'll start."

Abuela gives me a sympathetic nod.

I sigh and reach into the bag again and pull out the Mountain Dew, which I hold out for Lily as a peace offering. "I got this for you."

She glances over to see what I'm holding and can't hide the small smile that creeps across her face. "Thanks," she mumbles, reaching for the soda and immediately twisting off its cap.

"You're welcome. Enjoy the show," I say, making my way to the bathroom.

I close and lock the door behind me, dumping the contents of the bag onto the counter. With shaky hands, I pour some shave gel into my hands, rub them together as I would to lather up for my legs, and...realize I've never shaved my face before.

Is it the same as shaving your legs? Should I be in the shower? Is there any special direction I should shave in? How easy is it to cut myself?

Maybe I should've watched a YouTube video about this. But my hands are already covered in foam and I just want this to be *done*.

I'm quick with it: slather my face, wet my shaver, and slowly guide the blade over my skin, doing what feels right.

For a second, I lock eyes with myself in the mirror, face still half covered in shave gel, and nearly laugh out loud. If only end-of-junior-year, on-top-of-the-world Whit could see herself now.

A few more strokes before I'm done, then I wash my face, pat it dry, and inspect my work. My face is smooth, if a little red and blotchy from crying, but I'm hopeful my brown skin will tame the pinkness and everything will settle overnight.

I skip my pre–first-day-of-school ritual. Instead, I simply slip beneath the cozy blankets on my bed.

Patch starts to knead biscuits in my lap as I pull out my phone.

On social, I scroll and see a post from Marisol, who's posted a throwback photo of herself and her older sister, Natalia, with the poll: "Who was cuter? Me / Natalia"; a video about lettering styles for your bullet journals, which I save to watch later; and dozens of posts from classmates showing off their final night of summer.

But it's a video from Jay Martinez, a guy in my math class, that makes me sit up in my bed, startling Patch.

The video shows Jay and his friends skateboarding at a local skate park. That's not what catches my eye, though—what interests me is that I'm pretty sure he's hanging out with *Isaiah Ortiz,* my middle school boyfriend-turned-enemy.

Only it's a wonder what a summer has done to him. Isaiah is six feet tall and muscular, with skin the color of rich hickory. I scrub through the video more times than I care to admit, catching a glimpse of him here and there and wondering when the *hell* he got so hot.

Not that I'd ever tell him that.

Back in the day, sixth-grade Isaiah Ortiz was cute enough. We were always seated close together in class because of where our last names fell in the alphabet, so we got to know each other. He was obsessed with alt R&B and his beloved skateboard, and we got along well because he cracked dumb jokes that made me laugh. Eventually, we "dated" in that way middle school kids do: by passing notes back and forth. (I didn't have a cell phone yet, so the courtship was especially wholesome.)

But when we tried to take our relationship off paper and into real life, Isaiah ghosted. We had plans for our first real date at the movies, but he never showed...and then he immediately stopped talking to me. Even six years later, I'm not okay with the way he broke middle school Whitney's heart.

See? He doesn't deserve for me to even *think* he's cute.

As if to prove to myself he's not, I turn off my phone.

I get out of bed, agitated. At my desk, I load my notebooks into my backpack, and then let my gaze wander to the three-month calendar hanging above my laptop. It's normally brimming with notes, including dates with Aiden, hangouts with Marisol and Sophie, girls' nights with Lily and Abuela, solo craft nights for myself, notes about the return of my favorite TV shows.

But over the summer, I stopped filling the calendar out because I got sick of seeing nothing but work shifts and doctors' appointments. Instead, I just marked each passing day with a dramatic red X, so that August looked like nothing but a map with thirty-one hidden treasures.

September and October, which should be flooded with plans, are blank except for two things: FIRST DAY OF SENIOR YEAR and FALL FEST.

Long before my entire life fell apart, I decorated the seven days of this year's festival with tiny leaves and pumpkins as a reminder of what was to come—daydreaming of how Aiden would give me the perfect Fall Fest proposal; envisioning dress-shopping with Sophie and Marisol; picturing taking cheesy photos of me and Lily with Abuela so we could commemorate the day.

Something about those red Xs over all of August, marking all this time I've already lost, sparks a fire in my chest. I need this upcoming year to be better than the summer—and it's up to me to make it happen.

It's me and you now, fall. Don't let me down.

SEPTEMBER 2023

Sunday	Monday	Tuesday	Wednesday	Thursday	Friday	Saturday
					1	2
3	4	5 *first day of senior year!*	6	7	8	9
10	11	12	13	14	15	16
17	18	19	20	21	22	23
24	25	26	27	28	29	30

OCTOBER 2023

Sunday	Monday	Tuesday	Wednesday	Thursday	Friday	Saturday
1	2	3	4	5	6	7
8	9	10	11	12	13	14
15 *Fall Fest begins!*	16	17	18	19	20	21 *Fall Fest ends!*
22	23	24	25	26	27	28
29	30	31 *Halloween*				

Chapter Three

Even before my alarm goes off, the feeling of something on my forehead startles me out of my slumber.

"Wake up!" Lily whisper-shouts in my face.

I groan and swat her away.

She yanks on my blanket. "Come *aaaahn*."

I open one eye to squint at the kitten-shaped alarm clock beside my bed, which reads 5:58, a full thirty-two minutes before my actual alarm is supposed to go off. If I didn't love Lily so much, I might actually kill her. How dare she steal rest from me when I had so much trouble falling asleep last night?

I was up *late*. The calendar above my desk was daring me to add something—anything—meaningful to it, and I found myself needing to take control. Needing a plan. So I pulled out my notebook and, on the cream-colored first page, wrote this:

Whit's Totally Definitive Guide to the Perfect Senior Year

1. Make Aiden fall in love with me again.
2. Reignite my friendship with Sophie and Marisol.
3. Ensure that Lily's freshman year is memorable.
4. Find a way to get my PCOS under control.
5. Get elected president of the Fall Fest committee and make Fall Fest my entire personality.

All five action items really boil down to the same thing: stop letting life call the shots and take back senior year, so help me Goddess (Beyoncé).

"Good morning, my irritating baby sister," I say, rubbing the sleep from my eyes and welcoming her round brown face into focus. Her shoulder-length brown hair, curly like mine, is French-braided in two, likely by Abuela. Part of me is sad to have missed out on their TV-and-hair-braiding session.

"Aren't you ready for school yet?" Lily teases. "You're going to be late."

"I know I warned you that high school starts a lot earlier than middle school, but this is a bit much, don't you think?"

She ignores my question and instead says, "I *really* want to wear my pink-and-white backpack, but I can't find it."

If there's one thing I love about Lily, it's her unwavering sincerity. "Need some help?" I ask.

Lily takes this as permission to pull the rest of my comforter away from me with a grin.

As we tiptoe down the hallway toward her bedroom, the gravity of today hits me. I've been so worried about what this day will mean to me that I haven't given enough thought to what it'll mean for Lily.

Today, Liliana Margaret Rivera, my baby sister, will officially be joining me at Elmwood High School as an incoming freshman! Meaning: she's probably feeling just as nervous as I am.

Despite her annoying tendency to wake me up before my alarm (she will get hers, I promise), Lily is a bundle of delight: bright, caring, funny, creative, silly, totally obsessed with Intonation, a Mountain Dew–drinking champion, and autistic. She loves anything related to music, never lets me play with her Nintendo Switch, and purposely gets song lyrics wrong because she knows it bugs me.

I'll admit that I can be fiercely protective of Lily, as I think many older siblings are. But the fact that sometimes people don't "get" her makes me even more protective.

Lily can struggle to pick up on certain social cues, and people notice that. They also notice that she isn't terribly keen on close physical affection, like hugs (though she's perfectly happy with a high five or fist bump); that her happy mood may turn angry in the blink of an eye; that she rubs her hands together whenever she's excited. They make assumptions about who she is.

It hurts when our classmates poke fun at her, whether over missed signals or over "uncool" things she's done. Worse are the classmates who have tried to take advantage of her because she is so trusting. And don't get me started on the teachers who've lacked patience.

The best people see *all* parts of Lily.

I do my best to be there for her whenever I can, and now that we'll be in the same school again, this will be a little easier. (We'll need to work on the getting-up-way-too-early thing, though.)

In Lily's room, we start our search for her backpack in the closet. When that fails, we check her bureau, under the bed, and behind her laundry basket. We nearly turn the room upside down in our quest, making so much noise that we wake Abuela.

She pokes her head into Lily's disaster of a room. "¿Qué pasó?"

"I need my pink-and-white backpack!" Lily says.

"We've looked everywhere." I sigh. "Any suggestions?"

"Ay, Lily." Abuela clucks her tongue, her knees clicking as she kneels near Lily's bookcase before I can protest. In one swift motion, she reaches behind the shelf and pulls out the backpack. "Here it is."

"How'd you know exactly where it was?"

Abuela chuckles. "I tell you: se todo. Now, ¡vámanos! You don't want to be late."

This adventure with Lily has eaten up a good chunk of my morning, leaving me next to no time to do what I'd planned. Forget writing a bullet list or leisurely doing my makeup—I'll be lucky if I manage to diffuse my hair before racing out the door.

"Have you showered yet?" I ask Lily. She ignores me and searches through her backpack instead. *"Lily."*

"No," she confesses.

"Shoot," I mutter. "Well, hurry!"

Abuela corrals Lily toward the bathroom and I rush to the kitchen to grab some breakfast, mind racing. I have a full day of classes, including several AP courses I'm hoping will translate into college credit. And I need to show Lily around the school and make sure she can get to and from her classes and locker okay. And I promised Marisol and Sophie I'd meet them in the courtyard before the day even starts.

While I wait for Lily to finish her shower, I decide to text Aiden. It's his first day of school, too.

Me: Good luck today!

Aiden: With what?

Oh, you sweet, sweet himbo.

Me: Isn't it your first day at your new school?

Aiden: Oh, yeah. But I'm not worried! 😎

That makes one of us.

I wish he would send me a little encouragement back, even something small. But then I remember number one on my list, *Make Aiden fall in love with me again,* and push past that.

Me: You shouldn't be! You'll be great. 🖤

I try not to explode when Aiden like-reacts my text. It's fine.

Lily is taking her sweet, sweet time in the shower, and at this rate, I'm not going to have time to stop for a PSL on the drive; I may not even be able to meet up with Sophie and Marisol.

I march over to the bathroom and knock on the door. Lily's voice rings out in between the steady thrum of the shower as she's performing a one-woman concert.

"Lily!" I shout. "I need to get in there, too!"

No answer. I knock again, more forcefully this time. When there's still no response, I call out, "Abuela! Lily's taking forever!"

Abuela emerges from her bedroom shaking her head. "I've told Lily no Intonation in the morning. It gets her too distracted!"

This family's love for that boy band knows no limits. The three of us bonded over the five-member group ages ago, and our love is just as strong now as it ever was (though the older I get, the shyer I am about admitting that in public).

Abuelo loved to tease us about "our boys" and how often we would dance and sing along to their music. I was head over heels in love with them. I had committed everything about them—from their favorite colors to their birthdays—to memory; I made social media accounts dedicated to them; and I was even convinced I would someday marry Rider. (The wedding colors would be varying hues of his favorite color, green. Obviously.) Lily was similarly enthralled, though her number one was Lucas. Henry, the clean-cut, religious member of the band, was Abuela's cariño—so much so that sometimes we would joke that Abuelo should watch out.

We've been to two of their concerts, memorized the lyrics to all of their songs, and were appropriately devastated when they announced their sudden breakup during my sophomore year of high school. Lily took it the hardest of us all, and Intonation remains her favorite band ever. She plays their music near-incessantly, and talks about them as if they still perform. If only.

So believe me: I get why their music inspires my little sister to put on her own concert. If she feels anything like me, Intonation still sparks the most intense nostalgia, reminding us of simpler times, a shared love among the three of us, and the playful ribbing from Abuelo, which I think we all miss deeply.

But she needs to hurry up so I can have the shower.

When the bathroom door finally bursts open, I glance at the clock. We're absolutely, 100 percent going to be late.

I pull up my group text with Marisol and Sophie.

Me: I'm so sorry, but I can't make it this morning 😭

Sophie: But it's tradition!!!

Me: I know! I want to be there SO BADLY.

Me: Lily has been hogging the shower and I'm just now getting in. I'll make it up to you!

Neither of my friends replies, and I kind of don't blame them.

I take a cold shower and then dash out the door with Lily in tow. By the time we make it to school, we're not just pumpkin spice latte–less; we've missed homeroom. I have to literally run to get Lily to her first class before speeding to the other side of the school to find my own.

As I plop into the only open seat, sweating and out of breath, I realize that this one misstep has swiftly taken me out of the running for perfect attendance for the entire year.

So much for getting things back on track.

At least I look cute...but this moment of self-confidence doesn't last very long.

In second period, Brock Moore, one of the baseball kids, loudly clears his throat and says, "Whoa, Whit. You look...different." He makes a show of puffing out his cheeks. Only his best friend, Dom Taylor, laughs, but still.

All I can manage is an exaggerated eye roll at him, unwilling to let him see that my insides are shaking. I tell myself that at least I've gotten the first pointed insult out of the way. Now I can move on.

Throughout the day, I do my best to ignore the sideways glances, not-so-subtle lookbacks, and wide-eyed exchanges between friends and teachers.

I may have given up diets, but sometimes I wish I could give up this cruel society, too.

Chapter Four

Things That Go Wrong on My First Day of School

1. Lily uses all the hot water so I take an ice-cold shower.
2. I'm late.
3. I don't get to see Marisol and Sophie before school, even though I promised I'd be there.
4. I don't even get a pumpkin spice latte even though I deserve ALL the PSLs!!!
5. Brock Moore and Dom Taylor exist.
6. I spill water on my BRAND-NEW JOURNAL and waterlog a bunch of the pages.
7. The ink on Whit's Totally Definitive Guide to the Perfect Senior Year bleeds, and when I blot it with napkins, part of the list just disappears…a surefire sign that this senior year will be anything but perfect.
8. At lunch, I'm so stressed that Sophie and Marisol might be mad at me that I ask them if it's okay if I sit at their table. They look at me like I have five heads, and we sit through an A+ awkward lunch.
9. The sleeve of my blazer catches on my locker and the button rips off, which is really the icing on the cake of this craptastic day.

On top of all of that, Lily barely registers me when I show up at her locker to pick her up, and she simply keeps packing her things into her backpack.

"Hi, Lily!" I chirp. "How was day one of your freshman year?"

She shrugs.

"That good, huh?" I joke.

When she offers nothing, I tell her about my day instead—though I leave out the part about Brock and his puffed cheeks.

"I feel like my class schedule is going to be killer," I ramble, leading Lily. "I have a class with one of my favorite teachers, though, so that's nice." Lily's looking down at her phone while I talk, but I press on. "How were things with you? Any good classes?"

"It was fine," Lily says.

I push through the heavy doors that lead to the parking lot. "Just fine? I told you about my whole day. That's all I get?"

Lily rolls her eyes. "It was *school*. What is there to say?"

Only a million things! Were people generally nice? Which teacher was her favorite? How was it navigating school? What did she eat for lunch? Did anything funny happen?

I huff. "Sor-*ry*. I was just wondering if anyone noticed your backpack. They better have, given that searching for it helped make us super late this morning."

Lily stays quiet as we approach our car, and I instantly feel bad.

"I'm sorry. I shouldn't have said it like that." I shake my head, pushing some of my curls out of my face. "It's been a long day."

Lily pulls open the car door and throws her book bag inside before plopping on the seat. "Tell me about it," she mutters.

So badly, I want to probe and ask what went wrong. But she clearly wants to be left alone.

Instead, I let the quiet settle between us as we make the drive home. Frankly, I'm tired, too. I don't mind the silence, though I am startled when we turn onto our street and Lily gasps and points.

"It's Nora and them! Can you let me out here?" Nora is one of Lily's friends from our block. Though they're around the same age, Nora goes to private school, so Lily never gets to see her during the day.

"Sure." I ease the car to the side of the road and Lily hops out with her backpack.

When I turn into our driveway a moment later, I'm surprised to find Abuela grimacing from her seat on the front steps, rubbing her hip. In her midfifties, Abuela's not old by any means, but she does have a bad hip, which she hates talking about because she says it's an elderly-people problem and she's *not* elderly. Still, it acts up sometimes and reminds her she should take it easy.

Judging by the appearance of the thin headband that's keeping her short black hair from falling into her face—something she only ever puts on when she's doing physical work—I know there's no way she's been taking it easy.

"Abuela!" I call, rushing over to her and dumping my bag onto the step beside her feet. "What happened?"

"Nada," she insists, clasping her hands together like she wasn't just rubbing her hip. "I wanted to get all these decorations up before you got home as a nice surprise after your first day."

I glance around and see that my abuela has lugged out two plastic bins stuffed with fall décor onto our front porch. Not much has made it out of the bins just yet, but I'm irritated all the same. She knows better!

I point over at the bins. "Please tell me a big, burly lumberjack randomly carried those up onto the porch?"

Abuela gives me a sheepish grin. "Ay, don't worry about it."

"Abuela," I groan. "You have to take care of yourself!"

"I know, I know," she says, reaching for a hand. "Help me up, will you?"

Slowly, I guide her to her feet and over to one of the outdoor rocking chairs. "How about you watch *me* do some decorating?"

"Yes," Abuela says, in a way that sounds like "jes." "¿Dónde está Lily?"

"We saw Nora on the drive home, so she's over at her place," I explain.

"Ah, okay. So how was your first day?"

I wrinkle my nose at her. "Honestly? It kinda stunk."

"No! ¿Porqué?"

"Well, I was late, for starters." I reach into the bin and pull out some fake cornstalks, rummaging around till I find twine to secure them to the square porch columns.

Abuela tsks. "I'm going to talk to Lily tonight. Maybe if she takes her showers in the evenings, you can get to school on time."

"That would be great, actually. Thank you," I say, starting to arrange the stalks. "But I mean, it wasn't just that. After I missed homeroom, I felt like I spent the entire day catching up, not enjoying my final first day at Elmwood. I was rushing so much that I actually got caught on my locker and my sleeve ripped." I hold up my arm to show her.

"Ah, I can fix that, easy," she assures me with a wave of her hand.

"Thank you, Abuela." I smile, though it fades as I remember Brock and Dom. "Two of my classmates were huge jerks to me, too."

Abuela straightens her spine, her face instantly hardening. "What did they do?"

I wave a hand at her concern. "It's nothing serious. They just laughed at me."

"¿Porqué?" she demands.

I motion toward my midsection and laugh a little. It's not funny, but it sure feels incredibly awkward. "Mis chichos."

Abuela slaps her hands together in a way that makes me think she might be imagining Brock's and Dom's heads between her palms. "I'm calling the school."

The way school sounds like "e-school" softens my otherwise worn heart.

"No, no. It's not a big deal."

"It is!"

I shake my head. "If you call, it'll just let them know they upset me. I don't want that. Honestly, more than anything, the worst part of the day was just"—I busy myself with tying a length of twine around the column so I don't have to look at her as I say this next part—"that I didn't feel like myself, I guess."

I don't let on that it's been this way for a bit. I don't want her to freak out.

A sympathetic expression falls across Abuela's face. "Oh, nena. Why didn't you say something? We can schedule another follow-up with Dr. Delgado." Her voice drops to a whisper, even though it's just us. "Is it your tummy?"

Dr. Delgado has me trying metformin, a medication she says can help manage insulin resistance—one of the long-lasting, many, and varied symptoms of PCOS. A side effect of the medicine is that it can cause an upset stomach.

"It's not that," I say quickly, busying myself by draping a colorful maple leaf garland on the railing. "More like everything, I guess. This summer was *a lot* to deal with and maybe I haven't been processing it very well."

Abuela nods. "Ay, bendito. Come here."

I go to her on the chair, perching on its arm, and let her envelop me in a hug. She smells like a mix of Aussie hairspray and Jean Naté—a sweet, citrusy perfume Abuela's worn since I was a little girl. A wave of comfort washes over me at the familiar scent, and at being this close. I even let her stroke my hair.

This horrible day mixed with the ongoing exhaustion of dealing with an illness for which there is no cure might be catching up with me.

"Thank you, Abuela." I let her rock me back and forth for a moment. "Enough about me, though. How was work?"

"Bien, bien. Less fun than when you and your sister are around,"

Abuela says. "I'd gotten used to you both keeping me company in the shop!"

"I missed it, too," I admit.

Lily and I had made a habit this summer of helping Abuela at El Coquí, her tailoring and dry cleaning shop. If I find joy in lists and order, Abuela finds her joy in the art of fabric. She can breathe new life into any garment—patch holes, create new silhouettes, make any outfit fit like a glove. Her hands work so quickly, steady and confident, that I'm dizzy when I see her using her sewing machines.

Though I can do basic sewing, I'm not very good. Instead, I help with the bookkeeping and split cleaning and inventory duties with Lily, three things that used to fall to Abuelo. Lily also handles some of the marketing, like designing flyers and posting to our Instagram.

"Maybe you can ask Titi Mariana and Titi Luisa to visit you more," I suggest.

"*Oh* no. No, no, no!" Abuela wags a finger at me. "I am not inviting my older sisters to come in and boss me around." At this, I laugh. My tías *can* be pretty bossy, especially Titi Mariana. "I'd rather be in the quiet alone."

We rock in the chair a little longer before I rise to finish decorating the porch. I hang leaf garlands, twinkle lights, and a wreath made of synthetic pine cones and mums; arrange corn stalks and ceramic pumpkins; decorate the wicker rocking chairs with umber pillows; and set out a welcome mat that reads HEY, GOURD-EOUS.

When I'm done, I stand back to survey the work. Though our little one-story, pewter-colored bungalow isn't much, it's perfect for us. And for Abuela, who can easily access everything without having to venture up any stairs.

"This porch is looking just like fall. Abuelo would love it," she says, gesturing around us. "You did good, mija."

Chapter Five

Nothing is going to stop me from meeting up with Sophie and Marisol this morning.

I lay out my clothes. I prepack my bag. I prepare breakfast in advance. *And* I wake up extra early to shower, which I'm actually okay with—it avoids Lily waking me like a sleep-deprivation demon.

We're even out the door with enough time to swing by Starbucks to grab three PSLs and a strawberry iced tea for Lily. I walk my little sister to her homeroom, then practically sprint toward the school's courtyard. It's the one pretty spot at this ancient school, a grassy area with octagonal picnic tables surrounded by pink dogwood trees that turn salmon come spring. A giant elm tree in the center of the courtyard offers ample shade on the hot days.

When Marisol and Sophie show, I offer my best and most apologetic smile. "Hi!"

Sophie smiles back. "Hey!"

"Hi," Marisol says, voice flat, as if she's already bored with me. She's never too shy to make it clear how she's feeling. If it isn't obvious enough by her tone or mannerisms, she'll tell you, point-blank, no guesswork involved.

With the tips of my fingers, I scoot the tray of drinks toward the two of them. "Pumpkin spice latte?"

Marisol sniffs. "Somebody's sucking up."

I reach for one of the drinks. "I'm not ashamed to admit that. Look, I even waited to take a sip until you two showed up. That's love."

"That *is* love," Sophie agrees, reaching for her cup and sliding into the seat next to me. She bumps her shoulder into mine. "Thanks."

When Marisol doesn't budge, I turn the cup around to show her a tiny sun the barista drew beside her name. "Cute, right?" It's a reference to her nickname, Sol. When not even that impresses her, I get desperate: I pick up her drink and pretend to make it talk in a high-pitched voice. "Aww, c'mon, Sol. You know you want me!"

That makes her break, and the sound of her laughter is sweet relief. "Fine, you weirdo. I'll take the latte." She playfully snatches the cup away from me and sits, shaking her head. "Thank you."

I give her a little nod. "So, how'd the rest of the afternoon go for you guys yesterday?"

"It wasn't terrible. Most of my teachers are ones I've already had, so they all adore me." Marisol dramatically flips her dyed bronze curls over her shoulder.

"Except for Mr. Greene," Sophie says, wrinkling her nose.

Marisol groans. "Ugh. Don't even get me started on that pendejo."

My eyes go wide. "What happened?" I ask.

"She got stuck with Mr. Greene for AP History, and apparently he used to *love* Natalia," Sophie explains. "He was not shy about letting Marisol know it."

"He kept calling me Natalia Pérez's Little Sister. As if that's all I am!"

I make a face. "What? That's not okay at all!"

Sophie sighs. "That's what I said. But he's super tight with Principal Johnson, so he gets away with everything."

"He's probably going to make me suffer all year long because I'm nothing like the Supreme Teacher's Pet Natalia." Marisol rolls her eyes. "I'm obviously way better."

"Obviously," I say with a laugh. "But I'm sorry. What a douchebag."

"It's whatever." Marisol shrugs. "*This one* got quite the surprise, though."

Sophie can't hide the soft blush that creeps across her cheeks. "It was definitely a surprise."

"Well?" I press. "Don't leave me hanging. Spill!"

"Loverboy Noah had the hookup and somehow managed to switch a ton of his classes so they'd be on the same exact schedule," Marisol says. She clears her throat and makes her voice low, imitating Noah. "*Babe, I just can't fathom not being with you twenty-four seven. You're the air that I breathe, babe. Can I carry your books, babe? Should we get matching sweaters? Babe? Babe!*"

Sophie shoves Marisol in the arm. "Oh my God, shut *up!*"

"What?" Marisol asks, laughing. "That's what he sounds like! I'm surprised he's not texting you right now, like, *Babe! Babe, I haven't seen you in, like, hours. I need you, babe!*" A perfectly timed text sets Sophie's phone buzzing on the table, and Marisol dives for it. "It's him! I told you!"

The two of them erupt into more laughter, Sophie desperately trying to wriggle her phone from Marisol's grip. I laugh, too, though there is a small pang of jealousy in my chest as I listen to their easy banter. This is what I've been missing out on.

Sophie holds up her phone triumphantly, unlocking it to show us the notification. "See? It wasn't even him. It's a notification from my French teacher clarifying a homework assignment."

Marisol rolls her eyes. "*Boring.*"

"Speaking of my French teacher...Madame Dubois was saying there's a music internship program Elmwood is offering this winter—and it takes place in Paris."

I grip her wrist excitedly. "You have to apply!" I quasi-shout. I hardly know anything about this opportunity and I'm practically salivating on Sophie's behalf. She's dedicated the last three years to the violin, and her French is *parfait*. Not to mention the girl's *obsessed* with Paris.

"I'm thinking about it, but my parents would lose their minds." Sophie sighs. "It would require me to be in France for three weeks over holiday break."

"Three weeks is nothing," Marisol says.

"To Má and Ba, I might as well be abandoning the family and running away from home."

I take a sip of my PSL and consider this. "Okay, so, we'll have to figure out a creative way to sell them on this."

"*If* I even get the internship," Sophie adds. "You really think I should apply?"

"Oh, you're applying, and you're *getting* this internship. That's a promise," Marisol says. "We'll do some plotting this week."

"I'm in," I say with a nod. "And actually, I wanted to run something by you two."

Marisol looks over at me. "Oh, yeah? What's up?"

"I *really* want to be on the Fall Fest committee this year. Like, do the whole running-for-Fall-Fest-president thing, even. And I was kind of hoping you guys would join the committee with me."

I'm surprised when Sophie immediately exchanges a look with Marisol. "Oh, um. It's just that Marisol and I had talked this summer about maybe auditioning for the school play..."

After a long moment, "Oh" is all I can think to say back.

"I mean, you weren't around, so we couldn't exactly discuss it with you!" Marisol argues.

"But, I mean...it wasn't set in stone or anything. What does being on the committee entail?" Sophie asks. "Like, we'd have to organize everything?"

"Yes, exactly! Choose the themes and help execute the events," I explain.

Marisol wrinkles her nose, as if she's just smelled something sour. "It sounds like a lot of work."

My heart sinks. How can I convince them that this will be fun?

"It'll look really good on our college applications," I offer. "If I'm president, I'd handle all the heavy lifting with whoever is named senior officer. Honestly, you two could just be there for moral support!"

"Do you even know the first thing about organizing a huge event like that? It's a whole week of activities! Plus a dance." Marisol puts a hand on either side of her temples. "I'm overwhelmed just thinking about it."

"I understand it's a lot, but you guys know how organized I am, and you know how determined I can be if I set my sights on something," I say. "I can do this."

Sophie grimaces. "I know *you* can do it. But do *we* have to?"

"I could do it alone," I admit. "But I was hoping to share Fall Fest with both of you."

How much, exactly, do I love Fall Fest? Let me count the ways.

Mi abuela y abuelo, Paola Acevedo and Eduardo Rivera, met at the Fall Fest in the late seventies. But it wasn't some kind of instant fairy-tale romance. Abuela rejected him at first.

They were the only two Puerto Rican students at Elmwood (though that's thankfully changed!), and their friends insisted they had to get together—because a shared ethnicity destines two people to fall in love, right?

Abuela was insulted that everyone was trying to set up the only two brown kids. She admits that she stubbornly wouldn't speak to Abuelo for most of the night, despite their friends conveniently pushing them together at every turn. But it became hard to ignore him, Abuela says, because Abuelo was funny and charismatic and unbelievably cute with his black curly hair, deep voice, and sharp jawline.

Despite not exchanging much in the way of words, Abuela kept sneaking glances at Abuelo, and Abuelo wouldn't stop trying to charm her—with jokes and bravado and dance moves and a laugh that sounded like music. He was determined to make her smile, and the moment he did, catching sight of her dimples, he fell to his knees and pretended his heart was thumping right out of his chest. Abuelo was smitten.

He used to say it was as if a golden light had shone down on his Paola and his heart decided it had seen enough—she was everything.

They danced with fervor, with joy, with connection, the way only two people who long to be seen and understood can. They talked about their families; their traditions; our culture; the music and foods that felt like home...and somewhere between the fake leaves and scratchy haystacks they fell in love. Everything about that night felt like theirs and theirs alone.

It's a story they always shared fondly, and one I cherish.

But Fall Fest was only the beginning. They bought their house in the autumn; they got engaged in the autumn; and it was in autumn when their Julia, mi mami, was born.

We don't talk about her, though.

Sometimes I wish the story of her absence in my life was slightly more interesting than "She just left right after Lily was born." Couldn't she have been abducted by El Cuco or something?

First she had me. When my biological father (the sperm donor, as I call him) found out he and Mami's casual fling had resulted in an unexpected pregnancy, he booked it to Puerto Rico, leaving Mami to nurse a broken heart. But she didn't give up on love, and found another man, Lily's father, Andrés, shortly thereafter.

He didn't want kids, either, though: not any of his own and definitely not a talkative three-year-old that he'd inherit as part of the relationship. So after Mami, a hopeless romantic, gave birth to

Lily, Andrés convinced her to run away with him, and away from all of us—breaking Abuela's and Abuelo's hearts in the process.

The good thing is we were so young that Lily and I don't really remember any of that. As far as we're concerned, Abuela and Abuelo are our parents, and we've had the joy of extended family through our tías abuelas and tíos abuelos and their families. I know it has always been hard for them, though, to be estranged from their one and only little girl.

It's partly because of this that I think Abuela and Abuelo poured so much of themselves into us. They always ensured that Lily and I felt loved and appreciated. Part of that manifested in going big on all celebrations and carving out Rivera traditions, especially the one related to autumn, a season that brought Abuelo and Abuela so much joy over the years.

So fall feels like it's mine. Fall Fest isn't just a celebration of homecoming. It's a celebration of my family.

Is it so wrong, then, to want to share this with my best friends?

Sophie turns to Marisol. "Well...there *is* always the spring play..."

Marisol breaks, too. "Ugh. *I was hoping to share Fall Fest with both of you, my dearest companions.* Why'd you have to go and be all sappy?"

"You love that about me," I say.

"Do I?" she teases, and I stick out my tongue.

"First meeting's tomorrow. After school." I clap my hands together. "It'll be fun! Like old times."

"We'll go," Marisol agrees. "But if it ends up being trash, we're bailing."

I grin at her. "I think that's more than fair."

Chapter Six

The next afternoon, I walk Lily to the bus line in front of the school since I won't be able to give her a ride home. She's reluctant, seeming like she'd rather not put me out, but I'm just being a good sister.

My friends and I head to one of the small classrooms on the lower level of Elmwood. It's air-conditioned in this wing, thankfully, so we're not bogged down by the suffocating humidity that's lingering. I'm especially grateful because I chose to wear a chunky sweater today, convinced that I could somehow make autumn arrive via my wardrobe choices. Summer, can you please give it a rest already?

Once we're seated, I cast a glance over at Marisol and Sophie and give them a bright smile. "Excited?" I ask, lifting my shoulders and doing a little shimmy.

"Practically peeing my pants," Marisol says in a monotone.

Sophie swats at her arm and I laugh, taking a moment to survey the room. There are more than two dozen students, a mix from each grade. I recognize some of them, mostly the seniors, like Chloe Torres, an artsy fellow Boricua always covered in paint, and Cyrus Ali, who has the most incredible hair. If they're planning to run for Fall Fest president, they should know that I could crush them both like bugs. (Respectfully.)

As I'm plotting their demise, Ms. Bennett, my favorite teacher, waltzes into the room.

Though she teaches math, a subject I'm woefully bad at,

Ms. Bennett is endlessly patient with me. She never hesitates to sit me down and explain a stats problem (once, twice, and maybe even a third time). She also has a to-die-for wardrobe of quirky printed dresses. Today she's wearing one with little robots on it.

"Hello, hello!" Ms. Bennett says cheerfully. "I'm thrilled to be this year's Fall Fest advisor and I thank you all for coming." She looks around the room at us and smiles. "For those of you who are first-years, you may have heard rumblings about the Fall Fest, but let me give you a rundown."

"Fall Fest is Elmwood High's weeklong autumn-inspired homecoming. It usually happens the third week in October, when fall foliage is often at its peak. A committee of students is elected to organize the week and its central event—the dance. These students will hold all the planning power. Doesn't that sound incredible?"

YES, I think.

"Committee roles will be filled with a vote. In all, we need a president, a position open to seniors only; a senior officer, to assist the president; and class representatives for juniors, sophomores, and first-years. It will be a five-person board. Everyone else will be a valued volunteer and help as needed. Yes, you can still put that on your college applications."

Once Ms. Bennett has finished, she opens the floor for questions.

I'm surprised when Marisol's hand is the first to rise. "I'm wondering about the voting process for Fall Fest court. I know there has historically been a ban on campaigning for yourself, but has that changed this year?"

Two years ago, Davin Reed and Elsie Astor not only collectively used their parents' riches to hire a skywriter to write VOTE FOR DAVIN + ELSIE *in the freaking sky,* but were also found to be secretly bribing students to rig the vote for king and queen. Principal Johnson put a swift end to all campaigning efforts after that.

"Ah," Ms. Bennett says. "Fall Fest court rules are the same as always. Interested participants can self-nominate or be nominated, and then it's up to your peers to vote."

Marisol sighs. To me and Sophie, she whispers, "I was really hoping to campaign for me and Ari."

Sophie pats her hand sympathetically, and I mouth *Sorry* as Ms. Bennett calls on Hudson Moore, a sophomore, for the next question.

"Hi. So, I know that crowning has always taken place at the football game. And that's sort of what happens everywhere. But hear me out: How about crowning homecoming court at the homecoming *dance*?"

Leilani Mamea, a junior who always has her hair pulled back into fun hairstyles like today's space buns, leans forward in her desk excitedly. "Oooh, like prom?"

Hudson points a finger at her. "*Exactly* like prom! Not all of us love watching a bunch of jocks grunt at each other on the football field. To each their own, but I, for one, would enjoy skipping all that nonsense."

"Oh my gosh—I love this idea," I whisper to Sophie and Marisol as others start to agree, too.

Ms. Bennett holds up both of her hands. "While I appreciate this delightful enthusiasm, decisions like that can only be made by our committee, which we'll be voting for on Monday. If you're planning to self-nominate for a committee role, use this weekend to gather your materials: you can present your case at our next meeting before we cast ballots. If there are no other questions, we'll see each other Monday after school. Same time, same place!"

She pauses a beat to check for hands. I'm practically bursting with questions about the election process: Are there examples of successful campaign speeches given by past Fall Fest presidents? How long do I get to talk? Can I bring visuals? Once elected, exactly how much power will I have? But I keep my mouth shut and instead vow to email the questions to her later.

"Okay, then. Let's call it for today," Ms. Bennett says. "I'll see you all next week!"

Marisol, Sophie, and I start to pack our things and go, and I give Ms. Bennett a small wave on my way out.

"The fact that we can't campaign for court because two rich idiots bribed their way to the top is so frustrating," Marisol laments. "As if that's not the American way!"

"It does suck," Sophie agrees. "I'm sorry."

"Honestly, Sol—even without being able to officially push for votes, I think you'll get your place on court," I say, adjusting my backpack on my shoulders. "Everyone already loves you and Ari."

Marisol frowns. "Yeah, but we've never had a queer couple win court. I just figured if we could campaign ahead of it..." She lets out a long sigh. "Pero, it's whatever. Let's talk about something else."

Sophie frowns for a moment, but her face lights up as we step outside into the sticky September air. "Okay! Well, how about the fact that we have yet to live our best life as a pool trio?"

"Who needs your pool when it already feels like we're swimming?" I pull my long curls into a thick ponytail.

"I'm serious! How about tomorrow? I'm dying for you guys to visit." She cuts a glance my way. "*Both* of you."

Right. Because based on their social posts, I know Marisol has been to Sophie's house plenty this summer. It's me who's been woefully absent.

In my defense, the two of them live on the same street—in one of the wealthier parts of town, I might add—so even if I hadn't been slammed with medical appointments and shifts at El Coquí, I likely wouldn't have been around as much as they wanted.

I can try to be there now, though.

"Let's do it," I say with a nod.

Sophie squeals and throws her arms around me. "The Tran household hasn't been the same without you."

* * *

That is how I find myself standing in one of the three (!) pristine bathrooms at Sophie's house the next afternoon, staring at my reflection in the mirror.

The scene feels familiar enough. I've been to Sophie's house to swim hundreds of times. Her insulin pump is dutifully placed on the shelf above the towel rack, like always, and there is even a towel with the letter w that hangs from the back of the door—Sophie's mom had it monogrammed for me ages ago when they were investing in new pool gear. All of that's the same.

But I'm different.

Internally, my body is feeling a little weird. I'm tired. Still having to shave my face daily, still fearful that someone might notice the tiny nick I gave myself this morning. No period in sight. And externally, well...

It's complicated, okay? I'm hot...but I'm shy, too. Some days I'm thinking I'm such a freaking queen I want to rock a crop top and miniskirt and have people groveling at my feet. Other days, like today, my eyes seem to hone in on all the parts of myself that jiggle a little too much.

It's not like fat girls and pools have historically been on the best of terms. Like, shopping for swimsuits is hard enough as it is, but finding a plus-size swimsuit can be a downright nightmare. The selection has definitely gotten better, but most swimsuits for fat girls are still expensive as hell, and often not very cute.

After what felt like weeks of searching, I stumbled across a retro yellow halter one-piece that ties behind the neck. It practically cost an arm and a leg, but Abuela insisted I needed a bathing suit. It looks so cute. Yet...

My body is the biggest one here, you know?

I steal a glance out the window, where I can see Sophie, in a simple seafoam-green bikini, floating in the center of the pool on a bright pink flamingo. Her shoulder-length black hair is fanned out behind her, making her look like a tiny brown goddess. She bobs her head to whatever song is playing off Marisol's Spotify playlist. I can't hear it in here.

Marisol, meanwhile, is all curves with café con leche skin that seems to sparkle in the sun (likely from the shimmer lotion she obsessively applies well beyond summer). In her zebra-print two-piece, she's showing Sophie a dance that goes along with the song that's playing, the coils of her hair bouncing as she moves.

Last summer, the three of us spent nearly every day in the pool. I was totally fine joining in with the two of them with my smaller size fourteen body.

But I am beautiful like this. I am. I am. I *am*.

The white tile is cold beneath my bare feet. I use that sensation to ground me as I take a long, steady breath in.

Go, Whit. Just go.

I stride into the backyard as if I'm strutting down the runway. Fake it till you make it, right?

Outside, an in-ground pool is surrounded by a natural-stone patio. There's a small waterfall with a grotto at one end, which Soph and I used to use as our secret mermaid hideout, and a connected hot tub at the other. Almond-colored chaise lounges are lined up perfectly on one side. Even more amazing, the surrounding yard is so green it looks fake, with plants that spill over every surface (thanks to Sophie's dad's green thumb). Her backyard is my favorite part of her house, although her entire Tudor-style home, with its cottage-style brick-and-stucco siding, looks like it was plucked right from *The Secret Garden*.

Sophie is the first to spot me. Her face instantly transforms into a bright, toothy smile. "Okay, model!"

Marisol—who had since jumped into the pool—turns, wiping water droplets from her immaculate brows, and eyes me. "About freaking time. Love your suit!"

And just like that, the moment of revealing this new body of mine is over.

"Thanks, Sol!" I say, removing my sunglasses and setting them on the edge of the pool. Then I jump, letting the cool water wash over my skin and renew me. I swallow the guilt I feel for avoiding my two best friends for most of the summer just because I was insecure.

With a renewed confidence, I slip beneath the water's surface again and glide, enjoying how my body seems to remember every curve of the pool.

When I rise to the surface near Sophie, I smile up at her and put on a nasally voice. "Hi. You wanna play mermaids?"

The reference catches Sophie off guard, and she snorts, hopping off her flamingo and into the pool beside me. "Obviously! Sol? Mermaids?"

"First one to get across the pool is the mermaid queen!" Marisol shouts.

The three of us swim across the pool, flapping our feet together like fins, and when we break through the surface, we can't stop giggling. "Who won?" I ask.

"Who cares? We're *all* mermaid queens, as far as I'm concerned," Sophie says, hopping back up onto her float.

"Of course we are," Marisol agrees. "But I'm the queeniest."

I lean back and prop my arms on the edge of the pool. "So, I think I've come up with the perfect way to make this Paris internship happen."

Sophie arches an eyebrow at me. "Oh, yeah?"

"We switch places," I say with a shrug. "I could get used to living here. I'll just stalk around the house ensuring I'm heard but never seen, and we'll chalk it up to you being super intense about your violin practice. Obviously you'll need to record yourself practicing so I can play it on loop, but other than that, I think this plan will work."

"Ooh, can I get in on that?" Marisol asks. "I could use an escape from all the Natalia comparisons going on in my household. We'll pretend to be Sophie together!"

"Done!" I agree.

Sophie laughs. "Well, I'm glad you two have it all figured out."

Marisol kicks herself off the ledge of the pool and floats on her back, looking up at the sky. "In seriousness, Soph, have you told them you're applying for this thing?"

"Not yet. But I will."

"Maybe they'll surprise you and be incredibly supportive," I suggest, which earns me an eye roll from Sophie.

"Have you *met* my parents? The same parents who outlawed chewing gum in the house for fear I might choke?" She shakes her head.

"Fair enough." I forget sometimes that not everyone has an Abuela by their side. "It might still be worth trying."

Sophie idly runs her fingers through the water. "Maybe. We'll see how my next concert goes. Maybe it will remind them I'm actually really good at violin and deserve to go to Paris."

"When *is* your next concert, anyway?" I ask. "I want to be front-row so we can cheer super loudly. Right, Sol?"

"Don't do that," Sophie warns.

"Why not? We're also going to paint our bodies in the school colors and wear foam fingers with your name," Marisol teases.

Sophie narrows her eyes. "Don't do that, either!"

Marisol sighs dramatically. "You're no fun. It's just silly that the only context where it's acceptable to paint your body and scream is sports."

Sophie nods. "Fair enough. You're more than welcome to give it a try at someone else's performance."

Marisol sticks out her tongue. "I could keep arguing with you, and I would win, but since I respect you as a human I won't do that."

"Good. Leave the incessant arguing to debate club and keep me out of it, thank you very much."

Marisol has decided to put her immaculate skills of argumentation to use by launching a debate club at Elmwood, enthralled by the idea of getting to argue with people for fun. Bonus: it's a pretty great résumé builder for her eventual career as a lawyer.

"I will! I have big visions for this semester. Like verbally humiliating my peers just for the sheer satisfaction of it." She gives us a devilish grin.

"Get it, girl," I say with a laugh.

Marisol stands, pushing her wet hair back, and glances over at me. "Not to bring up the elephant in the room, but have you talked to Aiden at all since this past weekend?"

I visibly wince—because no, we haven't talked, unless a handful of painfully generic texts count. "Sort of. I mean, we've been texting a little here and there."

Marisol raises her eyebrows. "Texting a little here and there...with your *boyfriend*?"

"Ugh, I know," I groan. "I keep pushing, I swear! I've tried to start, like, several conversations with him. But he's the worst about texting me back. I don't know what to do."

"What about the video date I suggested?" Sophie asks.

"Aiden said he couldn't commit to that because football has him slammed."

At that, Marisol scowls. "Give me a freaking break. Like he's the only person in the world with extracurricular activities."

"I hate to say this, Whit, but..." Sophie glances down at the water glinting in the sunlight. "It almost sounds like he's not even trying."

"I'm with Soph. At this rate, why do you even want to be with him? What are you getting out of this?"

Marisol's question catches me off guard. What *am* I getting out of my relationship with Aiden?

Before he moved, that was easy to answer. I got the comfort of being around someone I cared about, I got to hang out with my friends in a gigantic group and laugh a ton, and I also got the physical affection—the hugs, the hand-holding, the kissing, the touching.

But now that all of that's gone, all we have is...conversation. As it turns out, maybe we weren't so good at that. "I *used* to get a lot out of it..."

Marisol cuts in. "Right. A lot of making out and fucking."

Sophie bursts into laughter. "A little crass, don't you think?"

But Marisol just shrugs. "What? It's true! And it's perfectly fine to come to the realization that a relationship has run its course. Maybe your interests were more physical than emotional."

"That's not true," I say defensively. We had more than just kissing, didn't we? The jelly beans! "I don't *want* it to have run its course."

Sophie chews on her lip thoughtfully. "Okay. Well, if you don't want it to be over, maybe some of the passion is what's missing. Send him AMAZING pictures of you so he'll race down that highway."

My cheeks get hot—that idea hadn't even crossed my mind. "I don't send him selfies. Is that a mistake?"

"No wonder your relationship is on life support!" Marisol practically shouts. "Come on, girl. Let's go." She hops out of the pool and holds out a hand to me. It's an order, and when Marisol gets that tone in her voice, I'm prone to listen. Just seventeen and she's somehow already mastered the deadly glance typically only deployed by grown Latina women.

In a moment, I'm by her side.

Without another word, Marisol reaches for the T-shirt she was wearing before we got into the pool and starts to use it to gently scrunch out some of my curls. It's an art form, getting your curls just right, and Marisol is a sculptor. She works out some of the water, tousling my long, wet hair and helping the ringlets spring back to life.

She points. "Chair."

"What, exactly, are we doing?" I ask.

"Obviously you're going to send your boyfriend a super-hot photo of you," Marisol says, as if it's the most obvious thing in the world.

Sophie claps her hands together. "Yay!"

"Can I at least do my makeup first?" I beg. "My bag's inside."

"On it." Sophie's gone and back in a flash, carrying my blue-and-white bag with the word CHILTON emblazoned on it. (A reference to *Gilmore Girls*, obviously. I use it to carry my emergency makeup.)

"Keep it natural, but hot. Okay?" Marisol instructs.

With an eye roll, I say, "I'll do my best."

Admittedly, I enjoy doing my makeup. There's something I find deeply relaxing in the precision of it, in its problem-solving, its creativity. It's something I do just for me. So it only takes me a few moments to fluff up my brows, add some dramatic mascara, peach-blush my cheeks, and finish things off with a glossy pink lip balm.

"Well?" I ask.

"Hot," Marisol confirms.

"Totally hot," Sophie agrees.

Marisol directs me this way and that as she moves around me to play with angles. Sophie fans me with a towel in an attempt to get my curls to come to life for an effortless *Oh-is-that-the-wind-or-am-I-just-a-total-goddess?* moment. We take some photos from above, while others are from behind with me looking back at the camera. Maybe this should embarrass me, but honestly? This whole afternoon is the most normal I've felt with Sophie and Marisol in months. I've missed letting them see the vulnerable parts of me.

It isn't long before we've selected a favorite for Aiden, and I have to admit, I actually do look pretty hot.

Heart pounding, I get the final picture ready to send. "What should I say?"

"Maybe just an emoji?" Sophie suggests. "Or something simple, like *Hi?*"

We both look to Marisol for her thoughts, but she looks back at me. "What do you *want* to say? This is your boyfriend."

I nod. I should be able to figure out what to say to my own boyfriend. Right? I think for a moment. "I kind of just want to send the picture. Let it speak for itself."

Sophie breaks into a smile. "I love that."

"Do it!" Marisol agrees.

"Okay..." I breathe. "One...two..." My finger hovers over the arrow that'll send the text. "Three!" I shout at the same time my finger smashes the screen.

Marisol and Sophie squeal and off the photo goes. Right to my boyfriend. Who I haven't seen in months.

My heart might just leap from my chest and run away. "Okay. Okay! We sent it. Now can I hide my phone? And can we please talk about something else?"

"I won't be able to rest until I know what happens next," Sophie admits.

Marisol points at her and laughs. "This one really loves a dirty text, no?"

Sophie playfully swats at her arm. "Shut up!"

"Well, I'm happy for a change of topic while we wait for Aiden's reply," Marisol says. "Can we sleep over tonight, Soph?"

"Way to barge into my life. What if I had plans with Noah?" Sophie teases.

"He can survive without you for one night, *babe*." Marisol nods toward me. "What do you say? You down?"

"*Only* if I can use someone else's phone to call Abuela and ask," I say as they erupt into over-the-top cheers.

Abuela is quick to agree. I do okay avoiding my phone for a little bit, but admittedly, in between episodes of bad reality television and belting out songs on the karaoke machine Sophie got for her birthday, I do sneak some peeks.

Aiden doesn't respond to my text all night.

• • •

When the three of us wake on Saturday morning, Sophie is the first to bring it up.

"Well?" she asks gently. "Did he write back?"

Without a word, I turn my phone toward her and Marisol so they can read the message.

Aiden: Nice

No punctuation. No emojis. No let's-FaceTime-right-now-because-you-look-so-good-and-I-need-more.

It's Marisol who gets angry first, erupting with a stream of expletives in Spanish that I don't even understand. Sophie, ever the levelheaded, gentle soul, just reaches over and puts her hand on mine. I fight the urge to cry.

How silly of me to expect anything other than this. Maybe Aiden and I really are doomed.

Chapter Seven

I channel my disappointment into working on my bid for the Fall Fest presidency throughout the weekend.

I jot down bullet points for a short speech, which I'll deliver during today's committee voting. I come up with a slogan. I even enlist Lily's help in filming a campaign video in the comfort of my room. She's excellent at video editing and graphic design, so she helps me piece it all together, ending with the slogan "Fall for Whit." I am *ready* for this meeting.

If all of this sounds like a little much, that's okay. I *am* a little much. Who would ever want to be less?

It helps to sort of distract me from thinking of Aiden and the nerve he had to follow up his *Nice* text with a text about football. Foot. Ball.

Those two texts back-to-back push away any visions I had of Aiden doing some kind of grand, romantic proposal for Fall Fest. At this point, I'd be lucky if he even drove down to be my date.

I push those depressing thoughts away as I drive Lily and myself to school on Monday. Once I've walked Lily to her locker, I pop in my headphones, put on a Spotify playlist of powerful female anthems, and march down the hall toward the courtyard, PSL in hand. I'm mentally reviewing my speech for the Fall Fest meeting later this afternoon.

"There is nothing I love more than fall and planning," I whisper to myself. "Pumpkin spice is in my bloodline, and I dream of spreadsheets."

I'm glancing down at my phone to check my notes for the next part of my speech when a voice yells, "Heads up!"

But it's too late. Suddenly someone is crashing into me, *hard*, knocking me, my belongings, and my coffee everywhere—including all over my favorite marigold-colored cardigan patterned with adorable mushrooms.

"Ugh!" I shout, landing on the floor with a thud.

"Oof!" the other voice says, sounding muffled over the loud music pulsating in my ears.

My wrist aches from where it caught most of my weight, I'm soaking wet, and my phone went flying. I look over to see who clotheslined me.

It's none other than Isaiah Ortiz—the ex I was ogling just days prior.

His skateboard is lying belly-up with the wheels still moving, the likely culprit for our collision.

If we were in one of the cheesy Hallmark movies Sophie is totally obsessed with, this *might* be a meet-cute—you know, a sweet little first encounter between two characters who eventually fall in love.

But this is Isaiah Ortiz, the bane of my existence *and* the reason my meticulously selected outfit is completely ruined. If he weren't my sworn enemy before, he definitely would be now.

I rip my earbuds out. "Can you watch where you're going, Isaiah?!"

"Can you?" he shoots back, dusting off his pants, speckled with grime from the dingy linoleum floor.

As he rises to his feet, I take him in: tall, dark-skinned, locs falling past his broad shoulders, long eyelashes, full lips, and a cool, casual, *I-don't-care-but-somehow-I-look-great* sense of style.

I swallow. Just because he's cute doesn't mean he's not still my enemy.

"Ex-*cuse* me?! I was minding my business," I huff, ignoring Isaiah's outstretched hand adorned with silver rings. I stand without his help, hastily gathering my belongings. "You're the one who was riding a skateboard in school!"

A smooth, easy grin spreads across Isaiah's face. His smile used to be my favorite feature, but right now, the sight of it makes me want to mop up what's left of my drink and put it back in my cup just so I can toss it in his face.

"Yeah. I totally was," he admits, running his hand through his dark locs. "But *you* weren't even looking where you were going. You were looking at your phone and whispering to yourself. What the hell was that about?"

My neck prickles. "It's none of your business."

Isaiah shrugs. "It was a mutual crash."

"That's the most ludicrous thing I've ever heard." I snatch my phone from the floor and breathe a sigh of relief when the screen is intact. The protector is scuffed, though.

"Is it good?" Isaiah asks.

"It's fine. Just a little scratched from these disgusting floors." I frown down at my phone and then at my now coffee-drenched clothes. "And I'm sopping."

"Shit, yeah. Sorry." Isaiah reaches to the back of his collar and starts to shrug off his oversize hoodie.

"What are you doing?" I demand.

He freezes, arms midair. "Letting you borrow this?"

My spine stiffens. Why on earth would I want to wear Isaiah's hoodie? I doubt it would even fit. "I'm good."

"So you're just going to walk around in a soaking-wet sweater all day?" Before I can come up with some kind of retort, he's pulled off his hoodie, revealing a dark gray T-shirt underneath. He tosses the sweatshirt to me. "Go on. I'll start cleaning up."

I take a peek at the tag and note that it's a men's XL, so where it was oversize on Isaiah, for me, it'll just fit. But my other choice is to walk around with a giant, ugly stain on the front of my sweater. Not cute.

"Fine," I say, as if he hasn't already moved on to picking up my spilled lid and cup. I duck into the nearby bathroom and start to blot myself clean. The stain only worsens, so I give up and slip into the stall, pulling off my cardigan.

Then I stare down at Isaiah's hoodie in my hand—soft, black, with a small teddy bear embroidered in the upper right corner—and laugh out loud. I woke up this morning with lots of thoughts, but not once did I picture myself standing in the girls' bathroom stall about to wear my middle school ex's hoodie to the most anticipated meeting of my high school career.

But it's fine.

It's cool.

When I emerge from the stall, I fluff my curls in the mirror, grateful I opted for a rust-colored corduroy skirt and some black tights, neither of which looks terrible with this top.

I hear voices as I push open the bathroom door and let myself back into the hall—Isaiah's husky one I expected, but there's someone else with him, laughing.

It's Death Glare Denise, the school's gruff janitor, who I have never even seen crack a smile, let alone laugh. She and Isaiah are squatting down mopping up the coffee with some of those thin brown paper towels every school seems to have.

Denise is notorious for reporting students for their hijinks. I don't blame her. She works hard to keep our school clean and for what? I can't imagine having to pick up after reckless teens day in and day out, some of whom are super privileged and purposely throw things on the ground and make remarks like "I'm keeping Denise employed." It's no wonder she's prickly.

Yet here she is. With Isaiah. Practically giggling.

"So these wheels might be working a little too good," Isaiah is saying, shaking his head.

Denise grins. "I tried to warn you!"

"I mean, what should I have expected from a set called Wildebeest?"

Another chuckle, then Denise stands and reaches for her mop. "Well, that's what you get for skating in school. You know linoleum gives the worst traction."

Isaiah stuffs the dirty paper towels into an oversize trash can. "Hey, now. I think ice might be slightly worse."

"Just barely."

"Well, consider it a lesson learned, D," Isaiah says, and my eyebrows go up. Did that crash...push me into another dimension...or something? What else might explain Isaiah and Denise bonding over skateboards? And did he call Death Glare Denise...D? "The wheels are sick, though. Thanks for the recommendation. And, seriously, thanks for helping me with this mess."

I clear my throat a little, and they both look my way. "Hi. Just wanted to say sorry about the coffee. And thank you both."

Denise points at Isaiah. "No worries. This clown told me it was all him."

"Ay, so now I'm a clown?"

"Always were," she teases. "Get going now, will you? I'm good here."

Isaiah nods at her, then turns to me with a sly smile. "Nice hoodie."

The way his eyes fix on me sends a ripple of excitement through me. I clear my throat and pull at the hem, looking for something to do with my hands. "I'll, um, wash it and get it back to you tomorrow."

He waves a hand at me. "Whenever. I did crash into you and ruin your coffee—let's be honest. I owe ya one. Okay?" Isaiah walks over to his skateboard and scoops it up from the floor. His brows furrow in concern as he surveys the damage.

"Is it okay?" I ask.

He nods. "Looks like it'll be just fine. Thanks."

I gather my things from the floor where I left them, pulling my bag over my shoulder. Other students have started joining us in the halls now. "Okay. Well. Thanks for the hoodie."

"Don't mention it."

Without another word, Isaiah hops onto his skateboard and starts weaving down the hall, leaving Denise shaking her head, and me bewildered at our first interaction in six years.

* * *

From homeroom, I sneakily send the same text to my group chat with Marisol and Sophie and to Aiden.

Me: Guess who I ran into this morning? LITERALLY.

Soph responds immediately.

Sophie: Who? 😌

Marisol: Is that why you ditched us in the courtyard AGAIN? We've been looking for you!

Me: I'm sorry! But ISAIAH ORTIZ skateboarded right into me!

Sophie: WHAT!!! Are you okay?

Marisol: Wait, THE???

Me: THE ONE AND ONLY.

Me: I'm fine. Mostly just a bruised ego, but SO glad no one was here to see the aftermath. Books, notebook, coffee EVERYWHERE.

Marisol: Noooo! That sucks!

Me: And now I'm wearing his hoodie?

Marisol: Um?

Sophie: ???

I send them a selfie, which they both heart.

Sophie: Your makeup looks so good!

Me: Thanks, boo!

Marisol: We're talking about your ex, right? Tall? Long locs? Super hot? And 🍑🍑🍑?

Me: How. Dare. You.

Sophie: So you're wearing your ex's hoodie...why?

Me: Did you not hear the part about coffee everywhere?

Marisol: He just stripped down in the middle of school for you, hmm? And you're not trying to admit that was lowkey sexy?

Sophie: Does it smell good?

Me: YOU. GUYS. Do we not all have partners? Why are we talking about Isaiah Ortiz's 🍑 and what he smells like!!!!

Marisol: It's unrealistic not to acknowledge attraction!

Me: This conversation is over. Love you. Byeeeee.

But just before the bell rings, I consider Sophie's text about whether the hoodie smells good.

I turn my head to the side and subtly press my nose to my shoulder, breathing in.

Isaiah's sweatshirt smells a little like some kind of cologne, mixed with firewood and adobo—just like I remember.

Chapter Eight

As if I didn't have enough to worry about, the crash with Isaiah rattles my nerves ahead of my Fall Fest presentation. Marisol and Sophie playfully tease me about it all day long, which I'm actually fine with because it reminds me that we're back in a good place.

They also tease me about the hoodie, which I'm less thrilled about. Even though things with Aiden haven't been great, I'm still his girlfriend.

In the period before last, Aiden finally texts me back.

Me: Guess who I ran into this morning? LITERALLY.

Aiden: Um . . . a wild turkey?

That makes me breathe a laugh, remembering the time a flock of turkeys somehow ended up on Elmwood's campus and Principal Johnson was among the group chasing them away—in heels, no less.

Me: I wish. At least that'd be funny!

Me: Remember Isaiah Ortiz?

Aiden: Skateboarder dude with locs?

Me: That'd be the one.

Aiden: Vaguely lol

Me: Well, he literally CRASHED INTO ME WITH HIS DUMB SKATEBOARD!

Aiden: Damn, that sucks.

Aiden: You good??

Me: I'm good. Thanks. ♥

It's not much, but it's something. I guess.

When the final bell rings, I check in with Lily to ask how her day went. She tells me she's finally starting to make a few new friends, and how much she's liking the teacher's aide, Ms. Kaminski.

"That all sounds really awesome." I smile at her and start to lead her down the hall toward the bus. But I stop when I notice she's not by my side. "Lil?"

She pulls her backpack tighter. "You don't have to walk me to the bus every time you need to stay after school, you know."

"I know. But I want to."

Lily tucks her hair behind her ears, eyes cast at the floor. "I can do it by myself."

I blink at her, surprised. "Oh. Well…okay. Are you sure?"

"I'm *sure,* Whitney," she says with a sigh. "I'm not an idiot."

"Of course you're not an idiot!" I say quickly. "I just wanted to be sure you're good. And you are. So…see you at home, then?"

I hold up my hand for a fist bump, which she returns, but half-heartedly. Then she walks past me and down the hall toward the buses.

I know I can sometimes be a little overbearing, but is it too much to want to ensure that she's comfortable and settling in okay?

With a sigh of my own, I make my way to the awaited meeting in a nearby classroom. I've come ready with my Fall Fest presidential speech and teaser trailer of what Fall Fest could look like under my leadership.

Marisol lets out a low whistle as she and Sophie enter the classroom. "Nice hoodie."

"Oh my God."

"I don't know, Whit—I bet it felt pretty nice when it came off Isaiah's body and went right onto yours," Sophie points out, making my cheeks flush.

"Sophie!" I hiss.

"We're just trying to distract you because we know how nervous you get before presentations," Marisol says, patting my shoulder. "Are we doing a good job?"

I narrow my eyes at her. "Almost too good."

"You're welcome." Marisol slides into the seat next to me, and Sophie sits on my other side.

"I hope you know there's nothing to be nervous about," Soph says. "You're a natural-born leader—driven and committed, and you have more vision in your pinkie than anyone else in this place."

"You're also freakishly organized," Marisol adds.

Sophie laughs. "Yeah. That, too."

I glance down at my notebook, which may or may not have carefully printed notes for me to reference as I speak to the group, and give them a playful grin. "I have no idea what you're talking about."

Ms. Bennett joins us a few moments later wearing a rocket-ship-print smock dress. "Are we ready to make use of our democratic right to vote?"

"The United States has long moved past democracy and into oligarchy," Marisol quips.

"Fair enough," Ms. Bennett says. "But democracy is alive and well in this classroom, so we'll vote. Thank you to everyone who submitted nominations over the weekend. Now let's run through our list of nominees, shall we?"

With that, Ms. Bennett notes that Hudson and Everly will each automatically become officers for their grades, and there is an audible exhale from Everly, who looks relieved she won't have to present. Tori Allen, Leilani Mamea, and Addison Bell will each present for junior officer. It's me versus Chloe Torres for Fall Fest president, and whoever doesn't win will automatically become senior officer.

When Ms. Bennett asks for a volunteer to go first, my hand can't rise fast enough. I stand and smooth my skirt, walking to the front of the classroom.

"I brought a presentation, if that's okay," I say.

Ms. Bennett looks surprised. "Oh! Wonderful. Please."

I take a second to connect the ancient laptop I checked out from the library to the projector and pull up the video trailer I've created, with the words FALL FOR WHIT visible on the screen.

Before I can hit play, Chloe raises her hand and politely says, "Actually, I'm happy to step aside so Whit can be president." She smiles at me, as if this is a huge favor.

But the logo!

The video trailer!

The hours of preparing!

The speech that I was certain was going to make people cry after hearing Abuela and Abuelo's love story!

Was it all for nothing?

"Okay! That certainly does make things easy, then, doesn't it?" Ms. Bennett asks, casting a glance toward me. "Are you fine as class officer, Chloe?"

Chloe wrinkles her nose, pushing up her lime-green glasses. "Honestly, I just want to help with the design-and-décor side of things, if that's cool."

I blink at her. Why the heck wouldn't she want to make decisions and boss people around?!

"Oh. All right…" Ms. Bennett looks around the room. "Is there anyone else interested in being senior officer, then? Whit's going to need some help."

When no hands go up—not even Sophie's or Marisol's, those traitors—Ms. Bennett just clucks her tongue. Then she looks at me. "I'll figure something out. In the meantime, congratulations, Whit! I can't wait to see what you'll dream up for this year's festival."

I give her a half-hearted smile. "Thank you."

Ms. Bennett calls on Leilani to present while I return to my seat. Sophie shimmies her shoulders in celebration, while Marisol silently snaps her fingers.

"Congrats, girl!" Marisol whispers.

"Thanks, guys," I whisper back, still a little dazed by how much work I put into my presentation for no real reason at all. Does *no one* appreciate my intensity?

At least I'm president. By the end of the meeting, I have a pretty solid-looking crew of officers to support me:

First-year Representative: Everly McDonnell
Sophomore Representative: Hudson Moore
Junior Representative: Leilani Mamea
Senior Officer: Vacant
President: Whitney Rivera

Given everything, would it be wrong to ask Ms. Bennett if I can serve as my own senior officer?

* * *

I'm still a little grumpy on my way to meet Abuela and Lily at El Coquí. I can't believe how much time I wasted on this president thing only for me to slide right into the role! The bells jingle as I push open the front door.

Abuela's taking measurements on a thirtysomething dude whose pants are way too long, while Lily is curled up in one of the chairs in the corner, watching Intonation videos on her tablet.

I wave to Abuela and let myself into the back office so I can get started sorting through any emails that came in and handle any other administrative tasks. When the bell chimes again, indicating that our customer has left, Abuela's voice calls to me.

"How was school?" she asks.

"Fine," I yell back. But when her head pops into the office doorway, I jump. "Jeez, you scared me!"

"That's all you have to say? After your big meeting and all?" Abuela narrows her eyes at me skeptically. "¿Y qué es esto?" She points at Isaiah's hoodie.

"Don't get me started," I mumble.

She plops into the chair on the other side of the desk. "What happened?"

"Isaiah Ortiz happened," I say, as if that answers anything.

Her eyes get big. "Zay? *Your* Zay?"

I bristle a bit, hearing the nickname I used to call Isaiah in the sixth grade. After being called Whitney my whole life, I suddenly became convinced I wanted everyone to call me Whit, and I wanted nicknames for everyone else, too. Isaiah was fine with me calling him Zay, but he called me Whitney when he wanted to tease me. I liked it. So, while the world knew the two of us as Isaiah and Whit, to each other, we were Zay and Whitney. It felt really special, just for us.

Hearing it again now brings back those middle school feelings in a way I didn't ask for. Gross.

"Not *my* Zay, but yes. The same one I used to talk to or whatever." My eyes meet hers, and I frown. "He bumped into me and I fell. I spilled coffee all over my cardigan."

"¡Bendito! Are you okay?"

"I'm fine." I reach down to my bag and pull out my stained cardigan. "This is another story."

She gets up and rushes to the sweater, inspecting the damage. "It's okay. Keep talking while I work on this. Come on."

I follow Abuela as she heads into the back room to soak the now-dry stain in a solution of warm water, dishwashing liquid, and some white vinegar. "The cardigan was a casualty of the run-in, which sucked. My wrist hurts a little." I rub at it.

Abuela looks up from my cardigan, jutting her chin back toward the office. "Ponte Vicks. I have some in my bag."

I swear, if I got hit by a car she would say, "¡Ponte Vicks!" and call it a day.

But I know better than to argue. I slink into the office and rummage through her bag, where I find a giant tub of the ointment and rub a little on the offending wrist.

"Other than that, the day was fine," I call to her.

"And the meeting?" Abuela presses. "Am I talking to the president or what?"

Shoulders slumped, I sulk back into the room. "Yes, I'm president."

"So why do you look like this?" She rolls her shoulders forward dramatically and puts on a deep frown, mimicking me.

I can't help but laugh. "Well, I'm happy about being president, but I'm not happy that I didn't even need to give the speech I'd prepared. The other person who wanted the role just... gave it to me."

"That just means you were the most qualified," Abuela assures me.

"I guess. It felt anticlimactic after all this anticipation." Abuela nods but says nothing. "I know I'm being dramatic. I guess I wanted to earn the role, you know?"

"You're being too hard on yourself again, nena." She dries her hands on a towel, then meets my eyes. "Are you feeling okay? Do you want me to make an appointment with Dr. Delgado?"

Ugh, no. The last thing I want to have to deal with is another doctor's appointment, even though I have been extra tired lately. It's annoying how many ways PCOS can disrupt your life.

I once started a list in my notebook and it nearly filled up an entire page:

Symptoms of PCOS According to Whit's Internet Sleuthing

- Enlarged ovaries with small cysts
- Irregular periods
- Excess androgen
- Type 2 diabetes or prediabetes
- High blood pressure
- Insulin resistance
- Excess facial and body hair
- Acne
- Hair loss and/or baldness
- Miscarriage or premature birth
- Liver inflammation
- Sleep apnea
- Depression
- Anxiety
- Eating disorders
- Excessive sweating
- Weight gain
- Difficulty losing weight
- Bloating
- Food cravings
- Feeling cold
- Chronic fatigue, difficulty falling asleep, and/or restless or disturbed sleep (or sometimes all of the above!)

Fall down a deep-enough rabbit hole and the symptoms bring out other symptoms. There's so little research, things sometimes feel hopeless. It often feels easier to stop talking about it altogether.

"It's not that," I assure her. "It's other things. Aiden, I guess."

Abuela puts a hand on each of my shoulders. "What did he do?"

How do I put into words that our chemistry seems gone now

that we can't physically be in the same room? Abuela would probably break out the chancla.

I go with a version of the truth. "The long-distance thing has been really hard. He hasn't even asked me to the Fall Fest yet."

Abuela nods. "Ah. Pero, he *will*. We have weeks before then! One way or another, you'll go, you'll have a wonderful time, and it will be everything you dreamed it would be."

I bite my bottom lip. "You think so?"

"I know so! And here's how I know." Abuela motions for me to follow her out into the showroom. On the way, we pass Lily, and Abuela waves at her to come, too.

Abuela stops at the closet holding garments she's intending to fix up. She reaches in to pull out what I recognize as her Fall Fest dress from the 1970s. Up till now, I'd only seen it in photos.

I realize that was for the best.

In person, it might actually be the most hideous dress I've ever seen. I mean, the seventies had some amazing fashion, but this? This is not it.

Chiffon with a pleated A-line skirt, this dress was a *choice*. Any beauty from the ripe-papaya color of the fabric is completely obscured by dizzying lace trim: along the V-shaped neckline, at the ends of the flowing sleeves, across the belted midsection, and for some terrible reason, along the skirt. An offensive lace bow sits at the center.

I understand now it wasn't so much the dress that made Abuela look radiant, but the other way around.

"Mira—I found my Fall Fest dress in the basement. It's a sign!" Abuela's dimples deepen as she wears a smile that's equal parts proud, nostalgic, and wistful.

I push away any initial negative feelings about the look of the dress, instead thinking back to the photos I've seen: how the color highlighted Abuela's caramel skin, how her big, soft curls framed her face. She looked beautiful that night, and more importantly, she has told us again and again that she *felt* beautiful that night.

"It's gorgeous," I say, smiling at her.

Lily shoots me a look. "How can you say that? That thing is hideous."

I gasp. "Lily!"

But Abuela is laughing. "No, Lily's right. This was gorgeous then, maybe, but not now," she admits. "I'm just happy I found it! It's got me thinking of redesigning it and seeing if I can sell it this homecoming season. We could make some good money and get you and Lily something nice to wear!"

My hand goes to my heart. "Sell it?!"

Abuela takes a step back, causing the dress's tiers to flutter. "Ay, I know it needs work, but come on! Have a little faith that your abuelita can make it beautiful again."

I shake my head. "It's not that. This is your dress. The dress you wore the night you and Abuelo met. You can't just sell it."

"Better than rotting away in the basement, no?" Abuela asks. "This way, someone will be able to love it again. Maybe have their very own night to remember."

It's a nice thought, but I'm frowning. Other people deserve to have their nights to remember—but not in Abuela's dress. This dress is our family's beginning.

"We should hang on to it," I insist. "Put it on display somewhere! Maybe in the storefront?"

Lily snorts. "And chase away all the customers."

I glare at her. "Don't be rude."

But Abuela is laughing again, sweeping the dress away, back to the closet and onto the rack. "Let me think about it, okay?" she offers. "But we could really use that money."

If it's money we need, fine. I'll get another job. As far as I'm concerned, though, that dress isn't going anywhere.

Chapter Nine

After school the next day, I start applying for jobs so I can save Abuela's dress. Our cat, Patch, keeps me company while I do. I take pride in the fact that he likes my room best and that he often snuggles up to me in bed. (It's probably because of all the natural light my windows let in, but I tell myself it's because I'm his favorite.)

In between job applications, I manage to schedule a FaceTime call with Aiden for that night, our first since right before school started. I should be excited about it, but I don't know. I want to keep my expectations low, I guess. A girl can only take so much disappointment.

The scheduled call at least saves me from having to fifth-wheel it when Marisol texts to invite me to dinner with her, Sophie, Noah, and Ari. My friends' responses are so perfectly them that it makes me laugh out loud.

Marisol: Tell him he's on thin ice. THIN. ICE.

Sophie: Ahh, yay! I hope it goes really well!

I decide to use the call as an excuse to pamper myself. I take a long, hot shower, slather myself in cocoa butter, paint my nails. While my hair dries, I put on some music and work on my makeup, going for something a little more sultry than my day-to-day look, though I'll admit it's not necessarily for Aiden—more for myself. I want to feel pretty. I want to feel desired. I want to feel wanted. Especially because I haven't felt any of those things lately.

In an attempt to drum up some excitement, I try to conjure up some of the sweetest memories I have with Aiden: our weekly date nights to his favorite sushi spot, whenever he invited me to watch him play flag football, all the different types of musical artists he introduced me to, like Fivio Foreign and Sleepy Hallow.

Only...as I go through each memory, turning them over in my head, I notice a pattern: the best times also seemed to include our *friends,* and what few one-on-one habits we developed sort of revolved around him: his favorite restaurant, his games, his playlists.

Aiden was lots of things. Patient. Usually kind. A little clueless. Excellent kisser, among other talents. But often a little preoccupied with himself and his own interests.

It's enough to make me scroll back through some of our recent texts. I note that most of our conversations began with me reaching out, rather than the other way around.

When was the last time Aiden texted me first? Sent me a photo? Initiated a FaceTime?

I wonder this as I select my outfit and my earrings, then spray some water in my hair to rejuvenate the curls that have gone limp. In the mirror, I look beautiful, but there is a pit in my stomach as I continue scrolling and come across that pool selfie I sent him. With some distance between me and the moment, I think I actually look pretty freaking good in it—and he responded with *Nice*? Of all things?

As the clock ticks closer to the time we've set for our FaceTime date, I find myself secretly wondering whether Aiden will even call.

Or maybe I'm hoping he won't.

I prop my phone up on my ring light and stare at it.

Don't ring.

Don't ring.

Don't ring.

I repeat this over and over, so many times I lose count, until long after we've passed the time when he was supposed to call.

But instead of crying, I send him a text.

Me: Thanks for blowing me off.

And then I silence my phone, pull open my laptop, and start to work on my digital vision board for Fall Fest, along with a spreadsheet of ideas.

I lose track of time, so deep in it that I don't hear the knock at my door, and only come to when Lily calls my name. When I look over at her, she's in an oversize Intonation T-shirt, and she's grinning.

"Oh, hey." I close my laptop. "Sorry."

"We're going to make some empanadas," Lily says. "You want to help?"

"That sounds nice. Be right there."

As Lily slips out of my room, I pull off the date-night outfit I selected and instead dig out my own matching Intonation T-shirt from my pajama drawer. I pile my curls into a giant, messy bun on top of my head and pull on some cozy socks, but leave the makeup. It looks good. Why waste it?

In the kitchen, Abuela is rolling out the empanada dough as Lily watches eagerly. When she spots my shirt, she motions between me and Lily with a laugh. "Twins!"

I come over and bump my hip into hers. "You know it."

"¡Que linda!" Abuela smiles. "Where's mine?"

"You want one?" I ask, pulling out my phone, ready and willing to buy one for her, too.

"No, no. I'm only teasing," she assures me. But I jot down a note to myself to get her one for Christmas. Hopefully I'll have a part-time job by then.

I take in a big breath, sweet and savory scents mingling over the stove behind Abuela. "What kind of empanadas are on the menu for tonight?"

Abuela starts listing them off on her fingers. "Carne, pollo, guava—"

"And pumpkin!" Lily adds. "Guess whose idea that was?"

I walk over to the stove and stir the pot of ground beef that's sizzling with chopped olives, potatoes, tomato sauce, sazón, adobo, and a mix of other spices. "Hmm, lemme think..." I blow on a small spoonful I'm totally planning to eat right out of the pot. "Could it be my genius little sister?" Lily nods enthusiastically and I bite down, letting the umami mixture of delicious spices dance on my tongue. "That's *so* good."

Abuela swats at my hand. "No tasting from the production line!"

"Yeah, *Whitney*!" Lily teases, sticking out her tongue. "I chose pumpkin because we all know how obsessed you are with fall."

"With good reason!" I argue. "So what's this big plan for your pumpkin empanadas?"

She shrugs at me. "That's as far as I got."

"Maybe a little brown sugar? Cinnamon?" I do a quick search on my phone for a recipe that might help. "This also suggests adding some nutmeg and cloves."

Lily nods vigorously. "That sounds really good."

"Couldn't agree more." I wash off the spoon I licked and put it in the dishwasher, grabbing a new wooden spoon to continue stirring the beef. "So, how has everything been going at school for you, Lil? Are you liking it so far?" I ask. Lily casts her glance down to the floor and gives me a small shrug.

"I remember having a hard time switching from middle school to Elmwood High," I reassure her. "It gets easier, though."

I open the guava paste and measure that, as well as the accompanying cream cheese, into a bowl.

"Actually, it's funny you mention that," Abuela says, using a circle cookie cutter on the dough she's just rolled out, alternating dough, parchment paper, dough, parchment paper.

I grab a whisk. "Oh, yeah?" Stir. "Why's that?"

Abuela catches my eye. "Lily was telling me she thinks she's ready to be a little more independent at school—getting herself to and from her locker and the bus, that kind of thing," Abuela says, keeping her voice light, gentle. "Isn't that great?"

"But *I* usually walk with her," I blurt out.

Lily shrugs. "I want to walk with my friends like everyone else does."

I pause. "Oh."

"It's good Lily's adjusting to everything so quickly," Abuela adds. "As it turns out, she's been reunited with one of her friends from middle school. Remember Ruby Davis?"

The name stirs something in the recesses of my brain. Was she the one who stole Lily's hat that one time? Or was that someone else? "Not really…" I admit, switching from the guava to preparing the pumpkin filling.

"Ruby lives near Nora's grandma across town. Nora would take me over there all the time two summers ago," Lily explains.

"And Ruby is a year ahead of Lily, so they were just becoming friends before she moved on to high school. Now they're back in the same school," Abuela explains. "She's a good girl."

I look over at my sister, who's reaching for the whisk I've just used to stir the guava so she can lick some of the remnants off. So much for not tasting from the production line. I hand it to her anyway.

"It must be nice to see her again," I say, and Lily nods. "That's great."

Abuela shoots me a thankful look. "This is a good thing, mija."

"Yeah. Definitely." But I can't help feeling a little sad about it. I had envisioned spending the year walking with Lily in the mornings and afternoons, assuming she'd not just need but *want* my guidance—plus the extra time to catch up. Guess not.

Abuela lets out a breath, wiping away some flour on her forehead. "Phew. Okay. The dough's all ready to be filled."

"Let's do it!" Lily says, and before I can let myself get too in my feelings, she pulls out her phone and the nostalgic sounds of Intonation fill the air.

Abuela starts to sing, loudly and off-key, which leads to Lily and me joining in while we make an assembly line of filling and sealing each empanada until they're ready to be fried.

Between misremembered lyrics and bad dance moves, we manage to prepare dozens of empanadas: half to be frozen, the other half ready to either cook now or share with our tías.

After we've sampled them all, the verdicts are in: Lily's favorite remains the guava, Abuela loves the carne, and—in a surprise to no one—I'm partial to this new pumpkin flavor.

Back in my room, I turn my phone on to see if Aiden's written back.

He hasn't.

So I settle back into bed with Patch, pull my Excel doc open, and dive in again, getting lost in the ease of organization.

If I can't have perfection in most parts of my life, let me at least have it here.

Chapter Ten

"*Did you seriously turn* down dinner so you could make the most irrational spreadsheet known to humankind?"

It's the first thing Marisol says to me when I arrive in the courtyard the next morning. I wouldn't call the spreadsheet irrational; to me, it's immaculate, a beautiful outline containing each committee member's assignments, as well as all tasks, subtasks, and sub-subtasks; budget items; and due dates. In my quest for serotonin last night, I emailed it to the committee to review before our next meeting.

I roll my eyes. "Good morning to you, too, Sol."

"Did you, though?" Sophie asks, eyes big. "We thought you had a date with Aiden!"

"He ghosted," I admit.

Sophie frowns. "Oh, Whit. I'm so sorry."

But Marisol looks annoyed. I expect her to call Aiden a slew of names, but instead, her annoyance is aimed at *me*. "Why didn't you text us?"

"I guess I wanted to wallow in my shame alone?"

"Well, that's stupid," she snaps. "Let us be there for you."

"Okay, I will," I say. "It's just that I don't know what I was expecting from him. Like, of course he's not going to bother replying to my texts. He didn't even want to write back to me when I was trying to sext. Shout-out to being abandoned." I try to make a joke, but just end up frowning. "You guys aren't going to abandon me now, too, are you?"

"What the hell are you talking about?" Marisol demands.

"Well, you're friends with Aiden's friends," I explain. "I don't want to put you in a weird position."

"First of all, Ari barely even likes Aiden. She pretty much just hung out with him because he was part of what we have here." Marisol motions between the three of us. "Second of all, if you keep talking like a dumbass, then I *will* abandon you."

Sophie pats Marisol on the arm. To me, she says, "Don't mind her. She has a lot of love to give and she gets offended when you reject it."

Marisol grabs me by the shoulders and shakes me, letting out a frustrated laugh. "Let. Me. Love. You!"

Which makes me laugh, too. "Okay, okay! I accept your love!"

"Are we interrupting something, mi luz del sol?" Ari asks with a grin. She uses the nickname she's given to Marisol—mi luz del sol, my sunlight—and I swoon inside a little. With her short, curly dark hair, big almost-black eyes, and the most eclectic collection of button-ups I've ever seen, Ari brings big masc-femme energy. Soft-spoken, thoughtful, yet a total badass on the rugby field, she's perfectly matched to Marisol. It's adorable, and I'm totally jealous.

"Kinda seems like we're interrupting something," Noah agrees. Speaking of couples that are disgustingly in love: Noah leans down to give Sophie a kiss, his floppy blond hair falling into his soft blue eyes. I always tell Sophie that in another life he is totally in a boy band. "Hi, babe."

"Hi, bubs," Sophie coos back.

"All you're interrupting is your girlfriend trying to kill me," I explain to Ari, "for being unwilling to accept her love."

Ari nods, running a hand over Marisol's curly hair affectionately. "She does love pretty hard. I get it."

"You all adore this about me," Marisol says, pouting. "But honestly, Whit was out of pocket, saying she was worried Soph and

I were going to *abandon her* now she's having issues with Aiden. He blew her off last night."

"Yes, please announce my pathetic love life to everyone," I say sarcastically.

Noah claps a hand on my shoulder. "Sorry to hear that. Dude's an idiot."

It makes me laugh a little. "Thanks, Noah."

"We've got your back," Ari adds. "No question."

The unexpected support makes my heart swell. Apparently letting people in can be a good thing.

* * *

What's not a good thing: the spreadsheet I sent out to the Fall Fest committee. As it turns out, I may have overstepped, which I swiftly find out later in the week when Ms. Bennett pulls me aside before our next Fall Fest meeting.

"Whit, you know I adore you and your commitment to things," she begins.

"It's part of my charm, right?" I ask.

Ms. Bennett nods. "It really is. But that spreadsheet may have been a little much. Reminder: this is your senior year. You should be having fun!"

"Spreadsheets *are* fun," I insist.

"Yes, but we haven't even had any brainstorming sessions as a group yet."

My shoulders slump. "Oh. That's true."

"Listen, your spreadsheet had some amazing ideas. I mean that. Let's start small, though. How about you spend the next meeting introducing yourself as the group leader?"

"Okay. I can do that."

Ms. Bennett gives my shoulder a reassuring squeeze. "Great. In that case, the floor is yours."

We reenter the classroom and she slips into a seat at the back while I walk toward the front, feeling more nervous than I thought I would. I'll admit that having my favorite teacher tell me my meticulous planning is all for naught has sucked the wind out of my sails. How could it not?

The group quiets as I stand at the front of the room, and I plaster on my brightest smile.

"Hey, everyone," I begin. "I wanted to start by thanking you all for allowing me to be your Fall Fest president. I am definitely someone with a strong vision, as you may have guessed from my intense spreadsheet."

There are a few polite chuckles, and I laugh, too, feeling the tension in my body ease a little.

"But I hope that serves as a testament to my enthusiasm, excitement, and organizational skills. I really want this year's Fall Fest to be great. I think we all do, so I also want to make sure everyone feels like their ideas are heard. So don't be shy about speaking up." (Just not over me, and definitely not with any ideas that suck, please.)

"If there are no questions..." I pause to give my classmates a minute to raise their hands. When none rise, I continue. "Maybe we can kick things off by sharing some thoughts about the Fall Fest as it stands, so we can figure out where we want to go with it?"

Marisol's arm shoots up. "Honestly, I hate how tacky everything was in years prior. Construction-paper leaves in the school colors do nothing for me. This isn't elementary school."

I grab one of the whiteboard markers and draw a line down the center with LIKES written on one side and DISLIKES on the other.

"Fair enough," I say as I write the word *tacky* under DISLIKES. I add *construction-paper crafts*.

Marisol's frankness seems to open the floodgates, and soon we have a whiteboard full of thoughts related to the Fall Fest—mostly that it's perceived as an outdated, dorky tradition that needs some serious updating. Unfortunately, our group hasn't listed many things under the LIKES column, meaning we have a lot of work to do.

As I stare at the list we've made, my brain starts buzzing with ways we might improve this perception of Fall Fest—when I suddenly hear something rolling down the hallway, like a teacher wheeling around a projector or one of those backpacks with the wheels.

A deep, husky voice says, "Sorry I'm late."

I turn toward the door and—*no*.

Because there, in the doorframe, is Isaiah, skateboard in hand, easy grin on that beautiful but supremely annoying face of his.

What is he doing here? In *my* Fall Fest committee meeting?!

"You're late," Ms. Bennett says, hand on her hip. "Very, very late."

He pushes his locs from his face. "Yeah, I know, Ms. B. My bad!" Isaiah comes into the class and puts his board on an empty desk. "I got caught up in chemistry class and stayed late."

"I need you to take this seriously," she reminds him. "We *all* do."

He holds his hands up in defeat. "I know, I know. I'm really sorry. It won't happen again. I swear."

Ms. Bennett straightens. "It better not," she says, as if Isaiah is planning to make repeat appearances at this meeting. I'm gonna barf.

"No, ma'am." He slides into an empty desk, neatly tucking the skateboard into the wire cubby attached to the bottom. "Please continue."

Ms. Bennett clears her throat. "I apologize for the interruption. Isaiah, as you can see by the whiteboard, we've been brainstorming possibilities for this year's festival."

Isaiah studies the board, grabbing a pen from behind his left ear and taking a few notes in a small Moleskine notebook that he pulls from his back pocket. How can he travel so lightly? I carry, like, four bags every day!

"And, team, I know we've already selected our class officers and president," Ms. Bennett continues, "but that vacant senior officer position needs to be filled."

Her eyes fall to me as she's saying this.

My heart starts pounding.

Because no.

No way.

"What do you mean?" I ask.

"I promised you I'd find someone to fill that role so you'd have the help you deserved, and I'm really excited to share that Isaiah has volunteered!" Ms. Bennett explains in a far-too-cheerful voice. "He will make a *great* number two."

I can feel my eyes go big without my permission. I'm embarrassingly bad at hiding my feelings, especially when I'm caught off guard. There might as well be a giant sign next to me that says WOW, I HATE EVERYTHING ABOUT THIS!!!

To make matters worse, Isaiah has the audacity to playfully waggle a few fingers at me in a wave.

"You're joking," I deadpan.

Isaiah pretends he's wounded. "Ouch, Whit. That hurts."

"Whitney!" Ms. Bennett says, surprised.

"I'm sorry! It's just that I thought *I* was going to be leading this thing."

"And you are," she confirms. "Isaiah is here to help with the execution of the ideas that you and your fellow officers decide on. I think it will be a really meaningful opportunity for both of you."

"Considering I'm usually more of a number one in most situations, I feel like this is actually a decent concession on my part," Isaiah teases.

I might dive across the table and start strangling him if not for Ms. Bennett and the hopeful—but stern—way she's looking at me.

"We can make this work, Whit? Right?" she asks.

But I'm not sure I can. I've been so focused on becoming the president of this committee, with late-night visions of me in this solo role, making the Fall Fest mine-all-mine, shaping it into the perfect homage to autumn I've always envisioned, that having to share with anyone else nearly cracks me right in half.

I made vision boards about this...only for ISAIAH ORTIZ to be my reality?! It doesn't seem right.

"Whit." The sound of my name in a hushed tone brings me back to earth. I glance toward the voice—Marisol—and take in a breath.

"Right. I'm good with that," I manage to say.

But really, all I can think is: *HOW ABSOLUTELY DARE YOU RUIN THIS FOR ME, ISAIAH ORTIZ?*

The group resumes its brainstorming, though I can barely pay attention. Instead, I shoot eye daggers at the side of Isaiah's face.

When Ms. Bennett dismisses our meeting, she asks me and Isaiah to hang back. I give a dramatic wave to Marisol and Sophie using both of my hands, because RIP me.

Ms. Bennett perches on the edge of the desk at the front of the classroom in that I'm-a-cool-teacher-I-swear kind of way and gives us both a warm smile. I mean, fine, she is cool, but I'm really mad at her right now.

"Okay, so. I know this felt a little abrupt," she says, "but I'm grateful that you're both willing to work together on this. Whit, you bring immense organizational knowledge, big ideas, and the most heart that the Fall Fest has ever seen. Isaiah, you're smart and creative, too, and I'm counting on you to be pragmatic, dedicated, and helpful. I think the two of you, together, will balance each other out well."

Why doesn't she just come out and say that Isaiah is essentially here to throw cold water over whatever big, gorgeous dreams I have for this event?

"Okay," I say, unable to help the sigh that escapes my mouth. "We can do that."

"We'll make you proud, Ms. B," Isaiah promises.

"I know you will," she agrees. "You'll both do a great job. Think you can get together sometime before our next meeting to start working through the list we made today?"

My gaze meets Isaiah's; he's standing there looking entirely too amused by my pain. The corner of his mouth quirks up into a smirk.

I grit my teeth and say again, "We can do that."

Ms. Bennett claps her hands together. "Great! Well, I'll leave you to it, then. Off to goat yoga." She grabs her tote bag and purse and gives us a wave before disappearing through the classroom door.

A look of disgust comes over Isaiah's face. "Goat yoga? White people are so weird sometimes."

I cross my arms. "Can we just set a time to meet up, please?"

"Sorry, didn't realize your time was so precious."

"Why'd you even volunteer for this, anyway?"

"You're not the only one who cares about things like college applications, you know," he scoffs.

"Fine. Can you meet Monday after school?"

He reaches into his pocket to pull out his phone, tapping a few times. "I don't have to be at work till six, so looks like it." Isaiah looks up at me. "Where should we meet?"

"Here," I say, as if it's the most obvious thing in the world. When he looks irritated at my unrelenting attitude, I soften. "Or...maybe out in the courtyard? It's supposed to be nice on Monday."

Isaiah tucks his phone away in his pocket once more and reaches for his skateboard. "Fine." He heads for the door, but turns back to add, "And, for what it's worth, I think this could be kinda fun. *If* we don't kill each other first."

I give him a thin-lipped smile. "Let's not bet on it."

Chapter Eleven

On Friday night, Abuela goes to Titi Mariana's to have dinner with her and her family, while Lily hangs out at Nora's house, leaving me alone with Patch. I'm not sure my life could get more pathetic, but here we are. The *only* silver lining from this week is that I got an email about an interview tomorrow morning for the cashier job at Nature's Grocer, a high-end grocery mart.

I eat a pathetic dinner of crackers and peanut butter standing at the kitchen sink, then flop onto the couch. All I have the energy for tonight is reruns of bad television and lurking on social media.

From the comfort of the couch, I find myself idly navigating back to Jay Martinez's TikTok account so I can watch that video of him and Isaiah skateboarding again. Though Isaiah seems to make plenty of appearances in Jay's videos, I can't find any evidence that might lead me to his actual account. So much for hate-scrolling.

Then my phone lights up with a call. It's Aiden. He *never* calls.

"Yeah?" is how I answer because I already know what he's calling to say.

"Whit?" he asks on the other end.

"The one and only."

"Oh…hey." Aiden pauses. When I don't respond with anything, he goes, "So, about the other night—"

"When you totally blew me off?" I ask bluntly.

"Yeah, that. It's just that I've been meaning to talk to you…"

"You're calling to break up with me," I deadpan.

"Uhhhh…"

I sigh. "No need to beat around the bush here. That's why you're calling, isn't it?"

"Well, yes, but I had this whole thing prepared—"

"It's fine, Aiden. Really."

"It's not like you haven't been great," he continues. "You have been! It's just, you know, I kinda met someone. It's—it's Moose, as you may have guessed."

This gets my attention and I sit up in bed, sending Patch darting out of my lap and into the hallway.

"*Moose?*" I ask. "As in, your new best friend?"

"Yeah. My new best friend..." His voice trails off. "She and I have been seeing a lot of each other."

"She," I repeat. "Moose is a girl."

A pause. Then, quietly, I hear Aiden say, "...Yes?"

And I can't help it.

A laugh bubbles in my chest and bursts out of me unexpectedly, like a hiccup. Another laugh follows, and soon I'm practically cackling. Moose is a girl. Moose is a girl!!! And Aiden's been hiding that from me!

It's not like I've ever been the kind of unreasonable person who would object to him befriending girls, but I definitely object to him obscuring that fact, like it's a dirty little secret. The only logical reason for Aiden to hide something like that is because he's been interested in Moose from the jump.

Suddenly, the way Aiden's voice always lilted up when he said her name makes sense. It clicks why he was constantly ignoring me to go do something with Moose, why he always talked about Moose, why Moose was so involved in every facet of his life—from the new clothes he wore to the new nickname he had.

I've been dumped by my first boyfriend, during my favorite season, in my senior year, when almost every single thing that can go wrong has, just weeks before a dance that became a legacy in my family, for A GIRL NAMED MOOSE, and all I can do is laugh.

"Okay, jeez. I'm gonna go," Aiden says, clearly annoyed—annoyed! As if he has a right to be!—on the other line. "Bye."

"Bye." I giggle. "Have fun with Moose!"

I hang up and, still giggling, I text Marisol and Sophie.

Me: As it turns out, Moose is a girl!

Me: A fact that Aiden has been hiding!

Me: And now he's dating her!

Me: After not replying to my angry text!!!

Me: Bahahahah skdjfsjdf

It's mere seconds before my screen is illuminated with a Face-Time request from Sophie. I accept. Marisol joins, too.

Sophie's the first to speak. "Okay, so, that's a lot to process. First: Are you good?"

"I'm about to drive up to New Hampshire and egg his car." Marisol scowls, then leans closer to the screen, squinting at me. "Wait. Are you laughing or crying?"

"I'm laughing!" I wipe at the corner of my eye. "And also crying. But from the laughing!"

The two glance at each other on their respective screens, Sophie concerned, Marisol amused.

"Because Moose is a girl! Like, of course, right? Aiden Miller was such a coward he couldn't even tell me he'd met someone. He made me do the emotional labor of trying to keep our so-called relationship alive, but he was always planning to cut out. And now he's free to live happily ever after with a girl named Moose. *Moose!* And that's just so, so funny to me."

"Is it possible you're on the verge of a nervous breakdown?" Sophie asks.

"Sounds to me like she's finally seeing Aiden for the walking dumpster fire that he is," Marisol says sagely.

Sophie nods. "There's no questioning *that*. But I can't believe he did this to you. I wouldn't blame you if you were heartbroken—breakup or no breakup. I'm so sorry!"

"I'm not. Want to know why?" I cup one of my hands around the side of my mouth for emphasis as I say, "He suuuucked. What did I even see in him?!"

"He was hot," Sophie says simply.

Marisol shoots me a look. "See? Told you it was all physical."

"You could do *so* much better than him," Sophie says. "Goodbye and good riddance."

"Bye, pendejo!" Marisol calls out, as if Aiden can hear. "Our bestie's going to find someone who stimulates her mind *and* her body now!"

It makes me erupt into laughter, which makes Marisol laugh, which then cracks a smile from Sophie, and soon, we're *all* laughing: the side-clenching, belly-aching kind of laughter that you feel in your whole body.

When we come up for air, Marisol asks, "But seriously, Whit. Are you really okay with everything?"

"You know, I am honestly not sure," I admit. "I feel simultaneously relieved and hurt and confused and embarrassed and sort of...angry. Resentful."

"*All* legit," Sophie says. "Can we do something to cheer you up?"

I sigh. "I don't know if I need cheering up so much as I need to punch something. Like, therapeutically."

Marisol snaps her fingers as if an idea has just occurred to her. "We may not be able to let you punch something, but how would you feel about stabbing a pumpkin?"

My brows furrow. "Excuse me?"

"Let's go pumpkin-picking! You love pumpkin-picking!" she exclaims. "Then we can carve them and you can get some of that pent-up frustration out. I mean, it's that, or we can create an elaborate catfishing scenario where I pretend I'm a blonde Bri'ish girl named Bridget and I get Aiden to emotionally cheat on Moose and—"

"Okay, let's go pumpkin-picking!" I cut in. "Pick me up tomorrow after lunch?"

"See you then," Sophie says. "And block Aiden's number, okay?"

Wiser words have never been spoken.

SEPTEMBER 2023

Sunday	Monday	Tuesday	Wednesday	Thursday	Friday	Saturday
					1	2
3	4	5 First day of senior year!	6	7 First Fall Fest meeting	8 Sleepover @ Soph's	9
10	11 Fall Fest committee voting	12 Date with Aiden	13	14 Fall Fest weekly meeting	15 BREAK UP WITH AIDEN!!!	16 Pumpkin-picking with the besties
17	18 Meet with the enemy!!!	19	20	21 Fall Fest weekly meeting	22	23
24	25	26	27	28 Fall Fest weekly meeting	29	30

OCTOBER 2023

Sunday	Monday	Tuesday	Wednesday	Thursday	Friday	Saturday
1	2	3	4	5 Fall Fest weekly meeting	6	7
8	9 Indigenous Peoples' Day	10	11	12 Final Fall Fest meeting before go time!	13	14
15 Fall Fest begins!	16	17	18	19	20	21 Fall Fest ends!
22	23	24	25	26	27	28
29	30	31 Halloween				

Chapter Twelve

It's a nearly perfect fall day when I wake: clear blue skies with the gentlest breeze in the air, a hint of the cooler weather that's to come. I throw open my bedroom window to soak it all in. *This* is what I've been waiting for.

After a shower, I put on some minimal makeup and layer a fitted white turtleneck to go under a vintage navy-blue crew neck sweater that reads CAPE COD over some black leggings and chunky sneakers.

"How cute do I look, Patch?" I ask. He doesn't look up from the sunbeam where he's napping, but I know he loves the outfit.

It's early, and I don't have my interview at Nature's Grocer for a bit, so I decide to take full advantage of the autumn vibes and make use of the leftover pumpkin puree from our empanadas. On my phone, I pull up a recipe for pumpkin muffins and make quick work of mixing ingredients, then pop the first tray into the oven. I settle at the table to work on some homework while they bake.

It isn't long before the air is filled with the sweet aroma of cinnamon, summoning Abuela into the kitchen. She's wearing a hot-pink velour tracksuit, her pajamas of choice, and it's a total vibe.

"Buenas dias, mija," she says, leaning in to give me a kiss on the forehead. "My mouth is watering! What're you making?"

"Pumpkin muffins! I figured I might as well, since I was up so early."

She rubs her hands together. "¿Cafecito?"

"Please!" I tuck my completed worksheet into my folder and sit back in my chair. "How was Titi Mariana's? Were the twins there?"

Abuela slaps her forehead. "Dios mío."

"So, delightful as always, then?" I tease. Titi Mariana's and Tío Johanny's youngest daughter, Ava, lives there with her husband, Juan, and their adorable but hyper five-year-old twins, who make every visit to their house...spirited? Or a straight-up challenge, depending on the mood you catch them in.

"One day, I'm going to go there and find Mari tied to a chair—just you wait!" Abuela shakes her head, laughing. "They are so cute, though."

"They really are."

The timer on the oven beeps. I grab an oven mitt to pull out the initial batch of muffins and place them on top of the oven. Abuela doesn't bother waiting for them to cool and starts to pop them out of the tin with her bare hands.

"Abuela! Doesn't that burn?" I ask, horrified. She always does this! I swear her fingers are made of Kevlar.

She waves away my concern, easing the final muffin onto a cooling rack. "Ah, it's okay."

"What smells so good?" Lily's voice calls down the hall.

"Whitney made muffins! Come, sit," Abuela says, pulling out plates and taking over breakfast prep, the way she tends to do any time we're in the kitchen. "Are you two coming to the shop today?"

"Can't," Lily says with a mouth full of food. "Going to Ruby's house."

I raise my eyebrows. "You're hanging out with Ruby a lot, huh?" She shrugs, taking another bite. "And sorry, Abuela. I have that job interview this morning, and then Marisol and Sophie are taking me to the pumpkin patch."

"Don't be sorry! That sounds fun," Abuela says. "Except for

the part about the job interview. I hope you know I don't expect you to work. Just focus on your studies and your well-being."

Now it's my turn to wave away her concern. "I'll be fine." Because Abuela is proud—and because I don't get my stubbornness from nowhere—I opt not to say that we could really use the extra money. I peek at my phone. "And I should get going so I'm not late. I'll swing by the shop to help you close up, okay?"

Abuela nods. "Okay, mija. Good luck!"

* * *

Maybe there was something special about Abuela wishing me luck because I get hired on the spot.

But it's more likely that wages for service jobs are so trash that Nature's Grocer was super desperate for bodies. Either way, I'll take the win.

I tell Marisol and Sophie about the success as we pile into Marisol's black Escalade. I admit that every time I slip into Sol's gigantic car—a gift from her wealthy stepfather, Robert, who is adorably sweet and dorky—I feel like a celebrity.

Sophie picks the music, and then we're off to the Knoll, an "Instagram-friendly" pumpkin patch. We went for the first time last year and, to our surprise, absolutely loved it. Of course you can pick pumpkins, which is the most important thing, but the Knoll also has a farmhouse that's been converted into an indoor haven for photos and selfies. Every inch feels photo-worthy, including a space that offers different backdrops, like a wall made of tiny white gourds and a neon-orange sign over some greenery that reads HI, PUMPKIN! When I tell you we spent literal *hours* here last year, I am not exaggerating.

"Okay, so, photos first this year, right?" Sophie asks.

Marisol nods vigorously. "Oh, yes. There is no way in hell I'm lugging my pumpkin around first and getting all sweaty again. I look cute. I need photographic evidence of it."

"Hard same. Let's take our time with the photos, and then we can grab some of the cider and get on the hayride," I say from the back seat.

Sophie turns in her seat to look at me. "Ooh, we should totally get some kettle corn, too!"

I grin. "It's like you're reading my mind."

I have to admit that it means a lot to have my friends dedicate their Saturday afternoon to something I love. I know they'll enjoy themselves, too, but after worrying we might have a hard time reconnecting after this past summer, this is a nice reassurance.

Still, there are times when I find myself feeling so, so guilty over not filling them in on my diagnosis. Though I'm not so ashamed of it anymore, it's almost like the longer I go without talking about it, the harder it is to *start* talking about it. I don't know.

We pull into the lot at the Knoll and climb out of the car.

"Shall we?" Sophie asks, holding out an arm to me and Marisol.

We link arms and head right into the farmhouse. It's not too busy yet, so we can take our time grabbing individual, group, and artistic shots. Sophie literally squeals when she sees a corgi dressed like a scarecrow having its photo taken while she's perched on a bale of hay. (Obviously we beg the owner to get our photo taken with the corgi, too. Her name is Pickles.)

Some cider and popcorn later, we hop in line for the hayride.

While we wait, my gaze falls to a hickory tree with leaves already turning golden. "God, the leaves already look so pretty," I breathe.

"One time, when I was younger, my mami took Natalia and me on a scavenger hunt for different shades of leaves so we could make a rainbow. Of course, Natalia kept saying the leaves I was picking were ugly, but I was only three! She complained so much that Mami had us each make our own," Marisol says with a huff. "But that yellow leaf would've been perfect for it."

"It's not too late to grab it and send a pic to Natalia. Show her how good your leaf selection skills have gotten," Sophie teases.

Marisol laughs. "Don't tempt me."

The tractor rumbles toward us, pulling a wagon full of people, each with their selection of pumpkin. A group of four girls, likely middle school age, are the last to hobble off the wagon. As they near, I can see the reason for it: heels.

I nudge Sophie and Marisol and pucker my lips in exaggerated sympathy.

When they're out of earshot, Marisol lets out a laugh. "God, that takes me back."

"Right? I'll never forget when we made the same mistake." I laugh, too, shaking my head.

Back in the tenth grade, the three of us got all dressed up to go on a haunted hayride at nearby McNally's Farm. So many of our classmates were going and we wanted to look cute, so we went all out with our outfits, including wearing heels—on a farm, in the middle of a rainy autumn. It was not our finest moment. Every few steps, we'd sink right into the ground and have to help one another walk. We thought the heels would make us look sexy and sophisticated. We were wrong.

"We all have to learn that lesson eventually," Sophie jokes. "I pray for their poor ankles."

"At least they look super cute. You know they got some good selfies back at the barn." I nod toward the wagon. "You ready?"

Marisol climbs aboard the wagon first, grabbing us seats on a hay bale toward the back of the ride. Sophie and I flank her.

"Tenth grade feels so long ago, doesn't it?" Marisol muses. "I was still chasing boys then. Gross."

"That's right! You had a huge crush on Erik Jimenez!" Sophie laughs.

Marisol makes a face. "Don't remind me!"

"Isn't he kind of a pyromaniac now?" Sophie asks.

"You really know how to pick 'em, Sol," I tease. "Hey, maybe we break out the heels at McNally's next weekend for old times' sake."

"I kind of think we should!" Sophie says suddenly.

"Speak for yourself," Marisol jokes, but Sophie's eyebrows are knit together in concern.

"Seriously, though! We'll never go to McNally's and foolishly wear heels again." She frowns. "And this could be the last time we pick pumpkins together."

I gasp. "Don't say that!"

"But it's true," she insists. "After we graduate, who knows what'll happen? I mean, Marisol is going off to become an incredible lawyer. I'll be studying music. Whit will be off making people's lives better. What if we drift?"

"No matter where we end up, we'll still be friends," Marisol says firmly. "You putas will *never* get rid of me."

Sophie lets out a big sigh. "I'm just starting to get sad thinking about things I'm enjoying that might become our last without us knowing. It doesn't seem fair."

Hearing her say that makes my heart ache, especially as I think back to the summer. Were there things I missed during that time that I might never do again?

"It *isn't* fair," I say. "I think all we can do is soak everything in now and make the most of it."

Sophie nods. "Consider me a sponge."

Chapter Thirteen

I arrive in the courtyard for my meeting with Isaiah well before he does. It gives me time to set up my three-ring binder of Fall Fest ideas, as well as my notebook. I may not be thrilled that Isaiah and I have been paired up, but I'm going to take this meeting seriously. I owe it to the Fall Fest. And myself.

Ignoring the sun that's making me a little too warm in my sweater, I start to review some of my notes. It isn't long, though, before I hear the now-familiar sound of wheels gliding across pavement. Isaiah. I look up and am immediately struck by the way his lithe body instinctively makes micro adjustments on his skateboard as he nears. He makes it look so effortless.

Today, his locs are pulled back into a high ponytail at the top of his head, and he's wearing a plaid button-up open over a band T-shirt, paired with jeans. My eyes involuntarily fall down his body as I remember Marisol's text from days ago—*We're talking about your ex, right? Tall? Long locs? Super hot? And* ↻ ↻ ↻?—and I feel my cheeks flush. She's not wrong, okay?

I push my curls over to one shoulder as he approaches.

"Hey," I call to him.

"Hey," Isaiah calls back, stepping off his board and kicking it with his heel so that it jumps up into his hand. "Am I late?"

I shake my head. "No, I'm just freakishly early to most things."

I reach into my bag to retrieve Isaiah's hoodie. Abuela laundered, folded, and wrapped it in tissue paper and twine, the same way she does with everything from El Coquí. I told her I could wash it myself, but she insisted, saying I had enough to worry about with school and my job training tomorrow night.

"Your hoodie, as promised," I say, watching as he joins me at the picnic table. He tucks his skateboard beneath his bench, then reaches for his shirt, the tissue paper crinkling in his hands.

"A ribbon!" Isaiah muses, even though it's clearly *twine*. "You do this just for me? I'm flattered."

"It was my abuela, but I'll tell her you liked it."

"You really didn't have to get it back to me so fast."

"I wanted to." Silently, I add, *Because I needed to stop thinking about how great it smelled.*

Isaiah places his hoodie on the bench next to him and then claps his hands together. "All right. So. Fall Fest."

I give him a firm nod. "Fall Fest. I already have so many ideas." I crack open my binder. "I thought we could start by breaking down the week in its simplest form. There are seven days of activities we've got to plan for, Sunday through Saturday. Although some things are pretty set in stone, like the Friday pep rally and football game, plus the dance on Saturday, we have creative freedom pretty much everywhere else."

Isaiah reaches into his back pocket and pulls out a Moleskine notebook, spreading it open to a new page. From behind his ear, he grabs a pen I hadn't noticed.

I watch as he writes down the days of the week with the activities I mentioned beside them. The shock of him actually taking this seriously throws me off, and when he looks back up at me, I realize I've lost my train of thought.

"So, um…"

"You were saying we have creative freedom outside of Friday and Saturday," he says.

"Right. Okay, so, over the last few years, the committee has typically gone with school spirit–type themes for early in the week, like wearing school colors or Pajama Day or whatever. I looked through a couple of old school newspapers online to see if that was always the case, and it looks like it has been since at least, like, the 2000s."

Isaiah lets out a thoughtful "Mmm," adding a few notes to his paper.

"Personally, I'm not totally in love with those suggestions just because I feel like it's been done. I'm not sure how you feel about it, but I would really love to freshen things up and offer some fun, traditional fall options. Really play up the autumn angle, you know? I mean, it's called the Fall Fest—why are we not making the most of that? We could have a Coziest Sweater Day or a pumpkin-painting contest. Maybe a bonfire."

I turn my binder around so he can see the vision board I've made for the weeklong event, feeling weirdly nervous he might not like what I've pulled together. I'm hoping to pitch a 1970s theme to incorporate into the dance itself, inspired by browns and reds and oranges and yellows that feel super retro—a subtle nod to when Abuela and Abuelo met all those years ago.

Isaiah's eyes scan the page, a smile spreading across his face.

"Something funny?" I ask, defensively crossing my arms.

"No. I just like this," he says. "I like this a lot."

My face brightens. "Really?"

"That seventies vibe is great, you know? *And* you managed to include imagery of us brown folks! I feel like we killed it in that decade and we never get enough credit."

I give him a small smile. "Yeah! Also, I always felt like there was this image of fall belonging to white Christian girls or whatever. But my grandparents met and fell in love during this season and it's really special to us, and it's just like...how can a season belong to a particular kind of person, you know? Anyway, the iconic colors from the seventies work so well with autumn, it seems like an obvious pairing. I figure the dance itself can be seventies-themed and we can all dress for the decade. Bell-bottoms, bell sleeves, popped collars, suit jackets—you get it. And Chloe can make all the posters and stuff look retro, so the Fest will actually feel cool and exciting again. Yeah?"

"Definitely. I think people are going to really like it, honestly," Isaiah says. "What else you got, Madam President?"

"Okay, so," I start, feeling my excitement rise at Isaiah's interest, "I want to open up the king and queen to any gender or sexual orientation. It's archaic that we haven't already done that. It should also be fine if there are two queens, two kings, whatever."

Isaiah nods, flipping through the binder. "Absolutely, yes. Could we add a nongendered title, too? To be more inclusive?"

"Oh, I like that." I jot it down in my notebook. "Any ideas for that new title?"

"Maybe Sovereign?"

"Monarch?" I suggest.

"Aristocrat," Isaiah adds, feigning a posh English accent.

I grin, putting on my own accent to match. "Your Majesty." We both laugh at that one, mostly because of how over-the-top it is.

Isaiah rubs his chin, thinking. "King…Queen…and how about just Royal as the third option?"

My face brightens. "I like it! It gives off big *Bridgerton* vibes and I'm here for it." I add this to my notes, too. "Who knew you'd come ready with the ideas?"

He taps a finger on his temple. "Believe it or not, sometimes I even have more than one."

I gasp dramatically. "No!"

"It's not something I want getting out, but yeah." Isaiah reaches for his phone and taps a few times, then turns the screen to me. "So, in *my* research for the Fall Fest, I saw that the original celebrations had a whole-ass after-school carnival—games, fair food, crafts. How dope is that? I think we should bring it back, but with your fall spin. We could have caramel apples, cider donuts, that type of thing."

I blink at him. How does he keep taking me by surprise? And how did I not think of this?!

Isaiah winces, pulling his phone back. "All right. You can just say you hate the carnival idea instead of staring at me all bug-eyed like that."

"No, actually—I *love* it!" I clap my hands together excitedly. "It's genius. I'm actually mad I didn't come up with it myself."

He breaks into a grin, smooth and easy, and rubs his chin. "So you're saying I'm a genius..."

I don't bother suppressing an eye roll. "Don't get ahead of yourself. I said the *idea* is genius, not you."

"Same thing."

"Not," I argue. "But okay, okay, okay. The carnival. What if instead of after school, we made that our kickoff event the Sunday before? We could turn it into an all-day thing so it's not wasted on just a few hours!"

"*Now* you're talking, Whit," he says, nodding. "From what I could find, the carnival was usually made up of donations from local vendors. With your enthusiasm and rumored love of spreadsheets—"

"Oh my God," I groan.

"—and my incredibly good looks and charm, it'll be easy. Plus, if we charge for things at the carnival, we'll recoup some of the costs and possibly then some."

"Can I just reiterate that I hate that you came up with this instead of me?"

"Told you I'd be an excellent number two," he says with a smirk. "But I'm dying to know. What's 'Fall for Whit'?" He points to the header on one of my binder pages. I immediately push his hand away, but he's way stronger than me and pushes right back. "Aw, come on! You put it on every single page of your Fall Fest plans and you won't even tell me?"

"It's nothing," I insist, using my free hand to grab at his, like him touching the words on the page is the problem and not the fact that I *forgot to delete that tagline from my documents before I printed them out*. In my defense, this binder was originally for my eyes only, not his. "It was a silly campaign I made to try to get elected president of the committee."

At this, Isaiah stops pushing my hands away, but he doesn't let go. He tilts his head to one side, one of his locs brushing against his cheek as he does. "You made a whole campaign to become president?" His voice doesn't sound judgmental, but curious.

"Yeah, I did. This is really important to me," I admit. "For college applications and all. But also, if I'm honest, it's important to me for other reasons, too. The Fall Fest means a lot in my family, so I want it to be special. I figured my best chance was to do it myself."

Isaiah's dark eyes study my face while I speak, and the intensity of his gaze makes me look away. "We're going to make it special. That's a promise."

When I glance down, I see that his hands are still holding mine, and I ignore my heart skipping a beat as I quickly pull away.

"Okay," I mumble, busying my now-free hands by smoothing the hem of my denim overall dress. "Fine."

He smiles at me. "Glad you see it my way."

I make a face at him. "Don't even."

And it makes him laugh with such warmth that the sound thaws part of my icy heart. Ugh, what is *up* with me today?

"I even made a video for the campaign," I blurt.

"Of course you did." He motions for me to hand my phone over. "And now you're going to let me see it."

I make a big show of reaching into the pocket of my dress for my phone, as if this is such a huge hassle, even though I'm the one who brought it up. "If you insist."

He takes my unlocked phone, where I've pulled the video up on YouTube. I gaze over his shoulder at the video, even though I've seen it dozens of times since Lily helped me cut it together, sneaking peeks up at him while he watches.

Part of me is convinced that Isaiah is totally messing with me right now, and at any moment he's going to burst out laughing at how extra this all is, at how no one in their right mind would take planning a high school homecoming dance this seriously.

But as it finishes and he hands me back my phone, he gives me a thoughtful look. "You really go for things, don't you?"

"I try," I say, tucking my phone back into my pocket. "Why bother unless you're going to really commit?"

"I think it's cool," Isaiah replies. "I mean, you can be a little intense. Maybe even a little scary..."

I scrunch my nose. "Shut *up*."

"But it's all good. You care. A lot. That matters." He closes his notebook nonchalantly, as if he hasn't just thrown me off-kilter by getting it—*seeing* me—in a way a lot of others probably don't. "Anyway, what is it about fall that's got you so sprung, anyway?"

"Everything, obviously. What's *not* to love about fall?" I challenge.

"I don't know. It kinda bums me out, since winter comes right after. I hate winter."

"Okay, yeah. But there's so much to love about the months before then, especially the beginning of fall. There's the foliage, of course. And apple fritters. Pumpkin spice everything. Mums, campfires, cozy sweaters, pumpkin- and apple-picking—"

Zay cuts in. "You're forgetting rain, mud, waking up in the dark, super-short days, death—"

"Death?!"

He smirks at me. "Fall is the death of all that's living! You're basically admitting that you enjoy watching nature crumble in on itself, Whit."

I scowl at him, crossing my arms. "That's not at all true! Fall is the necessary reprieve before a period of rest. It's like when a phoenix turns to ash so that it can be born again. It's part of rebirth—the last burst of light before a second chance."

His mouth goes to one side and he looks off, as if contemplating this. "You make it sound so serious."

"Only because my love for it *is*," I protest.

"There's that intensity." He shakes his head. "I'll admit that some of what you said might be true—"

"Ha!"

"—but the fact that the sun sets at four o'clock is practically criminal!"

"Well, I'm not going to argue with you on that one. That part really *does* suck."

"I'll cop to liking the pumpkin spice drinks, though," Isaiah admits. "Shit's fire."

"Right?! Absolute perfection," I agree.

"Maybe we can have pumpkin spice lattes at the carnival."

"Oh my gosh. Yes!" I practically squeal. "Look at you with the good ideas."

He grins, tapping the side of his forehead. "See? I'm good. I even think this could be fun. But it won't be anything without the seventies theme, honestly. *That* is cool, and *that's* what's gonna elevate the entire thing and keep it from going stale."

I meet his eyes, returning the smile. "Thanks. Well, I'm clearly living in some kind of other dimension, because I'm starting to think this could be fun, too."

Chapter Fourteen

Whoever decided fluorescent lights should be the standard in big-box stores was an actual masochist. They flatter no one, and I can say this with confidence now that I've spent four hours under them while working my first shift at Nature's Grocer—*farm-fresh food for a happy-fresh you!*

Yes, that's the terrible tagline I'm forced to utter whenever I finish ringing up a customer.

It's a small price to pay considering I earn a full five bucks more per hour than the other minimum-wage jobs I applied for. I even get to wear a forest-green apron and visor as I ring up organic groceries for wealthy people. Yay, capitalism!

Luckily, I've already gotten good at smiling through the pain. I'm telling myself I'm saying their tagline ironically, which helps a little.

By the end of my first shift, though, my feet are sore and I realize that wearing wedges was probably not the move.

I'm limping my way inside the house and all too grateful to be home when the scent of Abuela's delicious pollo guisado hits me. My stomach grumbles, since I've subsisted all day on nothing but a granola bar I had in my backpack for emergencies (because everything at Nature's Grocer is way out of my price range, even with the employee discount).

"¡Hola!" Abuela calls to me when she hears the sound of my keys dropping into the bowl in our entryway.

"Hi, Abuela!" I kick off my shoes and hobble into the kitchen, where Abuela sits at the table using her reading glasses to sew Lily's pink-and-white backpack.

"What happened?" I ask, surprised to see it torn.

Abuela shoots me a look. "Lily won't say, but when she came home, one of the straps on her backpack was broken."

"Do you think someone broke it on purpose?" I hate that that's my first instinct, but I'm always worried someone is going to pick on Lily.

She shakes her head. "No se. Maybe it just got caught on something and she's embarrassed. It's an easy fix."

"I hope that's what happened." From the cabinet, I grab myself a big bowl and start to spoon in some of the chicken stew, which is still warm on the stove.

"Why are you walking like a little old lady?"

"I'm not," I lie.

Abuela pushes her glasses up so they rest on her head. "I have eyes, mija."

With a sigh, I sit at the table across from her. "I learned the hard way that I wore the wrong shoes for my first shift." I show her my red and blistering feet and she grimaces.

"¡Ay! That looks painful. Let me get you something to soak them."

"I'm okay, Abuela, really." Of course, she won't hear it, immediately retrieving a bucket and filling it with warm water.

"Here," she says, setting it down in front of me.

The combination of sinking my aching feet into the warm water and taking a big bite of Abuela's savory stew makes me feel whole again. "Thank you so much."

She comes over and kisses the top of my head. "Siempre, mi amor." She rejoins me on the other side of the table.

"If you leave that, I can finish it," I offer.

But she waves her hand at me.

That's the thing with Abuela—she always wants to take care of everything herself, tending to everyone around her before caring for herself. Sometimes I like being doted on, but I do wish she'd occasionally let me and Lily dote on her, too.

I swallow another bite of the stew. "How was your day?"

"Bien, bien," she murmurs, focusing on the backpack. "Pero, this uppity woman came in to complain about a skirt of hers I hemmed three years ago."

"What?!"

"¡Sí! She says she hadn't had time to try it on until now and when she put it on, it didn't sit right. As if bodies can't change over three years?" She sucks in some air through her teeth, shaking her head. "Some people."

"That's wild, Abuela. What did you say?"

"I told her I would fix it for her."

"Abuela!"

"Well!" She huffs. "She had this cute little baby with her and I just turned to marshmallow. I couldn't say no while he was looking at me."

I smile at her, pulling my feet out from the bucket and drying them off. "You big softie." I rise to put my bowl in the dishwasher and give her a side hug on my way to the counter. "I like that about you."

She pats my arm and leans her head against me. I give her a kiss on her head. She works so hard for us; I'm happy I was able to get this part-time job to be able to give back to her, even if it isn't much.

Abuela is essentially a single mom, since we lost Abuelo years ago to cancer. Thankfully, Titi Mariana and Titi Luisa help fill in the gaps whenever they can. We know they'd be there if things ever got really bad, like a safety net. Sometimes the emphasis on family above all else in our culture can be a little toxic, but I lucked out to be part of a pretty wonderful one.

The three sisters get together a few times a month to play dominoes or trade chisme or go to the "club," which is actually a local community center that has a bimonthly 50+ Latin Night. Abuela never misses a chance to go with her sisters and dance with the crowd.

I think of Titi Mariana and Titi Luisa like yin and yang. They're both older than Abuela, but all three look younger than fifty by a lot. Titi Mariana loves when people tell her she seems too young to be a grandma. She's loud and bright and fun, while Titi Luisa, a devoted Catholic woman who never married, is softer-spoken and more reserved. We love them both fiercely.

After I load the dishwasher, I walk into the living room, expecting to see Lily, but she's not there. I check her room, which is a huge mess, by the way, and she's not there, either.

"Where's Lily?" I call out.

"Oh! She's staying over at Ruby's tonight," Abuela says from the kitchen. "And I'm off to Titi Mariana's for a little bit."

"On a school night?" I ask, and Abuela shoots me a look. "I meant that about Lily, not you!"

"¡Sí! You stay at Sophie's on school nights all the time," she reminds me.

"Oh. That's true."

"It's good for her, I think," Abuela continues. "I'm happy she's found a good friend."

"Yeah," I agree, though I find myself feeling a little skeptical of Ruby. "Me too. Anyway, have fun. Tell Titi I said hi. And don't stay out too late."

Abuela rolls her eyes at me, but leans down to kiss my cheek. "Yes, mami."

I watch her go. When the door closes behind her, the house feels eerily quiet. I wish Lily were here with me.

Since she started high school, it's felt like we've seen less and less of each other. Part of me is proud of her for settling in so nicely and so quickly. But the other part of me just misses her.

Chapter Fifteen

After my initial meeting with Isaiah, plus an idea that comes to me in the middle of the night (the best ones always do), I'm beyond eager for the next Fall Fest meeting.

I don't even mind that Isaiah will co-lead this meeting with me, especially because he lets me kick things off.

"So, it became pretty clear in our first meeting that the Fall Fest was basically on life support," I say.

"I've been brushing up on my CPR," Isaiah jokes.

"Isaiah and I spent some time envisioning what this new version of the Fall Fest could look like, and I think we've got things going in the right direction." I pull up a short presentation I threw together. "These slides will hopefully give you an idea of what we landed on."

"And when she says *we*, Whit really means herself. This is pretty much all her. Turns out her spreadsheet wasn't so outrageous after all," Isaiah teases.

I give him a well-deserved eye roll. "My thinking is that we can bring the Fall Fest back to what it was originally intended to be: an over-the-top, incredible ode to autumn and the harvest. For the dance, I would love to go with a retro theme, sort of 1970s. I feel like that's trendy and fun without being forced."

Sophie and Marisol are nodding encouragingly as I speak. I switch over to some color swatches and outfit examples, explaining that I think the dance itself should be seventies-themed, and then show off some sample decorations we could draw inspiration from:

disco balls, glitter walls, shiny red garlands, that kind of thing. I end on the vision board I showed Isaiah, the one that got him in line with my vision.

"The seventies theme is so good!" Sophie gushes. "I love that whole feel."

Hudson actually claps his hands together. "This is perfect, Whit. It feels so chic! So fancy! So...opposite of a homecoming dance desperate to be deemed cool!"

I practically beam, especially when some of the other class-mates chime in with their support. I grin at Isaiah, who tilts his head at me as if to say, *See? I told you they'd like it!*

"This is going to be so much better than those tacky other home-comings," Marisol says, flipping her hair over her shoulder. "People aren't going to know what hit them. Whit! You rocked this!"

"I'm so glad you all like this so far! And Isaiah actually had a pretty great idea, too..."

I kick things over to him so he can present on the carnival.

People are actually pretty enthused by his plans, and Isaiah even looks pleased with himself. But as he starts to wrap up, pre-paring us to move on to the execution discussion, I interrupt, rid-ing high from everyone's eager attention.

"There's one last thing I wanted to mention," I start, glancing at Isaiah. He shoots me a confused look, since this wasn't part of our presentation, but lets me continue. "So, while we're making changes to homecoming court, I'd like to propose adding an addi-tional couple of honorees called nobility to the court. I was think-ing these spots could honor some of the students at our school who are part of our special education program. What do you think?"

There's a soft murmur from some of the committee, but my eyes cut to Isaiah first—I'm hoping to gauge his opinion. I'm expecting him to be nodding along, maybe with his jaw open a little, impressed by this grand epiphany I had.

He doesn't really look pleased, though. In fact, the muscles in his jaw are clenched and he's not meeting my gaze at all. Confused by this, I look to my classmates, and I'm relieved when they appear to have received the idea much more positively. Everyone seems to approve.

"Thank you, Whit and Isaiah. Wonderful job," Ms. Bennett says. "Why don't you take your seats and we can open the floor for feedback and a vote?"

On my way back to my seat, Sophie squeezes my hand. "Such good ideas! You two killed it."

"You know I live for throwing a wrench in tradition, so I'm all in," Marisol adds.

After a brief discussion among the committee, the group votes. We easily agree to the seventies theme, Hudson Moore's suggestion to move homecoming court crowning to the dance from the football game, and the more inclusive homecoming court titles. The carnival is also enthusiastically approved, though my proposed Wear Your Coziest Sweater and Build Your Own Scarecrow days both get nixed. But I don't care because we end with a unanimous vote in favor of creating a new "nobility" category, just like I suggested. All I think of is Lily.

At the conclusion of the meeting, Isaiah slips out of the classroom before I can even congratulate him on a job well done.

"Great job today, Whit," Ms. Bennett says as I'm packing up my things. "I knew you and Isaiah would be great together!"

I smile at her. "Thank you. We had a surprisingly good first meeting. I'm feeling really optimistic."

"Wonderful! I hope it continues. We're making excellent progress already." She gives my friends and me a little wave, and the three of us walk out of school together.

"I'm *so* excited about officially opening the crown to everyone, without forcing folks to fit within a binary or deal with heteronormative bullshit," Marisol gushes. "I can practically taste the win!" She mimes putting a crown on her head.

"You know, *Queen Sophie and King Noah* has a nice ring to it," Sophie teases, pretending to rip the crown from Marisol and place it on her own head.

Marisol flips her hair over her shoulder. "Oh, it's on!"

"I'm teasing. You know I have no interest and would do anything for you and Ari to win."

"I know, Soph. I love that about you," Marisol says with a smile. "And how great is the idea of adding extra honorees to the court? I feel like Lily could be a total shoo-in, if she wanted!"

"I hope so!" I hold up my crossed fingers. "Hey, so, did Isaiah seem a little off to you in the latter half of that meeting?"

"Off how?" Sophie asks.

"Quiet?"

Marisol shrugs. "Hmm, I hadn't really noticed. Maybe?"

"Now that you mention it, he was definitely more talkative during the first portion when you were presenting," Sophie says. "Maybe he was just tired?"

"Hmm...maybe." But I'm not convinced.

Marisol pokes me in the side. "You worried about your man?"

"Yeah, you got me." I roll my eyes. "Anyway, can I catch a ride home with you guys?"

"*Only* if we can stop for iced coffee," Marisol says. "I've been craving one all day!"

It's not long before we're sipping Dunkin' as we cruise toward my neighborhood. Sophie starts talking about a new podcast she's created, but admittedly, I'm only half listening. What was up with Isaiah this afternoon?

I'm determined to find out.

* * *

The next day, I seek him out at lunch and find him and his friends skateboarding in the back parking lot just beside the courtyard.

My inner rule-follower notes that they're not *technically* supposed to be skateboarding on school property, but I tell her to shut up.

I catch Isaiah's eye from where I'm standing and wave him over. He skates toward me.

"What's up?" he asks, an edge to his voice as he continues skating.

"Hey. Sorry to track you down like this, but we didn't get a chance to catch up yesterday after the meeting. I thought it might be good for us to get together this weekend to talk about homecoming," I explain.

"I'm busy this weekend." Isaiah loops around me. "But you'll probably have no problem deciding everything for yourself. That's what you want anyway, right?"

"What?" I ask.

He grinds his board to a halt and kicks it into his hand. "I got that sense during yesterday's presentation when you totally blindsided me with an idea we didn't even talk about." He shakes his head. "You know, I thought we were on the same page, but if you're still stuck on calling all the shots, go for it."

"Wait, what? I wasn't trying to take over."

"Sure felt like it," he says. "Why else bring up an idea without even talking to me first? I'm supposed to be your number two."

"You are!" I insist. "I should've told you. Sometimes, I don't know. I guess I can be a little…"

"Bossy? Single-minded? Unbelievably frustrating?" he suggests.

My stomach drops until I notice the corner of his mouth curving into a slight smile. He's annoyed, yes, but also messing with me. So he can't be that angry.

I breathe a laugh. "You forgot *perfectionist*."

"Oh, I could've kept going. I just stopped for your sake."

"In that case, thank you," I say. "And I'm sorry. I got a little carried away. It was just that I came up with that idea late last night and I couldn't even text you because I didn't have your number or anything. I honestly didn't think you'd care!"

It feels like a perfectly logical thing for me to say, but I can immediately tell it wasn't. His face goes hard again. "Why wouldn't I care?" When I don't have an answer, he purses his lips. "Right. You assumed. I told you I thought this could be fun, and I meant it. I do care, and I feel like I've made that clear. And like I said, I have college applications to worry about, too, you know."

Right. Of course. I hadn't even stopped to consider that his interest was legitimate.

Embarrassed at my faux pas, I rush to apologize. "You're absolutely right. I'm really sorry, Zay." I don't intend to call him by the old nickname and I feel my cheeks go warm at the slipup. "Isaiah. I meant Isaiah. Sorry."

I expect him to be extra annoyed at the use of his old nickname—he's been known as Isaiah for *years* now—but instead, his lips tug into a true smile. "Wow. Haven't been called that in a while."

"God, I wasn't even thinking. On all counts, apparently."

"You're good, *Whitney*." And just like that, his icy demeanor is gone again and he's back to being warm, easygoing Isaiah. "I guess in fairness to you, you're right. You don't have my number, so you couldn't text."

"I really couldn't! And you're not on social media. I looked."

Isaiah's eyebrows go up. "Oh?" He motions with his hand and says, "Gimme your phone." I dig into my bag and pull it out, unlocking it and handing it over to him. A few quick taps and he hands it back. "Text me your big, brainy ideas next time, all right?"

I take the phone back and tuck it away in my bag. "Promise."

"And maybe we can get together this weekend and put in some work," he adds.

At this, I grin. "Thought you were busy?"

He tosses his skateboard on the ground and steadies it with his shoe. "I *think* something might've just opened up tomorrow night. But it probably won't stay open for long."

"Guess I better text you, then," I say.

Isaiah hops up onto his board. "Guess you better."

Without another word, he skates back to his friends, and I have to swallow down the jolt of excitement I feel at whatever this exchange just was.

Because I haven't even been broken up with Aiden for a week.

So there's no reason for me to feel electrified by this.

Whatever *this* is.

Or might be.

* * *

After school, Marisol and I plan to get a bite to eat before we head to Sophie's concert, the first of the semester.

"Where to?" she asks, buckling her seat belt.

"Mimi's?" I suggest, referring to a tiny mom-and-pop restaurant that serves the most delicious Puerto Rican food downtown.

"It's like you're reading my mind!" Marisol pops on her sunglasses and rolls down the windows so we can enjoy the surprisingly warm day.

We sing along to the radio on the drive over, shimmying shoulders and dancing. When we arrive at Mimi's, I offer to grab a table outside while Marisol goes in to order. Her Spanish is way better than mine, so I'm more than happy to let her take the lead, and I'll Venmo her after.

While I wait, I pull out my phone and send a text to Lily.

Me: Hello?

Me: Is this Lily?

She writes back immediately.

Lily: Ya

Lily: What do you want?

Me: Sorry, it's just been so long since I saw you, I thought maybe you'd changed your number, too!

Lily: 😕

Lily: I'm home tonight. Abuela and I are playing dominoes.

Me: The one night I have plans!

Lily: Omg. You're so dramatic.

Lily: Like you haven't been busy, too!

I sigh. She's right. I hate when she's right. Can't she just let me guilt her in peace?

Me: I know 🙄

Me: I just miss you, hermana!!!! ♥♥♥♥♥♥♥♥♥♥ ♥♥♥♥♥♥♥♥

Lily: BYE

"What's so funny?" Marisol's voice asks as she sets our tray of food on the table.

"Nothing. Just annoying Lily," I say, holding up my phone. "I've really been missing her lately, you know? It's like overnight, she just grew up."

"It must at least be nice to be in the same school now."

"You'd think, but I feel like I barely see her! She doesn't sit with us at lunch—"

"She has her own friends," Marisol points out.

"—and she won't even let me walk her to her locker anymore." I frown.

"She probably wants a little independence."

"She can be independent with me!"

Marisol makes a face. "That's the opposite of independence, girl. And you know it. Just let her live a little is all I'm saying."

"Yeah, I guess," I say.

Marisol unwraps her sandwich, the delicious aroma of her tripleta wafting through the air, while I pull the clear plastic top off an aluminum container and practically drool over the arroz con gandules and chicken in front of me.

Between bites, I change the subject and ask, "How's everything going with you?"

"It's going," Marisol says noncommittally.

"You're gonna need to give me more than that!"

She sighs. "Mami has been on my ass about college applications. How fair is it that just because my older sister is 'el ángel perfecto' and got into an Ivy League school, now I have to worry about that shit, too? Sorry Natalia is such a freaking loser she has no life whatsoever and can dedicate her entire being to studying, but that's not me. It's so irritating."

"Ugh, I'm so sorry," I say, feeling a wave of gratitude over the fact that Abuela mostly leaves me alone about that kind of stuff.

Marisol grabs a tostone from the plate we're sharing and pops it in her mouth, chewing thoughtfully for a moment. "It's fine, I guess. I know she wants the best for me, but I have it handled, especially now that debate club is a thing." She shrugs. "Anyway, what's up with you?"

I shake my head. "Nothing, really. Just obsessing over Fall Fest."

Her mouth quirks into a small smile. "I asked about *you*. Or are you Fall Fest?"

"Funny," I say dryly.

When we finish our food, we order a giant slice of dulce de leche cake to split with Sophie after her performance. Soon, we find ourselves in the auditorium of Elmwood High, snagging front-row seats so we can cheer loudly for her (though, sadly, we didn't bring foam fingers or paint our faces).

Sophie's violin playing is serene, beautiful, and even though I'm not much of a classical music fan, the entire orchestra kills it, which will make the celebratory dulce de leche that much sweeter.

Chapter Sixteen

When I go to text Isaiah that night, I struggle to find his name in my contacts. I try Isaiah and Ortiz first, but nothing comes up, despite the fact that I watched him enter his name into my phone.

Remembering our earlier conversation, I try one last thing.

Zay.

And there it is.

I spend no less than twenty minutes composing my text to him, reading, rereading, and then deleting the whole thing and starting again. Everything I type out seems robotic and unnatural, and I'm on edge even more than normal because of how thoughtlessly I hurt his feelings earlier.

I'm also maybe a little confused by how quickly he's gone from the bane of my existence to someone whose opinion I care about.

Eventually, I end up with this.

Me: Hey! It's Whit. You mentioned earlier that tomorrow might work to meet up? I'm around, so let me know!

Casual-ish, peppered with my usual smattering of exclamation points. Short. Simple.

After I send it, I hide my phone under my pillow and go to find Lily. She's lying on the carpet in her room, playing her Nintendo Switch. *Animal Crossing: New Horizons,* without a doubt.

Lily has played this game obsessively since its release, meticulously making and remaking her island, crafting custom items, and trading with players on Discord. I got into it with her for a bit, but every time I played my character, she complained I was messing up her island by letting too many weeds grow because I insisted they were pretty (true) and giving too many "ugly" clothes to Clay, an adorable hamster who loves being lazy and eating. She eventually deleted my character. Honestly, I get it.

"Ooh, are you talking to my boyfriend, Clay?" I tease from the doorway.

She doesn't even bother looking up, but I catch the gigantic eye roll she gives me. "I kicked him off the island."

"You what?!"

Lily shrugs. "I have a new theme and he didn't go with it!"

"What's the theme?" I ask.

"I'm turning the entire island into a giant karaoke bar." She tilts the screen toward me and I get down on the floor next to her to take a closer look. In the game, she's built a massive dance area with microphones, vertical speakers, colored lights, and twinkling palm trees. It looks pretty amazing.

"Um, this is incredible," I say, snatching the Switch to get a closer look.

"Hey!"

"I'll give it back." I move her character (who is wearing a head-set microphone, cute) around the island so I can look around.

But when I accidentally trample through some of her flowers, she yanks the console back. "You're done. You're done."

I pout and cross my arms. "Fine."

Lily shakes her head and turns completely around so I can't see her game, and I flop on the carpet dramatically, staring up at her ceiling, where she's stuck glow-in-the-dark music notes. Then I flop onto my side and start to poke her with my toe. "Is this distracting?" Poke. "How about this?"

"I'm ignoring you," Lily says.

From this angle on her floor, I can see everything that's under her bed, including some ancient board games we haven't played in forever, forgotten Hatchimals, and a few scattered Lego pieces. I can't imagine not being obsessive enough that you'd just have random Lego pieces outside of their original box, but whatever, that's why this is her room and not mine. I reach for the Hatchimal, an interactive stuffed toy that you teach to do things as if it's a baby. It comes to life and giggles.

"God, I forgot how creepy these things are," I say, tossing it back under Lily's bed. When that doesn't get her attention, I sigh loudly. "You're being boring."

"And you're being annoying."

"I'm your older sister. I'm supposed to be annoying."

Lily finally turns to me. "I think you have that backward."

"I think you have that backward," I repeat in a high-pitched voice.

She lets out a frustrated groan and turns her console off. "Fine. I'm done. Are you happy now?"

"Delighted," I say with a grin. "Can I do your makeup?"

"Really?" she asks, eyeing me skeptically.

"Really!"

"With your *good* makeup?"

"With my good makeup," I promise. Lily claps her hands together and nods a few times. "Yay! Let me go grab my stuff."

I'm back in a hurry with a Caboodle filled with different types of makeup, including the drugstore stuff I usually use for Lily's makeovers (oops) as well as the good stuff I hoard for myself (What?! It's expensive!). A promise is a promise, though, so I skip right to the items I've picked up from Ulta and hold out two different color palettes from which Lily can choose.

She opts for the Sugar Rush Tarte palette, a mix of bright colors

I rarely use, and I'm thrilled to have a chance to experiment with them on her. The colors will look great with her brown complexion.

"Can we skip the contouring?" Lily asks, wrinkling her nose when I reach for my foundation. "It makes my face itch."

"Ugh, but you won't get the full effect!" I whine.

"Don't care. Eyes only, please." She smiles smugly, knowing I'll give in.

With a long, dramatic sigh, I agree, and pat some primer on each eyelid.

"I feel like we haven't really seen much of each other lately. How's everything been going? You getting to and from your classes okay?" I ask.

Even though her eyes are closed, she opens them just to roll them. "It's going fine."

"Oh, okay. Good," I say, disappointed she doesn't want to share more. "Anything else?"

"School's okay. Kind of boring sometimes. One of my teacher's aides is super nice."

"Is that Ms. Kaminski?" I start to layer on the yellow at the inner corner of her eye.

"Yeah. We just call her Ms. K. She sometimes lets me listen to music."

"In class?" I ask.

Lily shrugs. "Sometimes."

Why is she letting Lily goof off and listen to music when she should be helping her focus on her studies? Though Lily struggles to read and write at her grade level, she's super smart, and I hate when authority figures can't see that.

"Is she supposed to be doing that?"

"It's only when we're between activities or a few minutes before the bell," Lily explains.

"Hmm" is all I say as I switch to the next color in the palette, a neon green, which I'll blend into the yellow on one side and eventually into the turquoise on the outer edge of her eye.

"Ruby thinks Ms. K is awesome, too," Lily adds.

"Is that so?"

"Yeah. The other day, Ms. K let Ruby bring in her Switch and show me her entire island. It's not as good as mine, but it's way better than the ideas you had."

"Hey! Watch what you say about the girl doing your makeup," I warn.

She opens the eye I'm not working on and laughs. "Sorry."

"What's so great about her island?"

"It's just really cool. She figured out how to make all these different levels and the houses line up kind of like a neighborhood. It's hard to explain, but I really like it," Lily says. "She's so good."

I blend the shadows out on her left eye, satisfied when they meld together. "Sounds like it. Other eye now."

"Abuela bought me the paid version of *Animal Crossing* so I can have Ruby to my island whenever I want."

"You can do that?"

I add the colors to Lily's right eyelid as I listen to her talk. "Yeah. Ruby showed me how. So now if she's on and I'm on at the same time, she can just come over to my island or I can go to hers. You can only do that if you list someone as your best friend, though."

"I see. And Ruby is your best friend?"

Lily laughs again. "Well, in the game, yeah. She has to be, otherwise it's harder to visit each other."

"Oh, right, right." I'm nodding despite her eyes being shut.

"But…yeah, probably in real life, too. That's why when she asked me if she could borrow my copy of the Intonation vinyl, I said it was okay."

This makes my hand pause midair. "The limited-edition one?"

"Yeah."

"But Lily, that's super valuable!" I protest.

Okay, so, in fairness, I don't actually know if it's that valuable. I haven't looked it up on eBay or whatever, but it *was* limited-edition. Seven years or so ago, the group partnered with a store to produce an extremely limited number of vinyl records featuring an exclusive remix of one of their singles. You could only get it by waiting in line at a physical retailer (as if it were the 1990s or something), and once the vinyls were gone, that was it! The remix isn't even on Spotify now. So why would Lily think it was a good idea to loan it to someone who's practically a stranger?

Her eyelids fly open and she scowls at me. "So what? Ruby wanted to borrow it so I let her. It's mine!"

"It's ours," I correct her.

"No, it's not. You don't even like Intonation anymore! You barely even listen to their songs. It's always your sad, sappy Maggie Rogers playlists."

"Um, I listen to Beyoncé, too!"

"Whatever!" Lily argues. "It's mine and I can do whatever I want with it."

"But Lily! How do you know Ruby's not just using you to get that vinyl?" Even as the words leave my mouth, I know it's a terrible thing to say, especially about Lily's new friend.

"Why would you even say that?" Lily's arms are crossed now. "God, you're so annoying. Just leave me alone and get out of my room."

"I didn't even get to finish your makeup," I protest.

"I said, leave me *alone*!"

Sheepishly, I grab my makeup kit and slink down the hall to my room, feeling her eyes watching me as I go.

For a minute, Marisol's words from earlier ring in my ears—*Just let her live a little*—but whatever. Am I such a bad person because I don't want Lily to be taken advantage of? She has this habit of giving in to whatever people want, always letting them borrow her belongings even if the person is a near stranger. Sometimes she gets the items back, but sometimes they come back broken or, even worse, are never seen again. I don't want this to happen to the Intonation album—not when it holds so much sentimental value.

Lily may be mad now, but she'll thank me for this later.

Chapter Seventeen

After my fight with Lily, I have a hard time sleeping. To add insult to injury, Isaiah takes forever to respond to my text.

When he finally replies, he just writes, *6? my house?*

It's not that.I was expecting more or anything, but...

Me: That works!

Zay: 👍

By morning, I've replayed my exchange with Lily about a hundred times over in my mind, and I feel awful for coming on so strong. I really just wanted to hang out with her last night because I missed her, and then I got so consumed with the idea of protecting her from Ruby that I was completely out of line.

In the shower, I work on an apology, silently acting out how I hope it'll go. But I'm startled from those thoughts when a large clump of hair comes out as I'm doing my hair routine. I gasp at the dark, wet strands splayed across my palm. It looks like *a lot* of hair—far more than normal.

There's a loud, abrupt knock on the door. "Mija, I'm heading to work. You're still coming to the shop today, yes?"

Crap. I totally forgot.

"Yeah, for a little bit," I say. "But I have to go to Isaiah's to work on Fall Fest stuff right after."

"Oh, okay. And tomorrow?" she asks.

"I have an all-day shift at the market, remember?"

"Ay, sí," Abuela says. "Well, I'll see you and your sister later then. Be good?"

"Of course," I promise.

In the mirror, I study my face for any new, rogue facial hairs that may have sprouted up while I let my hair air-dry. Then I finish getting ready and meet Lily in the kitchen.

I give her a soft smile. "Morning, Lil."

She doesn't look up from her oatmeal.

"I wanted to apologize for last night. I was a total brat and I shouldn't have been. I'm really sorry," I say. "I just want you to be careful, you know? I worry about you."

Lily huffs, dropping her spoon so that it clanks loudly against the ceramic bowl. Then she pushes her chair away from the table, its legs scraping against the floor, and goes over to the dishwasher. I resist the temptation to remind her she really should wash her oatmeal out first. She's mad enough at me as it is.

"Well, I am really sorry," I continue. "I hope you can forgive me."

She washes her hands, walking past me like I'm not there, and calls over her shoulder, "I'm going to Nora's."

"You have to ask Abuela first," I say.

Lily grabs her pink-and-white backpack and snatches open the door. "Already did!"

Then she slams the door shut behind her.

Great.

Now I need to lie down.

Normally, fights with Lily don't knock the wind out of me like this, but after pulling out a huge clump of hair this morning, I'm already on edge.

Lately, there are some days when I hardly feel like myself. One minute I'm riding a high and the next I'm exhausted and cranky, and I can feel myself taking things out on the people around me, the very people I care about, who don't deserve it. Every time I vow to be better, something else sets me off and the pendulum swings again. It's got me wondering if maybe I should tell Abuela so we can make an appointment with Dr. Delgado? Especially because I haven't managed to get my period in *months* now. (I took a pregnancy test, too, just to rule that out. I actually did a little dance when it was negative.)

Yet, for as much as I respect Dr. Delgado, a part of me is afraid to say anything, knowing how quickly my summer was completely engulfed by appointments and tests and solutions that all felt like Band-Aids rather than *actual* useful medical advice to take care of my PCOS. And that makes me angry, too.

How is it possible that there are no solid, useful treatments for this wretched syndrome? The fact that the best most doctors can offer me is the vague suggestion to lose weight is an epic failure of the medical system, and if I weren't so exhausted all the time, maybe I could actually do something about it.

Instead, I climb into bed to rest for a bit and then will myself to help Abuela at the shop until it's time to head to Isaiah's.

• • •

It's been six years since I've set foot inside the Ortiz house. And even then, I was only inside for a second to use the bathroom, because we were in the backyard: Isaiah was hosting a Halloween party at his house and invited some people from school, including me and Sophie. It was as tame and wholesome as sixth-grade Halloween parties can be. We mingled awkwardly with our classmates, listened to music way too loud, ate tons of food, and tried to show off for one another.

The house looks mostly like I remember it: a taupe split-level ranch with white shutters; a pristine green lawn; and, interestingly, elaborate Halloween decorations—including a comically large twenty-five-foot skeleton—despite it only being mid-September. It's such a weird time warp, like I've been sucked all the way back to middle school and I'm arriving at Isaiah's for my first-ever coed party. All that's missing is the black synthetic witch hat on top of my head. (Isaiah will just have to use his imagination.)

I ring the doorbell, and the door swings open almost instantly.

"*You're* not pizza," a small voice says accusingly. It comes from an adorable brown girl whose dark hair is worn in two puffs on either side of her head. My eyes go big when an identical girl—except with braids and barrettes in her hair—joins her at the door.

"False alarm!" the girl with the braids calls into the house, turning on her heel.

"Guys, I think it's for me," I hear Isaiah's voice say. He comes into view, wearing black socks, an oversize Champion crew neck sweatshirt, and jeans. "Hey, sorry."

The first girl crosses her arms and passes a look between me and Isaiah. "And who is *this*, Isaiah Caleb Ortiz?"

"Mind your business, Amaya!" a woman's voice calls.

Amaya pretends to dramatically flip her hair over her shoulder and stomps away. "Well, he invited a *girl* over!"

Isaiah rolls his eyes and opens the door. "That's my little sister, Amaya. The other one is Gianna. They're pretty cute, but..." He raises his voice. "They're also extremely nosy!"

"Am *not*!" They both yell.

He nods his head toward the living room. "Come on in."

The Ortiz home is the perfect mix of lived-in and lovingly decorated. Around the living room, fake spiderwebs, ghost figurines, purple twinkle lights, and black-and-orange Halloween décor match the spooky setup outside.

Homes that look a little too perfect and untouched sometimes make me feel like I shouldn't be there, but Isaiah's home gives off the total opposite vibe—like the moment you step inside, you're exactly where you're supposed to be.

There's some cumbia music spilling out from the kitchen and into the rest of the house, and a memory of Isaiah's mom, Mrs. Ortiz, rushes back.

Even though I only met her briefly at that Halloween party all those years ago, I remember thinking she had the biggest, brightest personality of any adult I'd ever met. Every time she joined us to check in or refill our snacks, she couldn't help but shimmy her hips to whatever music was playing. Isaiah physically shooed her away at one point, embarrassed by her presence, but I remember thinking she was the kind of mom I might want to be someday.

It's then that I hear her voice. "Mira, I told you, no pizza! Papi is grilling out back."

"But Mami!" either Amaya or Gianna yells, while the other goes, "Ugh!"

"Come on." Isaiah motions for me to follow him, and he leads me into the kitchen.

We find his mom standing at the stove getting started on what I can only guess is arroz con gandules, based on the caldero and the ingredients on the counter. She's shorter than I remember, and her dark hair is pulled into a tight ponytail that stretches to the middle of her back. She's fat like me, with round cheeks, thick eyeliner, and red lipstick. I instantly feel a connection with her, and I break into a smile when her gaze falls upon me. She returns the same kind of easy smile I've come to expect from Isaiah as he introduces us.

"Mami, this is Whit."

"Whitney Rivera!" she shouts, rolling the rs in my last name and throwing her arms in the air. "It's been so long!"

And then she sweeps me into a hug and presses her cheek to mine and I smell her perfume, something sweet, and let her kiss me on the cheek and rock me back and forth like we're old friends.

"Hi, Mrs. Ortiz! So good to see you," I say. "I can't believe you remember me."

She pulls back from me. "Of course!"

"Mami has a wild memory," Isaiah explains, an amused expression on his face.

"One time, we played a game of memory, and Mami got every single card right in one turn!" Gianna enthuses.

"Did she now?" I ask with a smile.

Gianna nods, studying me. "You have pretty hair."

I reach up to touch my curls. "Oh, thank you! So do you."

"Right? She looks so cute with her braids." Mrs. Ortiz reaches over to pinch Gianna's cheeks. Then she leans down to give Amaya, who is coloring at the kitchen table, a big kiss on her head. "And I love your sweet little puffs. ¡Que linda!"

Gianna and Amaya practically beam.

Mrs. Ortiz looks at me again. "Anyway, it's good to see you, nena. You're staying for dinner, right?" I look to Isaiah to get his opinion; I haven't eaten and had assumed we might have dinner here, but we never clarified. "No, no, no! I'm not asking him. I'm asking you."

"I'd love to stay for dinner," I say.

Amaya gives me the stink eye when she hears my answer, but Mrs. Ortiz doesn't catch it because it's then that the song changes and she's swaying her hips. "I love this song!"

"You need help with anything, Mami?" Isaiah asks.

"No, go do your work, mijo." She swats at him with a dish towel, still dancing.

Isaiah slips his feet into some sneakers by the door and pushes it open to his backyard. I follow.

It's a cool-but-not-cold September afternoon, though it might get chilly once the sun goes down. We step down onto a stone patio where Isaiah's dad is grilling some steaks, just like Isaiah's mom said. The backyard is as pristine as the front, with manicured grass, a fire pit surrounded by six white patio chairs, and two wooden picnic tables nestled beneath an open gazebo.

Mr. Ortiz—tall like Isaiah, dark-skinned, with a curly-top fade and trim beard, and wearing a tan bomber jacket over jeans and a white T-shirt—raises a hand in greeting to us. He and Isaiah look just alike, from their muscular build to their black hair and long lashes.

"It's a zoo in there," Isaiah says to him.

Mr. Ortiz smirks and shakes his head. "Why do you think I'm out here?" To me, he says, "Hey. I'm Victor."

"Whit," I reply. "Thanks for having me over."

"Of course. Dinner should be up shortly. Until then"—he drops his deep voice to a whisper—"enjoy the quiet out here."

I grin and follow Isaiah over to the fire pit, which already has a small fire going.

I take a seat next to him as he exhales a breath. "Phew. Okay. That was a lot."

My eyes widen. "I *loved* it."

"You loved all of that?!" he asks.

"My house is always so quiet! It's just me, Abuela, and Lily," I say. "Oh, and our cat, Patch, but he's so lazy he barely counts. The only time it ever gets loud is when my abuela's sisters visit."

Isaiah chuckles. "Fair enough. It can be a bit much sometimes, especially when Camila gets home."

"That's your older sister, right?" I ask.

"Right. She's taking some classes at the community college down the way but living at home to save some money. So it's a full house, like, all the time. And sometimes Mami's parents visit from Puerto Rico and stay with us in the basement. Then it just descends into absolute chaos. Good luck getting any work done."

"Oh, God, yeah. I can only imagine," I say. "Still, it sounds sort of fun. At least some of the time. But maybe I'm just saying that because I don't have to deal with it all the time."

He looks up at his house, where the music, laughter, and

shouting are currently contained. "Nah, it's fun. It is. Wild, but fun." Then he looks back at me. "Anyway. Should we get started?"

I pull my binder and notebook from my tote bag so we can start reviewing everything. We've already approved designs for the Fall Fest posters, made by Chloe Torres with witty copy written by Leilani Mamea. Those will go up starting Monday, thanks to Leilani, Hudson Moore, and Everly McDonnell, the class officers, who volunteered to plaster them everywhere. Once they're posted, the over-the-top homecoming proposals will likely start to roll in.

For now, our plan is to release Fall Fest dates without a full schedule just yet. This way, people can start to prepare for the event and have fun choosing their outfits and dates, but the committee still has time to work behind the scenes to secure its donations and partnerships with local businesses.

Though we're given a budget for the basics of the Fall Fest, if we want to go above and beyond, we need to rely on the kindness of those in the town or do some fundraising of our own. Thankfully, several businesses are repeat donors—offering up things like pumpkins and mums to help with decorating—but if we want to pull off bringing back the carnival this year, Isaiah and I will have some work to do.

We divide up the businesses that we plan to hit up—in person, because it'll be more difficult to say no if we're right in people's faces—and work on our pitch.

"Should we do some kind of fundraiser?" he asks. "It feels like a natural fit for this, you know? The administrators will probably love it, the local businesses get tax write-offs, and people don't mind spending money when it feels like it's for a cause."

"I like it. What did you have in mind?"

He shrugs. "I hadn't thought beyond that yet."

"And you once called yourself a genius," I tease, shaking my head.

Isaiah narrows his eyes at me, playing along. "What's your big vision, then?"

"Obviously, a bake sale! We can sell things like maple sugar donuts, pumpkin rolls, apple butter bars, whatever," I explain. "Lily and I make some pretty great pumpkin empanadas, too."

"Okay, I'm feeling this," Isaiah says, nodding. "Simple."

"Exactly. Simple is good." I sit back in my chair, watching as Isaiah jots down some notes in his notebook, and feel myself smiling.

He must feel my gaze because he looks up at me suddenly. "What? Something on my face?"

"No," I say with a laugh. "It's just that you're actually really good at this."

Isaiah narrows his eyes at me. "You always sound so surprised."

"I don't mean to—you've always had a good work ethic and all, but I guess I'd never have pegged you for someone interested in the behind-the-scenes grunt work of a school event. It's pretty thankless." I tilt my head. "What made you volunteer for this, anyway?"

He shrugs. "I told you, college applications."

"I know *that*. That's part of it for me, too, but you also know I'm doing this because of my grandparents and because of my love for fall!"

"More like your sick obsession," Isaiah jokes.

"Seriously, though. Is it just for college applications?"

He sighs. "I don't know. Maybe I just liked the idea of getting leadership experience...and getting to annoy you. Two birds, one stone." I stick out my tongue at him. "Maybe I'm still trying to make amends for spilling that coffee all over you. And for whatever happened between us back in middle school."

His gaze meets mine and holds it.

I swallow, a million thoughts racing through my mind all at once, but before I can say any of them, laughter from Gianna and Amaya spills outside and Isaiah's mom announces it's time to eat. Isaiah rushes to help his mom carry the caldero out to the picnic table. I head inside and help the twins grab plates, napkins, and utensils while Mr. Ortiz sets out the main course, and once we all sit down, it's as if what Isaiah just said is forgotten.

Away from the fire, there's a chill in the air as the sun sinks in the sky. As the blue darkness settles around us, a sea of twinkling lights I hadn't noticed before blink on, illuminating the tall white fence in a soft yellow haze. A string of lights is also draped under the canopy over the picnic tables. It's beautiful.

A loud voice cuts through the backyard chatter and shouts, "I'm heeeeere!"

I'm the only one who turns, this being an apparent nonevent to the rest of the Ortiz family, and see Camila, Isaiah's older sister, burst into the backyard. Her eyes zone in on me. "And please tell me you're Isaiah's new girlfriend?!"

Something about being called Isaiah's girlfriend—especially after what felt like a meaningful glance earlier—makes my pulse quicken, but Isaiah is fast to shut Camila down.

"This is my *friend* Whit," he corrects.

Camila rolls her eyes at this. "Ugh. I was hoping he'd finally grown a pair and moved on from Destiny."

And at the sound of that name, the backyard goes quiet, and I'm left in the dark wondering: *Who's Destiny?*

Chapter Eighteen

I suddenly feel like an intruder when Mrs. Ortiz narrows her eyes at her eldest daughter. "Ca*mila.*"

Isaiah's jaw clenches, and he casts a dark look at his sister. "You want to start this right now? Really?"

Camila flips her braids over one shoulder. "I don't want to start anything, Zay, but I'm not sorry for wanting you to just move on already."

"You need to shut your mouth," Isaiah volleys back.

Mr. Ortiz holds out a hand. "Ay, ay. That's enough."

"*She* came at *me,*" Isaiah says, and Camila rolls her eyes.

"I know, but let's just drop it." Mr. Ortiz points at the spread on the table. "I want a nice dinner. Okay? All of y'all can put your claws back and fight this out later. We have a guest."

"And she likes my braids." Gianna grins. "They're just like Camila's."

Camila lays a big kiss on Gianna's forehead. "Mami did such a good job. And this all looks so yummy." She goes to each of her parents and gives them a kiss on the cheek, then Amaya, and Isaiah, and me. "Sorry," she whispers in my ear.

"No worries," I whisper back.

Mrs. Ortiz claps her hands together. "Let's eat!"

My stomach feels like it just might burst by the time we're done, but everything tastes so freaking good I can't help myself. Tostones and arroz and steak and a simple salad with a dressing that has no business being that good.

Beyond that, I'm more than happy to be a spectator at this dinner, taking in all the conversations happening simultaneously: school, sports, college, work.

As it turns out, Mrs. Ortiz is a nurse practitioner who teaches dance classes on the side (perfect!), while Mr. Ortiz is in insurance and also serves on the city council. Camila bartends (and oh my God, does the girl have *stories*), while the twins play soccer and Isaiah tutors. (I had no idea.) They listen as I tell them about Abuela and Lily, and Amaya finally warms up to me when I mention I have a cat. She desperately wants one and is totally smitten when I show her pictures of Patch from my phone.

After dinner, we all help clean up. It's obvious this is a regular habit for them, as they all move around the kitchen swiftly like a well-oiled machine—minus the twins, who Mr. and Mrs. Ortiz instruct to settle down at the dining room table and do their homework.

"But it's the weekend," Gianna whines.

"And if you do your work now, then you won't have to do it later," Mrs. Ortiz says. "Vámanos. All of you. Papi and I will finish cleaning."

"You sure?" Isaiah asks.

She squeezes his shoulder. "Sí."

"Thanks so much for dinner. It was incredible," I gush. "Just, everything."

Mrs. Ortiz smiles. "Come back anytime."

I smile, too, and then Isaiah motions toward the backyard, where all our belongings are. "Should we get back to it?"

I nod. "Yeah, that sounds great."

From the dining room, Amaya's voice calls, "Zaaaay, can you help me with this?"

Camila chimes in. "He has his own work to do. I can help you."

"But you suck at math!" Amaya argues.

Isaiah bursts out laughing and looks at me. "Mind if I take a second?"

"No, go for it. I'm going to find the restroom, anyway."

He nods toward the hall. "Ah, that way, second door to the right."

I head in the direction he just nodded in. In the bathroom, after I wash my hands, I pause in the mirror to fix my makeup and hair. When I open the door, I'm startled to see Camila waiting just outside, tying her microbraids into one long side braid.

"Hey," she says.

"Hi," I reply, surprised.

She expertly weaves the three sections of her hair together. "Sorry again for making things weird at the start of dinner. Destiny is a bit of a sore subject in this house. They broke up, like, a month ago, and Zay is *still* not over her."

"Oh, wow." I feel like Camila is telling me something Isaiah probably doesn't want me to know, but I'm not sure what to do.

"Yeah. To be honest," Camila continues, "I didn't like her much when they were together—she made him act foolish, spending all his money, talking about how he'd go to the same school she did regardless of whether it made sense for him. After they broke up, I wasn't shy about my relief, and now it's become this *thing* where we, like, can't even say her name in this house. So, when I saw you...I don't know. I was hopeful! Like, maybe he was finally ready to move on and find someone who he could be a partner to rather than a loyal puppy dog with. But whatever. It's me and my big mouth." Camila shakes her head, taking the hair tie from her wrist and securing it around the end of her braid. "He'd kill me if he knew I was telling you this, but I didn't want you to think I was just a jerk."

"It's totally fine. I'm just sorry to hear about how it all went down."

She casts a glance toward the dining room, where we can hear Isaiah walking Amaya through the math problem they're solving together. "Me too."

"I should get back, though," I say, hoping to escape this deeply personal discussion. "It was nice meeting you."

"You too." Camila smiles at me. "And, hey. Be good to him."

"I will" is all I can think to say as I walk toward the dining room.

Phew. So, Camila is intense. Well-meaning, but a lot. I can't even picture Isaiah the way Camila just described—so over-the-top in his feelings that he can't think or act right. Which is not Destiny's fault, by any means, but from the way Camila described it, maybe they weren't good together.

There's only one Destiny in our grade that I can think of, but I don't know her well. Nosily, I make a mental note to look her up on social media later.

When I finally enter the dining room, Isaiah looks up. "Ah, good timing. We just finished."

"Great. Let's go." This time, I lead the way to the backyard, straight to the fire pit. I hold out my hands toward the flame, embracing its warmth.

"Okay, so, I *have* to ask. What is your laundry secret?" Isaiah asks, settling beside me.

"Excuse me?"

"Oh, come on! Don't hold out on me. My hoodie that you borrowed has literally never smelled better or felt softer. What kind of witchcraft is that, Whit?"

I laugh. "Oh, that! That was the magic of my abuelita. She owns El Coquí, the tailor shop downtown."

"No shit? Mami loves that place!"

"Really?" I ask.

Isaiah nods. "Won't get our clothes tailored or cleaned

anywhere else." He leans back in his chair. "Makes sense, then. She's just really good at her job."

I shrug. "I wouldn't rule out witchcraft, frankly."

"You never really can." Isaiah grins.

"Your mom is just as fun as I remember. All of them, really—although I think the twins were only, like, one last time I was here. At the Halloween party."

Isaiah groans. "Please, let's not talk about that Halloween party. It was so, so cheesy. I cringe just thinking about it."

"What?! I loved that party!"

He gives me a side glance. "Come on, now, don't lie."

"What? I really did," I say. "Sophie and I talked about it for months. We were so impressed you were actually able to throw a real party."

"Really?"

"Really!"

He glances to the ground, kicking at the grass with the toe of his shoe, and lets out a soft laugh, which makes me smile a little.

"What?" I ask.

Isaiah shakes his head. "Nothing."

"Oh, come on!"

"It's just funny, is all." He squints at the ground and then over at me. "You know I threw that party to try and impress you, right?"

I laugh. "No, you didn't."

He grimaces. "But I did."

I look at him like he's lost his mind. I mean, surely, he has. "You *didn't*."

"So, the thing is, I thought you were cute. And you had these little gold dangly pumpkin earrings you would wear."

At the mention of this, my cheeks go hot and I put my hands over my face. "Oh my God. Those earrings! I wore them, like, every day." They were a gift from Abuelo and I still have them.

"You did! And I remember overhearing you talking to Sophie about how much you loved fall. I mistakenly assumed you loved Halloween specifically, like us...In my head, I was like, *I gotta impress this girl somehow.*" He's shaking his head again, laughing. "Camila helped me convince our parents to do this dorky little party—which they were all for, because they're kind of Halloween freaks, as you can see." He motions to the house behind him. "Anyway, I invited you and I was so psyched because you *actually came*! But then I was too chicken to talk to you. Hence, the note."

He's referring to a note he wrote on a piece of notebook paper, which he had folded at least a dozen times until it was a teeny, tiny slip of paper, and then pushed onto my desk the following Monday. It read, *I like you. —Zay.*

I still remember how my hands shook as I read the letters scrawled across the page, wondering if it was a joke, or if the cute boy who'd been sitting next to me in one of my classes *really* liked me.

When I looked over at him at the desk next to me, he was watching me, and I knew it wasn't a joke. I wrote him back in pink pen: *I like you, too.*

And our note-passing-based relationship began.

We were just twelve, so it wasn't much, but we sometimes sat together at lunch. Our notes back and forth contained nothing but doodles or messages like *What's up?* and *How are you?* but it was sweet and wholesome until it wasn't.

Still, this information has me absolutely reeling.

I blink a few times at him. "I...had no idea."

He grins, that easy Isaiah smile. "How could you have?"

"I wish I had, though." I'm staring at him so intently, harder than I should be, but I'm touched knowing that what we had started out so sweet. "That's adorable."

"Sixth-grade crushes were something else, huh?" he asks.

"They really were," I agree. A silence falls between us, and I'm not sure what to think—it was so long ago, and we were just kids, yet…this comfortable feeling. The hoodie. The banter, the teasing. The way he smells. Zay. Even if he stood me up, I can't deny the way those other things feel so light in my heart.

I chew on my lower lip, studying his long lashes, wondering if maybe now's the time to finally ask him *why* things went wrong with us.

But after his earlier admission, there's another thought tugging at me. Maybe it's time to let go of the past and simply forgive and forget.

I clear my throat. "I think we're in good shape for the Fall Fest. So, maybe we can call it for tonight?"

His eyebrows go up. "Oh, no. I scared you away with my stalkerish story."

"No, not at all," I assure him. "I just need to get home. Abuela probably needs help with chores, and I need to be up disgustingly early for work tomorrow."

"Right, of course." Isaiah stands, too. "Let me walk you out."

"That sounds good."

I follow him, saying goodbye to his family that welcomed me like theirs, and all but run to the car. Alone, in the quiet for the first time tonight, I swallow a thought.

Some small part of me might have a crush on Isaiah Ortiz.

Chapter Nineteen

I try to swallow any thoughts involving *crushes* or *Isaiah Ortiz* or *whatever reasoning he may have had for volunteering to work with me on the Fall Fest in the first place.*

How dare he be so easy to talk to?

And how dare he be so committed to the Fall Fest?

And how dare he subvert basically all the negative opinions I've harbored for literal years?

I mean, what did he even mean by making amends for "whatever happened between us back in middle school"?

Doesn't he care that his even hinting at an apology might make me feel like I'm floating on a cloud?

What gives him the right?

Especially since there's Destiny and whatever unresolved feelings exist there, which I am reluctant to deal with. Based on how Isaiah reacted when her name came up, it seems pretty clear to me that he's still hung up on her. A month is both a long time and no time at all when it comes to breakups.

Still…how is my heart supposed to handle knowing Isaiah threw a whole Halloween party to impress me?

Again: How. Dare. He.

I'm stomping around my house the next morning thinking of all of these things and more. I go into the bathroom and splash my face with some cool water, staring at the mirror and pointing at my reflection.

"There will be no crushes in this house, Whitney Rivera.

Especially not on your middle school boyfriend who's hung up on his ex," I whisper.

The doorbell chimes.

Abuela is already at the shop, so I imagine it must be Lily. Things with her were still icy before she rushed out of the house to hang out with Nora and Ruby. She no doubt forgot her keys in the hurry; I definitely would have.

I open the door, preparing to lecture her about how she wouldn't have forgotten her keys if she'd given me the time of day, but my words catch in my throat when I see it's not my baby sister at all.

"What are you doing here?" I ask.

"Good morning to you, too," Isaiah says with a laugh. He glances down at my pajama bottoms, which I realize with sheer mortification are stitched with the word INTONATION up one of the legs. "Nice pants."

I scowl at him. "I'd like to see what *you* wear to bed." Then, realizing what I said, I add, "I heard how that sounded and I will not acknowledge it."

"Fair enough." Isaiah holds up a cup of coffee. "This is for you."

"For me?" I reach for the cup, the warmth from the drink transferring to my fingertips, still cold from the water I just splashed on my face.

"You said you had an early start this morning." He gives me a shrug, as if hand-delivering a coffee to my front steps is nothing to him. "I've got an early tutoring session and got myself a coffee anyway. Thought you could use one, too."

"Thank you," I say, feeling near speechless.

"It's pumpkin spice. Our favorite." He grins at me. "Oh! And I also wanted to drop this off."

Isaiah hands me a three-ring binder, similar to the one I've used for my notes, though this one is smaller than the one I've been using. "Those are some ideas for the carnival and the bake sale."

I blink at him. "But we just decided on the bake sale last night!"

"And I'm a natural at this planning stuff. I believe you have used the word *genius* several times?"

That earns him a well-deserved eye roll.

"With said genius, I present you with *my* version of the sacred Fall Fest binder." Isaiah grins. "Now I've gotta go to that tutoring session I mentioned..." He starts to walk backward toward the porch stairs. "But I trust you'll have those notes studied, memorized, and ready for further discussion by our next meeting?"

"Okay" is all I manage to say, my eyes darting back and forth between Isaiah and the items in my hands.

"That's the spirit!" Isaiah calls, unlocking the car.

"Thank you for the coffee!" I call back, watching as he opens the door and slips inside. "And the notes!"

He leans out of his window and taps the roof of his car. "Just channeling my inner Whit Rivera. I kinda like it!"

Without waiting for a response, he's gone, leaving me with warm pumpkin spice coffee in one hand, a beautiful, idea-filled binder in the other, and a heart brimming with feelings.

Chapter Twenty

In a daze, I get ready for my shift at Nature's Grocer, tying my wild curls back into a thick ponytail just to keep them out of my face so I can settle in for a long day of scanning, bagging, and chirping *Farm-fresh food for a happy-fresh you!*

I'm trying to focus on work—I really am—but I can't stop thinking about the coffee and the binder and Isaiah freaking Ortiz.

As I was saying: How. Dare. He!

Yet, in between the beeping as I ring up each item and the cheerful smiles I give to each new customer, I find myself dreamily crafting a new list to add to my notebook.

Things I Like About Isaiah Ortiz

1. His smile.
2. His laugh.
3. The way he makes me crack when I don't want to.
4. How infuriatingly frustrating he is.
5. His easygoing nature, of which I'm eternally jealous.
6. He's hot.
7. And cute. At the same time, somehow?
8. The way he smells.
9. How familiar being around him feels.
10. THE HALLOWEEN PARTY? HELLO?!?!?!
11. Those lips!
12. The special delivery of COFFEE TO MY DOORSTEP.
13. His natural gift for planning.

14. His dedication to the Fall Fest.
15. THE FREAKING BINDER.

Ugh, Whit, what are you doing?! Quick—make a list of the reasons not to like him.

"Excuse me, miss, but you seem to be in a daze. Can I please speak to your *manager*?" A voice breaks me from these thoughts. I look up to see it's actually Marisol standing there with Sophie, both of them giggling.

I break into a grin. "What are you guys doing here?!"

"Buying some caviar, of course, like everyone else," Sophie teases.

Marisol shakes her head. "Seriously, this place is *bougie*." She lowers her voice and leans in. "I was worried we might be followed around or something."

"You're good," I say. "This place is going for, like, rich-hippie-chic rather than WASP-y-racial-profiling. At least I think. I've only been here a week."

Marisol leans over to tuck away a curl that has come loose from my ponytail. "Well, you're killin' it."

"And you look so cute in your little visor!" Sophie gushes.

I pretend to tip it to her, then glance back to see that there are two other customers behind my friends in line. "Can I ring you out?"

"Oh, yes!" Sophie pulls some bakery items from the wire basket at her side and puts them on the belt.

"These look yummy."

"Yeah, but they'll be the most expensive donuts this girl's ever going to eat," Marisol says. "And we obviously didn't just come here for those. We wanted to see if you could hang out in a bit? Maybe fill us in on how things went at Isaiah's?" She waggles her eyebrows suggestively.

I frown. "I wish I could, but I'm actually here all day. Then I have my English paper to work on."

"All day?" Sophie asks. "Jeez! Is that legal?"

"Unfortunately, yes. That'll be seventeen dollars and eighty-four cents, by the way."

Sophie taps her credit card against the machine to pay, seemingly accepting my response. But Marisol isn't having it. "How about after you finish your English paper?" she asks. "We're all going to the movies. It'll be fun!"

"All?" I ask.

"Yeah, me, Noah, Sol, and Ari," Sophie explains. "I'll buy you some jelly beans!"

I'll admit that being the fifth wheel isn't ideal, but I don't want my friends to feel like I'm blowing them off. Without Aiden, this is just my reality now. Sometimes I'm going to be the Single Friend. And I like Noah and Ari, so how bad can it be, right?

"Okay," I say finally. "I'm in."

Sophie claps her hands together. "Yay! We'll text you details."

"Oh! That reminds me. Do either of you know someone at school named Destiny?"

Sophie shakes her head, but Marisol pauses to think. "Hmm, I feel like she might be friends with some of Ari's friends. Hang on."

I can see the customers in line starting to get impatient, and one even sighs. The last thing I need to do is get in trouble as the newbie for talking to my friends for too long—friends who, by the way, I wasn't even supposed to technically check out because of conflict of interest and all—but this is important.

Marisol turns her phone to me, showing me an Instagram profile. "Destiny Wright?"

"Yes! Text that to me, please, please, please," I beg.

"Already done." She points a manicured nail my way. "But you

know you don't get to ask a shady question like that and not offer an explanation. Fill us in later?"

"Done," I say. Catching sight of my manager, Pamela, nearing the register, I add, "Thanks for shopping at Nature's Grocer—farm-fresh food for a happy-fresh you!"

Sophie sees Pamela arriving, too, and winks at me. "Wow! Thank you so much. You might be the most personal and efficient cashier I've ever had. I don't know who you are, but you deserve a raise!"

"Couldn't agree more!" Marisol chimes in, putting on a British accent. "Above and beyond, really. Above and beyond!"

I apologize for the wait on my line and do my best to ring up the next few customers as quickly as I can. The millisecond Pamela dismisses me for a lunch break, I book it to the back room, where I pull up the link from Marisol and use it to scroll Destiny's account.

Based on her profile pic, I feel like I may have seen her when I met some of Ari's friends a while back. Her bio lists her as an artist, aspiring fashion designer, and Aquarius. I wrinkle my nose. Aquarius? Well, no wonder she and Isaiah—who's a Cancer, if my memory serves correctly—didn't work out. Aquarius-Cancer pairings have disaster written all over them.

From Destiny's most recent photos, she could easily be mistaken for Zendaya's little sister: slim but curvy, long microbraids, light skin, high cheekbones, and a killer sense of style. It's no wonder she's an aspiring fashion designer. She's also *gorgeous,* and if she weren't Isaiah's ex, I might have myself a new crush.

I know I've probably done enough snooping for one day, but I can't help myself and keep scrolling. Whether it's because I want to admire more photos of her or because I'm just nosy, I can't say for sure.

Suddenly, my stomach drops. In the second row of photos is a picture of her leaning on Isaiah's shoulder while he stands on his board. It looks like they're at a skate park somewhere. His face is scrunched up in a goofy grin, while she's sticking out her tongue at the camera. I check when it was posted. Six days ago.

Things I DON'T Like About Isaiah Ortiz
1. In the sixth grade, he asked me to the movies and then proceeded to stand me up and GHOST me, and that sucks, even if he is sorry.
2. He's absolutely, 100%, without a doubt still into Destiny Wright. See Instagram for proof.

* * *

I regret saying yes to this movie date the second I slide into Marisol's Escalade and I'm stuck in the back seat listening to Sophie and Noah whisper sweet nothings. I start to keep count of how often Noah says *babe* in a sentence, and I'm pretty sure it's in the dozens by the time the twenty-minute car ride is through.

From the front seat, Marisol and Ari are practically speaking in some kind of secret language. When I innocently mention how weird I think the Dunkin' billboard we pass is—it features a freaking shark—that sends them into a conversation all their own.

Marisol suddenly shouts, "There's a shark in the water!"

And Ari dons an Australian accent. "It encircles its prey!"

They both burst into laughter.

At the movie theater, my friends talk of splitting this and that with their partner, and I'm stuck ordering a kiddie-size popcorn and drink just for one, which practically screams: HELLO I AM SINGLE.

At least Sophie keeps her promise of getting me jelly beans.

But then when we go to choose our seats, Marisol and Ari want to grab something in the front, while I prefer the middle, and Sophie and Noah want the back (no doubt so they can make out).

We split up. I sit alone. And I vow never to agree to be the fifth wheel for a movie date again.

Chapter Twenty-One

After a jam-packed Sunday, including me staying up way too late to review Isaiah's binder of Fall Fest ideas, the very last thing I want to do is spend time after school helping out at El Coquí. But Abuela needs me so we can stay on top of the bookkeeping, and thus, begrudgingly, I drive there with Lily.

I'm quiet on our car pool to the shop, which is easy, since Lily is still not really talking to me.

When we arrive at the shop, Abuela instructs Lily to help organize some of her new supplies in the back room, while I head into the office with Abuela so we can go over the last month's expenses. We're in decent shape, but our sales have been slow this quarter, so I see why Abuela was hopeful she could sell her dress for a few hundred dollars. I still feel a little guilty that I selfishly want to hold on to it, but hopefully my first check from my new job will help.

Out of nowhere, Abuela turns to me and her face grows serious. "How are you doing, mija?"

I don't know why, but the question catches me by surprise. "I'm good," I reply, automatic, without thinking.

"No, I mean, how are you? Really."

"What do you mean?"

Abuela sits back in her chair. "You've seemed a little bit out of it lately."

"I am," I admit. "I have a lot going on with senior-year work, thinking about college applications, Fall Fest...this new job."

"I keep telling you you don't need to have this job," Abuela reminds me.

"I know, I know. But I want to help out around here. I'm old enough to be contributing now."

"Your only job is to go to school and get into college—or find a job, whichever—and be happy," Abuela says. "That's all I care about."

"Well, let me at least stick around a little more and we'll see."

"All right," she agrees. "What else?"

"I broke up with Aiden," I confess.

Abuela gasps. "Mija, are you okay?"

"I'm actually fine. We just hadn't been connecting, really, and he met someone else."

"Bastard!" Abuela shouts, taking me by surprise.

"Jeez, Abuela. Tell me how you really feel," I say, laughing. "Honestly...I'm kinda okay with us being done. I was hanging on to what we were when we first got together, but we'd been losing our momentum for a while. But...being single sometimes makes me feel like a fifth wheel around Marisol and Ari and Sophie and Noah...which I know is silly, but still."

"Oh, yes. I know you all liked hanging out as a group. But you can go alone, no?" Abuela asks.

"I mean, I *do*, but it feels weird! Last night at the movies, I ended up sitting by myself."

"Oh, no. That's too bad."

"Yeah," I sigh. "I'm just...tired."

"Tired? Are you not sleeping enough?"

I rub at one of my eyes wearily. "No, I am. I'm sleeping plenty. I just feel exhausted, no matter how many hours of sleep I get. And..." My voice trails off as I try to figure out how much I want to share. "My period still isn't here."

Abuela squints at me. "I thought it was just here a few weeks ago?"

"Ugh, no. I just bought tampons to hide the *other* reason I needed to run to the pharmacy."

"¿Qué?" Then her eyes go big with a realization. "No! ¡Ay dios mío! You're pregnant!"

Now my eyes go big. "What?! No! I'm not pregnant!"

Abuela puts her hand over her heart. "You scared me!"

"Why is that your first thought?!"

"Well! No period, tired all the time, mood swings—"

"Hey! Mood swings?" I scowl at her. "I didn't say I was having mood swings."

She rolls her eyes. "Come on, now. I get it. I was young once, too. But it's been like this." Abuela motions her hands up and down as if her palm is riding on a roller-coaster track. "No?"

With a sigh, I plop my chin in my hand. "No, you're right. I've been all over the place."

"But you were saying, about the pharmacy?"

I'm almost too embarrassed to say, don't want to choke the words out. This hairy face of mine has such a hold on my self-esteem lately. It makes me feel disgusting. Like I'm a boy, but I don't want to be. And I know there's nothing wrong with cis girls who have facial hair—truly, nothing at all—but it just feels like this huge, shameful secret I'm harboring, like it's weighing on my chest and I can't breathe. Before I even say it, I feel hot tears threatening to fall. "My face has been growing hair," I manage.

"Oh, mi querida! We're Puerto Rican. We're hairy, you know?"

I shake my head, one fat tear rolling down my cheek. "Not like that. Hair on my upper lip or my chin, I expect." I sniffle. "It's more like hair here. And here. And here and here and here. Just, everywhere." I'm pointing at my jaw and my chin and where my cheeks meet my hairline and along my neck. "And it's not even just that. But my curls—my beautiful, wild curls that I love so, so much—have been falling out in clumps."

Abuela clucks her tongue sympathetically and stands, stretching out her arms to me. "Ven aquí," she says, beckoning me to come to her. I fall into her open embrace, crying for the first time in weeks as she rubs my back. "Todo bien, mi amor. Todo bien."

The tenderness in her voice welcomes a fresh wave of tears. "I don't know what's wrong with me!" I cry.

"Shh, shh, shh." Abuela's rubbing my back in big, calming circles, and drawing in deep breaths in a way that instinctively encourages me to do the same.

It takes a bit, but eventually, the waves of tears slow, and I calm, settling like the ocean waves after a storm.

Abuela pulls back from me a little, but keeps both hands on my wrists, inspecting me. "¿Bien?"

I wipe my face and nod. "I'm good."

"Okay. I'll make an appointment with Dr. Delgado for you, yes?"

I'm too tired to protest. So I just nod. She gives me another hug and tells me to go home and rest.

Chapter Twenty-Two

The Fall Fest posters in all their groovy seventies glory are up at school. Chloe Torres *nailed* it. I want to frame one and hang it in my room, and if all goes well, I just might.

After an early-morning meeting with Isaiah to review the ideas he shared with me, I'm feeling pretty good about where we're headed for the festival, planning-wise. Even if I have sort of been lagging behind Isaiah in business outreach these last couple of days.

As I'm walking from third to fourth period, I do a double take when I spot Destiny Wright in the flesh, heading in the opposite direction. She's wearing a fitted, collared baby doll tee over some wide-leg pants painted with elaborate designs in bold colors, and I'm instantly struck by how truly gorgeous she is in person. *How* have I not noticed this girl before?

Suddenly, I see how Isaiah could still be hung up on her.

Great.

At lunch, while I'm sitting with Marisol and Sophie, I see Destiny again. And I can't help it; I stare.

"Helloooo?" Marisol playfully taps on the top of my head with her long nails. "You in there, girl?"

"I'm here, sorry," I say.

"What are you looking at so intensely?" Sophie asks.

Marisol shoots me a look. "Or *who*?"

"Remember that girl Destiny I was asking you about?"

Marisol crosses her arms. "Um, yes, and you still owe us an

explanation on that since you practically took a vow of silence since the movies."

"Well, she's Isaiah's ex. They were dating up until like a month ago. And now they're hanging out again."

Sophie furrows her brows at me. "And this bothers us...why?"

"Mm-hmm," Marisol adds, most annoyingly and unhelpfully.

I look between my two best friends. "Because—well, I...think I might have a crush on Isaiah."

Marisol lets out a shriek that gets most of the cafeteria looking our way, but when our classmates realize it's just Sol, they turn. Being loud is kind of her thing.

"Could you relax?" I ask, ducking my head down. "This is all super new. And anyway, in case you weren't listening, Instagram-model-slash-fashion-icon-slash-Zendaya-doppelgänger Destiny Wright is Isaiah's ex. Like I'd have a chance. And they're hanging out again!"

Marisol holds a finger up in the air. "Okay, first of all, no, I cannot relax."

Ari comes up behind her holding a lunch tray and nods. "Yep. Can confirm. Girl has no chill." She smiles at Marisol and swoops in to give her a kiss on the cheek. "Hi, by the way."

"Hi," Marisol coos back. Then she turns to me and holds up another finger. "Second of all, she really does look like Zendaya."

"I know, right?" I ask. "They're like twins."

Sophie and Ari exchange a playful eye roll at our quick diversion from the topic at hand.

"Third of all," Marisol continues, "I *know* you're not trying to imply that you somehow have no chance with Isaiah because Destiny is pretty—*as if you aren't fucking gorgeous your damn self.*"

I pause, taking a long sip of my drink. "That...is exactly what I'm implying."

"Oh, shut up!" Sophie exclaims—and it's so weird to hear her say anything even slightly less than positive that it makes the rest of us laugh.

"You tell her, Soph," Ari cheers.

I gasp and throw a carrot stick at Ari. "Traitor!"

But Sophie's not done. "Sol is right. *You* are a bi bombshell, and you're a freaking idiot if you don't see that. Just because you stayed with Aiden for way longer than you should have and he never treated you the way you deserved doesn't mean you're some, like, pariah destined to be alone. Everyone knows Aiden is a dummy. And we all make bad choices from time to time."

Marisol snaps her fingers in agreement.

Sophie grabs the carrot stick and points it right at me like it's a weapon. I put up my hands in surrender. "What you need to do is work on that self-image of yours and realize that you are a catch. And you downplaying that is not cute to anyone. So, if you *wanted* to go after Isaiah, you absolutely could."

Despite being lectured, I'm touched. "You *guys*," I say, making my voice soft. "That was the nicest scolding ever. And Soph! I'm so proud. Way to go."

She flips her hair over her shoulder. "Thank you."

"But everything she said is gospel. So you need to get right in the head," Marisol says. "Don't you agree, babe?"

Ari nods. "Of course I do, mi luz del sol." Then she leans toward me and whisper-shouts, "Happy wife, happy life!" Marisol gently swats at her shoulder.

"While I very much appreciate the love and support, the *real* issue is that Isaiah is hung up on Destiny." I sigh. "No amount of confidence or self-love I manifest is going to make it so that he forgets about her if his heart is still pining for her. Unless one of you is a witch and you have the ability to brew some kind of love potion."

"Well, let's not totally rule that out," Marisol says. "My titi Ines is a bruja."

I hold up a hand. "Um, stop. I need to hear absolutely everything about that immediately."

"How have you never told us this before?" Sophie asks.

"It's a long story. I'll tell you later. I don't want the gringos to overhear." She pretends like she's zipping her lips. "Anyway, how do you even know he's still hung up on her?"

"His sister told me, for starters."

"That'll do it," Ari says.

"Exactly," I agree. I pull out my phone and unlock it, showing them the photo I had pulled up of her and Isaiah. "And look at this. From six days ago."

Sophie inspects the photo. "They do look awfully cozy..."

"Let me see that." Marisol snatches the phone out of my hand and zooms in on the two of them. "That doesn't mean anything." She tosses my phone back and I just barely catch it, accidentally double-tapping the picture in the process.

"Shit! No! I just liked the picture!"

Ari goes wide-eyed. "You just made Whit swear."

"Hey," a deep voice says from behind me. I whirl my head around to see Isaiah, and I very smoothly drop my phone on the floor.

"Hey!" My voice sounds unnaturally high-pitched, hopefully drowned out by the others saying hello, too. I reach for my phone but Isaiah is faster. When he turns it over, praise sweet baby Blue Ivy that the screen is locked and not on the photo of him and Destiny.

I take my phone from Isaiah. "Thanks."

"No problem. And, hey, you actually left this at my house the other night..."

He reaches into his interior jacket pocket and pulls out a notebook. But not just any notebook: *my* notebook. The notebook where I keep all my silly little lists! (And, also, like, useful stuff like my agendas for the day and whatever, but THOSE LISTS ARE PRIVATE.)

"Oh my God, thank you!" I reach out to quickly take the notebook from his hands, far too eager to have it back in my possession. How did I not notice this was gone? I must really be out of it. "It would've been really embarrassing if my list ranking the hottest members of Intonation got leaked to the entire school."

He laughs. "Don't worry. I won't tell anyone Rider is your favorite."

Before I can respond, Isaiah is waving goodbye, and now I'm frantically flipping through my notebook for any indication that he *did* read it, because how the hell did he know Rider is my favorite member of Intonation? And do I actually have a list ranking the hottest members of the band that I don't remember writing?

"*Shit*, that was close," Marisol breathes.

"Too close," Sophie agrees. "Is your notebook okay? I know how much you love that thing."

I nod, scanning through the pages, including the waterlogged list for my perfect senior year. "It seems like it's all here. Crisis averted."

"Well...sort of," Ari says. All three of us look up, but Ari just juts her chin in the direction of the courtyard so that all four of us are watching as Isaiah rejoins his friends outside and Destiny Wright envelops him in a warm, chest-to-chest, we're-definitely-more-than-friends hug.

Suddenly my friends are murmuring, "Sorry, Whit," and I have no choice but to smile at them brightly and tell them it's fine—really. All good.

Chapter Twenty-Three

I'm ignoring my homework and neglecting my phone, instead curled up in my bed with Patch. We're snuggled up rewatching the first episode of *Gilmore Girls,* just because.

Thanks to Abuela's quick action, Dr. Delgado's office has already scheduled me for an appointment this week, so I don't feel quite so guilty leaning into the pity party for myself given how sluggish I feel, mentally *and* physically. Some days, it feels like I'm slogging through molasses while everyone around me is on hyperspeed. I even canceled the meeting Isaiah and I had set up to check in on Fall Fest things.

Something about the pop-culture-obsessed, coffee-addicted mother-daughter duo of Stars Hollow always brings me great comfort, though. For one, they're both from Connecticut, which is in New England, obviously, so it feels like I could pick up and visit Lorelai and Rory anytime I wanted. Everything about it, from the fast-paced chatter to the rich seasonal changes to the complex relationships among all the Gilmore girls to Paris Geller's entirely-too-much gene (I relate, okay?), feels like a steaming mug of warm tea.

I'm embarrassed by how many times I've rewatched the show in its entirety, including the Netflix additions, and I can quote so many lines from memory. (So many.) Like fall itself, everything about it is so cozy.

From the comfort of my bed, I hear Lily's voice down the hall. "Abuela, I need help with my homework."

This makes me snap to attention. I climb out of bed and pad down the hallway to where she's sitting at the dining room table, as if summoned. "I can help."

She and I have not been on speaking terms, but I *always* help with her homework.

Lily glares at me and calls, "Abuela!"

She comes into view from the laundry room, carrying a basket. "Sí, mi amor?"

"I need help with my homework."

Abuela peeks at me over the mountain of linens. "Can you help your sister?"

"I told her I would, but she's still ignoring me," I say, not hiding the irritation in my voice. Lily hasn't spoken to me in days now, and I've apologized so many times. What more can she possibly want from me?

"Lily, please let your sister help. I'm in the middle of something," Abuela says.

"I don't *have* a sister."

I gasp at the same time Abuela hisses, "Lily!" She slams the laundry basket down onto the floor and puts her hands on her hips. "Okay. Enough! You two have been sulking and giving each other the silent treatment and slamming doors for days now. I was trying to let you work it out yourselves, but I'm done. ¿Qué pasa?"

Lily narrows her eyes at me. "*She* started it."

"I told you I was sorry!" I argue.

"You didn't mean it!"

"Of course I meant it!"

Abuela claps her hands. "¡Basta!"

The edge to Abuela's voice tells us she means business. She orders Lily to explain. Then me. Lily shares her version of the story of how I was a total jerk. I offer a few corrections—I was *not* trying to hurt her feelings!—but mostly let it stand as she's shared it.

Abuela gives a weary sigh, and I'm certain she's going to turn to Lily and tell her she's overreacting.

But she turns to me. "Mija, I know you mean well, but Lily is growing up. You need to let Lily decide for herself what's good for her." I start to object but she holds up a hand. "I'm not finished. If Lily wants to let her friend borrow her belongings, including *her* vinyl record, that's her choice."

"What if she never gets it back? Or what if it breaks?" I practically whine, hating how I sound right now and yet unable to stop myself.

"That's not your business," Abuela says simply.

Lily nods. "And Ruby's not going to break it. She promised."

I huff. "But people accidentally ruin stuff all the time!"

"I don't care! I really don't." Lily's fists clench ever so slightly by her side. "You keep treating me like I'm a baby who can't do anything. I hate it."

That sucks the wind out of me, and I feel all the annoyance I've been holding dissipate, turning to shame instead. "You think I treat you like a baby?"

"You *do*. You made me walk with you to class like I couldn't find it on my own. You think Ms. K is bad for letting me listen to music. You tell me Ruby is just using me. You barely let me walk to Nora's house by myself." She shakes her head. "And it's not just that. You read things for me without giving me a chance to sound the words out. I at least want the chance to *try*. I'm not a little kid anymore."

As she lists her grievances, I realize I can't be mad at all. I *do* do all of these things, and maybe even more. There is a lump in my throat and I feel my eyes start to well, though I don't want to cry. Not when it's me who's been such a jerk this whole time.

"You're right. I guess I have been treating you like a little kid," I say softly. "I'm sorry, Lil."

Abuela gives me a very gentle smile and reaches out to take my hand. "It's hard to adjust to change."

I sniffle. "Yeah. It is. I just wanted to help Lily have a nice, easy transition to high school. I didn't realize I was making it worse." I look at Lily, whose gaze is on the floor as she rubs her elbow with her arm. "I'm sorry. I won't treat you like a little kid anymore. I know you're growing up, and you're smart, and you're capable, and you're a million other amazing things, too."

At this, Abuela takes Lily's hand as well. "You're both growing up—and I'm so proud of you. My Liliana." She kisses the top of Lily's hand. "And my Whitney." And then she kisses mine. "¿Está bien?"

Lily and I nod.

"Can Whitney help you with your homework now, Lily?"

"It's okay. I can do the laundry instead," I offer.

"No. I want your help." Lily is still looking at the floor, but her voice is warmer. "If you still want to."

I reach to give her an enthusiastic fist bump. "Of course I want to help if you want me to!"

She starts to push me away. "Ugh, don't be weird."

"Too late." I grin. "I'm *always* weird."

As I help Lily with her homework, I can't stop thinking about how my biggest fear for her—that people might not treat her with the dignity and respect she deserves just because she happens to have autism—came true. But it was *me* who was guilty of it. Me. How devastating.

I tell myself I'll be better not just for her sake, but for my own. Maybe I've let my Virgo, I-must-be-in-control-of-everything tendencies get the best of me.

It doesn't take long for us to finish Lily's homework, and by then, the tension between us seems to have dissipated entirely. That's what I love about being Lily's sister: we may break each other's hearts one minute, but the next we're plotting how to get Abuela to take us for ice cream.

There's no ice cream involved tonight, but Lily does show me an Intonation interview that was recently uploaded to YouTube. It's an old one, a snippet from one of their first concerts, before they skyrocketed to fame. She and I watched that concert on Netflix religiously. It was cut with interview segments between every couple of songs and we got to watch Intonation do normal things, like shop and play basketball and go bowling. Lily and I loved being able to see "our boys" being casual and normal, so much so that we ended up memorizing certain parts of the interview portions.

Parroting them back to each other as we watch this video feels so normal, but I know our normal is changing. It reminds me that—both for her sake and my own—I need to relinquish some control.

Chapter Twenty-Four

I take back what I said about the fluorescent light in grocery stores being the worst, because *clearly* the worst-lighting award goes to the doctor's office. At least in grocery stores you might find yourself surrounded by colorful flowers or freshly baked bread; in doctors' offices, it's nothing but the smell of alcohol burning your nose, nausea clawing at your stomach while you wait, wait, wait for it to be your turn and then wait, wait, wait to be seen.

I like Dr. Delgado. I do. But I don't like the uncertain feeling that washes over me every time we're discussing the dizzying array of symptoms I've been experiencing. And there are a lot. I wrote them down on the car ride over.

Whit's Excessively Annoying PCOS Symptoms
1. Excessive facial hair growth (Beard?! Is that normal?).
2. Excessive hair loss (And how can both #1 and #2 be true???).
3. Still gaining weight.
4. No period in sight (not that I'm complaining, but, you know).
5. So, so, so tired.

It's just five things, but they're five big things, at least to me.

In the waiting room, I show the list to Abuela so she can take a second look. She digs out her reading classes, perching them on the tip of her nose and holding the notebook out to read it.

"Bien," she says. "Pero, you should add mood swings."

"Abuela!" I hiss.

"See? Another mood swing." She breaks into a smile, and I roll my eyes. "Better to ask, no?"

I take the notebook from her with a sigh. "Fine."

6. Mood swings (according to my abuela).

The list only keeps my mind occupied for so long and then I can't stop fidgeting as we wait to be called in. I think of all the classes and assignments I'm missing to be here, and the fact that El Coquí is closed for the morning, meaning we could be missing out on money we need, and for what? I know Dr. Delgado is doing her best, and I don't mean to be so skeptical, but the idea of only being able to treat my illness one symptom at a time for eternity makes me bone-tired.

Abuela squeezes my knee and assures me everything will be fine, reminding me to breathe. But my leg doesn't stop bouncing up and down until we're in the office with all my vitals done and there's a soft knock at the door.

I clear my throat. "Come in."

Dr. Delgado's small frame emerges from behind the heavy door. Today, she's got her tightly coiled hair tied up in a gold-and-orange silk scarf. Peeking out from beneath her white coat is a black sheath dress, and she has yellow heels.

She smiles at me and then Abuela. "Whitney. Paola. How are you?"

"Good," Abuela answers.

"Okay," I say.

Dr. Delgado meets my eyes. "But could be better, right?" At this, I nod. "So, what brings you in today?"

"I don't even know where to start," I say, heaving a sigh.

"How's the metformin working?"

"I guess that's been helping. I'm not sure. I don't feel much different and sometimes it makes me feel sick if I eat carbs."

She makes a face. "Unfortunately, that can happen." She makes a note on her iPad. "Okay, what else?"

"Well, recently, all these other symptoms have been popping up and it's been taking a really big toll on me." I glance down at my notebook, splayed open in my lap, and turn it around so she can read it. "I made a list."

She gingerly takes it from me, nodding as her eyes scan the page. "Some list, isn't it?"

"Sorry," I mumble.

"No, no. I don't mean it like that. You should always, always feel comfortable sharing what's going on," she clarifies. "What I mean is: Wow, this is a *lot* for a seventeen-year-old to be dealing with, and look at you. Not only are you wise enough to be tracking all of this—paying careful attention to how you feel, just like we talked about—but I imagine you've also been managing everything else seventeen-year-olds need to manage, too. Yet you're here. You're saying your body needs help. And you're taking all the right steps to make that happen. That, in itself, is an accomplishment."

These words, combined with her reassuring tone and the gentle lull of her Dominican accent, make my face crumble. The tears come before I can stop them. "Thank you. It's been a lot," I admit, sniffling.

Abuela comes to my side and puts one hand over mine, rubbing my back with the other. "That's my Whitney. Always leaving me awestruck with how strong she is."

I give her a small smile, gently squeezing her fingers with mine.

"We are going to figure this out, Whitney," Dr. Delgado says. "I promise you that much."

. * .

I leave the doctor's office with a few things: a virtual appointment with a psychiatrist to discuss anxiety medication; an appointment for a sleep study to help with the drowsiness; and the satisfying validation of Dr. Delgado telling Abuela that while mood swings can be a symptom of PCOS, they're also symptoms of being human, so we'll revisit that one at a later date.

But it's still overwhelming.

In the car, Abuela rolls down the windows so we can enjoy some of the sunshine. She even makes a pit stop to get me a PSL. I sip and lean back in my seat and let her take the lead in picking up prescriptions, calling doctors from the pharmacy parking lot, and making decisions, while I just sit quietly. I feel numb and slightly beat up, despite the appointment going about as well as I could've hoped.

While Abuela is inside the pharmacy, I get a text from Marisol.

Marisol: The stupid dentist made you miss Noah's proposal! It was PERFECT.

Guilt again—this time at my white lie that I was going to the dentist.

A video follows Marisol's text. In the thumbnail, I can see that Noah is wearing a Mona Lisa T-shirt, holding up a sign that reads I LOUVRE YOU, SOPHIE. FALL FEST?

Okay. That's pretty adorable. Good job, Noah.

Yet with Aiden out of the picture, and no homecoming date prospects for me, I can't bring myself to watch the video in full. It's not fair, but it is what it is. I scrub through it so I get the basic gist, feeling at once genuinely happy for my friend and genuinely kinda sad for myself.

Me: OH MY GOD KJSFHHJKSDJKS SOPH!!!!! This is SO CUTE. CONGRATULATIONS!!!!!! So so happy for you! And so sad I missed it! Can't wait to hear everything

Sophie writes back a long string of heart emojis and I smile.

This is what Sophie deserves, and what Fall Fest and my dedication to it are all about. Even if it's looking like I won't get my own special night, I want it so badly for everyone else, especially those I love most.

Finally, we get to Elmwood. But when I reach for my backpack, Abuela stops me.

"Stay here," she says. "I'll be right back."

I don't even protest as she leaves the car running and strides up toward the building.

By now, it's lunchtime, and I see my classmates milling about: some of the seniors head to their cars to grab lunch off campus, some take a vape break (not technically allowed, but it happens, obviously). They're all trying to soak up the late-September weather while they can. We have little more than a month until fall shrivels up and turns cold, so we all spend as much time as we can outside before we're forced to shelter indoors.

"Whit?" a deep, familiar voice calls. I look to where the sound came from and smile when I see Isaiah standing idly on his skateboard. His locs are tied back and he's wearing that bomber jacket I think makes him look extra cute. He breaks into a smile. "Thought that was you."

"It's me," I say. "Hi."

With his foot, Isaiah gives a strong kick and skates over to the car so he's just outside the passenger door. He hops off the board and leans down so he's right at my eye level, and I get the faintest scent of cologne and firewood. It sends a small pang into my chest as I realize I've missed talking to him. It's only been a few days, and yet...

"Hi," he says, still smiling. "I've been looking for you. You hiding?"

"Not hiding. Just feeling a little under the weather," I say, even though I have kind of been avoiding him, too. After Destiny, I just can't.

His brows knit together in concern. "Oh, no. What's wrong?"

"Just a migraine," I lie. "I'll be fine."

"So, are you heading home, then?"

I nod. "Yeah. At least I think so. My abuela just ran inside and didn't tell me why."

"Well, it's good you go home and rest if you're not feeling well." His eyes search my face for a moment, like he's considering saying something else. "I've been worried about you, you know? After you canceled the other day and then there were no additional notes in our Fall Fest Google spreadsheet...I don't know. I thought you'd been abducted by aliens."

This makes me laugh a little. "Aliens, huh?"

He laughs, too. "It seemed like the most logical thing, honestly. I feel like nothing else would stop you planning. But I guess not feeling well makes sense, too."

"Isaiah!" a voice chirps from a distance. We both look over to see Destiny motioning to him. "You coming?"

He waves at her. "Meet you there." Then he turns to me. "I hope you feel better. Will you be at the committee meeting tomorrow, you think?"

"Probably. If this migraine goes away."

"Okay. Good. I hope it does."

We look at each other for a second, and I see that Destiny hasn't moved from where she was standing, waiting for Isaiah. "You should go, though. Destiny awaits."

He chuckles at the terrible pun and glances quickly at her, then back to me. "That's one way of putting it. All right. Well. I'll see you?"

I nod. "See you."

Isaiah walks, rather than skates, over to where Destiny is. She links an arm with his. I hear her say, "Finally!" and I slink lower into my seat. Seeing Isaiah felt so good, but with every breath I remind myself he's spoken for, so no matter how good the firewood and cologne smell, I need to let it go.

In the side mirror, I see Abuela making her way back to the car with Lily in tow.

"What's going on?" I ask as they both get in the car.

"Girls' day!" Lily sings, plopping in the back seat.

"But the tailor shop," I say.

"Pah. That can wait." Abuela waves a hand. "So, where should we go?"

"Midday movie?" Lily suggests.

Abuela waggles her eyebrows. "Ooh, the new Pedro Pascal one just came out! What do you think, mija? Should we go see my soon-to-be husband on the big screen?"

A movie where I'm not the fifth wheel sounds nice, and I can't be mad at two and a half hours ogling Pedro Pascal. I grin at Abuela. "Let's do it."

Chapter Twenty-Five

Homecoming proposals have officially taken over the school. There is an excitement buzzing in the air and it seems like every time Sophie, Marisol, and I turn a corner, someone else is being asked to this year's dance.

"Is it just me, or are a lot more people going all out this year?" I ask as the three of us walk away from a small crowd who just finished watching William Romano serenade Sydney Johnson with his guitar before asking her to be his date.

"Definitely," Sophie says with a nod. "And I feel like it's all your and Isaiah's doing."

"What do you mean?"

"You guys have really been working hard to get people excited! I mean, the theme, the killer schedule. People are responding." Sophie bumps her shoulder into mine. "Good work."

I smile. "Wow. Thanks, Soph."

"It really has been amazing," Marisol adds. "Even though I have to watch all these other people get their proposals and mine is nowhere to be seen." She heaves a sigh. "Tragic, really."

I shake my head. "Oh my God, Sol. You know Ari has something big up her sleeve. Give the girl some time! We still have two weeks."

She crosses her arms. "You mean we only have two weeks!"

Don't remind me, Sol. I'm falling behind on my Fall Fest duties as it is.

"It'll be worth the wait," Sophie promises.

But Marisol just flips her hair over her shoulder. "You only say that because you've already been asked."

As we turn the corner toward our shared English class, we spot a giant balloon archway at the end of the hall. In the center, in silver balloons, is the name HUDSON.

Marisol stomps her foot. "Oh, come on! Now the world is just being cruel."

It may be frustrating for Sol to have to wait, but now that I've moved past the initial jealousy phase (and yes, I did go back and watch Sophie's proposal in full and it was adorable), it's pretty cool to see everyone get as excited as me for this year's festival.

The buzz in the air permeates the afternoon, and at the Fall Fest committee meeting Ms. Bennett congratulates us on selling a record number of tickets to this year's homecoming.

We spend the first part of the meeting talking about the bake sale, which is happening next week to coincide with the official start of Fall Fest. It's all business—until Everly McDonnell asks Sophie to tell us all about the proposal from Noah. Our group loses focus and everyone starts to chatter excitedly instead of working. I get it.

Isaiah makes his way over to me. "You notice how happy everyone's been lately?"

"I have," I say.

"Is this part of that fall magic you're always going on about?"

I give him a smile. "Must be, right? Finally everyone is realizing this season's greatness. All thanks to us. We've made quite the team—and honestly, I just never ever expected we would."

He hops up onto the desk next to me. "Why's that?"

"Well, I wasn't exactly jumping for joy when you became senior officer, you know."

Isaiah quirks an eyebrow at me. "Because you hate me? Or because you're a control freak?"

This makes me laugh and I playfully swat at his knee. "I am not a control freak."

Now he's laughing. "You absolutely are! And you know it!"

I roll my eyes. "Fine, fine. I'm a control freak."

"I kind of like that about you, though," Isaiah admits, and I feel my cheeks go pink.

"And I don't hate you," I add. "Not even close."

"Oh?" he asks. "But you did, though, didn't you?"

"I mean...I won't lie, you weren't my favorite person. Not after—" I hesitate, gazing around the room. This is not the conversation I expected surrounded by all these people, but everyone else in the classroom is busy talking about who asked who to the dance, what they're wearing, plans for the upcoming weekend. No one's listening, so I go ahead. "Not after everything in middle school."

"Everything as in how you ghosted me out of nowhere?" There's a curve to his lip as if he's smiling, but his eyes tell me he's hoping for a real answer.

"What?! *You* ghosted *me.*" I lower my voice. "I was there at the movies!"

"No, *I* was there at the movies," he says. "*You* were nowhere to be found. Which is why I ghosted you afterward!"

"Oh my God—no, you *weren't,*" I insist in a loud whisper. "I was waiting for you like a fool in the freezing cold."

Isaiah blinks. "Oh, shit. You were waiting outside?"

"Of course I was! Our plan was to meet at the entrance to the movie theater...wasn't it?"

"I meant the mall entrance," Isaiah says. "So you wouldn't have to wait outside!"

I meet his gaze. "Wait...so you *were* there."

"And you were, too." He runs a hand along the back of his neck. "Damn. So, all this time, you thought I stood you up?"

"Obviously! Yes, I did! But...I guess that means you thought I stood *you* up?"

We look at each other, not saying anything for a minute, and then start to laugh. "I can't believe it!"

My giggle quiets, though, and I go still, imagining charming little Isaiah thinking I abandoned him for no reason. All these years. And even so, he was still so kind when he spilled coffee on my cardigan and has gone out of his way to help me ensure that Fall Fest succeeds. "God, that really sucks. I'm so sorry."

"*I'm* so sorry," Isaiah says. "I'm mortified that you think I wouldn't show."

"I was totally devastated," I admit. "Especially when you completely ignored me afterward."

Zay visibly cringes. "Yeah...my communication skills weren't exactly peak yet."

I arch an eyebrow at him. "As opposed to now?"

"Well, of course. I'm excellent at communication now." He grins. "But, yeah. I shouldn't have ghosted. That was cold."

"Pretty sure I got frostbite," I retort.

"Okay, corny," he teases, before his face goes soft. "I'm sorry for that. I know we were just kids, but I don't know. I was pretty into you." He glances down at his shoes as they dangle from the desk. "Who knows how things might've been different."

"Yeah. Who knows?" I agree. My poor heart hurts for little Whitney and little Zay. "What movie were we supposed to see that day?"

Isaiah laughs. "Some scary movie called *The Surrendering,* I think."

"We should see it together sometime," I suggest. "Make up for lost time."

He smiles at me, eyes twinkling. "That would be dope, actually."

I glance around the classroom, and Isaiah's eyes follow. I realize everyone has left, even Soph and Marisol, who must've slipped out while Isaiah and I were talking.

"Oh, damn. We cleared this place out," he remarks.

"Looks like it. Guess we should get going." I start to pack my backpack.

Isaiah slips off the desk. "Hey, so, how has your outreach to those businesses been going?"

"The meeting's over," I tease. "We don't have to keep talking about the Fall Fest."

"We barely talked about the Fall Fest at all, *Whitney*," he teases back. "And you seemed off earlier this week, so I wanted to make sure you're good."

Gently, I place my notebook in my bag beside my Fall Fest binder, which, admittedly, I haven't opened all week. "Well...it's been a little slow, if I'm honest."

Isaiah reaches for his messenger bag and slips it over his head. "You want some help?"

"Really?" I ask.

He nods. "Yeah. I mean, I'm already done."

"You're done with yours?! But we set a deadline for next Wednesday!"

"I can't help if I'm that good," he jokes. "But seriously. You free Sunday?"

I'm so behind I really could use the extra help.

"I think I can do Sunday," I say, keeping my voice casual. "Could you pick me up?"

He starts to walk toward the classroom door, his skateboard tucked under his arm. "I can do that. I'll text you?"

"Perfect."

Isaiah uses two fingers to give me the tiniest of salutes before he's on his board and skating away, leaving me smiling to myself without meaning to.

Because this is just Fall Fest business, I remind myself. Nothing more.

SEPTEMBER 2023

Sunday	Monday	Tuesday	Wednesday	Thursday	Friday	Saturday
					1	2
3	4	5 First day of senior year!	6	7 First Fall Fest meeting	8 Sleepover @ Soph's	9
10	11 Fall Fest committee voting	12 ~~Date with Aiden~~	13	14 Fall Fest weekly meeting	15 BREAK UP WITH AIDEN!!!	16 Pumpkin-picking with the besties
17	18 Meet with the enemy!!!	19 Shift @ Nature's Grocer	20	21 Fall Fest weekly meeting	22 Sophie's Concert with Sol	23 Fall Fest planning @ Isaiah's
24 Shift @ Nature's Grocer	25	26	27 Appointment with Dr. Delgado	28 Fall Fest weekly meeting	29	30 Shift @ Nature's Grocer

OCTOBER 2023

Sunday	Monday	Tuesday	Wednesday	Thursday	Friday	Saturday
1 Fall Fest outreach with Isaiah	2 Bake Sale + Fall Fest Schedule Announcement!	3 Shift @ Nature's Grocer	4 Finalize Fall Fest outreach	5 Fall Fest weekly meeting		7 Shift @ Nature's Grocer
8	9 Indigenous Peoples' Day	10 Extra Fall Fest meeting!	11	12 Final Fall Fest meeting before go time! Shift @ Nature's Grocer	13	14
15 Fall Fest begins! Fall Fest Kick-off Carnival (parking lot and fields)	16 Pumpkin-Carving Contest (courtyard)	17 Corn Maze Races (little gym—see your PE schedule for times)	18 Fall Feast hosted by culinary kids (cafeteria)	19 Bonfire (west lawn)	20 Pep Rally + Football Game (big gym and football field)	21 Fall Fest ends! Fall Fest Homecoming Dance (cafeteria)
22	23	24	25	26	27	28
29	30	31 Halloween				

Chapter Twenty-Six

Never in a million years did I imagine I'd hear the familiar, upbeat opening chords of Intonation's "Girl Be Mine" echoing down the hallways of Elmwood High. So when exactly that happens in the middle of the class exchange between periods five and six, I'm convinced I'm either imagining things or asleep, once again having that recurring dream I've had where they visit my school and Rider holds my hand and serenades me in front of everyone.

Neither ends up being true.

"Would Liliana Rivera please report to the rotunda?" Principal Johnson's voice asks over the intercom.

I text Marisol and Sophie immediately.

Me: OH MY GOD. IS THIS A PROPOSAL FOR LILY?!?!

Sophie: AHhhhhhhHhHhHh!

Marisol: I MIGHT CRY 😭 bb girl is growing up!!!

I speed-walk toward the rotunda, the central area in our high school where two staircases spill out onto the right and left sides of the building, dividing it exactly in the center. Already a crowd has formed on the edges of the upper circle, and there's excited chatter from some of my classmates. I squeeze into a spot right up against the railing and throw down my backpack just beside me, hoping to save a spot for Sol and Sophie. I glance down at the lower level, where there's a bouquet of flowers—delicate pink-and-white lilies, just like my sister's beloved backpack.

A lump forms in my throat at how thoughtful this is. Who *is* this?

Marisol finds me first, Ari just behind her, and it's not long before Sophie and Noah snake their way through the crowd to us, too.

"Did we miss anything?" Sophie whispers.

"Not yet," I say.

It's then that Lily walks up the bottom staircase, led by her teacher Ms. Kaminski, who instructs her to stand on the landing between the first and second sets of stairs. From up here, it looks a bit like a stage, Lily the central performer. But she's looking around just as bewildered and curious as the rest of us.

"Liliana Rivera..." a voice calls. And then it starts to sing along with the chorus of the song. "*Girl, be mine, smile like sunshine, girl divine, and so I pine...*"

Classmates whoop as Lily's friend Ruby ascends the stairs. She's wearing a gigantic, person-size version of the vinyl she borrowed from Lily, featuring all five bandmates. Ruby's off to the side as if she's the sixth member.

Suddenly, everything clicks: Ruby's borrowing the vinyl; Lily constantly talking about Ruby; the regular hangouts; their meet-ups in the virtual *Animal Crossing* realm. They like each other! Of course! My baby sister has her first mutual crush, and I can't help but beam at her, smiling and cheering with my friends, not hiding the happy tears pooling at the corners of my eyes.

Ms. Kaminski cuts the music pouring from the Bluetooth speakers, and in a shaky voice, Ruby asks, "Lily, will you be mine? And go to homecoming with me?"

Lily rubs her hands together excitedly. "Yes," she says into the mic, and Ruby pumps her fist in the air as the onlookers burst into cheers.

"Yeah, Lily!" I yell. She looks up at me, the purest smile I've ever seen illuminating her face. And maybe for the first time, I see her for who she is: not my baby sister, but my sister, a young woman in her own right.

Ruby gives Lily the best side hug she can given the huge cutout, and for the rest of our peers, it's over. But for Lily, this must feel like the start of something magical.

I grab Marisol and Sophie by the arms. "Come on!" Ari and Noah stay behind with our belongings while I practically yank my friends down the steps in a rush to get to where Lily's standing. She's giggling as Ms. Kaminski helps Ruby shimmy out of the costume.

"Lily!" I squeal, holding my hand up for a fist bump. "I'm so happy for you!"

"I'm so happy for me, too," she gushes.

"Yeah, girl!" Marisol whoops, holding up a hand for a high five.

Sophie grins. "Congratulations, Lily!"

Lily high-fives them both and I'm touched by how utterly thrilled my friends are for my little sister, who they've watched grow up, too.

I turn to Ruby. "And that was an incredible proposal."

"Seriously amazing," Sophie agrees, nodding. "You're a great singer!"

Marisol points toward the Intonation cutout. "Plus, all of that? Dedication. You nailed it."

Ruby smiles shyly at us. "Thanks. I wanted to make Lily feel special because she is." She glances over at Lily with green eyes full of adoration.

"We'll leave you to it," I say to Lily. "Just wanted to say congrats!"

Ruby's fingers reach for Lily's, and my heart practically explodes when Lily reciprocates.

There's another whoop from above that catches my attention, and when I look up, I see Isaiah standing just beside Ari and Noah. He waves at me, all smiles, too. I wave back.

And for the smallest fraction of a second, I let myself wonder.

What if?

What if Isaiah were standing there guarding my belongings the way Ari and Noah are holding Marisol's and Sophie's?

What if Isaiah handed my bag back to me and leaned in close, smelling like firewood and cologne, and whispered in my ear how happy he was for my sister? For me?

What if Isaiah put his hand on the small of my back, guiding me down the hallway toward my next class, the place where his palm rests warm from his skin?

What if, when I made it to my next class and we said goodbye, he leaned down...and his lips touched mine? Gentle, but urgent, a promise for later?

What if?

But then I see him turn back to Destiny, leaning in close as they exchange whispers, and all those what-ifs evaporate to dust, swept away in the soft September breeze like dandelion seeds.

I take a moment to look back at Lily—my sweet, lovely Lily—and know that as long as she gets her perfect homecoming, I'll be just fine.

Chapter Twenty-Seven

That night, I want to celebrate with Lily, but she makes plans with Ruby. A date. Her first. And I don't want to do my hovering thing that I tend to do, so it's a relief when Sophie asks Marisol and me to spend the night at her house.

Her parents are settled in the finished basement for a date night in, so we have free run of the house, but we choose to hang out in Sophie's room. I'm giving us each a full glam makeover because it's Friday and we want to and we don't need any other reason.

While I work on filling in Sophie's eyebrows, Marisol is painting her toenails a vibrant pink.

As she admires her work, she asks, "Can we please talk about how perfect Lily's proposal was?"

"It was absolutely everything," I gush. "I swear, just thinking about it makes me tear up again."

"I felt like I was getting to see my own sister have her dream moment!" Sophie says. "Hopefully this doesn't sound crass, but Whit, did you know? That she was into girls?"

I shrug a shoulder. "I mean...not really, no. But I'm also not super surprised. It's hard to explain. The way she had been talking about Ruby, it makes total sense." I pause. "I do wonder how Abuela will react to having two gaybies in the house, though."

The word *gaybies* sends Sophie into a fit of giggles, which makes me and Marisol laugh, too.

"She was fine when you came out, no?" Marisol asks.

I nod. "She and Abuelo both were. I wasn't expecting it at all, but they're pretty amazing that way."

"I think she'll be thrilled. Especially when she hears how happy the proposal made Lily," Sophie says.

Marisol blows on the wet polish. "Ugh, if Ari doesn't give me a proposal at least half as sweet as the one Lily got, we're done."

I add some blush to Sophie's cheekbones. "As if you'd ever leave Ari. You guys are *sickeningly* in love!"

"Yeah, but she's testing my patience," Marisol says, pouting. "I'm about to sic Titi Ines on her."

"The bruja?" I ask, and Marisol nods.

Sophie rolls her eyes. "Oh my God! Chill! Ari is working on something."

"What do you know, Benedict Arnold?!" Marisol demands.

"I'm sworn to secrecy. But it'll be worth the wait. Right, Whit?" Sophie looks to me for encouragement.

Ari texted us earlier this week for help in executing her plan, so we know it's coming. I nod enthusiastically. "You're going to love it!"

Marisol squeals, throwing herself back onto the fuzzy carpet we're sitting on. "I knew my baby wouldn't let me down!"

"You were just talking about breaking up with her!" I say with a laugh.

"I've changed my mind. My girl looooves meeeeee," Marisol sings. "And I just got some good news about the debate club! Now that the club is officially official, Ms. Singh says she can help me look into qualifying for the National Speech and Debate Tournament!"

My eyes go big. "Whoa, that sounds amazing!"

"It does!" Sophie enthuses. She waits a beat, then glances between us. "What does it mean?"

"I'm glad you asked, because I was just going to pretend I knew," I say with a laugh.

Marisol sits up dramatically. "It *means* that I might be able to represent our district and compete against over six thousand kids from across the nation! The top contenders are named national champions, and it looks so freaking good on your college applications," she explains. "Ms. Singh says she isn't sure we'll be able to get everything prepared in time to hold a proper competition, but she promised to do everything in her power to help."

Sophie claps her hands together. "Oh my gosh—that would be incredible!"

Marisol shrugs. "Well, I'd still need to win in our district to get sent to the national competition, but yeah." She tucks a strand of hair behind her ear. "It would be great just to participate. Oprah Winfrey is an alum!"

"Holy shit." I grin as I fill in Sophie's brows. "You and Oprah Winfrey!"

She laughs. "Let's not get ahead of ourselves. But we're basically besties, yeah."

"You'll definitely get into the national competition, and your bestie Oprah will have no choice but to call and congratulate you," I say.

"We'll see," Marisol replies, but she's smiling in a way that tells me she's flattered by our unyielding confidence in her. "Anyway, what's been up with you guys?"

Sophie gives us a devilish grin. "My stuffy music teacher broke his leg skiing so we have a substitute for the rest of the semester."

I gasp. "Oh my gosh!"

Marisol tightens the cap on her nail polish bottle and giggles. "Soph looks *way* too pleased about that news."

She shakes her head emphatically. "I'm not pleased about the injury, I swear! But..."

I arch an eyebrow at her. "But?"

"Well, the new substitute is amazing and has already said we can perform something contemporary for our winter show, so...sometimes the world works in mysterious ways, okay?"

Marisol shrugs one shoulder. "Or maybe you were secretly hoping for your teacher's demise!"

"I wasn't!" Sophie insists, tossing a pillow at Marisol, who laughs and ducks.

"Maybe it was Titi Ines's doing," I joke. Then I pat Sophie's knee. "You're all done, by the way."

Sophie grabs her mirror and admires her look. "Oh my God, I love it! What lip color is this?"

I hand her the lipstick. "It's Glossier Ultralip in Trench."

"My turn," Marisol says, scooting closer to me. I shift toward her. "While I have your focused attention: Can you please tell us what is up with you and Isaiah?"

I start to apply some primer to Marisol's smooth skin. "Funny you should ask. I actually just found out something pretty interesting."

Sophie's eyes go big. "Spill!"

"Well, you both know how I've always said Isaiah was my enemy because he totally blew me off for our date in middle school..."

"Of course. The worst," Sophie says.

"As it turns out, he didn't blow me off. He was actually there. We were apparently at different entrances," I explain. "So this whole time he thought *I* ghosted *him*, and I thought *he* ghosted *me*, when we were both actually committed to that date."

"Why didn't you text each other?!" Marisol asks, as if in disbelief.

I shake my head. "I didn't have a phone! We couldn't afford a cell phone back then."

Marisol puts her hand on her cheek. "This is way too tragic for me."

"It is super sad!" Sophie frowns, sticking out her bottom lip. "Zay-Zay! And Whit-Whit! Just two wholesome little babies thinking the other didn't want them." She turns to Marisol. "You didn't know him then, but he had these sweet little puppy-dog eyes that would just make you melt."

"Okay, staaaahp!" Marisol whines. "I'm depressed."

"I feel totally awful." I let out a sigh. "Especially because…"

"Because what?" Marisol presses.

"Well, because a few weeks ago, he told me this really cute story about a Halloween party he threw when we were in sixth grade. Do you remember that, Soph?"

"Oh my gosh, yes! We bobbed for apples and I won."

"Clearly the highlight," Marisol teases.

Sophie grins. "It absolutely was. But go on, Whit."

"Isaiah told me he sort of threw the party to impress me. Because he liked me." I put my hand over my heart. "Is that not the sweetest thing you've ever heard?"

"Okay, gross. Isaiah is, like, some kind of walking rom-com lead, because this doesn't even sound real," Marisol says, shaking her head. "First of all, the man is *foine*. Those. Cakes!"

"Sol!" Sophie cackles.

"Just because I'm gay doesn't mean I can't look. And believe me, when it comes to Isaiah Ortiz, I do. So he's, like, next-level hot, but also super smart and funny and kind and *also*, at twelve years old, the most romantic dude on the planet?" Marisol looks me square in the eye. "When are you going to nail him down?"

"He's into Destiny," I remind her.

Marisol arches an eyebrow at me. "But you also want to get into his pants, right?"

I shove her a little. "Oh my God!" She throws her head back and laughs. "But, I mean. Yeah."

"Whit wants to get her hands on those cakes!" Sophie shouts.

"She's coming for you, Zay-Zay," Marisol coos. "Get that butt ready!"

We laugh until our stomachs hurt, and our makeup is smudging, and every time we look at each other, we dissolve into giggles again—at nothing and at everything, and right now, I swear I'm using my whole heart to savor every beautiful silly second with these beautiful silly humans.

Chapter Twenty-Eight

Even if I'm going to be dateless at homecoming, I'm obviously still going to go. Who needs a date, right?

And because it's rapidly approaching, I have to buy a dress.

Buying a dress means I have to pay for it with money.

Paying for my dress with money means I need to go to work.

And this is how I will myself to get out of bed and go to Nature's Grocer for a long day of condescending customers who argue with me over prices, then get frustrated when they enter their credit card PIN wrong and act like it's my fault.

The day crawls by. I honestly feel like I might scream when I have to ring up an older white guy who comes through my line with a box of melted gourmet chocolates and attempts to return them because he left them in his car and they had the audacity to turn into "goo." Sir, how do you think the sun works?

By the end of my shift, my feet ache, my tongue is sore from a day of biting back what I wanted to say, and my stomach is rumbling.

Normally, I would head straight home and eat some leftovers prepared by Abuela. They're always delicious and it would save me a couple of bucks. But tonight, I just want to grab something greasy and warm and eat it alone in my car.

A cheeseburger and some fries later, my stomach is full and I'm just about to turn my car on and head home when I spot some people around my age across the parking lot. They're skateboarding, and a thought flickers in my mind. Could a tall, cute boy with locs somehow be part of that crowd?

Then I catch sight of the familiar hoodie. It *is* the tall, cute boy with locs—and his friends.

I have two choices: I can either turn on my car and peel out of the parking lot, avoiding being spotted by my classmates and the boy who makes my heartbeat quicken, content in the knowledge that crushes don't last forever and the next episode of *Gilmore Girls* is waiting for me at home.

Or I can fix my hair, add a touch of mascara and lip gloss, slather on some scented lotion, and march over there, in hopes of enjoying my crush—because crushes are fun and delightful and harmless and I deserve a little sunshine.

I guess the real question is do I go with plain or sparkly gloss?

As I walk toward Isaiah and his friends, the confidence that washed over me in the car starts to wane. Is this silly? This might be silly.

But I can't exactly turn around and run back to the car. Not when I'm this close, and not when—

"Whit?" Isaiah looks up, a confused—but pleased?—look on his face.

I smile at him, tucking a strand of hair behind my ear. "I thought that was you."

"What are you doing here?" he asks.

"Oh, you know. Just admiring the sunset from this delightful fast-food parking lot, as one does," I joke. "Actually, I just finished up a shift at my job and I needed sustenance ASAP. I was going to do the whole eat-shamefully-in-my-car thing, but then I spotted you and wanted to come by and say hi."

He gives me an understanding nod. "Ahh, I've lost count of the number of times I've desperately needed some fast food after I've finished up a tutoring session. I feel you. And I'm glad you came by to say hi."

But just how glad, Isaiah? Enough to forget your ex-girlfriend? Because if so...

Isaiah's hands go into the air like he just remembered something. "Oh! Let me introduce you to everyone." He kicks his board into the air and grabs it, then takes me by the elbow and gently guides me toward his group of friends. I savor the electricity that shoots through me at his touch. "So, okay, that's Malik." A chubby, adorable Black boy with a fade gives me a nod. "And that's Jay." Isaiah points toward a Mexican boy with perfect curls (whose social accounts I may have *lightly* stalked in search of Isaiah). Then he juts his chin toward a shaggy-haired, olive-skinned Chinese boy. "And that's Daniel over there. Guys, this is Whit."

I smile at them. "I think I've seen you all around. Hey."

"Hey," Jay says, giving me a warm smile back. "You're in my math class, right?"

I nod. "I am. But no judgments, please. Numbers are not my thing."

"Jay is kind of a math genius, but the nonjudgmental type, so you're good," Isaiah says.

"You skate?" Daniel asks, gliding on his board in a circle around me.

"God, no," I say with a laugh. "I wish!"

Daniel suddenly does something with his board that flips it in a circle. He lands perfectly on both feet, steady and grinning. "You could learn. Zay taught his little sisters to skate when they were, like, four. Now they're practically pros."

I shoot a look toward Isaiah. "Did you now?"

"Well, it was more like Amaya bullied me into it, but yeah," Isaiah says.

"That sounds like Amaya."

"We've *all* seen how intense that little girl can be. She once told me my mustache looked like dirt over my lip." Malik shakes his head. "Most savage burn I've ever heard."

"I notice you don't have a mustache anymore, man..." Jay teases.

"You think I was going to keep it after hearing that?! Nah, no way. She humbled me," Malik says, chuckling. "I think she might rule the world someday. And you know what? I'd be here for it."

"Me too," I agree. "I've only met her once and she's already kinda my idol."

"So, you down, then?" Isaiah asks. "To learn to skate?"

"Um, sure!" I hear myself say, because clearly my body is operating on pure adrenaline and my overthinking mind hasn't quite caught up yet.

Isaiah gently kicks his board toward me. "Hop on."

I look at him as if he has four heads. "Now?"

He shrugs. "Why not?"

Great going, Whit. Now you're going to fall over in front of all of these cute boys and you'll have no one to blame but yourself.

"Well, talk me through it. What do I do first?" I ask.

"Let's try to just get you on the board without falling to start. Okay? So, you can start by putting your nondominant foot on the area directly above the trucks," Isaiah says.

"Okay..." I move my sneaker toward the board, but pause midair. "What the heck's a truck?"

This makes them all laugh.

"She's a beginner, man," Malik reminds him. "Spell it out like you do for your tutoring kids."

"I've got it," Isaiah huffs. To me, he says, "The truck is a T-shaped thing the wheels are attached to. Right here." He points with his shoe. "Gently place your foot right there, so that your shoe goes across the board."

I do as he says, keeping my weight on my dominant foot. "Like this?" I ask.

"Exactly! Okay, so, actually, what I want you to do is add your other foot just beside it and try to balance. Do your best to keep your weight as centered as possible. You'll want to lean left or right when the board wiggles, but try not to."

The idea of stepping up onto Isaiah's board terrifies me. What if I fall? What if I break my neck? What if the board splinters beneath my weight? "I'm going to break your board," I blurt out.

He blinks at me. "Why would you think that?"

"I don't know!"

"Here." Isaiah holds out an arm to me, patting his forearm. "Hold me for balance." I hesitate for a second, but he meets my eyes. "I've got you."

I don't think and just do, adding my right foot beside my left. And when I realize I'm up, a laugh bubbles out of my throat. "I didn't die!"

"Yet," Jay teases.

Isaiah shakes his head. "Ignore him. You're fine."

I'm wobbly, though, and I find myself unable to straighten and find my center of gravity. Instead, I'm leaning, hard—just like Isaiah said *not* to do—and before I know it, I'm a tower of Jenga blocks crashing to the ground as the board zips out from under me and across the parking lot.

"Shit!" Isaiah swoops down toward me, and so do his friends. "You good?"

I'm stunned for a moment, just blinking, looking around at Isaiah, Malik, Jay, and Daniel. It takes a moment before pain surges through my legs and butt—not oh-my-God-I'm-dying-pain, but it hurts.

Yet I surprise myself when instead of hearing a yelp or a cry come from my throat, it's a laugh. A big, throaty laugh that echoes through the parking lot.

"I'm good," I say, lacing the words with giggles that come and go like waves, a signal to Isaiah and his friends that it's fine if they start cackling, too. They do. With each laugh, I feel like I'm also pushing away some of the tension and stress from the day. It feels nice.

Isaiah holds out a hand for me to take it, and I reach for him. His hand is softer than I expect, and warm despite the chill in the air. It eclipses mine and I find myself holding it longer than I need to as he helps to pull me up.

"Ow," I complain, rubbing my lower back, which took the brunt of my fall. "That hurt."

"We can be done," Isaiah assures me.

"No way! That's part of it, isn't it?"

"Absolutely! I still fall," Jay says.

"Mostly because you do stupid tricks, but yeah," Malik jokes.

Jay flips him the bird. Daniel, who took off after Isaiah's board, skates back into view. "Rescued this bad boy just before it almost knocked into an old lady carrying her food. Some might say I'm a hero."

"And not a single one of those people is here tonight." Jay grins at him, but it doesn't stop Daniel from proudly puffing out his chest.

Isaiah takes his board and sets it back down in front of me.

"Try again?" I ask.

"You sure?"

I surprise him by grabbing on to his shoulders and mounting the board. "I'm already up!" I shout victoriously.

Isaiah whistles. "Look at you!" He steps closer to me, putting a hand on either side of my hips and helping to steady me. The skin beneath my clothes where his hands rest feel like it's on fire—a rush of heat and tingling. "We're going to move now, okay? Just hold on to me. Don't be shy."

I gulp, worried he can hear from there how hard my chest is thumping. "Okay."

He starts to move me and it's rocky at first, the board jolting a bit under the cracks in the pavement, but once we have a little momentum and I get better at centering my weight, I feel myself grinning. "I'm not falling!"

"You sure about that?" A devilish grin comes over Isaiah's face. "I'm about to let go."

"What?! Don't!" I shout.

"You'll be fine," Isaiah says. "I promise."

I take a deep breath, not wanting his hands to leave my body, but nod. "Okay. Do it!"

Between Isaiah's gentle push and the momentum we'd already built, the board sails across the lot on its own. "You've got this!"

"I don't got this!" I yell back.

But I'm upright and alive. For just a few moments, it's me, my curls bouncing in the wind, this board, and the phantom feeling of Isaiah's hands on my hips, as I slowly sail across the parking lot.

Since I have no idea how to kick, it doesn't last long. It's enough, though.

When I successfully stop the board and get off it by myself, with no injury, to the far-too-kind and over-the-top cheering of Isaiah and his friends, I'm wondering if this is further proof I don't need to be in control of *every little thing* all the time.

Maybe sometimes, I can just glide.

Chapter Twenty-Nine

When I rise on Sunday morning after a long night of rest, the sun is shining, the birds are chirping, there are some scarlet maple leaves dancing in the breeze through my window, and I can still feel Isaiah's fingers on my hips—firm, but gentle.

In that dreamy, not-still-sleeping-but-not-quite-awake state, I imagine what it might be like if his hands had lingered on me, if they'd slowly trailed up my back, encouraged by the shaky breath I let out. One might slip its way toward the nape of my neck, palm warm and soft, before gingerly cupping my chin. Heat between us, skin touching, our heads would start to close the gap and—

My phone buzzes.

With a sigh, I open my eyes to grab it off my nightstand.

Marisol: Excited to go apple-picking today with your boo? 😊🍎🍏

Me: I am, actually. 🍏🧺😍

Marisol: Will you just tell him you like him already??

Me: Leave me alone and let me have this crush!

Sophie: You do you!!!

I smile to myself, reaching down to grab Patch off my feet and rub his head.

"I have a crush, Patchy," I whisper to him. He purrs in return.

Truly, I haven't felt this giddy since Aiden and I started dating. And I'd forgotten how much fun it is.

I like the constant state of butterflies in my stomach, of hoping against all hope that I'll bump into Isaiah. The thrill that rushes through me when it actually happens. The explosion of nerve endings at every accidental touch. Making up excuses to talk to him. Sneaking glances even when he's right next to me. Feeling my heart dance when that easy smile comes across his lips. Savoring the huskiness of his voice when he speaks, the way my name sounds when he says it. Imagining. Wondering. Daydreaming.

And with my revelation that perfection is not a thing I should be looking for, I scribble over what's left of Whit's Totally Definitive Guide to the Perfect Senior Year. I don't need it.

Once I'm showered with my teeth brushed, I take an extra-long time doing my makeup; embarrassingly, I need to cover up a tiny nick I got on my neck while shaving my face. I still haven't gotten this daily shaving routine down, but YouTube and TikTok tutorials have helped.

For my outfit, I tuck an oversize cable-knit sweater into my rust-colored corduroy A-line skirt. Opaque black tights are underneath, paired with dark brown Doc Martens boots Abuela and I scored while thrifting months ago. (Thrifting for clothes may sometimes be tough as a fat girl, but at least there's shoes!) A light-wash denim jacket completes the look.

As my long, dark curls air-dry, I join Abuela and Lily in the kitchen for breakfast.

"Good morning," I chirp, grabbing a plate and forking an omelet Abuela made with ham, onions, peppers, and tomatoes onto it (alongside some raspberries).

"Morning," Abuela murmurs. "Don't you look pretty?"

"Thank you." I take a seat beside her at the table and give her a kiss on the cheek. "I feel pretty."

A smile sweeps across Abuela's face at this. "Big plans today?" she asks, eyebrows rising.

"Just some Fall Fest stuff with Isaiah." I pop a raspberry into my mouth. "We've got a few more businesses to visit to see if they'll offer donations or sponsorships."

"Zay, huh?" Abuela casts a knowing look my way, a faint smile on her lips. "That sounds fun."

"Honestly, I think it will be. And speaking of fun...Lily, how was your date?"

Lily's cheeks go crimson and she looks away from me. "It was good."

But I'm dying to know more. "What did you and Ruby do?"

She rubs her hands together excitedly, leaning in. "We went to the arcade downtown. They were having a really cool *Animal Crossing* pop-up show! Lots of cool art and amiibos you can buy for your Switch and all," she explains. "Abuela gave me some money and I bought Ruby an Isabelle plushie. That's her favorite character in the game."

"Oh my gosh. You guys are so cute!" I gush, reaching over to squeeze Lily's hand. She tugs it away from me and rolls her eyes, but she can't hide the smile starting at the corner of her mouth.

"It sounds like you guys had fun," Abuela says.

"We really did."

"And that proposal?" Abuela puts her hand over her heart. "Ruby did good for our nena. Although I could do without the enormous Intonation cutout. I have no idea where we're going to store it."

"Did you bring it home?" I ask Lily.

"Of course I did! It's going to be my Halloween costume," she replies, as if it's the most obvious thing in the world.

I laugh. "Right, of course."

A text from Isaiah asks when he can come by. I give him a time, the butterflies I've learned to welcome flapping their wings in my stomach.

Vámanos, mariposas.

*　*　*

I'm not one for cars, but I am absolutely *tickled* when Isaiah pulls into our driveway in an old-school red Volkswagen Beetle, complete with black polka dots on the exterior and long, dramatic eyelashes on either headlight.

I duck down and through the cracked window say, "Um…add this car to the long list of things I didn't know I needed."

"*Don't* get me started. Camila took my car because it was parked on the end and left me with hers. When I texted her about it, she said I was a spoiled brat for not remembering that she had plans. When I pointed out that I, too, had plans, she said hers had been made first, and I was being disrespectful." He shakes his head. "Sisters."

"I'm honestly okay with all of this because it means I get to see this delightful ladybug car." I reach for the handle and let myself in, sliding into the passenger seat. "Thanks for picking me up. And for getting an early start with me."

"Of course," Isaiah says while I buckle myself in. "I mean, it's the least I could do, considering you're so behind and all. My reputation is on the line, too, you know?"

"Oh my God, shut up!" I laugh. "I've been busy!"

"Too busy for Fall Fest?" Isaiah shakes his head, but he's smiling. "Who even are you?"

"It's been a *weird* last few weeks, okay? And I've been working a lot," I admit. "But we're going to make up for lost time today. I present to you…Whit and Isaiah's Autumnal Adventure."

He arches a brow at me. "Excuse me?"

I reach into my bag and pull out my notebook, which I used to make a rough outline for the day's events. It's not nearly as elaborate as my plans usually are, but it's probably still A Lot by most people's standards. I wanted to make sure I could live up to my end of the deal, so I organized the list based on proximity to my house and when each location closes.

With the help of Google Maps, I've managed to sketch out a giant loop around our town, starting with a small farm stand just down the road and ending with my beloved Santiago's Orchard. It's just a few miles from home and therefore a place we visited a lot when I was growing up—so much so that the owner became a family friend known to me and Lily as Tío Sebbie.

The orchard has pick-your-own fields, like strawberries and peaches and pumpkins, as well as homemade pies and baked goods. But it's the dizzying array of apple trees that makes it really special, at least to me.

My family has visited this orchard every single year for as long as I can remember, making a daylong adventure out of it: apple cider donuts in the morning, walking the fields in the afternoon, taking our sweet time filling up our baskets and secretly sampling an apple or two as a reward for our hard work. Abuelo would lift me and Lily up on his shoulders as if we weighed nothing, just so we could reach the branches.

We got really good at learning to spot the best apples. By the time the day was through, we'd be dirty and sticky and carrying more apples than we knew what to do with. And then came the baking—apple empanadas, apple butter bars, apple pies, all of which we helped Abuela with—and she'd sell them at her store as a fall treat.

Knowing how special that place is, I don't think anyone would blame me for saving it for last. We probably won't be picking apples or anything, but it seems like the best way to end the day.

"I have everything all laid out in my notebook," I explain. "I've completely optimized our day so that we can get the most out of it and you can still make it home in time for dinner or whatever else you might want to do later."

"What, no binder this time?" Isaiah teases.

I stick out my tongue. "I know my binders can be a bit much. So I'm trying to dial back on some of that intensity. Just a page in my notebook today."

I don't mention the several other pages of notes I have on each place we'll be visiting, complete with facts like the owner's name, what I could dig up on them on social media that might help us curry favor with them, and what I hope they might donate versus what I think they'll realistically donate. A girl's gotta keep a *little* mystery, right?

"All right, hit me. What's our day look like?" he asks.

I turn the notebook toward him and show all six businesses I'm hoping we can visit and in what order. His eyes scan the page and he lets out a low whistle.

"Well, damn. We better get going, then." Isaiah starts to ease the car out of the driveway. "Be my copilot?"

I know he means this platonically and all, but the way he says *my* makes my heart skip a beat, as if there could be a universe in which we could be each other's.

Smiling, I pull out my phone and type the farm stand into Google Maps.

"Yeah," I say, keeping my voice light. "I'm yours."

Chapter Thirty

It only takes a few minutes into our visit to McNally's Farm, the first business on our list, before Isaiah has confirmed what I already knew: his charm is irresistible.

The way his eyes light up when he's talking to each person, like they're the only one who matters; the way he tilts his head just so, nodding as he listens; the generous laugh that ignites any conversation.

But it's the glances—small, subtle, just for me—when his dark eyes meet mine, his brows lifting just a touch as if to say, *See? We've got this.*

And I'm melting, full-on ice cream pooling down the grooves of a sugar cone under the hot summer sun.

Which is not to say I'm hanging back and letting Isaiah do the work. Sure, I do my fair share of ogling whenever he isn't looking, but I have a job to do and I came prepared.

We tag-team at McNally's Farm and the Law Offices of Nuñez and Quintilla, which are easy enough to get as repeat sponsors. They've funded homecoming dances in the past and I made a killer sponsorship package for this year's dance.

I let Isaiah take the lead at May Flowers, a new floral shop in town, once he surprises the owner—and me—with his robust knowledge of native New England plants. ("My abuela's *obsessed* with her garden," Isaiah tells me afterward, and my heart makes a secret wish to see it someday.)

It's my turn to shine at Petey's Sweeties, an adorable bakery that specializes in intricately decorated sugar cookies. I've followed them on TikTok for months and the opportunity to gush in person is too good to pass up. I even get to meet *Petey himself*, as well as his husband, Gil. When I tell them, briefly, about the Fall Fest's meaningful history within my family, Gil is so verklempt, they immediately sign on not just to become a sponsor, but also to generously donate a huge batch of cookies to the carnival that say FALL FEST.

"Did you and Petey just become best friends?" Isaiah teases once we're back in his sister's car.

"I think we did. He liked my dimples!" I bat my eyelashes and grin big, showing them off.

Isaiah reaches over and pokes the dimple in my left cheek, a playful smirk on his face. "How could he not? They *are* pretty cute."

My cheeks get hot, and I wrinkle my nose, my shoulder coming up to meet Isaiah's hand. It's easier to pretend he's tickling me than it is to admit that his touch has made my entire body hum.

He has a girlfriend! I remind myself as he pulls his hand away.

"Where to next?" he asks.

I pull out my phone, even though I don't really need to consult my list. I just need a distraction from the urge to grab his hand and put it back on my skin. "Um, looks like our next stop is Santiago's Orchard. And then we're done."

He blinks in surprise. "Wow. Already?"

"Flew by, huh?"

"It really did." Isaiah turns the keys and starts the engine. "But at least it's not over yet."

We don't say much more as he eases the Bug back onto the road. I'll admit that I'm still swooning over Isaiah calling my dimples cute...and his touch, *well*. Can I help that my mind is racing with hope? I understand it's not logical—there's Destiny, for one, and the fact that we haven't been a thing for over six years.

But...it felt the *tiniest* bit like flirting.

Or maybe those are just the butterflies talking.

Isaiah clears his throat. "So, I hate to admit this to the Harvest Holiness Herself—"

I laugh. "Did you just come up with that?"

"I did. You like it?"

"I do, actually," I admit, pulling out my notebook and jotting it down. "And I'm immortalizing it in my notebook. But please, continue. You were saying? Harvest Holiness Herself?"

He laughs, too, but continues. "Right. O Harvest Holiness Herself, I do have a confession: I've never actually been apple-picking before."

The gasp I emit is sharp and dramatic, and I clutch my hand to my chest. "You've *never* been apple-picking?"

He shrugs. "Nope. Never."

I blink a few times, shocked and wholly unsure of what to say. The boy has never been apple-picking!!!

I don't particularly enjoy being That Person who does the whole you've-never-done/experienced/tried/seen-whatever, mostly because I think it's a little elitist and ignores the fact that we all live varied, complex lives, which is what makes it so interesting when they intersect. But. Apple-picking is, like, in my blood. It's *such* a western Massachusetts thing! Like the ubiquitous Dunkin', there are apple orchards at practically every intersection in the rural towns.

Still, it's rude to make people feel bad about things they have or haven't done, so I'm readying myself to apologize for my over-the-top reaction when I catch the corner of his mouth quirking upward into a smug, playful smirk.

Oh my God. He's *enjoying* my disbelief.

Bolstered by this, I throw the back of my other hand onto my forehead. "I think I just blacked out. Because there is literally no way—no way in the world—that you've grown up here and you've never been apple-picking before. I don't believe it!"

"Believe it." Isaiah scratches his chin thoughtfully. "Come to think of it...don't think I've been pumpkin-picking, either."

"*Now* you're lying," I insist.

"What would I gain by lying about that?!" His voice is laced with laughter.

"You're trying to get me to drop dead so you can take all the credit for the work we've done today! Nice try." I cross my arms. "But I will continue living, thank you very much."

"And for that, I'm grateful. As a first-timer in the apple orchard, what should I know, Harvest Holiness?"

"God, where do I start?" I take in a breath. "Never pull the apple straight away from the tree! Instead, gently roll it toward the branch and give it a little twist."

"Roll and twist," Isaiah says, nodding. "Got it."

"You might think picking apples from the middle of the tree is, like, a nice little hack, but they ripen from the outside toward the center, so you might be picking apples that aren't ready to leave the tree yet. Instead, always start with the apples on the outside branches."

"Outside branches first. Noted." My phone directs Isaiah to take a right, so he does, before asking, "Anything else?"

I think back to all the apple-picking advice Abuelo and Abuela have given me and Lily over the years. In a softer voice, I add, "Yeah. One last thing. Apples are easily bruised, so always treat them with care."

Isaiah slows the car at a stop sign and glances over at me. "Treat with care," he repeats. His voice quiets, too. "I can do that."

My gaze meets his, and I take in a sharp breath. Are we still talking about apples? Or are we maybe talking about—?

Beep. Beeeeeeep.

Two honks from the car behind ours remind us we're just at a stop sign, and we look away from each other with a laugh.

"Massholes," Isaiah says.

"Massholes," I agree. Then I point, talking over my phone as it gives the next direction. "And, um, the orchard is right up here. It looks really sketchy, but I promise, once we get through this part right here, it's really cute."

"I'll take your word for it." Isaiah's eyes survey the sign that reads SANTIAGO'S ORCHARD—it's battered, faded, and weathered. Blink and you miss it, but it's there.

Once we're beyond the brush, the little Volkswagen Bug jostling us from side to side as we climb the gravel path, we come upon a clearing. Dozens and dozens of apple trees line the hillside, lush, green, and sprawling.

We park, and I unbuckle my seat belt. "Follow me."

Outside, we're greeted by the rich smell of earth, of damp soil as it mixes with the tang of fermenting apples, a result of the ripened fruit that has fallen to the ground. The trees in the orchard are still brimming with apples: Red Delicious with a sweet bite; tart Granny Smiths, which make your eyes water; and—my favorite—the aromatic McIntosh in red and green like Christmas.

I lead Isaiah away from the orchard and toward an old barn. Its tall wooden doors are propped open, welcoming visitors into a small store that's part gift shop and part farm stand: it has everything from freshly picked produce to homemade jams to kitschy wares (like dish towels that say IT'S WINE O'CLOCK SOMEWHERE and rooster-shaped mugs).

But instead of going into the shop, I pull open a door you might otherwise miss, and we start up the creaky steps.

"Okay, now. Just walking in like you own the place?" Isaiah asks from behind me.

I turn around and grin at him. "Maybe the nickname you've given me has gone to my head."

"Looks like it." He lowers his voice and hisses, "I'm all for adventure, but isn't this trespassing? I'm not trying to get killed by some white folks today, Whit!"

I keep walking up the steps. "Just trust me, okay?"

"If we die..." Isaiah lets his sentence linger and I can picture him shaking his head behind me, but he'll understand in a second. When we get to the top of the stairs, the door to the office I'm looking for is propped open, a Puerto Rican flag proudly displayed in its window. I give a gentle knock anyway.

Sebastian Santiago, the man who owns this orchard, is a medium-build, light-skinned Puerto Rican man with salt-and-pepper hair cropped close to his scalp and a matching beard. Tío Sebbie! I see him sitting at his desk.

He's not *actually* my uncle, but when you're Puerto Rican, everyone who's anyone becomes some kind of family: tío, tía, primo, whatever. Our connection to the island, however far from it we are, builds a bridge between us almost instantly, which is how Tío Sebbie and Abuelo first met so long ago.

At the sound of my knuckles on his door, he looks up and breaks into a smile, playfully slapping the stack of papers in front of him. "¡Ay, no! Whitney Rivera?!"

I grin at the way the *rs* roll off his tongue and the familiar way in which he wraps me into a hug. "So good to see you, Tío Sebbie."

"¡Sí, sí! How are you? ¿Y Lily? ¿Paola?" he asks.

"I'm great. Lily and Abuela, too! Busy," I say. "Abuela's especially busy, always working hard. You know how she is."

Mr. Santiago shakes his head. "Mira, she needs a serious vacation. Tell her I said so." He looks over to Isaiah. "¿Y tu novio?" He nudges me with his elbow.

"No, no!" I assure him with a laugh. "This is Isaiah. My *friend*."

Tío Sebbie extends a hand to Isaiah and shakes. "Hola. I'm Sebbie. I've known this one since she was practically in diapers."

"Tío!" I hiss, and Isaiah chuckles.

"To what do I owe this pleasure?" Tío asks.

"Fall Fest. I'm on the committee this year," I explain.

Tío Sebbie lets out a low whistle. "¡Felicidades!"

I grin at him. "Thank you! So I'm here on official business."

He chuckles. "Perdóname. I'm listening."

"We've been spending the day getting sponsors and donations for the event. We're bringing back the carnival for this year's
event—you remember it, I'm sure," I explain. "There's a lot of
pressure on us to make it good. So I wanted to visit my *favorite* tío
to see if you'd be willing to sponsor?"

He breaks into a smile. "Anything for Eduardo's nena. You
know I loved that man."

I smile at him. "You and me both." Something about Tío
Sebbie reminds me faintly of Abuelo, and it makes me feel warm
inside. "Thank you, Tío Sebbie."

"Seriously, thank you. We'll email you everything you need to
know, Señor Santiago," Isaiah says. "If that sounds okay to you."

Tío Sebbie claps Isaiah on the shoulder. "¿Señor? ¡No soy un
viejo!" He chuckles. "Pero, just let me know what you need."

"We will. I'll send an email before the end of the day tomorrow," I promise. "Now, if you don't mind, I'm on a very important
mission to take Isaiah on his first apple-picking adventure."

Tío Sebbie laughs. "A virgin!"

Isaiah grimaces and I feel my cheeks flush.

Before Tío Sebbie can say anything else, I grab Isaiah's arm
and start to lead him downstairs. "We'll be going now. Thanks for
everything, Tío Sebbie. Good to see you!"

"See you, mija! Tell everyone I said hello!" he calls after me,
amusement still in his voice.

I give him another wave before Isaiah and I step outside the
barn.

"He seems like a good dude," Isaiah says. "Clearly impressed with you, too."

"He and Abuelo were really close back in the day," I explain. "He's one of the few farmers of color in the state, and he works really closely with some of the cities nearby to help provide fresh foods in schools that really need it. Got this plot of land through the Northeast Farmers of Color Land Trust and really turned it into something incredible. I admire him…even though he can be just as embarrassing as any other tío. As you witnessed."

"Families always have a way of doing the most." Isaiah laughs. "Now, we going to pick some apples or what?"

I smile at him. "Thought you'd never ask."

Chapter Thirty-One

We spend the afternoon amid the rustling trees and drying grass, laughing and chatting and choosing apples. We reminisce about our middle school days. We make a game of trying to remember the silliest moments, like that time Dave Renner stole some chemicals from the lab and accidentally burned part of his shoe off, or when one of our science teachers accidentally said "orgasm" instead of "organism" and it became a scandal for, like, a week.

In between remembering mortifying moments we wish we could forget and picking fruit, I mentally make a list of firsts for Isaiah Ortiz and his inaugural apple orchard outing.

Isaiah Ortiz's Afternoon of Firsts
1. Visited an apple orchard.
2. Took a hayride.
3. Tried La Manzana, Tío Sebbie's special hot apple cider drink topped with a cinnamon sugar apple donut, and practically saw God.
4. Realized the hard way that wearing nice sneakers to stomp around an orchard is a terrible idea, slipping on a patch of mushy apples and nearly taking himself out.
5. Made me realize I am hopelessly, helplessly in over my head with this crush.

Sigh.

If you had told me a few weeks ago that I'd be spending a Sunday with Isaiah Ortiz, my ex–middle school boyfriend who I loved to hate, doing one of my favorite activities and *actually* enjoying myself, I'd probably have told you that you'd obviously lost your mind.

Because in no universe would I willingly give up my time to spend time with that heathen. I certainly would not be doing my best to catch his eye, or accidentally-on-purpose brush against his shoulder, or make him laugh in that dulcet way he does—all while secretly watering the seeds of affection blooming in my chest.

As the sky dims and we get back in the car, heading toward my house, I find myself wanting to extend the fun. I could ask him to stay for dinner?

Orrr I could let today be what it was and move on. He has a *girlfriend,* I remind myself.

I try to push away the thought as Isaiah eases the car in front of my house and parks, leaving the engine idling.

"Well, thank you so much for today," I say, reaching for my satchel of apples. I look over at him. "We did good."

Isaiah grins at me—easy, open, inviting—and all the thoughts I had about him having a girlfriend and not extending the night seem to dissolve. "We did do good," he agrees. "And now you have to admit that I was right."

I cross my arms, eyeing him. "About what, exactly?"

"I *told* you when this started that it would be fun if we could just figure out how to work together. You only needed to trust me." He points a finger my way. "Admit it! You had fun with me today."

That elicits a dramatic eye roll from me, but I can't suppress a smile. "I'd rather die, thanks."

He huffs, shaking his head. "Wow, she lies—and right to my face? I'm hurt."

I sigh. "Okay, fine." Then, glancing at him out of the corner of my eye, I add, "I had fun when you slipped on those rotten apples and fell."

Isaiah leans back in his seat so hard the car rattles. "Yoooo, you said you were never going to mention that again!"

"I said I wouldn't mention it to anyone else! It's fair game between you and me," I insist. "And yes, there was great satisfaction in watching your life flash before your eyes."

He narrows his gaze. "You're cold, Whit."

"Solid ice."

Isaiah laughs, his hands resting in his lap. "Well, I had fun, at least. Not *that* part. But the rest of it was nice."

"I'm happy for you," I tease. I should use this as my chance to say goodbye. Grab my bag and thank him and move on. Instead, I hear myself asking, "Hey, do you, um, want to come inside?"

I watch as Isaiah cuts his gaze to my house and then back to me, a question in his dark eyes. "Oh! Uhhh—"

"To have dinner with my family," I add quickly.

He breathes a laugh, and for a moment, I wonder what he was thinking, but then he smiles and surprises me by saying yes.

Yes. He said yes. And now we're going to spend the evening together.

In an instant, I'm leading the way up my familiar front walk to the Rivera house. Home.

Isaiah follows me as I cross the porch, unlock the teal-colored front door, and step over the threshold into the house. The smell of mofongo, one of Abuela's specialties, greets us, and Isaiah takes in a deep breath.

"Shit, that smells good," he murmurs.

"Aren't you glad I invited you for dinner? You're welcome," I tease. "You can take your shoes off here. Just watch for Patch. He likes to try and make a run for it." I point to a mat near the entryway, bending to unlace my boots.

"Patch?"

"Our cat!"

He snaps his fingers. "Oh, right!"

"Yeah, he's lazy, but sometimes he tries to sneak outside. He's done it before, and he figured out if he pretends he's a stray, he can get free food from the neighbors."

"Impressive little dude," Isaiah says, kicking off his sneakers.

"Right?" Then I call, "Abuela! I'm home! And I brought apples!"

"In here, mija!" she calls back to me. "How did everything go?"

I lead Isaiah to the kitchen and step inside. "Good. Isaiah's actually going to join us for dinner, if that's all right?" I probably should have called and asked first, so I lift my brows up in apology, hoping Abuela will let it slide.

Her face brightens when her gaze lands on Isaiah. "Of course, of course! Hola, Isaiah." She wipes her hands on a dish towel and pulls him into a hug.

"Nice to see you again, Abuela."

"It's been so long, no?"

Isaiah chuckles. "It's been a minute, that's for sure. But you look exactly the same as when I last saw you!"

Abuela's cheeks go pink and she swats at him with her dish towel. "Noooo," she insists. "Mira, dinner's almost ready, okay? Can you set the table? And get your sister to help."

"Of course, Abuela."

I lean over and kiss her cheek. She holds me there for a moment and whispers, "¡Que guapo!"

"Abuela," I hiss, worried she's said it loud enough for Isaiah to hear. But thankfully Isaiah's expression doesn't change, so I assume we're good. I pull back from her and nod toward the hallway, saying, "Lily's room is this way."

We hear the Intonation song well before we get to Lily's room, the sounds escaping from beneath her door.

"Her favorite band," I explain.

214

He smirks. "Don't play. I know they're yours, too."

"Oh, whatever." I knock on Lily's door, loudly, knowing she won't hear me otherwise. When she doesn't call back to me, I knock again. "Lily! I need you to help me set the table."

"I'm busy!" she calls.

"Abuela wants you to help, *please*."

Her door whips open and Lily stands in front of us wearing a curly brown wig tucked under a ball cap and a drawn-on beard and sideburns.

The laugh that erupts from my throat is loud and unexpected, but so is her whole look!

"I'm making a TikTok," Lily deadpans.

"Dressed as Lucas?!" I giggle.

She gives me a look like I'm an idiot. *"Obviously."*

"Well, can you take a break and come help set the table? We have a guest." I motion toward Isaiah.

"Great, then maybe he can help you." She smiles at me.

"Lily!" I don't mean to whine, but I definitely am.

"You like Intonation?" Isaiah asks her.

She arches an eyebrow at him. "Do you?"

"Of course I do. Number one bestselling boy band in the US." He grins at me.

"Whit loves Intonation, too. She's basically obsessed," Lily says.

Isaiah looks far too amused by this. "I knew it!"

"I'm not obsessed," I insist. "I mean, maybe I was, but—"

Lily cuts in. "She loves Rider. She used to kiss his poster on her wall *all* the time."

"Lily!" I say again, louder this time, my eyes going big. Isaiah is laughing now, and can I blame him?! My little sister just told him that I used to kiss a poster on my wall! Which is not *not* true, but oh my God. "I didn't!"

"Yeah, you did." Lily shrugs. "Anyway, can I finish this?"

"You need someone to hold your phone while you make your Tik-Tok? You can tell me more about how Whit's obsessed with Rider."

My jaw drops. "Now who's ice-cold?"

"Actually, Isaiah, that would be great," Lily says, opening her door wider to let him in. He steps inside, grinning at me, a playful twinkle in his eye. To me, she says, "I'm almost done, okay?"

"We won't be long," he promises. "Just long enough for me to get more blackmail material."

I scowl at both of them. "You're the worst. Hurry up and film your TikTok and then dinner's ready."

"Kbye." And Lily shuts the door in my face.

Fifteen minutes later, we're all seated at the table watching Lily's TikTok, which Isaiah ended up weaseling his way into. We're laughing so hard we're crying. Then we feast on Abuela's mofongo and tell her about all the progress we made for the Fall Fest, and, having a fresh set of ears to listen to her love story, Abuela regales Isaiah with the tale of how she and Abuelo met and fell in love there. Soon Lily's excusing herself for her virtual date with Ruby in *Animal Crossing*, and then Titi Luisa calls to gossip with Abuela—and it's just me and Isaiah left to clean up after dinner.

"I'll take care of all of this," I say, rising from my seat and starting to pack away the leftover mofongo.

Isaiah stands, too, and reaches for our cleared plates. "No way. If Mami found out I went to someone's house and didn't help with the dishes, she'd smack me upside the head."

That makes me grin. "I like your mami."

"You would," he teases. "Now, about this Rider guy..."

I groan. "I'm going to kill Lily!"

"I'm just saying, it's very interesting that the bad boy had you so sprung." He scrapes bits of food into the trash, clearing off the plates. "I'd have pictured you liking the squeaky-clean one. Maybe the artistic one."

"How do you even know this much ab

loading up two sets of Tupperware with the

"I have sisters. I know things."

I arch an eyebrow at him. "So, you didn'

where I rank the members in order of how hot tl

"You really made a list?!" Isaiah asks in disbe

"No!" I laugh. "But now I know you didn't pe

"I would never," he promises, chuckling. "I gu

Rider. He is the cutest, after all."

"Totally is. Rider just always seemed really swe

him, being the token brown boy in the band, you knov

"Plus, he's hot."

"*There* it is." Isaiah grins. "Now we know why you

poster so much."

"Ugh. You're never going to let me live this down, are y

"We could call a truce, you know. No more mentions

busting my ass at the apple orchard for no more mentions of

epic makeout sessions with a poster?"

"Easiest truce ever," I say with a laugh.

We fall into an easy rhythm. I tell him about the apple pastelillo

Abuela and I will likely make with our share of the fruit. He fills me

in on his work as a tutor. He helps middle-school-aged kids in the

town over from ours, and my heart swells as I imagine those kids

having someone like Isaiah to look up to.

I bet he's so good with them, the way he was with Lily tonight.

He swooped right in and won her over. It takes someone pretty

special to be able to make connections that fast.

I think this as we're saying goodbye and I'm loading him up

with Tupperware and practically rushing him out the door because

this night has been one of my favorites in recent memories, and it

can't mean a thing.

So it won't.

Chapter Thirty-Two

school, the energy is intensifying the nearer we get to
Fall Fest. While every academic year starts out fine enough,
eventually all start to pine for the festival, just so we can have a
ell-deserved break after weeks of studying and test-taking. (Also,
he Fall Fest proposals are getting on another level.)

I busy myself with checking in on the bake sale. Leilani, Everly,
and Hudson, our class officers, are staffing it, but I still make sure
to stop by. I _would_ invite Isaiah, but a little cooling-off period is
what I need right now.

"Whoa, this looks amazing," I say, admiring the faux leaf
archway under which Leilani, Everly, and Hudson sit at a table
piled high with sweets. They have everything from maple sugar
cookies to cider donuts to pumpkin rolls to sweet potato pie. We
scored most of this from the upper-level culinary classes, which are
also catering Fall Feast, and it looks delectable.

"The culinary kids nailed it, right?" Hudson asks, beaming.

"They really did!" I enthuse.

Everly claps her hands together. "We've already sold a bunch
of goodies."

Leilani nods and drops her voice to a whisper. "I'm gonna
hit up the vape kids when they come back in from their lunch
break."

"Excellent idea. How's everything been going so far?" I ask.

"People are loving it," Leilani says. "They're super excited
about the return of the carnival!"

"I'm personally looking forward to the bonfire," Hudson adds. "It's just so romantic."

Everly giggles. "You think everything is so romantic."

"Because it is!" Hudson argues.

I grin at them. "You're all doing an incredible job. Keep it up!"

In my afternoon study hall, Isaiah texts me.

Zay: sooo, mami was BEGGING me for your abuela's mofongo recipe

Zay: but if your abuela is anything like mine, there probably IS no recipe

Me: No recipe, just ✦ vibes ✦

Zay: gotta go break Mami's heart, then

Me: Noooo! I'll get Abuela to give me ingredients and approximations and let you know what I find out

Zay: 🙏

Me: I didn't get a chance to thank you last night for all your help. We're in such good shape for the dance now. And I really DID have a fun time.

Zay: i knew it!!!

Me: 😳

Me: RELAX

Zay: no bc after hearing your abuela's story about how much the fall fest means to her, i've made it my mission to ensure it's perfect. i finally get why you're so intense about it

Me: I'm not intense!

Zay: . . .

Zay: oh ok

Me: FINE

Me: But yeah. It means a lot to her, so it means a lot to me

Zay: i gotchu

At the natural end to our conversation, I pull up the group chat with Marisol and Sophie.

Me: Okay. It's not just a crush. I definitely like him 😳
Marisol: GIRL WE KNOW
Sophie: 🍑🍑🍑
Marisol: Tell us all about it when we go dress-shopping!!!
Marisol: Or else 🔪

I use the rest of my study period to send emails, including the one I promised to Tío Sebbie, and try to tie up a few loose ends for the carnival and dance before getting ready to meet my friends. We're going to the really nice shopping center a few towns away, so I'm not convinced I'll be able to find any dresses in my size (or in my price range), but that won't stop me from tagging along. We're hoping to each find something retro to go with the theme of the dance.

As the three of us bob in and out of stores, Marisol fills us in on debate club and the latest annoying thing Natalia did. Sophie shares more details about that winter internship in Paris. And I fill them in on my day with Isaiah—but not just the day itself. The feelings. The glances. The touches. And the lamenting that it's *just not fair* that I've finally accepted my crush on him and he's taken by someone else.

"He was mine first," I half joke, half whine while browsing through a section of peach-colored dresses. Is this because I have peach emojis on the brain?

Because let's not, brain.

I admire a flowing gold-and-ivory gown with a plunging neckline and internally groan when I check the price tag. Add it to the growing list of pieces I've looked at that either didn't fit or I couldn't afford, like the emerald-green lace dress with a sweetheart neckline that I felt was cover-of-a-book gorgeous.

In this fat body of mine, good dresses are hard to come by—and they're usually priced way above straight-size options.

I've saved up a decent amount from my job, but clearly not enough.

"That's not how that works. You can't claim someone just because you dated them first," Sophie reminds me.

"Rory Gilmore did," I pout.

"Rory Gilmore also stole a yacht and all she got was community service," Marisol says. "White people shit."

"Fine," I sigh, riffling through some other dress options, only half looking.

Sophie stands back and holds up an ice-blue fitted dress with elf sleeves. "What do you think of this color?"

Marisol wrinkles her nose. "Don't you want something sexier?"

"I want something my parents will let me leave the house in." Sophie sighs. "They've been really on my case lately. I came home two minutes late for curfew the other night and they immediately blamed Noah and said if this keeps up, I can't see him on weeknights anymore. Yet if they had bothered to let me explain, they'd know I was late because Noah stopped to help a baby raccoon out of the road on the drive home."

"Noah's a real Snow White, huh?" Marisol jokes.

Sophie scowls. "That's not the point, but yeah, he kind of is!"

Sensing that a quip was maybe not the right move, Marisol's face softens. "I'm sorry, Soph. That really sucks."

I nod. "It's totally unfair. You deserve a little trust from them. You've never done anything to make them think otherwise."

"Yeah, but I'm their precious little girl." She crosses her arms. "Why do they have to be so overprotective?"

"It can be a hard habit to break," I say. "I just learned that the hard way with Lily. Maybe you should talk to them."

Sophie makes a face. "Yeah, right. So, anyway, this is a no?"

"I actually really like it," I offer. "That color would look beautiful on you."

"And shoulders are sexy," Marisol adds.

Pleased, Sophie adds the dress to the growing pile she'd like to try on. Marisol's selection looks a lot smaller, though I realize that's just because there seems to be way less material on the dresses she wants to try on, and I love that for her.

"Should we head to the fitting room?" Sophie asks.

"Let's do it." Marisol eyes my empty arms and gives me a quizzical look. "You didn't find anything?"

"Oh, no. Not really. Everything has been a little expensive," I admit.

For some reason, it's a little easier to share that reason than to tell my friends that hardly any of these dresses come in my size.

"Nothing says you can't try things on anyway." Marisol winks at me.

She's not wrong, so I grab the dress I'd been eyeing, following Sophie's lead toward the fitting room toward the back of the store. We each disappear behind our respective doors, slipping out of our clothes and into our dresses.

I pin my hair up on my head with a clip, a few curls escaping and cascading along my neck, and then turn around to look in the mirror. It fits pretty well, actually, though the chest is a little too big. There's a slit that travels all the way up my leg that I hadn't noticed when it hung on the hanger and, honestly, this dress on this new, soft body of mine looks *good*.

"Okay, let's all come out on three?" Marisol calls. "One… two…three!"

I dramatically swing open the door to my dressing room and pose. Sophie lets out a squeal and when I see her in an olive-green silk halter dress I have to squeal right back. She looks elegant and beautiful.

"We look so hot!" Marisol practically yells. The shimmery, fitted jumpsuit in ruby red ties at her neck and flares at the ankles. When she twirls around, it's backless and sheer magnificence on her.

"*Okay*, Selena!" Sophie gushes, before pointing at me. "And *you* look like pure magic."

I take in our reflection in the mirrors. "God, we really do look amazing."

"Selfies?" Sophie asks.

"Obviously!" Marisol grabs her phone and starts to pose us. Dozens of photos and dresses later, Sophie and Marisol have successfully settled on their final looks: the first outfits they tried on.

We decide to get some celebratory boba tea and people-watch from the window of the tea shop, which offers a perfect view of downtown. Everything among the three of us has felt so easy and normal that it occurs to me that now *might* just be the right time to tell my friends why I disappeared this summer. I can't keep it a secret forever—nor do I want to. Not anymore.

I clear my throat. "So...I have to tell you guys something."

"Is it that you're going to take me up on my offer to put that dress on Robert's credit card?" Marisol asks, referring to her stepdad. He's incredibly generous and kind. And also superrich. "Because girl, you looked like a movie star."

I laugh a little. "No, it's not that. But thank you again."

Sophie puts down her drink, as if sensing that what I might say next is a little serious. "What is it?"

"This is really weird to share," I say, as if they might need a warning.

Marisol gives me an encouraging smile. "You know you can tell us anything."

I nod. "You're right. Okay, so...you know how I was kind of MIA over the summer?"

"Uh, yeah. At one point, we thought you ran away to marry Aiden or something." Marisol pretends to gag. "Thank God *that* wasn't the case."

"Yes, of course, and we missed you," Sophie says. "Did something happen?"

"Sort of. I started having all of these things happening to my body. Like, missed periods and...I don't know. Losing my hair and stuff. I started getting fatter." Marisol reaches out to put her hand on mine as I go on. "It was a lot of things all at once and, anyway, Abuela took me to the doctor and I got diagnosed with this thing called polycystic ovarian syndrome—PCOS. It's this really infuriating syndrome where, like, your body makes extra male hormones and these cysts form on your ovaries."

"Whit..." Sophie's face is gentle with sympathy as she speaks. "I'm so sorry."

"Oh, querida," Marisol murmurs. "We had no idea."

I don't know why, but the tenderness in their voices makes my eyes prick with tears. I swallow. "I didn't *want* you to have any idea. So I just kind of went away. I was embarrassed, really. About everything happening. And, honestly, I was really frustrated, too. When I finally got the diagnosis of PCOS, part of me was relieved to finally have a name for all these symptoms I'd been experiencing, but the other part was just so angry, especially because there's really no research or cure for it. I just have to learn to manage it and deal."

"Ugh, that's bullshit," Marisol says. "I'm so sorry that the medical industry has failed you like that."

Sophie nods, her hand joining Marisol's. "You deserve better."

"We all do," I say, nodding, too. I sniffle and wipe at the corner of my eye, but not because I'm sad. It's because I'm so relieved to have finally spoken this out loud and I'm grateful to have been heard in such an open and empathetic way by two people who mean so much to me. "Thanks, guys. I'm sorry I didn't tell you sooner."

"Don't apologize for that. Nobody tells you how hard it can be to admit chronic illnesses," Sophie says. "There is all this shame associated with it for no reason. Like, it's fine to break an arm or whatever because everyone knows that heals, but when you're sharing something you'll deal with forever, people get really weird about it. I feel the same way whenever I tell people I have type one diabetes."

I've seen firsthand how weird people are when Sophie has shared that, even people who are so nosy they feel totally fine loudly asking, "What's that?" and touching her insulin pump. It always makes my blood boil. Marisol has cussed out more than one person for their crassness.

As if hearing my thoughts, Marisol adds, "*Fuck* those people." She turns to me. "And I will kick anyone's ass if they have something to say about you. You know that."

I smile at her. "I do know that. Thanks, Sol. Honestly, just having you both know feels like a huge weight off my shoulders."

"We'll always have your back," Sophie says.

I pick up my boba tea and hold it in the air. "Cheers to that."

When I come home from dress-shopping empty-handed, Abuela promises she'll take me and Lily shopping at a different store—a better one, she insists—so we can find something.

As much as I want Fall Fest to be here, I also don't want to rush toward it—I want to savor the anticipation of it. Though there are still some logistics to sort through, Ms. Bennett has been great about keeping us on track, and the team Isaiah and I work with have been busting their asses to get vendors paid and invoices tracked.

I'm feeling good.

But I'd be feeling a lot better if I had a date and a dress.

Chapter Thirty-Three

Fall Fest has been keeping Isaiah, me, and the entire committee massively busy.

Everly took on the task of working with McNally's Farm. They've offered to donate an obscene number of pumpkins for our pumpkin-carving contest on Monday.

Leilani volunteered to organize the delivery and setup of the hay bales so Tuesday's corn maze races can happen.

Though they're not officers, Sophie and Marisol are helping with the Fall Feast on Wednesday—mostly because Noah is part of our school's culinary program. There are a lot of details to sort, and I don't envy them.

Finally, Hudson has taken on the bonfire, slated to happen on Thursday on the west lawn of the school. (Admittedly, Hudson said he wanted that for the chance to flirt with firefighters.)

And all of us are pitching in to help with the pep rally, the carnival, and the homecoming dance, since these huge events bookend the week and require the most work. We have to do things like manage deliveries from May Flowers and Santiago's Orchard, pick up Fall Fest cookies from Petey's Sweeties, and confirm so (!) many (!) things (!) with Wild Amusements, a local rental company that helps pull off elaborate events like the carnival.

At least the football game is handled by athletics, thank God.

For today's agenda, though, Isaiah and I are taste-testing caramel apples in the school kitchen to determine which flavors we should offer as part of the carnival. Did we volunteer for one of the easiest assignments? Yes. But have we also been working our butts off on everything else? Yes. So don't we kind of deserve something simple and tasty?

The two of us spend our lunch break in the culinary arts classroom, wearing black aprons alongside Noah, who graciously volunteered to help us.

"All right. So. I've got you two all set up with everything you need." Noah points at a glass bowl beside a bag of caramels and some sugar for melting. Next to that, he's set out an assortment of toppings, like sprinkles, different types of nuts, and chocolate chips. Isaiah and I are supposed to choose which toppings work best. "Utensils are over there. Bowls are on the stovetop. Skewered apples are already chilled in the fridge." He motions behind us.

"This is some serious service. No wonder Sophie's into you," I tease.

Noah lets out a laugh. "I aim to please."

Isaiah nods. "Yeah, thanks for doing this, man. So, can we just…do our thing?"

"Go for it. Just make sure you wash everything and clean your station when you're all done. I'm actually going to duck out and grab lunch with my girl," Noah says. "Assuming you guys aren't going to get into any trouble."

"We'll be perfect little angels," I promise.

Noah unties his apron and slips it off. "I'd expect nothing less. I'll be back after lunch to check on you." He walks toward the door and hangs his apron on one of the hooks. "Don't make a mess, okay? Mr. Elder will kill me."

"Throw caramel all over the walls. Got it," Isaiah teases.

"Don't even joke," Noah scolds.

"Tell Sophie we said hi!" I call after him, and he gives us both a wave as he slips out the door.

"Okay, so…what do we do first?" Isaiah asks.

I reach for a piece of paper lying on the counter. "Looks like Noah left us instructions."

Isaiah leans closer to me to take a look. " 'Step one: melt the caramel,' " he reads. Then he looks at me. "That's it?"

"I don't know how, do you?" I sigh. "To Google."

Isaiah takes the lead as I read out instructions for him to follow. It seems simple enough to microwave the caramel in thirty-second increments, then mix in some salt and heavy cream. I watch Isaiah's muscles flex as he expertly whips the ingredients together.

Yes, I'm totally ogling.

He proudly holds up the bowl for me to see. "Look how good this looks. I'm basically a chef now."

"Basically," I agree, grabbing the chilled apples from the fridge and bringing them over to the counter. "Ooh, Noah was meticulous with these skewered apples."

"What a talented dude."

I slide the tray onto the counter. "Next, we dip."

The two of us work together, me calling out instructions and Isaiah following along dutifully. Before long, we have six beautifully coated caramel apples—one with nuts, one plain, one with a dash of salt, one with chocolate chips, one with sprinkles, and one with crushed pretzels.

I choose to sample the plain one, while Isaiah goes for the one with pretzels. We bring our apples together and cheers them as if they're drinks, then bite.

The caramel is still warm, so it's at once decadent, gooey, and salty-sweet. The Granny Smith apple just beneath offers a tart contrast, making for the perfect bite.

"That's delicious," I say between bites. "I've never had a caramel apple before!"

"What?!" Isaiah asks. "You gave me so much shit for never

going apple-picking and now you drop the bomb that you've never eaten a caramel apple?"

"I mean, I've had caramel and apples together before, but not like this." I lick my finger. "I don't even need to taste the other type of apple. This is the clear winner."

Isaiah nods. "I'm with you. I've never really liked the regular candy apples, honestly. But here. Try this." He holds his apple out to me.

I let out a laugh, not sure if he's messing with me. "Really?"

"You'll like it. I promise."

At his gentle urging, I lean forward to take a small bite, my heart starting to beat faster. Something about leaning in to take a bite while it's just the two of us in this room feels so...I don't know. Intimate? He watches while I chew, waiting for me to say something.

The salt from the pretzel adds an extra element. "That's so good," I murmur, meeting his gaze.

He tilts his head to the side. "Isn't it?"

The sudden urge to get on my tiptoes and kiss him overcomes me. I shouldn't find any bit of this romantic—it's the middle of a Tuesday, we're in a classroom, and we're doing what's essentially free labor for the school.

And yet.

His hands are still near my face, and I can practically feel heat emanating off his body. I watched as he flexed his muscles while stirring the caramel. We're sharing food.

I could do it. I could close the gap between us. I could pull him close. I could, if not for the bell.

"Shit. We should clean up," Isaiah says.

I let out a shuddering breath, tethering myself back to reality. "Definitely. Before Noah gets back."

And before I do something I can't take back.

Chapter Thirty-Four

It's proposal time for Marisol. Wednesday afternoon, as classes let out, I lead her to the courtyard where Ari (with the help of Sophie) has strung a sun-and-cloud garland between two trees and hung a sign painted in perfect calligraphy that reads MI LUZ DEL SOL—MY WORLD REVOLVES AROUND YOU.

Marisol squeals loudly when she sees how beautiful it looks, and even I have to gasp when Ari gets down on one knee and presents her with a golden crown that looks like the rays of a sun.

"My sun, my light, my love—will you join me at the Fall Fest?" Ari asks.

"Of course I will, babe!" Marisol squeals, pulling Ari to her feet and into a kiss.

Sophie and I cheer as Ari gingerly places the glittering gold crown on Marisol's head. It glints in the sun, as if she were born to wear it.

I'm beaming at them until I feel a familiar sensation, like I've just gotten my period—a reminder that my body calls the shots, not me.

Right now? *Seriously?*

With my friends in full celebration mode, I don't want to ruin this moment and instead excuse myself and rush off to the bathroom. In my panic, I grab nothing. Not my backpack with its emergency tampons and pads. Not my purse, which might have some change so I can buy some from the machine in the restroom. And, of course, thanks to one parent who took major offense to free period products being offered in *all* bathrooms in school, the school removed the items entirely.

In the stall, I survey the damage and see that bright red blood has already seeped into the seam of my underwear. Of course my first period in months is going to be the equivalent of a torrential downpour. With little choice, I wad up some toilet paper to create a makeshift pad until I can waddle to the nurse's office for a tampon.

As I wash my hands at the sink, the door to the restroom opens. Of all the hundreds of Elmwood students it could be, it's Destiny. Her microbraids are swept up into a half bun on top of her head and she's wearing a sporty T-shirt under some distressed overalls, which looks super cute.

I give her a tight-lipped smile. The kindness in the one she returns causes shame to leaden my chest. Maybe I shouldn't have been flirting so much with the guy she's talking to. Or dating? It's unclear, actually.

"Hi," she says brightly.

I toss my paper towel in the trash. "Hi. You're Destiny, right?" As if I haven't stalked her on social media.

She looks over at me. "Hi...Whitney, right?"

I nod. "Sorry to bother you, but do you happen to have an extra tampon on you?"

"Oh my God, girl, of course! Hang on." She reaches into the canvas bag slung over her shoulder and feels around until she finds what she's looking for. When her hand comes back out, she's holding a tampon, as promised.

I reach for it as if it's the most precious item in the world. "Thank you so, so, so much. You just saved my life."

She laughs at that. "It's no problem at all. We've *all* been there. You want me to check you?"

My gaze falls to the mustard-colored skirt I'm wearing. I would hope I didn't bleed through, but you never know. "Could you?"

"Of course!" Destiny says, and I turn around. "You're all good."

I breathe a sigh of relief, turning back to her. "And I'll be even better thanks to this." I smile at her—a real smile this time—grateful. "Thank you again. I owe you."

She waves a hand like it's nothing. "Don't even worry about it."

"I love your outfit, by the way."

At this, her face lights up. "I sewed it myself."

"What? That's amazing!" I gush.

"Thank you," she says, readjusting her bag on her shoulder. "I'll see you around?"

"Yeah, for sure!"

And then Destiny and her radiant kindness are gone, and I'm left feeling like a real piece of garbage for being so jealous of her.

Chapter Thirty-Five

Abuela has plans to meet up with her sisters for dinner and drinks, so it's just me and Lily. We decide to make the most of things by skipping a proper dinner, picking out snacks at the dollar store instead, and then spending the night watching old movies we loved when we were kids. I even rope her into watching an episode of *Gilmore Girls* with me.

When it ends and I push NEXT EPISODE without asking, Lily huffs. "I could be hanging out with Ruby, you know."

"And yet you're here with me, your amazing sister, watching her favorite TV show." I give her an exaggerated grin and she rolls her eyes. "So that's a no on another episode, huh?"

She crosses her arms. "What do you think?"

"Okay, fine." I turn off the television with a sigh. "What do you want to do instead?"

Lily thinks, and then her face goes bright. "Have you heard the new Intonation song?"

"What?!" I practically shout. "New song? Since when?"

Intonation has been broken up for years. How can they possibly have a new song? And how can I possibly not know about it?

Lily starts to get excited at my interest. "Yeah! Here, listen." She pulls out her phone and pushes a few buttons at the same time as I whip my own phone out and start hunting for information. I'm shocked and embarrassed I didn't know this new piece of information about the boys! I mean, yeah, I don't follow their every move like I used to, but I'll always love them.

Google tells me the group reunited for this new single, "Hope," as a one-time-only thing, in hopes of helping to raise money for charity.

I listen intently as it blares from Lily's phone, savoring the thrill of hearing their familiar voices singing something new.

"It's good, right?" Lily asks.

"It's amazing. I love it!" When the notes fade out, I jump to my feet. "Play it again!"

We dance along, trying to commit the lyrics to memory. When Spotify starts shuffling Intonation songs, we keep going, sing-screaming the words at the top of our lungs.

I almost miss the knock at the door. Figuring it's Abuela, having misplaced her keys at the bottom of her purse again, I twirl my way over to greet her.

But it's Isaiah who greets me on the other side, eyebrows raised in amusement.

"Isaiah!" I turn to Lily. "Can you pause that, please?"

"Don't break up the party on my account," Isaiah says with a laugh. "I *knew* you still had a thing for Rider."

"You got me," I joke, hoping it hides my embarrassment. "What're you doing here?"

Isaiah holds up a gigantic tinfoil tray. "Delivering pasteles. Mami wanted to repay your abuela for the mofongo. And maybe bribe her to give up the recipe."

"Pasteles? Those are no joke to make. Your mom must really want that recipe." I reach for the tray. "Abuela's not here right now, but I promise I'll ask her about it tonight and text you."

"Thank you. I can't take much more of Mami's nagging."

"Is that Isaiah?" Lily asks, coming to the door. "Hi!"

"Hey, Lily!"

"He brought us pasteles," I explain. "And you never greet *me* that happily."

She ignores me. "You want to come inside for a dance party?"

"I'm sure Isaiah is really busy, Lil."

"Actually, I'm not. And I would *love* to come inside for a dance party."

I raise my eyebrows at him. "You would?"

"Like that's so weird?" Isaiah steps into the house, shrugging off his coat and hanging it on one of the hooks by the door. "I have dance parties with my little sisters all the time. I'm great. Watch."

Lily hits play again and Isaiah dances freely and without hesitation. As it turns out, he's good—because apparently my heart needed another reason to crush on him. Isaiah is even content to sing along with Lily, too, and when she suggests they make another TikTok, he's game.

The notes of another one of Intonation's singles, "Easy," fill the room.

Sweatpants, messy bun,
I know I'm not the only one
Who sees how beautiful you are.
Yet somehow it's me you chose,
And my love for you, it grows,
Loving you (yeah), loving you is easy.

I perch on the couch, watching them and smiling to myself, before Isaiah invites me to join them and suddenly Lily's teaching us the choreography to the song that plays next.

Our dance party only comes to a halt when Lily gets serious about editing her TikTok.

"Come on," I say to Isaiah, nodding with my chin toward the kitchen. He follows. From the fridge, I unwrap three apple pastelillos Abuela and I made together earlier in the week. "Snack?"

He nods. "Please."

"Great." I place the pastries on a sheet in the toaster oven and turn it on. "They're better warm. Does your mom ever make these?"

Isaiah shakes his head. "She has in the past, but not often. She doesn't like baking very much."

"That's totally fair. We cheated with these and used frozen dough, but they're still delicious," I say. "Also, can I say that I'm a little jealous of how much my sister likes you? She was so excited when she realized it was you at the door!"

"I have that effect on people," he jokes.

I lean back against the counter and face him. "Well, I appreciate that you've been so kind to her. Thank you."

"Of course. Why wouldn't I be?"

"I don't know. People can sometimes be...weird about the fact that she has autism, you know? They don't know how to act around her. Or they baby her. Even *I* can sometimes be a little much with her. So it's nice that you're just you with her."

"Damn, what a shame," Isaiah says. "Lily's dope."

"I think so, too," I agree. A few minutes later, I ease the pastelillos out of the oven and onto three separate plates. "Any interest in eating these out on the porch? It'll let Lily edit her TikTok in peace."

He nods, reaching for one of the plates. "Okay, yeah. That sounds nice."

"Take two, and give one to Lily?" I suggest. "She won't yell at you for interrupting her since you're her new favorite."

His gentle laugh fills the kitchen and I laugh a little, too. He heads toward the living room, while I slip into a jean jacket and boots and linger by the door.

Isaiah proves he really is the favorite when he calls Lily's name and offers her the warmed pastelillo, complete with a dad joke about an apple—"An apple a day keeps the doctor away—as long as you throw it at them hard enough!"—and she laughs and thanks him for the treat instead of shooing him off with a threat like she would me.

When he joins me at the door, he does a little happy dance. "She likes me better than you."

I stick out my tongue. "Yeah, yeah."

Isaiah shoves his feet into his shoes and reaches for the door to open it for me. "It's only fair. Amaya and Gianna have not stopped asking when you'll come back. Well, okay, mostly Gianna, but still."

"Amaya is a tough one, but I will win her over." I settle into one of the chairs on the porch, propping my plate in my lap.

Isaiah closes the door behind us and grabs the seat next to mine. "We'll see about that."

"Whatever." I reach for my pastry, finally cool enough to touch, and hold it up to Isaiah. "¿Salud?"

He holds his up, too. "¡Salud!"

As we enjoy our pastelillos, I suddenly become hyperaware of the fact that Isaiah and I are hanging out, intentionally, just because. At that realization, my pulse quickens and I feel my senses sharpen. Do I look okay? Smell okay? How's my hair? I had been having an epic veg-out session followed by a dance party with Lily mere seconds before Isaiah showed up, and I didn't look in the mirror in between.

I can't sneak my phone out of my pocket without making it super obvious that I'm checking myself out, so I settle for smoothing my hair and hoping for the best.

"Damn, this is good," Isaiah murmurs.

"Told you it would be."

He puffs out his chest. "And *I* helped pick the ingredients. It's almost like I had a hand in making them."

"If that's what you've gotta tell yourself, sure," I joke.

"Well, you and Abuela are the real bakers here, right?" Isaiah asks.

"I helped with the filling a little."

"It's delicious." He pops the last bite into his mouth, chewing thoughtfully. "I would pay a lot for these, frozen dough or not. You should be a baker."

I giggle. "No way. I'm way too much of a control freak and I feel like baking requires a lot of trust in the oven, which I don't have." I take my last bite, too, dusting the crumbs off my fingers and putting my now-empty plate on top of Isaiah's. He sets them on the table between us. "I do think I want to be an occupational therapist, though. I'd love to work with kids and teens like Lily."

"That sounds really nice..." Isaiah shoves his hands into the pocket of the vintage Aaliyah hoodie he's wearing. "Although I have to admit I have no idea what an occupational therapist does."

"I didn't either until I started searching for jobs that let you work with people who have autism," I admit. "Occupational therapists work with people to help make their day-to-day lives a little better. They basically help them use whatever's around them to be successful."

"So, like, teaching people how to adapt to new situations?"

"Exactly like that! OTs can work with people who have illnesses, disabilities, whatever, and basically help them figure out tools to live their lives without the assistance of others," I explain. "I think I'd be good at it. I'm a control freak, yeah, but also obsessively observant and empathetic. Good with details, you know? And stubborn. So I wouldn't be deterred if we tried something and it didn't work right away."

Isaiah sits back in his chair, a thoughtful look coming over his face. "Yeah, I could see that. You'd actually be awesome at that."

I toy with a strand of hair that freed itself from behind my ear, suddenly feeling self-conscious. "Thanks. How about you? I mean, not that I believe in the whole we-are-our-occupations thing, but you have me curious."

He chuckles at that and stretches his long legs to push himself back in the chair so it rocks ever so gently. "Nah, I feel that. I think I want to teach."

"Yeah?"

"Yeah. I've told you about how I tutor kids in math and they're just incredible. They're so smart, and some of them barely even need my help—it's just that the system is built against them, you know? So they just need access and, like, someone to actually invest in them the same way wealthier towns invest in their students. It's bullshit the way everything is set up." Isaiah starts to rock a little faster in the chair. "The institutional racism is never more evident than in the way our public school systems are set up. The fact that property taxes fund public education means the system is absolutely rotten from the inside out—especially when you consider the fact that Black and brown folks have historically been barred from owning property and thus are less likely to have generational wealth."

Hearing him get so passionate about this is amazing. "Absolutely. It's awful," I agree.

"Yeah, I talk about this with my pops a lot. Our communities often get pushed into cities that don't have the right infrastructure to support them, so people work jobs that don't pay enough," he continues. "Meaning they can't live in wealthy areas. Meaning they can't build wealth. Meaning their kids can't get the education they deserve because the tax base isn't there. It's this messed-up cycle and it breaks my heart."

"It's horrible, and obviously a strategy to ensure that marginalized communities stay marginalized," I say. "It's hard to fight systemic injustices when you're just worried about putting food on the table."

Isaiah nods vigorously. "Exactly! I know I can't fix the system from the inside, but I just feel like if I can maybe be an example of an Afro-Latino teacher and show these kids what they're capable of, that might help in some way. I don't know." The fervor in his voice, mixed with his anger and frustration, makes it so that it takes everything in me not to reach out and take his hands. Isaiah looks over to me, his dark eyes meeting mine for just a moment before he quickly averts his gaze to his shoes. "Sorry. I didn't mean to do all that."

"I love a good rant. And you're absolutely right. The system is broken." I keep my voice gentle. "Someone like you could really make a difference."

"Maybe," he says, shrugging a shoulder.

"Really. You could. I can tell how much you care."

"Yeah, well. Someone has to." Isaiah sighs. "If I don't become a middle or high school teacher, then I think I'd still want to teach in some capacity. Maybe be an Afro studies professor or something. Do, like, a teaching and research combo."

"You'd be amazing at that, too."

He chuckles. "You're being suspiciously nice to me right now."

"Don't get used to it," I say with a laugh. "Whatever you choose, though, I know it'll be good."

"Thanks," he says. "I'm hopeful this Fall Fest stuff will help with my college applications when the time comes. I really owe Ms. Bennett for hooking me up."

"Is that why you joined?" I ask.

He nods. "Yeah. I mean, I tutor, yes, but I wanted a real leadership role on my résumé, and Ms. Bennett said she'd help." Isaiah smiles at me. "I didn't know I'd end up liking it so much."

"I'm glad you did."

"Oh, yeah?" He arches a brow. "Because I thought you were going to strangle me when she made the announcement that I'd be your number two."

I laugh at that. "But that's only because I *was* considering strangling you."

"Right, right."

"The good news is that our work seems to be paying off," I say.

"Yeah, people seem excited," Isaiah agrees. "The proposals have been getting wild this week!"

"Oh my God, I know! Did you catch Pilar Aguilar's? Her boyfriend hired a mariachi band!"

"Shit, I missed that. And how about you? You're going with your boy, right? Andrew?"

"Aiden?" I offer.

"Aiden, that's right."

I shake my head. "No, we've been broken up for a while."

Isaiah stops rocking his chair, surprised. "What? I had no idea. I'm sorry to hear that."

"I'm not. Not really, anyway. It was for the best. We weren't right for each other and, weirdly, I don't miss him." It's true. I haven't thought about Aiden in...well, since I saw he posted that photo of him and his new girlfriend? "So, yeah, I'm not going with anyone. Just Sol and Sophie—and their dates, of course. Will I be the fifth wheel? Yeah, sure. You could say that. Or! It's empowering and I'm bucking tradition!"

This makes Isaiah laugh. "I'm not going with anyone, either."

My hands fall to my lap in surprise. "Not Destiny?"

He furrows his brows. "Why would I be going with Destiny?"

I glance down, fiddling with one of the buttons on my jacket. "Aren't you guys dating? Or, like, I don't know. Talking or whatever."

"God, no. We're just friends." His voice has a slight edge to it.

"Oh, sorry," I say quickly. "I didn't know."

But then he looks over at me and his face softens. "It's all good. We do hang out, and—well, she's been wanting to try again. But I'm not interested. Not after everything."

I think back to what Camila told me when I was at their house, but don't press.

In the silence, Isaiah continues, "I didn't like who I became with her, you know? *She* was great—it was me. I just didn't feel like I could be myself when we were together. I was worried she wouldn't like me—the real me, whatever that means—so I kept trying to morph into whatever I thought she wanted." He shakes his head. "We're so much better as friends. I'm way more chill now." Then he breaks into a grin. "Plus, Destiny would never give me the Fall Fest proposal I deserve."

I return his grin. "So you want a *proposal*, then?"

"Why not? I think I deserve it after all my hard work," he teases. "And anyway, just to be clear: Things with Destiny are done. I've moved on."

"Oh, yeah?" I ask.

"Yeah." Isaiah clears his throat. "I, uh—I like someone else."

My gaze meets his and I swallow, hard, feeling the quickening *thump, thump, thump* of my heart beating in my ears.

But before I can ask, before I can think, before I can do or say anything, the bright flash of headlights is in my vision and I squint as an unfamiliar black SUV pulls into the driveway.

We weren't doing anything, but the two of us scramble to our feet as Abuela emerges from the back of the car, a wobble in her steps. It must've been a great night with her hermanas; she's totally tipsy. She slams the door and doesn't even realize we're on the porch until she's walking up the steps, and then she gasps.

"¡Ay, dios mío!" Her hand goes to her heart as she bursts into a fit of giggles. "You scared me."

"So sorry," Isaiah says.

At the same time, I laugh and say, "Sorry, Abuela. Fun night?"

"Sí, sí." She kisses my cheek and reaches out to pat Isaiah on the shoulder. "And now, I sleep. Buenos noches, queridas. Don't stay up too late."

Then she gives me a not-at-all subtle wink and moves past us to let herself into the house. Once the door is closed, Isaiah and I laugh, a little awkwardly.

"So, I should probably get going," Isaiah says, checking the time on his phone. "It's later than I thought it was."

I tuck my hands into my jacket. "Right. School tomorrow and all."

"Thanks for letting me hang out. And please say good night to Lily for me."

"I definitely will," I promise. "Thanks for delivering the pasteles. Given Abuela's state, I may not get that recipe tonight, but tomorrow for sure."

Isaiah chuckles. "Yeah, no worries."

"Great."

I expect Isaiah to move toward the stairs, but he doesn't yet. He just looks at me, like there's something he wants to say.

Hope sprouts up in my chest when he licks his lips and steps a little closer.

"I noticed something the other day, you know. At the apple orchard." His voice is soft, low.

"Yeah?" I ask, nearly in a whisper.

"Your hair..." He reaches out, his hand stopping just before touching a strand, hesitant, then gently taking a curl between his fingers and pushing it back behind my ear, sending a shiver down my spine. "It looks like an apple tree."

A giggle escapes my throat before I can stop it. "What?"

Isaiah shakes his head. "That came out wrong. I just meant...I can finally see why fall is so great. Your curls, the way they fall, how they kind of sway whenever there's a little bit of a breeze? It reminds me of those trees in the orchard. Beautiful, you know?" He pulls his hand back, though I wish he hadn't moved away from me at all. "Anyway. I should really go."

I want to utter something—*anything*—to convince him to stay. Put your hand back in my hair. Tell me more. Come close. Compare me to the earth. Touch more than my curls. *Kiss me.* Instead, when I find my voice, I simply say in a whisper, "Okay. Good night, Isaiah."

"Zay," he corrects. "Good night, Whitney."

Chapter Thirty-Six

What am I supposed to do with myself now?

That boy waltzes up to my house, brings pasteles, bonds with my little sister, dances to my favorite boy band, confirms he's over his ex, compares my hair to a tree (but, like, in a romantic way?), touches my curls, insists I call him my old nickname for him, and then has the absolute *nerve* to call me *Whitney.*

Curse you, Isaiah Ortiz. Because how am I supposed to sleep? Or do *any*thing except pine with my whole being?

He hardly touched me and my entire body feels like it's electric.

I'm pretty sure if Abuela's Lyft hadn't pulled into the driveway exactly when it had, Isaiah was going to say that he liked me.

And when he reached for my hair, I think he wanted to kiss me.

Or at least *I* wanted him to. With all my heart. I wanted Zay to pull me close and let me melt into him.

I'm a mess. I barely sleep. When morning comes, I wonder if I can avoid seeing Isaiah until my mind can catch up to the Zay-shaped hideaway my heart has run off to.

Unfortunately for my brain, it's Thursday, so we have a scheduled Fall Fest meeting. One way or another, I'm seeing the boy I can't stop thinking about.

That afternoon, I do my best to act normal around Zay and everyone on the committee. I can't lose focus on the Fall Fest—not when it's right here.

So, without fanfare, Isaiah and I return to our regular banter. We give an overview of final tasks. We hand out assignments. We review feedback, including a motion from Everly McDonnell to add a photo booth to the carnival. (Her aunt has a wedding photo booth business, so she has an in. Easy.) We review plans with Ms. Bennett. I call him Isaiah. He calls me Whit.

Before long, the meeting's over, and I'm rushing to a shift at Nature's Grocer, and Isaiah is scrambling to his tutoring gig.

It's almost like we can ignore the thing that nearly happened on the veranda.

Almost.

* * *

My weekend gets swallowed alive by work—first at the grocery store, and the next day at Abuela's shop, where I've been seriously slacking lately. In fact, I need to spend the whole day updating the books because of it. But that's okay. In the back room, I can avoid classmates I don't feel like talking to as they come and pick up the dresses and suits Abuela has tailored for them.

Homecoming and prom season make lots of work at El Coquí. It's a full load for Abuela, Lily, and me, and the only respite comes the next day—Lily and I have the day off from school for Indigenous Peoples' Day—when we're on the hunt for formal wear.

"I'm so sorry we haven't gotten around to shopping until now, nenas," Abuela says as she drives us across town. "Claro, I would've just made you something myself if it wasn't busy season." She sighs.

"Don't be sorry, Abuela. We're going to find something today and it'll be great," I assure her.

"Yeah, it'll be fine," Lily echoes.

"Yo no se..." Abuela mutters, mostly to herself.

"You know what might make Abuela feel better, Lil? How about that new Intonation song?"

"On it."

Moments later, the sounds of our favorite boy band fill the car and Abuela is tapping her hands on the steering wheel in time with the song. When Abuela's favorite, Henry, croons with a solo, her cheeks stretch into a smile. "¡Mi cariño!"

As we pull into the shop Abuela has mentioned, Lily claps her hands in excitement. I join her, because this *is* exciting! It's finally hitting me that I'll be going to homecoming with my little sister.

The sign on the window of the store reads NEVA'S—it's a second-hand clothing shop owned by an old friend of Abuela's. Inside, Abuela greets Neva, a short, plump woman, in Spanish and kisses both of her cheeks. Neva has her short caramel-colored hair pulled back into a low bun, and wears mauve lipstick to match her wrap dress. They go back and forth for a minute before Neva pulls out measuring tape and tugs at the shoulder of my pea coat.

"Off," she instructs.

I look over to Abuela, who shoots me a look that says I'd best not argue. I shrug off my jacket and hand it to Abuela, letting Neva take her measurements of my body. She does the same for Lily and then starts buzzing around the store, draping items over her forearms.

"Doesn't she need to know what we like?" I ask.

Abuela shakes her head. "Not yet. She does measurements and then picks things she thinks will work. If you're not happy, she lets you browse. But people are rarely unhappy with what she chooses."

The three of us watch as Neva starts fitting rooms for me and for Lily. She motions us over once she's collected a few items for us each to try on.

I slip into the first item Neva has hung—an A-line, off-the-shoulder dress in lilac. I like it except for these tufts of fabric that are intended to loop around my upper arms as if to say, *Please ignore this fat part right here.*

The second option I nix almost immediately. It's a lovely shade of sage but the cut is not for me.

It's the third dress I love: a sleeveless ball gown with beaded lace appliqué reminiscent of old Hollywood. The color of white magnolias, the tulle stretches to the floor. It makes me feel like a princess.

I open the door and step out of the dressing room to show Abuela. Her gasp is as big as her heart, her brown eyes going wide. "¡Que bella! Turn around," she says, twirling her fingers in a circular motion. When I do, she chants, "Model! Model!"

I laugh and turn toward the three-way mirror to take in my reflection. It does look good on me, a kiss of winter in a gown.

Neva comes up behind me and unclasps the clip that's holding my messy bun. My hair cascades down my back and I reach up to fluff the curls. Neva disappears and returns with long sapphire-colored gemstone drop earrings and a matching barrette, which she uses to pin back the hair on the left side of my face.

"You like?" she asks.

I hold up the earrings, admiring my reflection, and nod. "It's beautiful. Thank you."

A pleased smile comes across Neva's face, and she goes over to Lily's door to check on her. Abuela comes up to me in the mirror and helps straighten the bottom of the dress.

"Do you really like it?" she asks, keeping her voice low.

"I like it," I say firmly with a nod.

What I don't say: this dress is lovely in all the right ways and I should absolutely adore it, but it doesn't feel like the One. It checks all the right boxes, though: it's affordable, it fits, and it makes me feel pretty. So it's good; great, even. Just not *perfect*. You know? And even though I've been trying to focus less on perfection, part of me still secretly hoped to find it in a homecoming dress.

Abuela squeezes my shoulder. "Bueno."

Neva's voice interrupts us. "Mira."

We turn toward her and she pulls open the door to Lily's

dressing room. Out Lily steps in a plum-colored two-piece velvet suit. With a simple collared white shirt beneath the jacket, the pant legs cuffed once, and her short, curly hair held in the same clip Neva used for my own hair, a few tendrils framing her face, she is transformed.

Abuela gasps once more at the sight of Lily, and tears spring to my own eyes. Sweet Liliana Margaret Rivera looks so grown-up.

"Lily, you look *beautiful*," I choke out.

At the crack in my voice, Abuela rushes over to me and swats at my arm. "You don't cry! Now I'll cry." And she wipes at her own eyes.

"*Guys,*" Lily whines.

"You just look so...mature," Abuela says wistfully.

I nod, taking Abuela's hand in mine. "This suit is perfect."

Lily looks down. "Think Ruby will like it?"

"She'll *love* it, mija." Abuela reaches for Lily's hand with her free one, pulling her to where we're standing.

We look up at our reflections in the mirror, my eyes still wet with tears, and just like that, the Rivera girls are ready for Fall Fest.

* * *

That night, I find myself thinking of all the reasons Fall Fest is so special to me. I thought I had a sense of it when I originally made it such a huge part of my vision for senior year and—let's be real—my identity. But I realize now that my fervor for this dance boils down to something simple: love.

It was love that brought Abuela and Abuelo together on that night and made us a family. Though our tiny three-person family is probably not what Abuela had ever envisioned, it's ours.

So maybe I want to start focusing on the love I'm fortunate enough to have in my life.

I use a fresh page to list the five most important people in my life right now.

Lily
Abuela
Marisol
Sophie
Zay

I want to find one meaningful gift for them between now and homecoming. And, for the first time in my life, I have the money to make it happen.

Because we went secondhand for my dress and Neva gave us a great deal, it was much cheaper than I thought it would be and Abuela insisted on paying. All I'd been saving from Nature's Grocer can now be given back to those who mean the most to me. I'll use some of it on my people and the rest will go back to Abuela to help us build a cushion so perhaps she doesn't have to work so much.

I fill each page in my notebook with possible ideas. By the end of the night, I've narrowed my list.

For Lily, I want to track down a pair of earrings that match what Lucas was wearing in her favorite music video. They're silver, gem-encrusted snakes. When Lily first saw them, she flipped out over how cool they were. In the music video, Lucas wore only one earring, so a pair will be enough for Lily and Ruby to share. Sentimental *and* romantic.

For Abuela, I order the same Intonation T-shirt that Lily and I already own. More importantly, I vow to give her a day off. She deserves time to rest more than anyone, especially after this busy season. I'll work with her sisters to gift her a day of pampering, and I'll happily request the time off work and run El Coquí that day.

For Marisol and Sophie, I commission a high-quality print of one of the photos a generous stranger took of us at the Knoll. As we were posing, I tripped and the three of us burst into laughter. Even though we weren't perfectly posed, the person who took our photo took our picture anyway, and I'm so glad they did. This is one of my favorites.

Lastly, for Zay, using all the courage I can muster, I decide that I'll give him his big, public proposal.

I just need a little help to make everything happen.

Chapter Thirty-Seven

First thing the next morning, I text Marisol and Sophie and ask them to meet up with me in the courtyard before school. When they arrive, I'm toting their favorite warm drinks—vanilla latte for Sophie, black coffee for Marisol, PSL for me—and a mischievous smile.

Marisol immediately narrows her eyes at me. "What are you sucking up for?"

I put my hand to my heart, feigning shock. "Can't a girl just buy her best friends some no-strings-attached coffees?"

"I'm fine with that." Sophie grabs hers and blows before taking a sip.

"But...I mean. Since you *are* my best friends and all, it would be great if you wouldn't mind helping me with something."

Marisol points a finger at me. "I knew it!"

I reach for her hand and pull it closer. "Ooh, I love your nails!" They're plain at the base but the ends are rounded and accented with gold glitter polish.

"As much as I hate to give my sister credit for anything, Natalia did them when she was visiting this weekend," Marisol says. "And, you know, we actually kind of got along? She even defended me to Mami."

My jaw drops. "Whoa! That's...a first?"

"Yep. It was so weird! But maybe going away to college is making her into a decent human," Marisol says, laughing. Then she turns to me. "But don't change the subject! You do want something from us."

"Totally guilty," I admit. "But hear me out! I really want to do something nice for Lily and Abuela ahead of homecoming as a way of celebrating them and all we've been through—and just to let them know I love them."

"Aww, that's so sweet," Sophie gushes.

"Thank you! I have my tías helping me with organizing a relaxing girls' day for Abuela, but for Lily, I really want to get her these replica earrings that Lucas from Intonation wore in one of their music videos. I stayed up late last night searching everywhere for just the right ones—you know how particular she can be—and I finally found some."

"That's great! But where do we come in?" Marisol asks.

I frown. "The earrings are at this vintage store an hour away." I grab my phone and pull up the store's Instagram feed. "See? They list all their items online but you have to get them in person. I DM'd the owner begging her to hold them for me and she said she would, but only until the store closes at six tonight. So...I was hoping you guys might be down for a road trip after the Fall Fest meeting today?"

"Easiest favor ever," Sophie says. "I'm in!"

Marisol grins. "When it comes to shopping, you *know* you never have to ask me twice. Let's do it!"

* * *

I see Isaiah for the first time since the almost-whatever-happened, at Tuesday's Fall Fest meeting.

Between that loaded moment and the decision to ask him to be my date to homecoming, I realize I have absolutely no idea how to act around him anymore.

Do I go back to calling him Zay? Do I flirt openly and with

reckless abandon? Do I play hard to get? Do I throw caution to the wind, grab him, and kiss him (but ask for consent first, of course)?

Instead, plagued by the overthinking goddesses, I greet him with a head nod, a casual "Hey," and then I...hold my hand up for a high five?

Confusion washes over his face, but he nonetheless returns the high five.

"Hey back," he says. "Since when do we high-five?"

I shrug. "I'm trying something new."

He blinks at me and says nothing for a second. "All right. So, did you get a chance this weekend to reach out to Wild Amusements to double-check we're all set for the carnival? I didn't hear from you."

There's a slight edge to his voice when he says that last thing.

I mean, yes. There were moments when I could've texted. But he could've, too! I had no idea what to say. I couldn't exactly text, Hi, I think you like me, and I like you too, but just wait for me, because I have a plan, okay? I swear.

At least I made time to call Wild Amusements, though.

"I did! And, yes, sorry, this weekend was super packed. I worked at Nature's Grocer and Abuela's shop and we had to get dresses for homecoming, so. It's just been really chaotic," I say.

He nods, suddenly looking a little embarrassed. "No worries— you don't need to explain. I just realized that what I said came out a little harsh. I just..." His voice trails off, like there's something he wants to say. Instead, he shakes his head. "Never mind."

"Oh. Okay."

And our conversation ends.

* * *

Less than one hour after that high five, Sophie, Marisol, and I are cruising down the highway toward the vintage shop so I can score those earrings for Lily. I DM the shop owner to let her know I'm on my way, and I even take a picture of us in the car and send it to her as proof.

It's a little much, but I want to ensure she knows I'm serious. I need those earrings!

"Are you guys getting excited for Fall Fest?" I ask from the back seat once I hit send.

"Beyond excited," Sophie says. "I finally put my foot down with my parents and I got them to extend my curfew to one o'clock that night."

"Oh my gosh, Soph! That's huge!"

"And! I may have floated the idea of the internship in Paris…"

"Holy shit," Marisol says. "What did they say?"

"After my mom stopped crying—" Sophie begins.

I wince at that. Oh, jeez.

"—she said we could discuss. Which means it's at least a possibility!" She practically beams at me. "I'm so excited I took your advice and talked to them."

"Our little Sophie is growing up," Marisol teases. "But I'm so proud of you. I know that must've been really hard!"

"It was, but I told them I needed them to trust me and have faith that I'll do the right thing," she explains. "I feel like I really got through to them and we might really make some progress. I'm just sorry I didn't try sooner."

"God, that's amazing. Good for you," I say. "Maybe by the time prom rolls around in the spring, we can actually get a hotel together."

Sophie wrinkles her nose. "Let's see if they say yes to Paris first. I'll know in just a few weeks if I've been accepted!"

"And please don't rush prom! It's not even homecoming yet." Marisol starts rubbing her temples. "I'm getting a headache just thinking about all the college applications we'll have to fill out."

I reach into the front seat and give Marisol a sympathetic pat on the shoulder. "Your mom is still being impossible, huh?"

"Don't even get me started! Mami and I fight practically every day about it because she thinks my plan of going to State means I'll never get into law school. It's all about the prestige with her." Marisol sighs. "But whatever."

"I'm sorry, Sol," Sophie says. "That really sucks."

"Seriously. Sorry not everyone wants to get into mountains of debt." I shake my head. "It's so messed up. And I'm sorry I even brought up prom, really. I've just been getting so sentimental knowing this is our senior year. Everything feels so big, you know? Like what if this is the last road trip we take together before we go to different schools?"

Sophie casts a sharp glance back at me. "Don't even say that, Whit!"

"You're the one who started this whole what-if scenario way back at the pumpkin patch!" I argue. "Now I can't stop thinking about whether every little thing we do might be the last."

"We have plenty of time for road trips," Marisol cuts in.

"You know what I mean! I'll just miss you guys," I say. "I'll miss this."

Marisol turns around in her seat and puckers her lower lip. "Staaaahp! You're making me sad."

"Me too. I don't want to think about not being with you guys all the time." There's a hitch in Sophie's voice. "Great, now I'm crying."

"If you cry, I'll cry," I say, feeling tears start to well.

"You guys! It's literally October!" Marisol shouts. "We're not doing this yet. I refuse." She pulls out her phone and connects it to Sophie's radio. "Bad Bunny has a new song out. So we're going to listen to that instead. Okay? And by the time we're done, all of this sad shit is going to evaporate from the car. You hear me?"

Sophie glances into the rearview mirror and makes eye contact with me and we both burst out laughing at the seriousness in Marisol's voice.

"Yes, Mom," Sophie teases.

"Repeat after me: No crying allowed when listening to Bad Bunny," Marisol says. "Say it!"

"No crying allowed when listening to Bad Bunny," Sophie and I say in terrible, disjointed unison.

Marisol rolls her eyes. "Pitiful. Again! And mean it this time!"

"Okay, ready?" I ask.

Sophie nods, and we both shout, *"No crying allowed when listening to Bad Bunny!"*

"Good," Marisol says. "Now, was that so hard?"

Chapter Thirty-Eight

We score the earrings for Lily, and I even pick up a necklace I think Abuela will like. It feels nice to be able to cross two things off my list. More importantly, I have the *best* time with Marisol and Sophie.

The next part of my plan involves a little sneaking around. In order to execute my vision for Isaiah's perfect proposal, I need to enlist the help of his friends.

Thankfully, his best friend is in my math class.

While our teacher is lecturing up by the board, I slip Jay a note:

> I have a huge crush on Isaiah and he told me he wants a big proposal for homecoming, which I'm down to do, but I need your help. You in?
> CIRCLE: Yes / No / Girl, you wild.
> —Whit

I watch the back of his head while he slowly unfolds the crinkled paper. He lets out a little chuckle, shakes his head, then leans over the note, refolds it, and very carefully drops it over his left shoulder onto my desk.

When I open it, I see that Jay has circled both *Yes* and *Girl, you wild*, which is absolutely fair. I return the note to him with my cell phone number and ask him to text me when he can so we can figure out next steps without making Isaiah suspicious.

The text comes next period.

Jay: should we have code names?

Me: I think that's only fair in a situation like this.

Me: What do you want yours to be?

Jay: gossip girl

I have to stifle my laugh when I read his reply, lest I disappoint Ms. Bennett (I'm so sorry, Ms. Bennett, for not paying attention—I swear this is for a good reason!).

Me: I'll be Veronica Mars

Jay: nice

Jay: hang on

A few minutes later, I get a different text from Jay in a new group thread with two numbers I don't recognize, but who I can only assume are Malik and Daniel.

Jay: aight, identify yourselves

Malik: Malik

Jay: by your code name man, cmon bro

Malik: My bad

Malik: Hannah Montana

Daniel (I assume): I feel a vision coming on ... Raven Baxter

Me: Veronica Mars

Jay: and we already know im gossip girl, obviously

Jay: ok i showed them the note

Jay: what do u need??

Me: Can you teach me how to become a better skateboarder in, like ... a week?

Daniel: 💀

Me: I KNOOOOW

Me: But here's what I'm thinking: big proposal at the football game next Friday?

Me: I skateboard in around halftime (hopefully with you guys as backup if you're going)

Me: Sign says something cute I haven't come up with yet???

Malik: 😴

Me: Too much?

Jay: no no no

Jay: well, ya

Jay: but he'll like it

Daniel: You want to practice after school today? We were going to the skate park anyway.

Me: No Isaiah, right?

Daniel: He's tutoring tonight, so you're good

Me: I'm in!!!

Me: Thank you

Me: Oh and also, if you tell anyone, I WILL have my bff Marisol's tía, who is a bruja, curse you for life

Jay: we're not saying shit, promise

Malik: Later, Veronica

Chapter Thirty-Nine

I wish I could say that after an afternoon with Jay, Malik, and Daniel, I had unearthed some secret talent for skateboarding. Alas, the only thing I managed to discover was how uncoordinated I am. I fell more times than I care to admit and the most humbling part was that I did it while wearing Daniel's little brother's *Paw Patrol* helmet.

But they reminded me that that was all part of learning and that all I needed was more confidence, which would come with more practice. If I can just figure out how to stay on the skateboard without falling flat on my face, I'll be happy.

"Hi, nena," I hear Abuela's voice say to Lily, who's watching TV in the living room. "Where's your sister?"

I'm lying in bed working on my English homework (or at least trying to, but Patch keeps climbing onto my keyboard as I try to type because it's so warm).

"I'm in here!" I call.

"Can you come here? I have a surprise for you!"

"Coming!" I give up my fight with Patch and let him settle on my keyboard, heading to the living room. Lily's eyes follow me as I enter, her brows raised with expectation, and Abuela is practically beaming at me. An El Coquí garment bag is draped over Abuela's arm. Okay. They're up to *something*. "What's up?"

"Well, you know how I've been working a lot lately," Abuela begins.

I nod. "Yeah, it's busy season."

"It is, sí. Pero, I've also been working on something for you."

My eyes widen. "For me?"

"You're going to loooove it," Lily sings.

I feel myself smiling at the palpable thrill in the air. "What is it?"

Abuela pushes the garment bag toward me. "Here!" I take it from her, confused.

"Open it!" Lily urges.

I hold the hanger in one hand and unzip the bag with the other to reveal orange satin fabric that looks familiar. My eyes dart to Abuela, then back to the bag, which I unzip faster.

"Is this...?" I ask.

"That was mine," Abuela says, and when I look at her, her eyes are wet with tears. "And now it's yours."

I swallow hard, gingerly lifting the dress in the air to get a better look. "But Abuela! How?"

Gone are the lace trim, the skirt that dusted the floor, and the gigantic bow. What's left is a simple, stunning sleeveless knee-length A-line dress. Without the lace accents, the pleated skirt is elegant, the orange fabric is vibrant, and the bell sleeves are ripply and free.

"Try it on," Lily says.

"Can I?" I ask Abuela.

"It's yours!" she reminds me.

I rush to my room and rip off my clothes, slipping into this dress—Abuela's dress, *my* dress—holding my breath the entire time. How did she let it out so that it fits me? How did she manage to get rid of all the worst parts of it and make it something entirely new and yet still perfectly Abuela's? Is this what has kept her so busy these last few nights?

When I turn to see myself in the mirror, I let out a small gasp. It's absolutely, positively perfect, cascading over my soft curves, the bodice nipping at my waist. The color is a sliver of sun against my skin and it fits like it was meant for me...because, I realize, it was.

I open the door to my room to find Abuela and Lily standing, waiting. Their faces light up with joy as they take in the sight.

"What do you think?" I ask, smoothing the fabric over my hips.

"Nena..." Abuela's voice cracks, her eyes soft as she looks me over. "It's perfect on you."

"I think so, too. Oh, Abuela. I love it!" I throw my arms around her neck and squeeze her. "I love it so, so much. Thank you." Her arms wrap around me and she rubs my back, and I find myself so overcome with emotion that I start to cry. "I love you. Thank you."

"I love you, mija." Abuela pulls back and cups my face in her hands. "You deserve this."

"You do. And if you were worried about it going to you instead of me, don't. I wouldn't have been caught dead in that dress in any form," Lily deadpans. "No offense."

The honesty makes the three of us erupt into laughter.

Abuela clucks her tongue, still smiling, and wags a finger playfully at Lily. "Fresh."

Lily grins back. "I mean, it looks great on both of you, but you gotta admit I look awesome in a suit."

"The suit! Neva's!" I slap my forehead and look to Abuela, panicked. "*The other dress!* You paid for it and now I've wasted your money! There was even a sign on the door of the shop that said all sales final, so we can't even return it, and—"

Abuela puts a hand on my arm. "Mija, I already returned it for a refund from Neva."

"You did?"

She nods. "We're old friends and she knew I might need to return the dress. I told her what I'd been working on."

"So this *is* what's been keeping you late at the shop." I frown. "You shouldn't have."

"I wanted to! I could tell that the other dress wasn't what you really wanted. And I had the idea to make this one yours since I found it, but with how busy I'd been, I wasn't sure I could finish it in time for your dance. That's why I had you get something at Neva's—just in case."

"You're amazing, Abuela," I say.

Abuela grins at me. "I know."

Chapter Forty

I have never once said this about a Fall Fest meeting, but the final one is nearly pointless.

It lasts all of twenty minutes, and that's only because Hudson brought in cupcakes for us all to celebrate a job well done. I thought for sure we'd be scrambling to get everything done ahead of the kick-off carnival on Sunday, but...we're actually kind of good? Apparently, all the planning Isaiah, I, and the committee did up until this point has paid off.

Afterward, I curse myself for accepting a shift at Nature's Grocer, because I'd much rather be practicing my skateboarding skills with Jay, Malik, and Daniel than ringing people out.

Still, I show up for the miserable four-hour shift.

The work is mind-numbing, but sadly not enough to distract me from the terrible sensations in my ovaries. My period has been raging since that day with Destiny in the bathroom—but today I feel a sudden pain in my lower belly so sharp it steals my breath away.

Is this what my periods will be like now? Is this what they were like before? I can't even remember.

I'm so lost in my thoughts, trying to keep my breaths steady and even despite the occasional rush of agony, I almost think I'm hallucinating when Isaiah comes into view.

He offers me a small smile. "Hoped I'd find you here."

"Zay," I say, doing my best to mask how I'm feeling. He can't know. I make my voice bright. "Hi!"

At the sound of his nickname, the smile on his face grows. "Just picking up a box of these." Isaiah holds up a package of pumpkin cheesecake cookies, which are made right in the store's bakery.

"You're going to become hooked. I apologize in advance to your wallet," I joke.

"Small price to pay for cookies that I believe you said 'taste like a little slice of autumnal heaven,' if I'm remembering correctly," he says with a laugh. "And I brought you a coffee."

I give him a look. "What for?"

"Not that I need an excuse to bring you a coffee, but you may remember that I spilled one all over you a few weeks ago." He chuckles. "I told you I owed you, and I meant it."

"You didn't have to—"

But another wave of pain hits and cuts my sentence short. I suck in a sharp breath and grip the counter in front of me.

"You okay?" Isaiah asks.

"Fine," I manage through gritted teeth.

"You don't look fine..."

"I am," I insist, but another pang causes me to squeeze my eyes shut.

"Okay, no, you're not." Before I can respond, I feel his hand on the small of my back, and he's guiding me away from the register and over to a nearby bench. "Sit down. I'm going to get you some water."

I just nod, waving him away. Then I look back at the line of customers I'm supposed to be ringing out. "Sorry," I croak. "Just a minute."

"No. Sorry, folks, but she's closed," Isaiah says, voice firm.

"Her light is on," an older woman argues. "And I've been waiting!"

"She's clearly in pain and is in no state to work right now, so you're going to need to find another lane that's open and move on."

"Oh, for God's sake," the woman mutters. "I'm calling a manager."

"Please do!" Isaiah says. He turns to me. "What hurts?" I grab my lower abdomen and he nods. "Okay. I'm going to get help." He abandons the coffee he'd been holding and taps Anna, the cashier at the register next to mine, on the shoulder. "Hey, can you watch her while I grab some water? She's not doing too well."

Anna looks over at me and her blue eyes go big. "Oh my gosh! Okay. Let me page Pamela." She calls for our manager into her walkie and then rushes to my side. I don't know Anna well, but she's suddenly my bestie, especially once Isaiah disappears to get me something to drink.

"What's wrong?" Anna asks.

"I'm having horrible pain in my abdomen," I gasp. "It's making me queasy."

She takes my hand. "Pamela's coming. Not that she's a warm and reassuring presence or anything, but she'll help."

When Pamela rushes over, she immediately notes my register's now-long line and walkies for backup ASAP. Then she asks us what happened. Anna explains on my behalf. "She's hurting in the lower abdomen. It's really bad pain. She might be having appendicitis or something."

When Isaiah returns and hands me a water bottle, Pamela asks him if we should call an ambulance.

"No! *Please*," I beg, knowing we really can't afford an ambulance bill right now.

"I can take her to the hospital," Isaiah says immediately. "Just—just stay with her while I get my car, okay?" He squats down to look me in the eye. "Take a sip of water. Breathe. I'll be right back."

I nod, more appreciative than he knows, but unable to express it properly right now. The pain has made me break into a sweat and all I can think about is how I know I need another tampon and pad—I had to double up because my period was so heavy—but I feel too weak to even go to the bathroom on my own.

"Let's get you outside," Pamela says.

"I'll get her things," Anna offers.

I climb to my feet and Pamela helps me hobble to the doors. Isaiah pulls his car right up to the curb and hops out, rushing to my side and helping me into the passenger seat.

"I need something to sit on," I say.

"Here." Anna appears, handing me my bag and draping my coat on the seat. "Feel better."

I slide into the seat and give her a weak smile. "Thank you."

"I'll call you tomorrow to check in," Pamela says. "Drive safely."

Isaiah nods, shutting my door. When he climbs into the driver's seat, I turn to him. "Please just take me home."

"Are you out of your mind? You can barely stand!" he argues. "You need to go to the hospital."

It's only then that I start to cry. "Our insurance is really bad. A hospital bill will kill us."

Isaiah's face goes soft. "Please don't worry about that right now. Shit, I'll help if need be. We'll figure that part out later. We just need to get you taken care of. You're not okay."

"It's just my period," I protest.

"Listen. I grew up with an older sister, and let me tell you something: periods should not be doing this to your body."

Panicked, I blurt, "But mine can be really bad. I have PCOS."

This may not have been the way I envisioned breaking that news to Isaiah, but what choice do I really have?

"I don't know what that is, exactly, but I still don't think this is okay. You need to get checked out. Please, just let me take you."

I stare at him, at the concern in his furrowed brows and all over his face, and finally nod, reluctantly.

"Call your abuela," he instructs, pulling the car away from the curb. "She can meet us there."

I do as he says. When Abuela picks up on the other line, the sound of her sweet "Hola, nena" inspires a fresh round of tears. "Abuela, I'm not feeling well," I croak. "Something's not right. Isaiah is taking me to the hospital."

"¡Mija! I'll be right there. Te amo."

I sniffle. "Te amo. Hurry."

Chapter Forty-One

Abuela and Lily meet us at the only hospital in town. Though Abuela thanks Isaiah profusely when she arrives and assures him he can head home, he doesn't. Not even when the emergency room is full. Not even when the staff says it could be a while before I'm seen. Not even when Abuela goes on a rant about the health care system in the US.

While we wait, I take advantage of a reprieve from the pain and head to the bathroom so I can change my pad and tampon. I'm met with so much blood that my underwear is ruined. Between waves of nausea, I clean up as best I can.

When I exit the bathroom, the hospital staff is finally ready for me.

I turn to Isaiah. "You should take off. You can't give up your entire night for me."

"Of course I can." He meets my gaze. "I can wait here until there's news. I don't mind."

"But I do. Go home, rest, and I'll text you," I say. "You've already done so much. Thank you."

He looks as if he wants to protest. But with a sigh, he says, "Just…please let me know how you're doing, all right?"

"I promise, Zay."

Isaiah gives me a small smile. "See you soon, Whitney."

* * *

Add the hospital with its sterile, blinding fluorescents to the list of places with terrible lighting. I get that surgeons and nurses need to be able to see what they're doing, but at what cost?

In case you couldn't tell, humor is my brand of coping, and it's exactly what I rely on once I've been given enough pain relief medication that I can finally think again.

Between tests they run on me, Abuela and Lily distract me by playing Heads Up!, that word-guessing game you put on your forehead, and M.A.S.H., the game that decides your future: where you'll live, who you'll marry, and how many kids you'll have. Abuela is all too triumphant when we tell her she'll be a millionaire living in Puerto Rico with Pedro Pascal and their seventy-five kids.

Finally, after hours of waiting and plenty of casual fatphobia ("Losing weight would be really good for you," one of the tech nurses suggests all too cheerfully), we get a diagnosis: one of my ovarian cysts has ruptured.

The doctor surmises that, due to my PCOS, the egg likely didn't release from the ovary during ovulation, resulting in a functional cyst. Though the cysts don't often rupture, it does happen, she explains.

"Lucky me," I mutter.

"Call Dr. Delgado," Abuela tells the attending physician. "She'll help." But the doctor explains that that's not how that works, it's far too late in the evening, and I'll just have to make a follow-up appointment.

Though I don't need surgery, the on-call doctor says she'd like to monitor me overnight just to ensure everything is okay. I try to say I'm fine to go home, unable to shake the guilt over the hospital bill that I know is creeping up by the second, but Abuela hushes me.

She waits until the doctor leaves before unleashing a stream of curse words in Spanish, especially when I get moved to my room and she realizes I have a roommate. There won't be enough space for all three of us to stay here overnight, Abuela argues; we need a private room.

The attendant gently explains that the hospital is at maximum capacity, and Abuela huffs and calls Titi Mariana to arrange pickup for Lily. I can hear Titi Mariana's voice heavy with concern as they speak.

When Abuela hangs up with her sister, she turns to me. "¿Y tu? ¿Qué quieres?"

"I'm good," I say. Between what the hospital offers, the near pharmacy Abuela carries around in her purse, and my work bag, I should have plenty to get me through the night, right down to an extra phone charger. "You staying with me is plenty."

But Abuela, who I think just needs to busy herself after the scare of her eldest being rushed to the hospital, excuses herself to hunt down some extra pillows and blankets.

It's just me and Lily.

"Sorry to ruin your whole night," I say to her.

"Yeah, I'm so mad at you." She rolls her eyes. "How dare you be in so much pain you needed to go to the hospital."

I laugh. "You're right. I'm being silly."

"Obviously." She huffs. "But I do have something that might help."

"Oh, yeah?"

Lily reaches into her backpack and pulls out her tattered, well-loved stuffed giraffe, Stretch, which she's had since she was a kid. "Abuela gave me exactly six seconds to grab anything I needed before we left the house. I panicked, so I grabbed my Switch and Stretch. I thought it would help calm my nerves. She was acting like you were dying!" Lily shakes her head. "Anyway, now that you're okay, I was thinking you might need Stretch more than I do."

"Really?" I ask.

She holds the giraffe out to me. "Really. He's good company. Promise."

I reach for Stretch, stroking his soft belly with my thumb. "Thank you, Lily. I promise to take good care of him."

"You better. If you lose him, I'll never talk to you again."

I grin at her. "I promise he won't leave my sight. Right, Stretch?" I hold him up and make him talk in a silly voice. "We'll be good, Lily!"

"That's not what his voice sounds like," Lily chides, and I laugh.

Abuela whisks back in, arms loaded with linens and pillows. "Okay, this should be enough." She starts to situate some under and around my head, then tucks another blanket around my legs even though I'm not cold. "There."

Lily holds up her phone. "Titi Mariana's here."

Abuela eyes me. "I'll only be a second. If I come back and you've gotten out of your bed, you're in trouble." I attempt to move my legs in a dramatic show of just how tightly she's tucked me in.

"Even if I wanted to move, I couldn't," I say.

"Bien," Abuela says. To Lily, she nods toward the door. "Okay. Vámanos."

Lily gives me a fist bump, then the two disappear down the hall. Alone, I text Marisol and Sophie to give them an update on how I'm doing. I can practically feel the relief in their responses as they promise to come first thing tomorrow to check on me.

Then I pull up my messages with Zay. It's late now, but I need to update him, especially after all he did for me tonight.

Me: Sorry it took so long for me to text. Abuela has been next-level extra (in her adorable way). But I'm finally settled. I'm fine now

Zay: thank god. are you on your way home?

Me: I wish. They're keeping me overnight just for observation

Zay: do you need anything? i can drop it off if so. or run to your house if it's something there

Me: No, no, I'm good. I swear. Thank you

Zay: what did they say happened?

Zay: i mean

Zay: if you want to share

Zay: no pressure

Me: It's okay. One of my ovarian cysts ruptured 🫠

Me: Thankfully, I don't need surgery or anything, just rest

Zay: fuck, that's scary. i'm so sorry

Me: Thanks. I don't know what kind of fate made you decide to pick up your pumpkin cheesecake cookies tonight, of all nights, but I'm so grateful you did

Me: Thank you, Zay. Truly.

Zay: of course. you would've done the same for me. like the time i almost fell at the apple orchard and you, lemme check, doubled over in laughter

Me: NOT THE ORCHARD

Me: I laughed because I knew you were fine!!!

Zay: okay, sadist

Zay: can i come see you tomorrow? even if it's at the hospital?

Me: I'm not sure how long I'll be here

Zay: oh okay

Me: But yes. Come

Zay: good. i will. now rest and i'll see you tomorrow.

Me: Please ♥

Chapter Forty-Two

From the moment I wake up the next morning, it's a revolving door of visitors. It starts with Marisol and Sophie, who arrive the millisecond visiting hours begin.

They bring travel toothbrushes for me and Abuela so we can freshen up, plus PSLs and breakfast sandwiches. Have I mentioned my friends are actual angels?

Sophie settles on the end of my hospital bed by my feet. "God, we were so worried about you. How are you feeling?"

"I feel okay now. Mostly tired because it felt like I was being woken up to have my vitals checked every hour." I sigh. "And I'm already over this period from hell. But good otherwise."

"Good. Now, I hope you rest and don't think about anything except taking care of yourself," Marisol says, giving me a stern look. "Especially not the Fall Fest. Isaiah is more than capable of handling anything that arises, and he has the other class representatives, plus me and Sophie as backup. Then, as the backup to the backup, there's Ms. Bennett. We're *fine*."

I frown. "So, what you're saying is you don't need me?"

Marisol throws her hands up into the air. "Ay dios mío." She glances at Abuela. "This is what you deal with?"

Abuela tsks. "Stubborn, that one."

"Tell me about it," Marisol agrees.

"I think Marisol is trying to say that we've got your back," Sophie says with a laugh. "I already made a plan to pick up any of your missed assignments at the end of the day, but since next week is the Fall Fest, you can pretty much coast."

"Thanks, Soph." Then I sigh. "I still can't believe that after everything, I'm going to miss so much of Fall Fest."

"That's the last thing you should be worrying about right now," Abuela scolds. "You need to rest."

Easy for her to say. She hasn't dedicated the last six weeks to planning the kickoff carnival, which is happening just two days from now! I *know* I'm going to be down in bed for that.

Marisol lovingly squeezes my shin. "I'm sorry."

Sophie checks her phone. "Ugh, we've gotta go if we're going to make it to school on time." She turns to me. "If you're still here after school, we'll be back."

"Hopefully she's home by then," Abuela says, rising to her feet. "Thank you, girls." She gives them each a hug. Sophie and Marisol lean in to give me a hug, too, as best they can with the metal railing of the hospital bed in the way.

"Text me everything," I call after them as they leave.

"Rest!" Marisol calls back.

From there, Dr. Delgado pays me a visit, apologizing profusely for the fatphobic nurse I mention to her. She assures me she'll have a word with her about professionalism. She also recommends getting me on hormonal birth control to help regulate my periods and prevent any future ruptures.

Then Titi Luisa drops by, blessing me, telling me how she had all her candles lit and she'll be praying for my speedy recovery. I'm deeply touched because I know she is a true believer.

At lunch, Lily and Titi Mariana visit with some home-cooked food, and just one bite feels like home. So much better than gross hospital food.

All of those visitors are wonderful, but when I get a text from Zay confirming he's on his way, my heart flutters.

With Abuela's blessing, I hobble to the bathroom to freshen up a little. My hair is a frizzy mess, and nothing will restore it except a shower, which is impossible with the IV I'm hooked up to. Oh, well.

In the mirror, I inspect my chin—a ritual that has become second nature these days—taking in the black hairs that sprout along my jawline. Without daily shaving, the hair just grows and grows, and I don't have a razor right now.

That's not *oh, well.* It breaks the dam of tears I'd been holding in, and I start to cry.

A soft knock comes on the bathroom door.

I sniffle, wiping at my face. "Yes?"

Abuela's voice is concerned on the other side of the door. "Are you okay, nena?"

"No," I admit, and my voice wavers. Abuela eases the door open and the sight of her makes me start to cry more. "I think everything is finally catching up with me. I don't want to be here. I don't want to be missing the Fall Fest. I don't want to be left out."

Abuela rubs a hand on my back. "I know, mi amor. I know. I'm sorry."

I sniffle. "To top it all off, I look awful."

"Don't say that. You are beautiful," Abuela assures me.

I shake my head. "Maybe to you, but I practically have a *beard.*"

My voice quivers on the last word. I've been so diligent these last few weeks, making sure I shaved every single day so I could experience some semblance of normalcy, like this illness hasn't completely eclipsed my life and taken full control, and now I'm in the hospital because of it, on the cusp of missing the festival I've dreamed of for months, and I can't even do this *one tiny thing* to help me feel a little better about myself.

Abuela's face goes soft. "Mija, you don't."

"I do," I insist, lifting my chin. "Can't you see these little black hairs?"

She sighs and steps closer to me, tentatively, as if she doesn't want to appease me on this but will. After a moment, she says, "I see, but only when I'm this close and purposely looking." Abuela takes a step back and puts her hands on my shoulders. "But when I'm looking at you, mi princesa, all I see is you. I promise. It's more noticeable to you than anyone else."

I rub at one of my eyes. "What if it gets worse? Becomes more obvious?"

"Then you'll still be beautiful, and for so many reasons. Your hair like a mermaid's, your eyes that light up when you smile, and of course your dimples—the most amazing dimples, como tu abuela," she teases. "But more importantly, you are beautiful because you are a good person. Kind. Generous. Willing to do anything for the people you love. I'm proud of you, mi amor. And for all of those reasons, nothing can ever dull your shine."

Her words cascade over me. They are a gift, a gentle reminder that I'm too hard on myself, that I'm more than any one feature on my body. That I'm whole, and human, and complex, and every part of me together is what makes me me.

I give her a smile and turn to my reflection in the mirror: puffy eyes, frizzy hair, stubbly chin... but also golden skin, full lips, and dimples como mi abuela.

"Even with a beard?" I ask, half joking, half sincere.

She meets my gaze in the mirror. "*Especially* with a beard."

I breathe out a laugh, and Abuela smiles at me. Then, without another word, she reaches for my long hair and uses her fingers to comb through it. I close my eyes, her fingertips cool against my scalp, and feel her start to gently work the frizzy strands into a crown braid.

"It's been a long day, I know," Abuela murmurs. "I'm sorry

you're going through this. If I could take on all of this for you, I would."

"I know you would. I don't want that, though. I'm strong. I can handle this."

"Of course you can. But it's okay to be mad about it, too."

A lump forms in my throat. "It's just not fair." A lingering tear escapes the corner of my eye.

"No. It's not." A silence settles between us as she weaves my hair between her fingers. Then, quietly, she says, "Zay is a good boy."

I open my eyes to see that a soft smile has come across her face. "He is, isn't he?"

"I knew he was good, but after last night—well. He cares for you. Deeply."

I smile at that. "I really like him, Abuela. We almost kissed, you know."

"¿Qué?" Abuela asks, her voice going up with intrigue.

"The night you came home tipsy. When we were on the porch."

"I was not tipsy," she insists, even though she totally was. "Pero, I *did* feel like I'd interrupted something."

"It's okay," I say. "We'll get there."

"Yes. You will." I feel her tucking the end of my hair into the braid she's already completed. She steps back to admire her work. "There. So pretty."

And when I look in the mirror, it is—and so am I.

"Thank you, Abuela."

She kisses the top of my head and, without another word, guides me back to my bed.

Moments later, there's a light knock on the door.

"Am I interrupting?" Isaiah asks, poking his head inside. In his hand, he's holding a yellow vase of sunflowers.

"Not at all. Come in, come in!" Abuela welcomes him into the room. Then she makes a big show of looking down at her wrist and checking the time. "You know, now that you have company, I may run home to shower and get changed." Her eyes meet mine. "You don't mind, do you?"

"I don't mind," I say. "You've already done so much."

She leans down and kisses my forehead. "Never too much for you, nena. I'll be back." Abuela turns to Isaiah. "Good to see you again."

He nods at her. "You too, Abuela." She gives us a wave and then she's gone. Isaiah turns to me, holding up the flowers. "These are for you."

"They're beautiful, Zay." I point for him to please set the vase on my side table. "Thank you."

"Of course." Isaiah shoves his hands in his pockets. "Should I sit?"

"Please," I say, motioning toward a chair. He drags it closer to my bed.

"You know, I had to fight off my family just before I left. They all wanted to come and wish you well." He chuckles. "I told them that would be overwhelming and they needed to just let me go."

"That's super sweet. But totally the right call on your part." I laugh. "I didn't sleep well last night and I look a mess."

"You don't," Isaiah assures me. He leans over and tugs on a tiny curl at the nape of my neck, too short to be wrapped in the braid. "You look shockingly beautiful for someone who's just spent the night in the hospital."

My neck flushes, both at the compliment and at the space where his fingers grazed my skin. He starts to pull his hand back but I grab it before he can. "Sit here," I say softly, patting the space right beside me on my bed.

Isaiah swallows but obeys, helping me ease the metal handrail down so he can perch beside me. Our legs touch, and I feel the heat from his skin through the thin sheets. "I have something to tell you," he says.

"What is it?" I ask.

"So, remember the other night, when I brought over the pasteles?"

"Of course I do," I say, smiling. "That was a good night."

"Really good." Isaiah looks down at his hand, which I'm still holding on to, then up at me. "I almost kissed you."

Now I swallow, and my voice turns to a whisper. "Why didn't you?"

He lets out a little laugh. "Honestly? Nerves." His eyes meet mine. "I like you, Whitney. I have for a while. I just thought—well, up until that night, I thought you had a boyfriend. So I didn't say anything. But I really, really like you."

My breath hitches in my throat. "I really, really like you, too."

A little chuckle escapes Isaiah, and he squeezes my fingers with his. "Thank God."

I laugh and tug at his hand, guiding it up to my cheek. "You should kiss me."

With his thumb, Isaiah strokes my cheek, and a chill travels down my spine. "What if I start and can't stop?"

"I think I'd be okay with that," I whisper.

Isaiah licks his lips and slowly starts to close the space between us. My heart is thudding so loudly I can feel it in my ears. I close my eyes, leaning into him, and the moment our lips touch, the mariposas in my belly shiver throughout my entire body. He wraps his free arm around my back, and I suck in a breath, my lips parting to deepen a kiss that already feels so powerful it's as if we're making our own electricity. I breathe him in, feeling jittery but so, *so* alive.

When we part, Isaiah lets out a contented sigh. "I've been wanting to do that for weeks, Whitney," he admits.

"Me too. So we should do it again, right?"

Isaiah grins at me and comes closer, this time all confidence and eagerness. We kiss with urgency, with tension, with joy, and I find that as each second ticks by, I forget every little thing I'd worried about just moments earlier. None of that matters.

This matters.

This, this, this.

I pull back after a few moments, flushed and a little breathless. "Wow."

He lets out a breathy laugh, nodding. "I can't believe that's what I've been missing out on."

"You and me both." I reach for his hand, entwining my fingers in his. "I should've asked if you were single sooner."

"I can't believe fake relationships kept us from this." He holds up our interlocked hands.

"At least we know now." Then my face falls. "Wait, no!"

A panicked look comes over Isaiah, his eyes darting over me. "What? What is it? Are you hurt? Should I get a nurse?"

"No, no, nothing like that. It's just that I had a whole plan!" I frown. "I was going to ask you to the homecoming dance."

He blinks at me. "What?"

I nod. "I had it all planned out. You said you wanted a big, public proposal, and after that night on the porch, I made up my mind to give it to you," I explain. "But I hadn't perfected everything yet."

Isaiah shakes his head. "Not *everything* needs to be perfect."

"I'm learning that." I give him a sheepish grin. "But old habits die hard."

"You do tend to pine for perfect," he says.

"Not true. I pine for *you*," I correct him.

"Same thing," he teases. I playfully swat at him, trying to ignore how firm his chest feels beneath my hand. "You know what I mean, though. Perfect isn't real. But this?" He motions between us. "This is."

At that, I smile. "That's true. But can you kiss me again? Just so I can be sure?"

He grins. "I can do that."

Kiss after kiss after heart-stopping, skin-tingling kiss, Isaiah makes it clear that he's choosing me, and I him.

I'm ready to open my heart to this incredible boy I've been swooning over, who threw an entire Halloween party in sixth grade just to get my attention, who gave me his sweatshirt the day I spilled coffee all over myself, who teases me for my obsessive binders and spreadsheets and color-coded everything, who simultaneously makes me laugh and infuriates me, who is willing to drop everything to drive me to the hospital and spend the night checking up on me with no strings attached, who wants to kiss me and touch me and caress me while I'm unshowered and fuzzy-faced, wearing an ugly hospital gown and IV.

As it turns out, the mariposas in my belly were right all along.

Chapter Forty-Three

Because hospitals have essentially become the drive-thrus of health care, I get sent home barely more than twenty-four hours after *a cyst in my ovaries ruptures*.

The discharge takes about as long as I'd waited to be seen in the ER. It's enough time that I am able to mentally make a list of all the things I'm going to do when I get home.

Things Whit Is Dying to Do Once She's Home
1. Shower.
2. Moisturize until I feel like a slug.
3. Give Patch all the behind-the-ear scratches.
4. Ask Chloe Torres about secretly being my eyes and ears at the kickoff carnival (and possibly other events, depending on how long I'm down for the count).
5. Watch that old Intonation documentary-slash-concert Lily, Abuela, and I were obsessed with years ago.
6. Kiss Zay again.
7. And again.
8. And again.

Those last few might be hard to execute now that Abuela has essentially told me I'll be housebound and resting from now through eternity.

As proof, she drives about five miles per hour the entire way home, concerned that if she hits a bump in the road, it might cause me pain—despite me reassuring her that that's not how it works. Lily is irritated, too, because she's supposed to meet up with Ruby. But Abuela takes her sweet time, cussing out any driver that honks at her and simply turning up the radio.

I head straight to the shower once we're home and take one that's long and hot. When I emerge, my fingers and toes are wrinkly and my skin feels like it's been steamed in a sauna. I love it. It helps me feel like a human again. I take my time putting on some lotion and running some coconut oil through my hair before settling into my comfiest pajamas and climbing into bed.

Patch joins me, rubbing up against my hand and purring, which he never does. Bendito. He missed me. I missed him, too.

There's a knock at my door.

"Come in," I say.

It pushes open and in comes Abuela with a tray full of rice, cold water, ginger ale, crackers, my prescription pain meds, and a giant jar of Vicks VapoRub. A heating pad is draped over her shoulder.

I laugh out loud. "What's all this?"

"To make you feel better," Abuela says, as if it's the most obvious thing in the world. She rests the tray on my nightstand and hands me the heating pad first. "The doctor said this will help. And it always helped with my cramps, too."

She plugs it in for me and then pulls back my blanket and positions it on my lower stomach. Then she reaches for the Vicks.

"Abuela, I don't need that," I protest.

"You *always* need Vicks VapoRub." The adorable way Abuela pronounces *VapoRub* like "vaparoo" is what ultimately makes me acquiesce.

"At least let me do it," I say.

"Okay, okay." Abuela hands me the jar. "What else do you need?"

"This is plenty, Abuela." As if she doesn't believe me, she looks around the room, straightening some things on my messy vanity, picking up some wool socks I left on the floor, taking a pen on my desk and placing it back in the cup where it belongs. "Abuela," I say, keeping my voice soft. She meets my gaze. "I'm okay. Really."

She lets out a sigh, her shoulders slumping. "I was really worried."

I give her a soft smile. "I know you were. But I'm okay. I just need to rest."

Abuela arches an eyebrow. "Are you sure?"

I nod. "Yes. I'm taking my medicine every four hours, just like I'm supposed to, so the pain is manageable. The heating pad will help. And the Vicks."

Abuela comes over and kisses me on the top of my head. "Okay, nena. I love you."

"I love you. Can we watch the Intonation concert tomorrow?"

This eases the worry lines on her face. "Of course we can. I'll ask Lily to look up where we can find it. Now, sleep if you can."

"Okay. I will."

When the door closes behind Abuela, I slather a little Vicks on my abdomen, just like I promised. Then I pull out my phone, text Marisol and Sophie to let them know I'm home, and FaceTime Zay.

He's already grinning when he answers. "There she is," he murmurs.

"Hey," I say, keeping my voice soft.

"Hey yourself. Looks like you made it home okay."

"I did. Now I'm resting after Dr. Abuela made me cover myself head to toe in Vicks VapoRub."

He laughs. "What is it with Latina matriarchs and that stuff? Do they have stock in it or something?"

I laugh, too. "They must."

A silence falls between us. It's the first time, I realize, that Isaiah and I have ever talked by phone. And phone calls are notoriously awkward, aren't they?

I wrinkle my nose. "God, this feels a little weird, doesn't it?"

"Yeah, a little," Zay admits. "I mean. I guess I didn't really envision what comes after the girl you like gets rushed to the hospital and the adrenaline causes you to profess your feelings. Do you just go right back to small talk?" He puts on a mocking voice. "How about that weather?"

"In my defense, I didn't intend to get rushed to the hospital. I'm dramatic, sure, but not that dramatic," I joke.

"I'm just glad I showed up at your job like a creep."

"It's not creepy to want to try those delicious cookies!"

He gives me a look. "Do you really think I went there for the cookies?"

"So, wait—you came just to see me?"

"Of course I did. I had this whole thing where I was going to ask when your break was and see if you wanted to split the cookies with me." Isaiah chuckles. "Guess you're not the only one who plans things out."

I put my free hand over my heart. "I'm touched."

"You sure you're not weirded out?"

"Not even a little bit," I promise. "Especially because I'm a little embarrassed with how you found out about my health issues. Talk about weird." My gaze drops. "In fact, I'm actually pretty mortified you found out at all."

"What? Why?" Isaiah asks.

"It isn't something I have practice talking about, for one thing. I'm used to keeping it a secret—even from Marisol and Sophie. I didn't tell them until recently."

"Oh, Whitney" is all Isaiah says.

"Yeah, it's been hard to—I don't know—come to terms with it all, I guess." I blink and look back at his face on the screen, which has taken on a soft expression as he listens. "This is terrible, but it just sometimes makes me feel like my body is a little broken." My voice hitches on the last word and I try to cover it up by forcing a laugh.

"I'm so sorry you feel that way," Isaiah murmurs. "I hope you know that nobody who matters thinks that. Not even close."

I bite my lip. "Maybe. It's difficult not to feel that way when there are so many symptoms to manage. It's never-ending." Despite my best efforts, I sniffle. "I was so worried that if my friends found out—if *you* found out, that maybe…" My voice trails off.

"That maybe what?"

"That maybe you'd decide I wasn't worth liking."

"Hey," he says gently. "I get what you're saying, and I respect your feelings. But I also want you to hear me when I say *nothing* like that could make me not like you. Okay?"

A wave of relief washes over me. Maybe it's silly, and maybe I shouldn't need this validation, but hearing him say those words out loud helps more than I'd like to admit. I've been so fearful of how others might view me once they knew I had this mysterious illness that manifests in dozens of strange and unpredictable ways that this reassurance is beyond welcome. Maybe it's okay to sometimes need that reminder.

"Really?"

"You've already admitted you like me, too, so you're kinda stuck with me," he teases.

I laugh at that. "What if I laugh at you again if you fall in another apple orchard?"

"Well, in that case, it's immediately over, obviously," he says, grinning. Then he glances quickly at something off-screen. "Yooo. You ever heard of knocking?"

"I need you to move your car," Camila's voice whines.

"Why can't you move it? I'm a little busy right now."

"Doing what?" Isaiah suddenly disappears from the screen

and he shouts "Hey!" as Camila comes into view—her face shifting from a scowl to a surprised smile.

"Whitney?"

"Hi, Camila!" I say, all too grateful that she didn't seem to catch any part of the heavy conversation Isaiah and I were just having. "How are you?"

"I'm fine. How are *you*, sweetie? You doing okay?"

I nod. "Yes. I'm doing much better, thank you."

"Okay, okay, give me back my phone," I hear Isaiah demand.

She raises the phone above her head so that I'm looking at the top of Isaiah's bedroom wall instead of either of them. "In a minute!"

"Now!"

"Ugh," I hear her say, before Isaiah comes back into view. Camila pokes her head up from behind him. "Are you guys dating yet?" I smile sheepishly and nod. Camila shrieks and jumps onto Isaiah's back. "I knew it!"

Isaiah rolls his eyes. "You have no chill whatsoever, damn. Get *off* me."

"What's going on?" a small voice asks from off-screen.

"Can y'all leave me alone?" Isaiah asks, unable to mask the irritation in his voice. "I'm in the middle of something!"

"He's talking to Whitney—they're dating!" Camila squeals.

"Oooh, I'm telling Mami!" the voice says.

"Amaya!" Isaiah calls after her.

More chaos, and then Isaiah's mom is in frame, with Amaya and Gianna in tow, and they're all gushing over me and Isaiah and asking a million questions. *Are you feeling better? What do you need? Is Isaiah treating you well? When did this start? Are you in love?* (That last question from Gianna.)

"Can you all stop being so nosy?" Isaiah asks. "Damn!"

"He swore!" Amaya yells.

"Let's leave your brother alone," Isaiah's mom says as she comes into view. "Hi, Whitney! It's so good to see your face. We've been praying for you, mija."

I laugh more. "Oh, thank you so much. I'm feeling much better."

"What do you need? Can we bring you anything?" she asks.

"*Mami,* chill," Isaiah warns. He looks at me. "I'm so sorry. I'll text you."

Then the screen goes black and I'm still chuckling to myself. Chaos or not, I appreciate Isaiah's family and their concern for me. They always make me feel like I belong.

Getting Isaiah is enough—but getting his family along with him is icing on the cake.

Chapter Forty-Four

Chloe Torres is thrilled to report back to me on everything Fall Fest–related. I originally tried to pry information out of the officers, but Leilani, Everly, and even Hudson had all been sworn to secrecy by Marisol. To my delight, though, she never managed to warn Chloe.

That's why Chloe is perfectly happy to send me several paragraphs detailing all that I'd missed at school on Friday, including some gossip about how Leilani and her friend, Addison Bell, got into a huge fight because they bought the same dress.

Since I'm stuck in my room until I feel better, this tea is pretty much the most riveting thing that's going to happen to me, so I soak it in.

Sophie stops by on Saturday morning to drop off my homework, a singular worksheet from my bio teacher, who is the absolute worst and always assigns homework on principle. Marisol tags along with her. Abuela reluctantly gives me permission to practice doing their makeup for the dance so long as I don't leave the bed.

As I work, they tell me stories to distract me.

Then, keeping her voice gentle, Marisol says, "So…what should we tell people when they ask why you're out?"

I stop blending the eyeshadow over Sophie's lids. "What do you mean?"

"Well, yesterday, people were already noticing you weren't at school. It was easy enough to say you were sick, but if you're not at the carnival this weekend, people will wonder."

"It's not their business," Sophie adds, opening one eye to peek at me, "but we wanted to check in with you."

"We can say whatever you want," Marisol offers.

I think for a moment. Months ago, having everyone know about my PCOS was one of my biggest fears. I was so, so worried what people would think, that they'd pity me because they assumed it would mean I can't have kids someday or they'd be disgusted by the fact that the syndrome makes me grow facial hair or they'd just feel sorry for me because there was something "wrong" with me. I was convinced I'd want to hide it forever.

But who cares if they know? I'm tired of keeping this a secret. This syndrome is shitty enough without having to worry what others think about it.

"Just tell them the truth," I say with a shrug. Sophie opens both eyes in surprise. "If they're annoying about it, that's their problem."

Marisol grins. "Yes! To hell with anyone who has something smart to say. I'll personally kick their ass."

"And I'll cheer her on," Sophie says.

"You guys are the best. Besides, there will be other drama to distract them soon enough."

Sophie arches an eyebrow. "Spoken like someone who knows something..."

I grin and, as I go back to working on Sophie's makeup, fill them in on Leilani vs. Addison.

"How do you even have access to this gossip?" Sophie asks.

"Chloe Torres. We've been texting," I admit.

At that, Marisol crosses her arms. "Why are you texting with Chloe Torres?"

I shrug. "We're friendly."

"Not *that* friendly," Sophie says.

"We both like Intonation," I add.

"So? They broke up years ago." Marisol eyes me skeptically. "Are you trying to get info out of her about the Fall Fest?"

I feign ignorance. "What?"

Sophie's eyes fly open, smudging the eyeliner I was working on. "Oh my God, you totally are!"

"Can you blame me?! You guys have barely given me a crumb of information! And close your eyes again, Soph, please." I work quickly to try to salvage the liner.

"Because you don't need to know!" Marisol argues. "We have it handled."

"Well, maybe I'm just nosy," I say. "And feeling a little bummed that I'll be missing out on everything tomorrow. The timing of this whole thing is awful."

"It really is. You've worked so hard for this," Sophie says.

"I was hoping I'd feel better and still be able to swing by the carnival, but when I mentioned that to Abuela, she nearly bit off my head."

"Good. Your stubborn ass needs it sometimes!"

"Sol," Sophie chides, but the corners of her mouth quirk into a smile she's trying to hide. I poke her in the ear with the blush brush in my hand and she giggles. "It's probably best if you just take it easy."

"If you rest now, then you might bounce back in time for the dance," Marisol says. "So don't push it."

They both have a point, but God, that makes me sad. I don't want to miss out on any part of the Fall Fest.

"So you're saying you guys won't sneak me out of the house and into the carnival tomorrow?" I sigh. "Some friends you are."

Marisol grabs one of my pillows and threatens to hit me with it. "Don't make me do this."

Sophie pretends to pick up her phone. "Hello, 911?"

We laugh, and Marisol drops the pillow. "I wouldn't hit you for real anyway. You haven't done my makeup yet."

Unfortunately, over the weekend, there's no miraculous recovery. Abuela is as stern as ever. I'm stuck at home.

Abuela at least lets me join her and Lily in the kitchen so I can drown my sorrows in café con leche and galletas de mantequilla.

Then Lily leaves to go to the carnival with Ruby, promising to bring us back a souvenir, and Abuela and I settle on the couch to watch TV, but I keep sneaking glances at the time on my phone, thinking, *Oh, the team is probably doing a run-through now. And now they're likely letting people in. Bet the selfies look amazing. Someone's probably eating a caramel apple. I wonder if people are having fun yet?*

Like a good friend-slash-informant, Chloe texts me updates, as promised, but there isn't much to tell because everything seems to go off without a hitch. She does send me pictures, though, which I very much appreciate.

All morning, I do my best not to bother Isaiah, since he has to do the work of two people, but it's killing me. No kickoff carnival *and* no Isaiah is cruel.

When Abuela leaves to go to El Coquí for the remainder of the day, I'm left alone with just my thoughts. By late afternoon, I'm so antsy I consider marching to the high school just to feel something. Thankfully, Isaiah texts me as I'm contemplating whether I can really get away with my plan.

Zay: how's my girl doing?

The butterflies go wild in my belly.

Me: Just dying a slow, painful death knowing absolutely everyone from school is at a carnival that you and I organized while I'm sitting at home by myself

Zay: i'm so sorry, whitney

Zay: i know it must be so shitty

Me: It is. We spent so much time working toward this and now I can't even enjoy it 😭

Zay: would you feel better if i brought the carnival to you?

Me: ??????

Zay: come to the front door ☺

I want to run, but Abuela's voice is in my head reminding me to take it easy, so I walk instead.

When I open the door, Isaiah is wearing a charcoal bomber jacket over jeans and a crew neck T-shirt with a jack-o-lantern and the words GET LIT. His locs are pulled back into a ponytail and he's holding a box full of caramel apples, a stuffed pumpkin, flowers, cinnamon sugar donuts, and several other items from the carnival.

"You didn't," I breathe.

"I knew you were upset that you'd miss out, so..." He grins at me. "Amaya and Gianna helped me choose what to bring. They may have gone a little overboard."

I reach for his arm and pull him inside as he points out each thing that's in the box. He holds up the stuffed pumpkin and makes it give me a little kiss on the cheek.

Touched by this display of pure kindness, I throw my arms around his neck, not caring that I'm in an old, oversize T-shirt and cat slippers. I kiss him until his hands reach for my hips and pull me closer.

When we part, I look up at him. "Is it okay that you're here? Don't they need you at the carnival?"

He shakes his head. "I got everything handled."

I smile at him. "So you can stay, then?"

Zay leans down and presses his forehead to mine. "Why? You offering?"

I glance over at the box of goodies. "Who else is going to help me eat those donuts?"

He grins. "Hand one over."

Chapter Forty-Five

Things I've Missed During Fall Fest Week Because of My ~~House Arrest~~ Painstakingly Slow Recovery

1. A last-minute proposal from Jack O'Reilly to Melissa Finch featuring a bunch of adorable puppies.
2. Zachary Lin, the football quarterback, revealing himself as an artistic genius during Monday's pumpkin-carving contest when he created a realistic rendition of our black squirrel mascot.
3. A very sweet reconciliation between Leilani and Addison, who are now embracing the fact that they'll be twins at the dance and making their dates dress the same, too. Drama officially squashed.
4. Cyrus Ali crushing the timed corn maze races in PE.
5. Principal Johnson accidentally leaving her loudspeaker on after she'd finished with the announcements and letting the whole school overhear her rapping along to an explicit song on Spotify.

Marisol, Sophie, Chloe, Lily, and Isaiah fill me in on these details and more, and what they don't share, I find on people's social media accounts. I know so much it's almost as if I'm there. Almost.

Each day that passes, I grow more forlorn. Until Abuela surprises me on Thursday night while I'm pathetically scrolling through my classmates' posts about the bonfire and says I can go back to school on Friday.

I could cry pumpkin-spice-flavored tears of joy.

* * *

The pep rally takes place Friday afternoon. The teachers accept that getting any work done is futile, letting us mostly goof off until it's time to be led to the gym for the afternoon's festivities.

Principal Johnson kicks things off with a brief speech about teamwork and how it's not about whether we win or lose the game, blah blah blah. Our squirrel mascot, Hazel, joins the dance team, and we go absolutely wild when she drops to the ground and starts to do the worm. Who the hell is in that costume and why are they so good?

I turn to Zay as the cheerleaders rush in and start to announce the football team. "I'll be right back!" I shout over the crowd. "I have to pee."

He nods, and I climb down the bleachers to meet Malik, Jay, and Daniel just outside the gymnasium. Operation Publicly Propose to Isaiah is officially underway.

"Hey, Whit," Malik says with a smile. "You ready?"

"To humiliate myself in front of the entire school?" I ask. "Ready as I'll ever be."

Daniel forks a thumb toward the gym. "You hear those fools? They are absolutely losing their minds over the football team. And that team suuuuucks. I feel like they'd cheer for just about anything right now, so you and your very adorable plan will go over great."

Jay nods. "It may not top Hazel basically humping the ground—"

"Gross, man. She was doing the worm!" Daniel protests.

"—but it'll be good regardless," Jay says. He grabs the sign I finished the night before and hands it to me. "Here."

I take it. "Thanks. And thank you all for doing this with me."

"Of course. Isaiah's a good dude," Malik says. "It's the least we could do."

From inside the gym, I hear Marisol's loud voice bellow over the speakers. "And now, please give it up for one of the chief masterminds behind this absolutely epic Fall Fest. Whitney Rivera, get in here!"

There's cheering, and Daniel gives me a little salute. "Do your thing, Veronica," he says, a final nod to our secret code names.

I jog into the gym, excitement in my chest and adrenaline coursing through my veins. Marisol gives me a side hug as I take the microphone from her.

You've got this, she mouths.

Whew. Let's hope.

Into the microphone, I say, "Elmwood High! It's Fall Fest week!"

They cheer, and I'm overwhelmed by the enthusiasm. Daniel was right. This crowd would cheer for just about anything right now.

I catch Isaiah's eye and he gives me a confused look. But I just lift my shoulders and smile at him.

"I'm super excited that *you're* excited, and that you seem to have enjoyed yourselves this week. I want to start by giving a quick shout-out to the incredible Fall Fest committee, without whom none of this would be possible: Ms. Bennett, for being an incredible leader, and our class officers Leilani Mamea, Hudson Moore, and Everly McDonnell; helper angels Sophie Tran, Marisol Pérez, and Chloe Torres; and, of course, our incredible senior officer, my partner in crime, Isaiah Ortiz."

More cheering.

"Now, I am hoping to take one more minute of your time for something super selfish. As you may know, I ended up in the hospital late last week, and yes I am totally telling you that to garner sympathy so you are nice to me as I put myself out there and do this next thing."

There's some polite laughter from the crowd, and one person whoops loudly.

"While in the hospital, I realized I *really* liked this guy I'd been working on the Fall Fest with, and that I wanted nothing more than to spend as much time with him as possible," I say. "So, as I've been watching these incredible Fall Fest proposals happen, I decided I wanted to do one of my own…"

My classmates start to cheer and clap, realizing what's happening, and their chants get louder as Daniel, Malik, and Jay skateboard into the gymnasium. I take a moment to place the mic in its stand so I can use both of my hands to hold up the sign I've placed by my feet.

I hoist the sign above my head, just as Isaiah's three friends encircle me.

In big, bold letters, it reads: ZAY, I WHEELIE LIKE YOU. Daniel holds a sign that says FALL, Malik holds a sign that reads FEST, and Jay rounds us out with the sign that says DANCE?

"Isaiah Ortiz…" I say, leaning into the mic. "Will you make me the happiest girl at Elmwood and go to the Fall Fest dance with me?"

It feels as if there's a lifetime between when the words echo out of the loudspeakers and the moment when Isaiah breaks into a huge, goofy grin—but it comes, and my heart soars as he shouts, *"ABSO-FUCKING-LUTELY!"*

Our classmates erupt into loud cheering and Zay rushes to me, lifting me off the floor and twirling me around, both of us laughing so hard it hurts.

Principal Johnson tries to restore order, but it's no use. We've devolved into pure chaos, some students leading the way toward the football fields, others congregating in groups, some taking selfies with Hazel (who's *in* that costume, anyway?).

Zay uses the opportunity to pull me close and says, "You're absolutely wild, you know that, right?"

"You wanted your big proposal!" I laugh. "This is the least I could do."

"And you guys!" He looks over at his friends, who tease him as boys do, while Marisol and Sophie join me in a group hug.

"You killed that!" Sophie squeals.

"So proud of you, babe," Marisol gushes.

"My original plan of skateboarding in and doing an ollie would've been better," I joke. "But this is good, too."

Somehow, in just a few weeks, I've gone from the girl who would give anything not to be noticed to the girl standing in front of her entire school professing her feelings for a boy she likes. Yet I feel more like me than ever before.

Chapter Forty-Six

At long last, the morning of the Fall Fest homecoming dance—the day I've been counting down to for literal years, the thing I've hyperfocused on throughout my entire summer and the first few weeks of my senior year, the remarkable occasion that helped bring the Rivera family into existence—arrives.

It comes in like a cool autumn breeze, gentle and welcome.

There is a sleepy smile on my face as I awaken. I take my time enjoying the sweet thrill of anticipation in my belly, yawning and stretching beneath the warmth of my blankets.

Until I hear them.

Las tías.

Or, more accurately, Titi Mariana and Titi Luisa, whose loud voices I'd recognize anywhere.

My eyes fly open as I sit up in bed, and Patch darts right out of the room at my sudden movement.

In all my visions for how this morning might go, I hate to admit that none included Titi Mariana or Titi Luisa. But of course they'd want to be here to help Lily and me get ready and to support their sister, Paola, on this night that is likely a mixture of joy and melancholy. It is a bittersweet reminder of Abuelo, after all.

It's embarrassing that this is only now occurring to me, and I think perhaps I should approach Abuela with gentleness, even if it means I need to swallow some of my excitement. It's worth it if it means I can be there for her on this day.

I brace myself as I pad out to the living room in my jammies, using the scrunchie that's on my wrist to swoop my hair up into a messy bun atop my head while I walk.

Though I expect to find my tías doing their best to cheer Abuela up, I instead find the three of them sitting on the couch, poring over a photo album, howling with laughter. Abuela is in the center, a sister on either side, and they're in such stitches I can almost picture them as children doing this very same thing.

I clear my throat. "Good morning?" I venture, in a voice that sounds like a question.

Abuela looks up and breaks into a bright smile when she sees me. "¡Mija! You're awake!"

"¡Buenas días!" Titi Luisa chirps.

Titi Mariana sighs. "Buenas días, nena. What's it like to sleep past nine o'clock in the morning? It's been years since the twins let me." She shakes her head. "You want to borrow them for a day?"

I laugh. "They're adorable, but I think I'm good," I say, giving each tía a kiss on the cheek. "What's got you guys laughing so hard?"

"Tu abuelo y él bigote." Titi Luisa curves a finger over her lips to mime a mustache. "¡Como una oruga!"

My eyes go wide. "Abuelo had a mustache?" I can't remember him as anything other than clean-shaven. Lily and I always made it a point to wriggle away from his kisses whenever he had an unexpected five o'clock shadow because we insisted it was too scratchy.

"Mira." Titi Mariana points at one of the photos in the album that's tucked behind the glossy paper, and yep, there's Abuelo, maybe in his mid-thirties or so, with thick black hair above his upper lip.

"Oh my gosh! He looks so…"

"Handsome," Abuela breathes dreamily.

Titi Mariana and Titi Luisa exchange a look, eyebrows raised.

"I was going to say *different*, but sure," I offer with a grin.

"It was a phase, but I liked it," Abuela says, turning the page in the album to reveal more photos. There are pictures of her and Abuelo at a party together; a photo of her posing in front of a Christmas tree; of Abuelo flexing his arm muscles while wearing a silly expression. Her face is wistful as she takes in each photo, remembering. I reach out to touch her shoulder.

"It's a big day, huh?" I say.

Abuela looks up at me. "It is. I wish he was here to see it all." Titi Luisa reaches out to squeeze Abuela's knee. "Abuelo would be so proud of you and Lily."

"I wish he were here, too." There is a hitch in my voice as I say it, and I swallow, not realizing how heavily Abuelo's absence might weigh on me, too, on this day. For so long, it's just been us three, but on this morning, with so much meaning, it's hard not to feel his absence in the pit of my stomach.

"Why don't I make us some breakfast?" Titi Mariana offers. She stands from the couch. "Lulu?"

Titi Luisa stands, too, with a firm nod. "Vámanos."

I settle beside Abuela on the couch, flipping through old photos, listening as she tells me this story and that—some I knew already, and some I'd never heard before. The shuffling of pots and pans and chatter wake Lily. She comes from her room with a scowl on her face, but joins us on the couch with a sheepish grin once Titi Mariana offers her a giant pan de mallorca dusted with powdered sugar that she picked up on the drive over.

While my aunts work in the kitchen, Lily, Abuela, and I take turns eating bites of the warm, sweet, buttery bread, one of Abuelo's favorites, and settle into the past. The new memories we'll make tonight can wait a little longer.

* * *

"Stop fidgeting!" Titi Mariana hisses.

We've moved well beyond sweet reminiscing and well into the

chaos of getting ready. Titi Mariana is pinning what feels like the millionth bobby pin into the back of Lily's hair.

"I'm not!" Lily whines, but she totally is. I don't blame her, though; her style is taking much longer to do than mine did, and she's getting anxious.

Titi Mariana has swept Lily's hair back into a soft braided updo with some of her dark waves left loose, and she has used an ungodly amount of hairspray and pins to keep it from moving while Lily dances.

My own hair is divided into a middle part with a small French braid on either side that wraps around my head like a crown. A few loose curls frame my face, while the rest of my long, wild coils are loose, cascading down my back. It feels like the perfect celebration of the hair I have, made fancy. I love it, even if it looks a little silly right now with my kitten-print pajamas.

"Okay, okay, I think we're good," Abuela says, rushing to Lily's rescue. She cups Lily's face in her palms. "It looks *beautiful,* nena."

Titi Mariana steps back to admire her work and breaks into a smile, elbowing Titi Luisa. "Not bad, eh?"

"Perfecto," Titi Luisa agrees, reaching out to wrap one of my curls around her fingers. "You have the most beautiful curls."

I beam. "Thank you, Titi." I turn to Lily. "Should I start on your makeup?"

"Fine, but no foundation!" Lily reminds me.

It doesn't take long for me to give her a natural look that enhances her long eyelashes and bronze skin. Titi Mariana and Titi Luisa watch as I apply the makeup, as if in a trance.

"This is so relaxing," Titi Luisa says with a soft laugh.

A gentle knock on the door grabs all our attention. Abuela tsks at me when I rise to answer. "You still need to be taking it easy," she warns. She hurries past me to do it herself, and her expression brightens when she sees Sophie and Marisol, each with their gowns draped over their arms. "¡Hola!"

"Hola, Abuela," Marisol says, leaning in to give her a kiss on the cheek.

Sophie does the same before hanging her dress on the coatrack near the door and glancing over at me. "How are you feeling?"

I grin. "I'm amazing, especially because you guys are right on time."

"Well, we know how neurotic you are, and we didn't want you to be mad at us when you're the one doing our makeup," Marisol teases, adding her dress plus a linen tote to the coatrack.

Lily laughs. "She *is* super neurotic. Especially today."

"Shut up, Lily!" I nudge her with my elbow, laughing, too.

She shrugs. "What? My makeup's already done, so I can say whatever I want."

This gets my tías to laugh and exchange a knowing glance.

"Aren't sisters the best?" Titi Luisa asks.

Titi Mariana checks the time on her phone and claps her hands together. "It's already after three! We still need to do Sophie's and Marisol's hair, Whitney needs to get going with the makeup, then you all need to get on your dresses, and your accessories, and take pictures. ¡Rápida, Lulu!"

At this, Titi Luisa rolls her eyes. "See what I mean about hermanas?"

Lily uses this moment to escape, which I respect. The rest of us settle down to create a makeshift salon in the center of the living room.

Titi Luisa keeps us hydrated and Abuela turns on music so we can find a rhythm while we work, and soon we're all swept away in delightful and dizzying excitement of getting ready for homecoming.

I handle the makeup for me, Soph, and Marisol, while Titi Mariana fixes their hair.

Before long, Marisol's copper curls are held back on one side by four gold pearl-studded pins, the rest of her long corkscrews flowing down her back. She has an expertly applied red lip, long lashes, and a dramatic winged eye, with matching rosy cheeks.

Sophie's dark locks are wavy and expertly tousled. Her dark eyes pop under lash extensions and a bold orange lid, which she's paired with simple, clear lip gloss.

For myself, I've dusted gold, shimmery shadow across my lids, accented by dark brown liner. Bronzer highlights my cheekbones and shoulders. Like Sophie, I've chosen a clear gloss. I feel beautiful.

"Should we get into our dresses now?!" Sophie squeals.

Marisol grins. "Let's do it!"

Sophie and Marisol grab their dresses and I usher them toward my room, but not before I hear Titi Mariana ask, "Is it time for wine now?"

I duck into the bathroom while my friends head to my room. Thankfully, my period has lightened significantly, so I should be able to relax a little at the dance without worrying. Still, I grab a handful of tampons from under the sink so I can tuck them into my clutch, just in case.

In my room, I find Marisol emptying the contents of her tote—jewelry and shoes for what looks like both her and Sophie—onto my bed. I stash the tampons in the gold clutch that matches my strappy heels, then meander over to my bedside table, where I've stored the gifts I got for them.

"I have a little something for you." I hold up the thin rectangular packages artfully covered in sparkly paper with a white ribbon in the center.

Marisol puts her hand on her heart. "You've been on bed rest and you somehow managed to get *us* gifts?"

"Oh my gosh, Whit." Sophie reaches for the present and gingerly takes it in her hand. "Should we open them now?"

"Please," I say, nodding.

While Sophie shimmies the ribbon off the gift and tucks it into her bag—no doubt to repurpose it later—and then tears into the wrapping paper, Marisol rips off the ribbon before using a long, manicured nail to carefully slice into the Scotch tape on either side of the package. It's a small but delightfully appropriate embodiment of who they are: Sophie, ever the sentimental one, loving ferociously, and Marisol, tough on the outside but oh-so-sweet and resilient on the inside.

I smile to myself as they study the framed prints—the ones that capture the three of us mid-laugh during a perfect afternoon at the Knoll—before them.

Marisol presses her fingers to the picture. "This is beautiful, Whit. Thank you."

Sophie hugs the frame to her chest. "Thank you so much. You really shouldn't have. . . but I'm really glad you did."

"I'm so happy you guys like it! It's just a little something for each of us to remember this fall. To celebrate how amazing this friendship is."

"And how hot we looked that day," Marisol adds with a grin.

"Not as hot as we're going to look today," Sophie says, pulling out her phone and putting on some music. "Shall we?"

An upbeat reggaetón song fills the room moments later. We pull off our clothes and climb into our dresses, dancing and laughing. I am thrilled when I find I'm not even consumed by thoughts of hiding my body; I'm in the moment with my friends, clasping a necklace here and asking to be zipped up there and having a good time.

I save putting on my gold dangly pumpkin earrings—the ones from Abuelo, the ones Zay always admired—for last.

And then we're staring in the mirror, our reflections adorned in the colors of autumn, skin sparkling, smiles big. We look *stunning*, and excitement ripples through my chest. Tonight is going to be one of the best nights of my life. I can already feel it.

Chapter Forty-Seven

Lily looks like a rock star when she emerges from her room in her suit.

Abuela squeals in delight, leaving sloppy kisses on both our cheeks, and the tías snap pictures on their phones. They even make Lily do a mini–runway walk, shouting "¡Wepa!" when she surprises us with an unexpected twirl.

It already feels like I've crammed a lifetime into this day, and we still have photos, dinner, and the dance itself.

Abuela is looking at me and Lily with hearts in her eyes, growing weepier by the minute.

"Abuelo would be so proud of you girls," she says again, putting a hand on each of our shoulders. "We need to take some pictures. ¡Vámanos!"

But she's only half right, since we need everyone to arrive before we can really do that.

We wait out on the autumn-decorated veranda. Sophie's parents show up first, her dad a sharp-jawed, dark-haired Vietnamese man with kind eyes, her mom a slim, graceful woman who always wears a bright smile. Marisol's mami, Lisette (who looks more like Marisol's sister than her mother), gets there next with Marisol's stepdad, Robert, a polite blond-haired green-eyed dude.

Then comes Noah, who has fully embraced the theme in a white, brown, and squash plaid tux, with his dads; Ruby, in a gorgeous, almost-floor-length halter dress with a dramatic collar and a daisy print, with her aunt; followed by Ari in a scarlet suit with a ruffled pink button-down; and, finally—finally, finally—Zay and his entire entourage: his mami, papi, and sisters.

The sight of him nearly makes my heart leap right out of my body.

His locs fall to either side of his face. He's wearing a cocoa-colored bell-bottomed suit with oversize lapels and a cream-colored button-up—a color combination that goes so perfectly with my dress, it's almost as if he planned it. He looks unbelievably good, and I think he means to say the feeling is mutual when his eyebrows go up at the sight of me and he mouths *Wow*. When he flashes me that gentle, easy grin of his, it takes everything in me not to run at him, full speed, and tackle him with a hug. Or a kiss. Maybe both.

Instead, I keep my feet firmly planted on the veranda, insides trembling as I watch him walk toward me. He leans in to give me a chaste kiss on the cheek, the two of us acutely aware of everyone, who all seem to be staring at us. It doesn't stop electricity from shooting through my body.

"You look fucking incredible," he whispers, voice low.

"All I want to do is sneak away and make out with you right now," I whisper back.

Isaiah laughs and shakes his head, like he needs to push away the thought.

A hand touches my shoulder and I turn to see Isaiah's mom. "How are you feeling, querida?" she asks, her question hanging heavy in the air.

It's the first time tonight that anyone has even hinted at my recent hospital stay, though I could feel the question coming well before she asked.

I nod at her and smile. "Much, much better."

"And she'll feel even better if we get to our dinner reservation on time—right, Whitney?" Isaiah asks, catching my eye.

turn it into a group hug.

Then I pull back from them and furrow my
d your parents actually agree to this?"

, I *will* speak with them," Marisol says

shared the good news, my dad spoke with my
hat I should go. . . I already accepted the spot.
to Paris!" Sophie squeals.

ons, Sophie!" Zay says. Lily, Ruby, and Ari
congratulations. I'm nearly buzzing on behalf of
picturing her at the Eiffel Tower and Versailles.
lly need to celebrate," Marisol insists. "In honor
good news, Robert may just buy the whole damn

s at her. "Oui!"

I smile at him, grateful. "Right! So, picture time?"

"Picture time!" Marisol shouts.

All at once, the veranda erupts into chaos. Titi Mariana and
Marisol's mom emerge as the natural leaders, directing us to pose
like this and that, substituting one of us for another, snapping
photos of the families, friend groups, and couples, with the couples exchanging corsages. We hit just about every combination
imaginable.

Forty-five minutes later, with cheeks aching from the nonstop
smiling, the eight of us actually attending homecoming manage
to extract ourselves from the smothering oohing and aahing and
cram our bodies into Marisol's black Escalade.

"That was a lot," Lily muses once we're settled in and moving.

"Sweet, though," Ruby adds.

Lily smiles at her, reaching for her hand, and they interlock
fingers. I'm seated next to the happy couple way in back, while
Sophie, Noah, and Isaiah are in the second row, and Ari and
Marisol lead us up front.

The car heads toward Friendly's, a New England staple known
for its ice cream and burgers, which we've agreed is the most ridicu-
lous place to show up in our homecoming outfits. Anyone who has
grown up in the area has been to a Friendly's, and the one nearby is
among the few left in the state that still does indoor dining.

I will also absolutely be getting myself one of its iconic Monster Mash Sundaes, which uses M&M's and Reese's Peanut Butter
Cups to create the eyes and ears of an adorable monster face. Its
nose is a cherry. *Obviously.*

My clutch vibrates from an incoming text on my phone. I smile
to myself when I retrieve my phone, seeing that the notification is
from Zay—who, yes, is sitting right in front of me, but still.

Zay: heyyyyy

Me: Hiiii

Zay: kinda wish we could sit together

Me: Same

Me: But at least we'll sit together at dinner?

Zay: of course

Zay: the real question is: which flavor ice cream are you getting?

Me: Cookies and cream!

Me: As part of the Monster Mash Sundae, of course

Zay: oh, of course

Zay: that's the one with the peanut butter cup ears, right?

Me: Yes! Cutest sundae known to humankind, really.

Me: What're you getting?

Zay: easy. chocolate ice cream, peanut butter topping, reese's pieces sprinkled all over

Me: That sounds amazing

Me: Should we do the cute date thing and split one?

Zay: no offense

Zay: but

Zay: absolutely not

Zay: get your own ice cream sundae!

I stick out my tongue at him (though I'm grateful—I really have my heart set on my monster sundae!), just as Marisol pulls her car into the parking lot of Friendly's.

Our group piles out, and the juxtaposition of all eight of us in fully beat faces, wearing tuxes and sparkly dresses, against the retro red-and-white Friendly's sign reminiscent of old-timey diners feels hilarious.

Noah and Sophie lead the pack, Noah grabbing the door and holding it open for the rest of our crew as we pile inside. We're just on time for our reservation, and our server leads us over to the area where several tables have been pushed together to make room for us all.

Zay reaches for a chair and pulls it out, smiling at me and motioning for me to sit.

I grin b

"Anythi
into the seat

Marisol s
being cute. Che

"Nothing w
Lily clears he

Isaiah tilts hi
that, best friend?"

Lily grins at hin
food?"

"Of course we're
Lily high-five. "We have

"We really do! Like

I laugh. "I meant mor
what? That works, too."

"Personally, I'm celebr
Marisol jokes, and Ari stick
course. I'm also celebrating
from her clutch. "It's on the ste

"What? No!" Sophie shak
to pay."

Marisol shrugs. "He *insisted*

Noah tips his chin at Sophie. "
Especially in celebration of your goo

All eyes fall to Sophie. "What go

"Tell us or Robert's credit card ge

"Well…I just found out that I've
internship in Paris," she says, a soft smi

"Sophie! Oh my gosh!" I squeal.

Marisol leaps from her seat at the ne
around Sophie. "Congratulations! This is a

I join Marisol and
"So proud of you!
brows. "But, wait—d
"Because if no
ominously.
"Actually, after
mom. They agreed
I'm officially going
"Congratulati
chime in with thei
my friend, already
"Now we re
of Sophie and he
place."
Sophie grin

Chapter Forty-Eight

When I catch sight of the entrance to Elmwood High, my breath hitches in my throat. It's *beautiful*.

The faded brick entrance is lined with carved pumpkins that glow, spelling out FALL FEST. White, orange, and yellow mums overflow from cream-colored pots to guide the way into the school.

Just outside the doors, propped on an easel, is a display of sepia-toned photos showing off happy students from prior Fall Fest dances.

I step closer to the pictures. "Is that...?"

Lily's eyes must be drawn to the same photo, because she finishes my thought. "Abuela and Abuelo."

I grab her hand and pull her toward me so we can take a closer look. Sure enough, nestled in the center of this tribute to the history of the homecoming dance is a striking monochrome photograph of our beloved grandparents—on this very night, all those years ago. Dimples in both of Abuela's cheeks surround her coy smile, while Abuelo's dark eyes are bright with hope, just like I remember.

"There they are," I whisper.

"They look happy," Lily says quietly.

I squeeze her hand. "I think it's because they were. They really, really were."

Then I swallow the lump in my throat, willing myself not to cry because I spent so goddamn long working on this makeup and I am not about to ruin it before we even get into the photo booth.

I turn to my friends. "Did you guys do this?"

Marisol gives me a small nod. "We know what this night

means to you two, and to your abuela, so we wanted to do something special."

"We love you guys," Sophie says. "None of this would've been possible without you."

I rush to my friends—my thoughtful, kindhearted, incredible, ride-or-die, stuck-with-me-till-the-end-of-time friends—and throw my arms around them. "I love you guys so much."

"Fiercely and loyally," Marisol replies, squeezing me tight. "Get your ass in here, Lily!"

Lily laughs but dutifully comes over and pats the three of us on our backs in her best effort to participate in the hug, which we happily accept.

"Well, *that* was wholesome as hell," Ari says with a laugh.

When we turn, we see that she, Ruby, Noah, and Zay are all holding up their phones.

"Got it all on video," Noah proudly announces. "Now you can all gush over this forever."

"Nice! I went a little artistic with portrait mode," Zay muses.

Ruby holds up her phone. "Live photos over here."

Ari grins. "And I got some regular ones. Damn. We're *good*." She turns to us. "How'd you all get so lucky with us?"

Marisol rolls her eyes but grabs Ari's phone so she can start browsing through the photos. "Oh, gosh. We look so happy." She turns the screen so that Sophie, Lily, and I can peer at it. We do.

"This is going to make me cry and ruin my makeup," I whine. "Can we go inside now so I can ooh and aah over the rest of this amazing work you've all done?!"

"And take our photos," Sophie adds. "I can already feel my hair starting to go flat!"

Noah wraps his arm around her waist. "You look gorgeous, Soph."

She grins at the compliment.

"I think I see our friend Margot," Lily says, pointing a thumb behind her. "Mind if Ruby and I head in?"

"Go! Have fun," I urge, giving her a little wave. She and Ruby hurry to catch up with their friend, with Sophie and Noah and Marisol and Ari in tow. That leaves just me and Zay outside. We step to the side, letting our classmates into the school, and he reaches for my hand. I take it, interlocking my fingers through his.

"You excited?" he asks.

I nod. "Beyond. And also...a little nervous." He tilts his head, his locs falling to one side of his face. "I've just hyped this night up in my head for so long. I really, really want everything to go well, you know? Plus, it's weird that I had absolutely no hand in the final planning for tonight."

Isaiah's brows furrow. "Wanting everything to go well I get—but saying you had no hand in tonight? Are you kidding me?" He motions toward the entrance. "You may not have physically put everything together, but the instructions you left were meticulous. Sophie and Marisol ensured they were executed to a T. Even Sophie was barking orders, reminding folks that this was an important night for you."

"Seriously?" I laugh. "I can't picture Sophie bossing anyone around."

He breathes a laugh, too. "It was pretty scary, honestly. But she and Sol kept us all in order. For you. And, not to brag, but I think I made a *pretty great* substitute president. I mean, not as great as you, of course, but not half bad."

I smile at him. "I think you did wonderfully."

Isaiah nods toward the entrance. "Only one way to find out for sure."

We push past the beaded curtains hanging in the cafeteria doorway to see our hypothetical Fall Fest dance realized.

A long, wavy rainbow made of brown, yellow, and orange electrical tape (Chloe's idea!) welcomes us inside like a red carpet. The long, picnic-style cafeteria tables have been cleared out to make room for a dance floor with colored lights and a shimmering disco ball gleaming at the center. Vibrant paper daisy cutouts decorate the walls.

The photo booth from Everly's mom is off in a corner, complete with retro props, like a bright honey-colored landline phone, feather boas, and a light-up peace sign. There's a selfie wall made of vinyl records and a glowing neon display that says GROOVY.

Tall, round cocktail tables line either side of the room, each topped with a coffee-colored tablecloth and a bouquet of sunflowers. The TV in the corner of the room that usually tells the time or offers that day's lunch menu is replaced with a looping video of Lava Lamps. The DJ toward the back is even wearing a powder-blue tuxedo.

"Oh my gosh," I murmur.

"That mean we did all right?" Isaiah asks.

I turn to him. "More than all right. This is stunning. Better than I even imagined."

"Great job, you two," a familiar voice says from behind us. When Isaiah and I turn, we see Ms. Bennett in a floral jumpsuit with bell sleeves and a necktie. "What a team."

"Thank you, Ms. Bennett," I say.

"Yes, thank you," Isaiah echoes.

"I had a feeling you might be good together. Glad you were able to work things out." She winks at us. "Now, I think I see a student getting a *little* handsy over in the corner, so I need to go handle that. Have fun. You deserve it."

I shake my head as she sails past us, a woman on a mission. "She should add *sneaky little matchmaker* to her résumé."

Isaiah laughs. "For real. We owe her."

"That we do," I say, nodding. "Now...are you down for a few more pictures? Or should we dance?"

Just then, the song switches over to something by Kenny-Hoopla, and we have our answer when Isaiah's face lights up. "I love this song!"

"Then let's dance."

Chapter Forty-Nine

We dance. We take selfies. We cram far too many bodies into the photo booth and trade photo strips like they're collector's items. We take girls' trips to the bathroom. We freshen our makeup. We laugh, a lot. We dance some more—in a group as friends for the fast songs and together as couples when the music slows.

During a break, Zay reaches for my hand.

His voice is low as he whispers in my ear. "Come on."

He leads me through a crowd on the dance floor toward the side door of the cafeteria that opens to the courtyard. The door closes behind us, drowning out the loud music, leaving us in the quiet of the autumn night. The stillness of the courtyard compared to the loud hum of music, laughter, and voices is stark.

Though a few classmates are out here, too, it feels as if Zay and I have stepped into our own little world. The courtyard is all dressed up for the dance, illuminated with delicate string lights and the same vibrant mums that adorn the front of the school. Disco balls the size of my palm decorate the branches of the elm tree, catching the moon's light as they sway. Out here, there are actual mini–Lava Lamps glowing on each table. I totally want to steal one.

"Well, *this* is magical," I breathe.

"Thought it might be nice to just take a minute away from everything." Isaiah leads me over to one of the picnic tables to take a seat. "How are you doing?"

"I'm having the time of my life," I say. "Though...I am getting a little tired."

Zay tilts his head at me. "You *did* just get out of the hospital, you know."

"I know. It's like I can hear Abuela's voice in my head reminding me to take it easy." I laugh. "And I hate that she's right! Everything has already been so surreal, I almost want to head home after the crowning."

"We can do that, you know," Isaiah says.

I shake my head. "We can't go home early!"

"Why not?" he asks, leaning in close to me. "It's *our* night, after all. We get to decide what we do."

As much as I don't want to admit it, going home sounds amazing. My whole body is tired, my feet hurt, and I just want to snuggle up next to Isaiah. Maybe that makes me sound like I'm a hundred years old, but the reality is this is the most I've done in more than a week. If nothing else, maybe my hospitalization let my body rest, and I think I needed the reminder that rest is not a luxury; it's survival.

"I don't want this night to end, though..." I protest.

Isaiah reaches for a curl by my face and gently tugs. "Who says it has to? We can go back to your house and hang out. Curfew's not till midnight, right?"

I shake my head again. "I can't have you miss out on this."

He leans in even closer. "As long as I'm with you, I'm not missing out on a thing." His voice is low as he says this, and it sends a shiver down my spine.

I reach for him, pulling his face to mine, and kiss him. It's slow and soft and gentle and I melt into him as he tugs me still closer.

From inside, I hear the music cut out and the DJ's muffled voice call that it's time to announce homecoming court. As much as I want to stay out here with Zay, kissing under the stars, I also very much want to celebrate whoever gets crowned.

Reluctantly, I pull back just a little. "That was nice," I murmur.

"*Really* nice," Isaiah whispers.

"But we should head inside," I say. "The crowning is about to happen."

Isaiah sighs. "All right." He rises to his feet and holds out a hand for me, which I'm all too happy to take.

I lead the way back inside as Principal Johnson takes the microphone from the DJ and starts her speech about another close race for this year's homecoming court. She launches into a rundown of the expanded homecoming court.

I reach for one of Marisol's hands, while Sophie takes the other; beside me, Lily looks nervous.

Principal Johnson clears her throat. "Let's begin with the nobles. We'll select one person to take on this historic, prestigious title to represent our phenomenal special education students." She reads off the list of nominees, and a thrill ripples through my heart at the sound of Lily's name.

"And, without further ado, Elmwood High's inaugural noble is"—she pauses, and I hold my breath—"Margot Isaac!"

My heart sinks.

But as the crowd erupts into applause and cheering, I cut my glance to Lily, who seems far from disappointed. In fact, she looks relieved as she and Ruby clap and holler for their friend.

Margot, a petite girl with red hair, makes her way toward Principal Johnson and adorably curtsies after getting her crown placed on her head.

"Yeah, Margot!" Lily shouts, cupping her hands around her mouth. She looks over at me and grins. "That's my friend!"

"You're okay that you didn't win?"

Her eyes go big. "Are you kidding me? I'm *glad* I didn't win. I didn't want to have to wear a crown and have everyone watch me dance!"

And it's like…of course, right? Lily, who has never enjoyed being the center of attention, wouldn't want to have everyone staring at her. Instead, she's beyond content to be celebrating one of the new friends she and Ruby have made.

The proudly serene expression on Margot's face as she looks around at our classmates who voted her in as nobility reminds me that, although *I* may have wanted Lily to win, this entire event is about so much more than me. It's about the incredible moments tonight is affording us and the history we're making. Suddenly, homecoming court has taken on new life, ushering in the next era for Elmwood High, which hopefully will be more inclusive and accepting of students who have traditionally been left behind.

"Way to go, Margot!" I shout, and she shoots me a thumbs-up.

"And now, for our first-year king and queen…"

She goes on to list the nominees and winners for the first-year, sophomore, and junior classes. For the first time ever, we end up with a royal (!) in the junior class, plus a gender-swapped king and queen for the sophomore class, which warms my queer little heart. Loud cheers and applause erupt for each pair of winners as they make their way to the front and receive their crowns, taking their rightful place beside Principal Johnson.

"At long last, I am beyond honored to announce Elmwood High's senior king and queen." She rattles off the list of nominees, including Ari and Marisol. I cross my fingers. *Please, please, please.* "Our senior winners have traditionally embodied all of the wonderful things about Elmwood High. They are driven, smart, kind, and valued members of our student body. Previous senior homecoming court winners have gone on to do remarkable things. I have no doubt this year's winners will do the same. Now, it is with great pleasure that I announce: King Ari Garcia and Queen Marisol Pérez."

The scream I emit surprises even me, but I can't help it: that's my best friend!!!!!!

Sophie and I throw our arms around Marisol and Ari, jumping up and down to celebrate this absolutely incredible moment in time—no, in history, as our school's first-ever same-sex couple glides onto homecoming court.

Happy tears roll down Marisol's cheeks as she makes her way toward Principal Johnson, who gives her and Ari both a hug.

"Congratulations, Marisol and Ari," she says. "You deserve this."

Seeing Marisol and Ari standing together, poised with crowns on their heads, brings tears to my eyes. Our group is whooping and hollering and cheering like our lives depend on it.

"They did it!" Zay whispers.

"They did it," I sigh, clasping my hands together over my heart.

The only thing that gets the crowd back under control is when the DJ announces that the court will now lead us in a slow dance.

As Ari reaches for Marisol, Zay extends his own hand to me. I close the gap between us, welcoming the warmth of his skin against mine. Together, we gently sway to the music.

"Can you believe just a few weeks ago I ran you over with my skateboard?" he asks.

"I could've killed you." I laugh.

He laughs, too. "I would've deserved it."

"There were many moments over these last few weeks when I wanted to kill you, actually," I tease.

"I can't say I wanted to kill you, but I *definitely* enjoyed getting you all riled up. And making your life harder."

"Trust me, I know," I say, grinning. "But I kind of like it. I hope you never stop."

He smirks. "You think it's kinda hot when I mess with you, don't you?"

I roll my eyes. "Don't get carried away."

He gives me that easy smile, eyes twinkling. "It's tough not to when I'm around you."

I press my cheek to his, letting him lead me gently around the dance floor.

When I started this year, I was so convinced I knew exactly what perfect looked like. More than that, I thought I needed perfect—I yearned for it, so consumed with the idea that if I could control everything, I would finally fix everything that was wrong with me.

As it turns out, the only thing that was really wrong with me was my need to fix everything.

So much of what I've learned over the last few weeks is how much happier I am when I embrace things just as they are. I don't need perfect or anything even close to it.

I need friends I'd do anything for. I need a sister who knows her worth. I need an abuela who supports me. I need tenderness from a boy who sees me.

I need people who don't just *let* me obsess over boy bands and make my silly lists and daydream about pumpkin spice lattes, but *love* me for it.

I need a life brimming with moments like this—chest to chest with Isaiah, hearts beating together as a reminder that we're here, and we're happy.

As the song we're swaying to comes to a close, I catch sight of Lily up by the DJ booth saying something I can't quite make out.

A moment later, though, it becomes clear when the familiar notes of Intonation's "Girl Be Mine" fill the air. I lock eyes with my sister and squeal.

She rushes over to me, pulling Ruby with her, and Sophie and Marisol dance their way toward us, mouthing the opening lyrics.

"It's your boys!" Marisol laughs. "I hope Zay doesn't get jealous."

I grin. "He knows about my first loves, don't worry."

"Let's show everyone what our living room concerts look like," Lily says, giggling.

"Now we're talking, Lil!" Sophie shouts.

The four of us dance along with the music and, surrounded by them, I feel lighter than I have in weeks, so full of joy I could float up and away, especially when Zay, Noah, and Ari join right in and somehow know the chorus to the song.

Soon, between fits of laughter, we're all singing along at the top of our lungs, forming the silliest boy-band dance circle to ever hit the floor at a homecoming dance.

Looking from my best friends to my little sister to Zay—my Zay—I find that all at once, I'm overcome with emotion over this entire night. My life feels as if it's been plucked straight from a teen movie.

Once the song ends, leaving us giggly and amped, Zay places his hand on the small of my back.

He leans down to my ear and whispers, "Jay just texted me that he and his date are leaving, if we want to catch a ride with them. Do you want to stay or should we go?"

As much as I enjoyed our incredible dance party, I think leaving now is probably the right call. Abuela will be happy I took it easy, my body will thank me, and I truly can't imagine anything that could make this night better.

"Let's get going," I agree.

With that, I give hugs and kisses to my friends, and we head back to my house.

A while later, when Jay's car pulls up in front of my bungalow, I see that Abuela has left the front porch light on for us.

"Can you stay a little?" I ask.

"Of course I can," Isaiah says with a smile.

eliciting tingles that ring throughout my entire body. My toes curl when I feel his fingers toying with the ends of my long curls.

Zay pulls back but keeps his face close to mine. He nudges his nose against my forehead, dropping a kiss there, too, and softly says, "I know you're beyond the whole perfection thing, but still—I hope tonight was perfect for you."

"It wasn't," I whisper. "It was better."

Chapter Fifty

In my ongoing quest to be less of a control freak, I let Isaiah pick our Halloween costumes.

That's how I find myself in a long black dress and a straight black wig that reaches all the way down my back, wearing a smoky eye paired with crimson lips, and carrying a bouquet of red roses. Isaiah's dark locs are pulled back into a ponytail and he's wearing a black-and-white pinstriped suit with a fake phantom hand affixed to his shoulder.

Zay has been describing us to everyone as brown Morticia and Gomez Addams, aka "the perfect couple," according to him.

We actually look pretty amazing as we meander around Sophie and Marisol's wealthy neighborhood hoping to score some full-size candies for Gianna (dressed as the sweetest Mirabel from *Encanto*) and Amaya (a terrifying zombie hungry for brains, obviously).

For this part of the night, we're joined by Noah and Sophie, who are a French chef and Emily from *Emily in Paris*; Ari and Marisol as Danny and Sandy from *Grease*; and Zay's parents, Mr. and Mrs. Ortiz, as a late-nineties J.Lo and Diddy, back when he was apparently known as Puff Daddy.

Though my friends and I have claimed we're accompanying Gianna and Amaya for *their* sake, the truth is we're loading up our own trick-or-treat bags, which we carry like precious loot.

Noah pops a mini-Twix into his mouth and chews thoughtfully. "God, I love free candy."

Sophie laughs. "Me too! It somehow tastes better."

Ari goes rooting through her bag. "We got too much chocolate, though."

I wrinkle my nose at her. "Are you really complaining about that?!"

She frowns in response. "Chocolate's fine, but I really like sour candies! And anything gummy," she explains. "When I was a kid, I'd eat those Nerds Ropes like it was my job."

"Your taste buds are wrong, babe," Marisol says, shaking her head. "But you know I'm down to trade with you. I've been grabbing extras for you whenever we went to a house that offered something you liked."

Ari's face lights up and she pulls Marisol into an unexpected bear hug. "¡Mi vida!"

"Aww, ya big softie," Zay teases.

Marisol whips around to glare at him. "Tell a soul and you're dead."

He leans in close to me and whispers loudly into my ear, "And the scariest Halloween costume award goes to…" which makes me laugh.

Marisol pokes Zay in the side. "I *heard* that."

"Only because I wanted you to!" he says with a laugh.

As the sky around us darkens, the streetlights blink on all at once, an indicator that the window for wholesome trick-or-treating is coming to a close.

Zay's dad shouts to us from up ahead. "I think we're going to call it," he says, cradling Gianna like a baby. "This one's feet hurt."

Mrs. Ortiz points toward a shrieking Amaya. "And that one is clearly suffering from a sugar high. We need to get them home. You coming?"

Zay glances over at me. "I think we'll walk. It's not far."

"You just want to get some more candy, greedy," Gianna teases.

"That's not fair!" Amaya whines, stomping her feet. "I need more candy!"

Mrs. Ortiz puts a hand on Amaya's shoulder to steady her. "What you need is a bath and to get ready for bed. Let's go."

There's more whining as Zay's parents shuffle the girls toward their car, which is parked at Marisol's house. Our group meanders behind.

"What are you all getting up to tonight?" Zay asks.

"I'm helping Ari's family paint some calaveras ahead of tomorrow," Marisol explains.

"Don't worry. She'll be rewarded heartily with the most delicious foods as part of our Día de Muertos celebration," Ari adds.

"One of my band friends is throwing a little party that Noah and I thought we'd check out for a bit," Sophie says. "And you two?" Her eyebrows go up as she smirks, knowing what I've got planned for tonight.

I shrug a shoulder, playing it off. "I think we're just going back to Zay's for a bit."

Zay nods. "Yeah, we're just going to hang out. Maybe raid Amaya and Gianna's candy stash while they sleep." He grins. "But this was really fun. Thank you guys for coming."

"Are you kidding? I *love* trick-or-treating," Marisol says. "It was nice to finally have an excuse to do it!"

Noah nods toward Isaiah. "Thanks for the invite, man."

We hug and exchange goodbyes, readying to go our separate ways. Marisol hangs on to me for an extra second and whispers, "Have fun on your redo date!"

With a final wave, Zay and I meander down the sidewalk in the direction of his house. For the first time tonight, it's just us. He reaches for my hand and idly strokes his thumb over mine, sending a tingle up my arm.

"You know, I really loved hanging out with everyone," he says. "Buuuut I'm kinda glad it'll just be us for the rest of the night."

"Me too. I've missed you today."

He wrinkles his nose. "Oooh, you *like* me."

"Here we go," I groan.

"You have a huge crush on me!" Zay teases. "I mean, I don't blame you at all. I'm extremely good-looking. Smart. Funny. Charming as hell. And this ass?"

I laugh. "Oh my God!"

He grins. "Admit it! You like checking it out!"

"There are *children*," I hiss between laughs—not because I'm actually offended, but because he likes when I pretend I am.

"Aww, c'mon. Say you like me!"

And I giggle, defiantly raising my chin in the air. "Never!"

Suddenly, Zay pulls me toward him firmly, closing any gap that may have existed between us just seconds before. He kisses me so hard I lose my breath.

When he pulls back, one hand still in mine and the other entangled in my hair, he whispers, "Well, I like *you*. A lot."

I press my forehead to his. "I guess I'm coming around to you. But maybe you should do that again so I can be sure."

Zay grins, accepting the invitation, and I melt into him again, overcome at how every single nerve in my body feels like it's on fire; at how I'll never, ever get sick of this; at how in just a few short weeks, he has managed to help make me feel like me again, only better. And hotter.

"Well?" he asks when I step back from him.

"Okay," I admit with a breathy sigh. "I like you a lot, too."

He raises his eyebrows at me. "Maybe we can continue that once we're back at my house, Morticia?"

"That's a promise, Gomez."

We're just steps from his house when an alert goes off on my phone and I pause to dig it out of my candy bag. My cell phone has been permanently on vibrate since...forever? The only sound notifications I've set are for Intonation's official Twitter account, but they haven't posted in years.

Which is why I gasp when I check the notification.

Because there's no way.

"What?" Zay asks. "Everything okay?"

"One sec." Hands trembling, I pull up the tweet to make sure it's real. It *is*. "Oh my God!" I grab Zay's forearm and squeeze, not prying my eyes away from the post that's already racking up likes and retweets.

@intonationofficial: We're baaaaack.

"What is it?" Zay asks, more urgently this time.

I turn my screen toward him. "Intonation is reuniting!"

"Wait, for real?"

"For real!" I shout, fingers scrolling through tweet after celebratory tweet, hungry for more information.

@enews: BREAKING: Following the release of their latest single, "Hope," bestselling boy band Intonation will reunite for a charity show called One Night in Vegas on Aug. 17, according to frontman Lucas Thomas. More soon!

"They're doing a charity show in Las Vegas!" I throw my arms around Isaiah and squeal, eliciting a laugh from him. "I have to call Lily and Abuela!"

"Of course you do!" Zay says.

I FaceTime them both, insides shaking with glee. Lily picks up on the first ring, her face mostly entrenched in shadows because she's outside waiting in line for a haunted hayride with Ruby.

"Hey, what's up?" Her voice is way too casual, so I know she hasn't heard yet.

I grin. "I have huge news!"

Then Abuela joins the call, but her video is pitch-black. "¡Hola!" she chirps, and I can tell by her voice she's already tipsy. She's at Titi Luisa's Halloween party and probably living her best life.

"It's a video call, Abuela," I say.

"Oh!" is all she says before Lily and I watch her video shift as she pulls the phone away from her ear. Her face finally comes into view, revealing the now slightly smudged, but still adorable, cat nose and whiskers I drew on her earlier in the evening. "Better?"

Lily nods. "Much. So? What's the huge news?"

"Intonation is reuniting for a one-night-only concert in Las Vegas!" I shout, not caring that my voice is echoing throughout the neighborhood.

"What?!" Lily asks, her eyes widening. "Are you joking?"

"I wouldn't joke about this! It's on Twitter!"

Abuela's hand flies to her heart. "¿En serio?"

"Yes! It's not till next August, but we *have* to go," I insist. "This could be our last chance to see them in concert!"

"We're going," Lily says firmly.

"Do you need my credit card?" Abuela offers.

A laugh bubbles out of me at their shared enthusiasm. "Tickets aren't on sale yet, but I'll let you know when they are. I have money saved, too. Ahh, I can't believe it! We're going to get to see them in concert again!" I do a little dance.

Lily gazes off-screen, then back. "I'm sorry, Ruby and I are next up for our ride, but this is amazing!"

"Go, go!" I urge. "I just wanted to share the good news."

She smiles at me. "I'm so happy you called."

"Henry, mi cariño, here I come!" Abuela laughs. "Good night. I love you, nenas."

I blow her a kiss. "Love you."

I'm still beaming when I click off the call. When I look over at Zay, he's beaming, too, even though this isn't even his news.

"I promise I'm not going to let this news completely overtake our night. I'm just so freaking excited."

"As you should be! Celebrate the hell outta this. These are your boys," Zay says. "I'm happy when you're happy."

And hearing him say that sends a flutter of appreciation through my heart.

A text from Lily comes in.

Lily: Just did the math. 291 days till the show!

I reply to Lily and send one other quick text to Zay's older sister, Camila.

Me: We're outside!

Camila: ON IT 🎁 🎬 💜

Zay puts a hand on the small of my back. "You know, as much as I'm dying to hang out with you, I won't even be mad if you want to bail. I feel like it must be killing you not to be researching the fastest route to Las Vegas and plotting exactly how your road trip with your abuela and sister is going to go."

"There will be plenty of time for that. Lily just texted me that we have two hundred ninety-one days until the show," I say. "But tonight? You and I have a date to get to."

He narrows his eyes at me. "What are you up to, Whitney?"

"You'll see." I take his hand. "Come on!"

I lead him behind his house. With the help of Camila, part of the backyard has been transformed into an outdoor movie theater for two. Earlier today, I packed a bag with a cozy blanket, popcorn, drinks, and the makings for s'mores, which I dropped off with Camila. She graciously lit the fire pit, took care of setting up an outdoor projector, and loaded up the movie, *The*

Surrendering—the scary film Zay and I were going to see during our first date back in middle school.

"Hi, lovebirds," Camila says, looking up from her phone. She rises from the picnic table, where she'd been sitting, and hands me a bowl of freshly popped popcorn. "Enjoy."

"Did you poison this or something?" Isaiah asks, eyeing his sister skeptically.

"No, dummy. I'm being nice!" She rolls her eyes. "But not for you. For her. Seriously, Whit, how you put up with this shit is beyond me..."

I laugh. "Thank you, Camila. Have fun at your party."

"I will. Don't get too wild now!"

With a wink, Camila is gone, leaving me with a confused-looking Isaiah.

"Fill me in, please?" he asks.

"Well, I realized we kinda skipped over that whole first-date thing and went right into just being together. Which is amazing! But I thought it might be fun to give us another chance at our *first* first date—the one from middle school. I had Camila help me set this all up, and, if you're down, we're finally going to watch that scary movie and eat snacks and hold hands, like we were always meant to," I explain. "So...Zay, will you go on a redo first date with me?"

Zay glances around the backyard, everything suddenly clicking. He leans down to kiss me. It's so heartfelt I feel like I could cry.

His hand reaches for a strand of my curly hair, and he gently tugs. "I've been waiting years for this."

We set out a blanket to lie on beneath the twinkling stars and snuggle under a mountain of cozy blankets, costumes and all.

"S'more?" Isaiah asks, holding a plate out to me with a perfectly golden marshmallow sandwiched between two graham crackers and a layer of gooey chocolate.

"Please." I take the plate from him and let him assemble a second s'more for himself, then nestle into the crook of his arm.

He hits play on the movie. We settle in, Isaiah pulling me close, body warm against mine. Sitting under the moon with him, fire crackling, sharing s'mores and kisses and electric touches, I swear I could stay like this forever.

Because with Zay, I'm finally settling into who I am. I'm making room for myself. I'm embracing who I am in every single moment, and not apologizing for it.

So tonight, with this boy who has always seen me, I swear I might just let myself fall in love.

Countdown to Intonation's One Night in Vegas: 291 days

Acknowledgments

What I wouldn't have given to read something—ANYTHING—about PCOS when I was a teenager diagnosed at 16. I didn't know anyone else in the world who shared this syndrome with me...and now I get to share a book about it with the world. It feels surreal, and I'd like to thank everyone for their ongoing kindness and support. I genuinely can't believe I'm getting to publish my third book, and it's all because of you.

My stories would go nowhere if not for the enormous efforts of the entire Holiday House team: Sara DiSalvo; Mora Couch; Terry Borzumato-Greenberg; Michelle Montague; Mary Joyce Perry; Amy Toth; Kerry Martin; Chelsea Hunter; Mary Cash; Alison Tarnofsky; Melissa See; Alex Aceves; Bree Martinez; Derek Stordahl; Miriam Miller; Erin Mathis; Elyse Vincenty; Annie Rosenbladt; Kayla Phillips; Rebecca Godan; and all of the folks who play meaningful roles in making a book from start to finish.

Thank you to my brilliant editor Mora Couch, who always manages to make my books ten times better with her wisdom, wit, insightful edits, and hilarious commentary. Your continued support throughout everything means so much.

Thank you to my fellow Stars Hollow-obsessed bestie Sara DiSalvo for always ensuring my books get out into the world and for fielding the endless deluge of emails from me.

Special thank you to Alex Aceves for generously lending her

bilingual talents to this book and making sure I didn't make a fool of myself with my rudimentary Spanish skills!

Endless thanks to my incredible agent, Tamar Rydzinski, who is forever championing for me and my work. There's no one I'd rather have by my side as we tackle the publishing world!

Thank you to Monica Rodriguez for always thinking creatively about branding and marketing and being willing to hop on a call or email to brainstorm.

Thank you to illustrator and artist Ericka Lugo, who entered the book world at the same time as I did and who brings my characters to life in ways I never could have imagined.

Thank you to students and readers who take a chance on my stories and who always ask the very best questions. That you see yourself in my characters is beyond healing. I hope I can continue to create stories that celebrate you for all that you are. Always remember you deserve the best.

Thank you to the incredible book community on social media—Instagram, Twitter, TikTok, and even Facebook—for all of the work you do. You ensure marginalized books and authors are supported and celebrated, and I appreciate you so much. I'm especially thankful for Carmen (@tomesandtextiles) for celebrating Latine books, as well as some of the most amazing bookstagrammers who have uplifted me and my stories, including Caro (@sanjariti); Julith (@nerdy_little_julith); Mélanie (@thebookoffaerie); Dany (@tearoomwithme); Delia (@aventuras.en.esl); Hayle (@bookishbluebird); Yanitza (@yanitzawrites); Paola (@guerrerawr); Chrystal (@curls.into.books); Linda (@linda.reads); Alicia (@akernalofnonsense); Ali (@2nd2lastunicorn); Keara (@theboricuabookworm); April and Christi (@thispodisoverdue); Cierra (@onedetailedteacher); Julia (@thebookshelfbitch); Alex (@thereadingcornerforall); Carina (@astoryofsorts); and so many more. Thank you for seeing me and loving these characters as much as I do!

I am so grateful for the support I've been shown from librarians, educators, booksellers, and book clubs, including Sarah Ressler Wright; Abby Rice; all of the incredible NEIBA folks; the entire team at High Five Books (with special shout out to Lexi and Kinsley) and The Odyssey (one of my all-time fave bookstores celebrating 60 years); Montrose Regional Library and Public Schools (hi, Addy!); Worcester Academy (hi, Marilyn!); J. Sterling Morton West High School; Print: A Bookstore; Cafe con Libros; Politics and Prose; Astoria Bookshop; Porter Square Books; University of Washington Tacoma; Omaha South High School; Bank Square Books; UConn; and on and on. I am humbled by your support and generosity in welcoming my stories into your classrooms, libraries, and bookstores in your corners of the world. How lucky that these characters get a chance to be part of your lives and meet readers who need them most—all because of you.

Olivia Abtahi: you are the best friend a girl could ask for and I consider myself so lucky to have someone in my life who gets it. And by "it" I mean everything. Obviously. Thank you for always being willing to suffer through the roughest drafts and celebrate all of the highs together.

Angela Velez, my glitter girlie, I'm so thankful for our friendship. You are walking sunshine.

Thank you to Writers Row—Judy, Jane, Cait, and Kerri—for your humor, friendship, and joyful gatherings, which are my favorite.

Thank you to all of my beautiful family members and friends. Your support means everything.

Thank you to my Renz for being the most amazing brother. You being proud of me means more than you know.

Special thank you to my father-in-law, Bill, for actually reading my books. It means a lot.

Thank you, Grandma, for all that you do and for the generous love you give. I love being your little chickadee and I am so grateful Maya gets to be your little munchkin.

Thank you Justin for being the best brother/cousin of all time, as well as my 90s Con partner-in-crime.

Thank you Brosh and Veatch for being part of our village, and to Cait, Paige, Kerri, Del, Laraine, Anne, Nikki, Annie, and all our littles; to Samm and Heather for always being willing to deep dive into our 90s obsession; to my OG internet besties for helping me find my way and reading my early Backstreet Boys fanfic; and to my author friends who are the best champions and supporters a girl could ask for.

Nothing in my author life would be possible without childcare so thank you specifically to Christine Magnani for taking Maya in and treating her like one of your own. The best compliment I get is when Maya accidentally calls me "Christine" because I know this means she is beyond loved in your care, and that's all I could ever ask for.

Thank you to my higher ed communities and friends, including my friends from Springfield College and UMass Amherst, and for their warm reception and support.

Thank you to my therapist, Jessica, for helping me put feelings into words and value myself.

Thank you to everyone who's purchased, borrowed, shared, exchanged, posted about, felt something for, or celebrated my books.

Thank you to Obi for being the perfect nap buddy.

Thank you to Maya Papaya for reminding me every day that life can be silly and fun and full of love and laughter. I hope my stories someday make you proud.

Thank you to my Bubby. After 17 years together, our relationship is officially as old as we were when we met. Doing everything and nothing with you has been the best adventure of my life. Look what we built together. Isn't it beautiful?